NIGHT WORLD

Also by L.J. Smith

Night World

Volume 1: *Secret Vampire, Daughters of Darkness* and *Enchantress*
Volume 2: *Dark Angel, The Chosen* and *Soulmate*
Volume 3: *Huntress, Black Dawn* and *Witchlight*

Other titles published by Hodder Children's Books

Beautiful Dead
by Eden Maguire

1: *Jonas*
2: *Arizona*
3: *Summer*
4: *Phoenix*

Darke Academy
by Gabrielle Poole

1: *Secret Lives*
2: *Blood Ties*
3: *Divided Souls*

VOLUME TWO

DARK ANGEL
THE CHOSEN
SOULMATE

L. J. SMITH

A division of Hachette Children's Books

First published in the USA in 1996 as three separate paperbacks by
Pocket Books, a division of Simon & Schuster Inc.

The Night World: Dark Angel first published in Great Britain in 1997 by
Hodder Children's Books

The Night World: The Chosen first published in
Great Britain in 1997 by Hodder Children's Books

The Night World: Soulmate first published in Great Britain
in 1997 by Hodder Children's Books

This bind-up edition published in 2009
by Hodder Children's Books

7

ISBN-13: 978 0 340 99663 8

Typeset in Meridien and Neuland by Avon DataSet Ltd,
Bidford on Avon, Warwickshire

Printed and bound by CPI Bookmarque, Croydon

Hodder Children's Books
a division of Hachette Children's Books
338 Euston Road, London NW1 3BH
An Hachette UK Company
www.hachette.co.uk

The Night World . . . love was never so scary.

The Night World isn't a place. It's all around us. It's a secret society of vampires, werewolves, witches, and other creatures of darkness that live among us. They're beautiful and deadly and irresistible to humans. Your high school teacher could be one, and so could your boyfriend.

The Night World laws say it's OK to hunt humans. It's OK to toy with their hearts, it's even OK to kill them. There are only two things you can't do with them.

1) Never let them find out the Night World exists.
2) Never fall in love with one of them.

These are stories about what happens when the rules get broken.

DARK ANGEL

For Janie, Cathy and Karen

CHAPTER 1

Gillian Lennox didn't mean to die that day.

She was mad, though. Mad because she had missed her ride home from school, and because she was cold, and because it was two weeks before Christmas and she was very, very lonely.

She walked by the side of the empty road, which was about as winding and hilly as every other country road in southwestern Pennsylvania, and viciously kicked offending clumps of snow out of her way.

It was a rotten day. The sky was dull and the snow looked tired. And Amy Nowick, who should have been waiting after Gillian cleaned up her studio art project, had already driven away – with her new boyfriend.

Sure, it must have been an honest mistake. And she wasn't jealous of Amy, she wasn't, even though one week ago they had both been sixteen and never been kissed.

Gillian just wanted to get home.

That was when she heard the crying.

She stopped, looked around. It sounded like a baby – or maybe a cat. It seemed to be coming from the woods.

Her first thought was *Paula Belizer*. But that was ridiculous. The little girl who'd disappeared somewhere at the end of this road had been gone for over a year now.

The crying came again. It was thin and far away – as if it were coming from the depths of the woods. This time it sounded more human.

'Hello? Hey, is somebody in there?'

There was no answer. Gillian stared into the dense stand of oak and hickory, trying to see between the gnarled bare trees. It looked uninviting. Scary.

Then she looked up and down the road. Nobody. Hardly surprising – not many cars passed by here.

I am *not* going in there alone, Gillian thought. She was exactly the opposite of the 'Oh, it's such a nice day; let's go tramping through the woods' type. Not to mention exactly the opposite of the brave type.

But who else was there? And what else was there to do?

Somebody was in trouble.

She slipped her left arm through her backpack strap, settling it on the centre of her back and leaving her hands free. Then she cautiously began to climb the snow-covered ridge that fell away on the other side to the woods.

'Hello?' She felt stupid shouting and not getting any answer. 'Hi! Hello!'

Only the crying sound, faint but continuous, somewherc in front of her.

Gillian began to flounder down the ridge. She didn't weigh much, but the crust on the snow was very thin and every step took her ankle deep.

Great, and I'm wearing sneakers. She could feel cold seeping into her feet.

The snow wasn't so deep once she got into the woods. It was white and unbroken beneath the trees – and it gave her an eerie sense of isolation. As if she were in the wilderness.

And it was so *quiet*. The farther Gillian went in, the

deeper the silence became. She had to stop and not breathe to hear the crying.

Bear left, she told herself. Keep walking. There's nothing to be scared of!

But she couldn't make herself yell again.

There is something *weird* about this place . . .

Deeper and deeper into the woods. The road was far behind her now. She crossed fox tracks and bird scratches in the snow – no sign of anything human.

But the crying was right ahead now, and louder. She could hear it clearly.

OK, up this big ridge. Yes, you *can* do it. Up, up. Never mind if your feet are cold.

As she struggled over the uneven ground, she tried to think comforting thoughts.

Maybe I can write an article about it for the *Viking News* and everyone will admire me . . . Wait. Is it cool or uncool to rescue somebody? Is saving people too *nice* to be cool?

It was an important question, since Gillian currently had only two ambitions: 1) David Blackburn, and, 2) To be invited to the parties the popular kids were invited to. And both of these depended, in a large part, on being cool.

If she were only popular, if she only felt good about herself, then everything else would follow. It would be so much easier to be a really wonderful person and do something for the world and make something important of her life if she just felt loved and accepted. If she weren't shy and short and immature looking . . .

She reached the top of the ridge and grabbed at a branch to keep her balance. Then, still hanging on, she let out her breath and looked around.

Nothing to see. Quiet woods leading down to a creek just below.

And nothing to *hear*, either. The crying had stopped.

Oh, don't *do* this to me!

Frustration warmed Gillian up and chased away her fear. She yelled, 'Hey – hey, are you still out there? Can you hear me? I'm coming to help you!'

Silence. And then, very faintly, a sound.

Directly ahead.

Oh, my God, Gillian thought. The *creek*.

The kid was in the creek, hanging on to something, getting weaker and weaker . . .

Gillian was scrambling down the other side of the ridge, slithering, the wet snow adhering to her like lumpy frosting.

Heart pounding, out of breath, she stood on the bank of the creek. Below her, at the edge, she could see fragile ice ledges reaching out like petals over the rushing water. Spray had frozen like diamond drops on overhanging grasses.

But nothing living. Gillian frantically scanned the surface of the dark water.

'Are you there?' she shouted. 'Can you hear me?'

Nothing. Rocks in the water. Branches caught against the rocks. The sound of the rushing creek.

'Where *are* you?'

She couldn't hear the crying anymore. The water was too loud.

Maybe the kid had gone under.

Gillian leaned out, looking for a wet head, a shape beneath the surface. She leaned out farther.

And then – a mistake. Some subtle change of balance. Ice under her feet. Her arms were windmilling, but she couldn't get her balance back . . .

She was flying. Nothing solid anywhere. Too surprised to be frightened.

She hit the water with an icy shock.

CHAPTER 2

Everything was freezing confusion. Her head was underwater and she was being tumbled over and over. She couldn't see, couldn't breathe, and she was completely disorientated.

Then her head popped up. She automatically sucked in a huge gasp of air.

Her arms were flailing but they seemed tangled in her backpack. The creek was wide here and the current was very strong. She was being swept downstream, and every other second her mouth seemed to be full of water. Reality was just one desperate, choking attempt to get enough air for the next breath.

And everything was so cold. A cold that was *pain*, not just temperature.

I'm going to die.

Her mind realized this with a sort of numb certainty, but her body was stubborn. It fought almost as if it had a separate brain of its own. It struggled out of her backpack, so that the natural buoyancy of her ski jacket helped keep her head above water. It made her legs kick, trying to stand firm on the bottom.

No good. The creek was only five feet deep in the

centre, but that was still an inch higher than Gillian's head. She was too small, too weak, and she couldn't get any kind of control over where she was going. And the cold was sapping her strength frighteningly fast. With every second her chances of surviving dropped.

It was as if the creek were a monster that hated her and would never let her go. It slammed her into rocks and swept her on before her hands could get hold of the cold, smooth surfaces. And in a few minutes she was going to be too weak to keep her face above water.

I have to grab something.

Her body was telling her that. It was her only chance.

There. Up ahead, on the left bank, a projecting spit with tree roots. She *had* to get to it. *Kick. Kick.*

She hit and was almost spun past it. But somehow, she was holding on. The roots were thicker than her arms, a huge tangle like slick, icy snakes.

Gillian thrust an arm through a natural loop of the roots, anchoring herself. Oh – yes; she could breathe now. But her body was still in the creek, being sucked away by the water.

She had to get out – but that was impossible. She just barely had the strength to hold on; her weakened, numb muscles could never pull her up the bank.

At that moment, she was filled with hatred – not for the creek, but for herself. Because she was little and weak and childish and it was going to *kill* her. She was going to die, and it was all happening *right now*, and it was real.

She could never really remember what happened next. Her mind let go and there was nothing but anger and the burning need to get higher. Her legs kicked and scrambled and some dim part of her knew that each impact against the rocks and roots should have hurt. But all that mattered was the desperation that was somehow, inch by inch, getting her numb, waterlogged body out of the creek.

And then she was out. She was lying on roots and snow. Her vision was dim; she was gasping, open-mouthed, for breath, but she was alive.

Gillian lay there for a long time, not really aware of the cold, her entire body echoing with relief.

I made it! I'll be OK now.

It was only when she tried to get up that she realized how wrong she was.

When she tried to stand, her legs almost folded under her. Her muscles felt like jelly.

And . . . it was *cold*. She was already exhausted and nearly frozen, and her soaking clothes felt as heavy as medieval armour. Her gloves were gone, lost in the creek. Her cap was gone. With every breath, she seemed to get colder, and suddenly she was racked with waves of violent shivers.

Find the road . . . I have to get to the road. But which way is it?

She'd landed somewhere downstream – but where? How far away was the road now?

Doesn't matter . . . just walk away from the creek, Gillian thought slowly. It was difficult to think at all.

She felt stiff and clumsy and the shivering made it hard to climb over fallen trees and branches. Her red, swollen fingers couldn't close to get handholds.

I'm so cold – why can't I stop shivering?

Dimly, she knew that she was in serious trouble. If she didn't get to the road – *soon* – she wasn't going to survive. But it was more and more difficult to call up a sense of alarm. A strange sort of apathy was coming over her. The gnarled forest seemed like something from a fairy tale.

Stumbling . . . staggering. She had no idea where she was going. Just straight ahead. That was all she could see anyway, the next dark rock protruding from the snow, the next fallen branch to get over or around.

And then suddenly she was on her face. She'd fallen. It seemed to take immense effort to get up again.

It's these clothes . . . they're too heavy. I should take them off.

Again, dimly, she knew that this was wrong. Her brain was being affected; she was dazed with hypothermia. But the part of her that knew this was far away, separate from her. She fought to make her numbed fingers unzip her ski jacket.

OK . . . it's off. I can walk better now . . .

She couldn't walk better. She kept falling. She had been doing this forever, stumbling, falling, getting up. And every time it was a little harder.

Her cords felt like slabs of ice on her legs. She looked at them with distant annoyance and saw that they were covered with adhering snow.

OK – maybe take those off, too?

She couldn't remember how to work a zipper. She couldn't think at all anymore. The violent waves of shivering were interspersed with pauses now, and the pauses were getting longer.

I guess . . . that's good. I must not be so cold . . .

I just need a little rest.

While the faraway part of her brain screamed uselessly in protest, Gillian sat down in the snow.

She was in a small clearing. It seemed deserted – not even the footprints of a ground mouse marked the smooth white carpet around her. Above, overhanging branches formed a snowy canopy.

It was a very peaceful place to die.

Gillian's shivering had stopped.

Which meant it was all over now. Her body couldn't

warm itself by shivering any longer, and was giving up the fight. Instead, it was trying to move into hibernation. Shutting itself down, reducing breathing and heart rate, conserving the little warmth that was left. Trying to survive until help could come.

Except that no help was coming.

No one knew where she was. It would be hours before her dad got home or her mother was . . . awake. And even then they wouldn't be alarmed that Gillian wasn't there. They'd assume she was with Amy. By the time anyone thought of looking for her it would be far too late.

The faraway part of Gillian's mind knew all this, but it didn't matter. She had reached her physical limits – she couldn't save herself now even if she could have thought of a plan.

Her hands weren't red anymore. They were blue-white. Her muscles were becoming rigid.

At least she no longer felt cold. There was only a vast sense of relief at not having to move. She was so tired . . .

Her body had begun the process of dying.

White mist filled her mind. She had no sense of time passing. Her metabolism was slowing to a stop. She was becoming a creature of ice, no different from any stump or rock in the frozen wilderness.

I'm in trouble . . . somebody . . . somebody please . . .

Mom . . .

Her last thought was: It's just like going to sleep.

And then, all at once, there was no rigidity, no discomfort. She felt light and calm and free – and she was floating up near the canopy of snowy boughs.

How wonderful to be warm again! Really warm, as if she were filled with sunshine. Gillian laughed in pleasure.

But where am I? Didn't something just happen – something bad?

On the ground below her there was a huddled figure. Gillian looked at it curiously.

A small girl. Almost hidden by her long pale hair, the strands already covered in fine ice. The girl's face was delicate. Pretty bone structure. But the skin was a terrible flat white – dead looking.

The eyes were shut, the lashes frosty. Underneath, Gillian knew somehow, the eyes were deep violet.

I get it. I remember. That's me.

The realization didn't bother her. Gillian felt no connection to the huddled thing in the snow. She didn't belong to it anymore.

With a mental shrug, she turned away—

—and she was in a tunnel.

A huge dark place, with the feeling of being vastly complicated somehow. As if space here were folded or twisted – and maybe time, too.

She was rushing through it, flying. Points of light were whizzing by – who could tell how far away in the darkness?

Oh, God, Gillian thought. It's *the* tunnel. This is happening. Right now. To me.

I'm really dead.

And going at warp speed.

Weirder than being dead was being dead with a sense of humour.

Contradictions . . . this felt so real, more real than anything that had ever happened while she was alive. But at the same time, she had a strange sense of unreality. The edges of her self were blurred, as if somehow she were a part of the tunnel and the lights and the motion. She didn't have a distinct body anymore.

Could this all be happening in my head?

With that, for the first time, she felt frightened. Things

in her head . . . could be scary. What if she ran into her nightmares, the very things that her subconscious knew terrified her most?

That was when she realized she had no control over where she was going.

And the tunnel had changed. There was a bright light up ahead.

It wasn't blue-white, as she would have expected from movies. It was pale gold, blurred as if she were seeing it through frosty glass, but still unbelievably brilliant.

Isn't it supposed to feel like love or something?

What it felt like – what it made her feel – was awe. The light was so big, so powerful . . . and so Just Plain Bright. It was like looking at the beginning of the universe. And she was rushing toward it so fast – it was filling her vision.

She was in it.

The light encompassed her, surrounded her. Seemed to shine *through* her. She was flying upward through radiance like a swimmer surfacing.

Then the feeling of motion faded. The light was getting less bright – or maybe her eyes were adapting to it.

Shapes solidified around her.

She was in a meadow. The grass was amazing – not just green, but a sort of impossible ultragreen. As if lit up from inside. The sky was the same kind of impossible blue. She was wearing a thin summer dress that billowed around her.

The false colour made it seem like a dream. Not to mention the white columns rising at intervals from the grass, supporting nothing.

So this is what happens when you die. And now . . . now, somebody should come meet me. Grandpa Trevor? I'd like to see him walking again.

But no one came. The landscape was beautiful,

peaceful, unearthly – and utterly deserted.

Gillian felt anxiety twisting again inside her. Wait, what if this place wasn't – the good place? After all, she hadn't been particularly good in her life. What if this were actually hell?

Or . . . limbo?

Like the place all those spirits who talked to mediums must be from. Creatures from heaven wouldn't say such silly things.

What if she were left here, alone, forever?

As soon as she finished the thought, she wished she hadn't. This seemed to be the kind of place where thoughts – or *fears* – could influence reality.

Wasn't that something rancid she smelled?

And – weren't those voices? Fragments of sentences that seemed to come from the air around her? The kind of nonsense said by people in dreams.

'So white you can't see . . .'

'A time and a half . . .'

'If only I could, girl . . .'

Gillian turned around and around, trying to catch more. Trying to figure out whether or not she was really hearing the words. She had the sudden gut-trembling feeling that thc bcauty around her could easily come apart at the seams.

Oh, God, let me think good thoughts. *Please*. I wish I hadn't watched so many horror movies. I don't want to see anything terrible – like the ground splitting and hands reaching for me.

And I don't want anyone to meet me – looking like something rotting with bones exposed – after all.

She was in trouble. Even thinking about *not* thinking brought up pictures. And now fear was galloping inside her, and in her mind the bright meadow was turning into a nightmare of darkness and stink and pressure and gibbering mindless things. She was terrified that at any moment she might see a change—

And then she did see one. Something unmistakable. A few feet away from her, above the grass, was a sort of mist of light. It hadn't been there a moment ago. But now it seemed to get brighter as she watched, and to stretch from very far away.

And there was a shape in it, coming toward her.

CHAPTER 3

At first it looked like a speck, then like an insect on a lightbulb, then like a kite. Gillian watched, too frightened to run, until it got close enough for her to realize what it really was.

It was an angel.

Her fear drained away as she stared. The figure seemed to shine, as if it were made of the same light as the mist. It was tall, and had the shape of a perfectly formed human. It was walking, but somehow rushing toward her at the same time.

An angel, Gillian thought, awed. An angel . . .

And then the mist cleared and the shining faded. The figure was standing on the grass in front of her.

Gillian blinked.

Uh – not an angel, after all. A young guy. Maybe seventeen, a year older than Gillian. And . . . drop dead gorgeous.

He had a face like some ancient Greek sculpture. Classically beautiful. Hair like unburnished gold. Eyes that weren't blue, but violet. Long golden lashes.

And a *terrific* body.

I shouldn't be noticing *that*, Gillian thought, horrified.

But it was hard not to. Now that his clothes had stopped shining, she could see that they were ordinary, the kind any guy from Earth might wear. Washed and faded jeans and a white T-shirt. And he could easily have done a commercial for those jeans. He was well built without being over-muscly.

His only flaw, if it could be called that, was that his expression was a little *too* uplifted. Almost too sweet for a boy.

Gillian stared. The being looked back. After a moment he spoke.

'Hey, kid,' he said, and winked.

Gillian was startled – and mad. Normally, she was shy about speaking to guys, but after all, she was *dead* now, and this person had struck a raw nerve. 'Who're you calling kid?' she said indignantly.

He just grinned. 'Sorry. No offence.'

Confused, Gillian made herself nod politely. Who *was* this person? She'd always heard you had friends or relatives come and meet you. But she'd never seen this guy before in her life.

Anyway, he's definitely not an angel.

'I've come to help you,' he said. As if he'd heard her thought.

'Help me?'

'You have a choice to make.'

That was when Gillian began to notice the door.

It was right behind the guy, approximately where the mist had been. And it was a door . . . but it wasn't. It was like the luminous outline of a door, drawn very faintly on thin air.

Fear crept back into Gillian's mind. Somehow, without knowing how she knew, she knew the door was important. More important than anything she'd seen so far. Whatever was behind it was – well, maybe beyond comprehension.

A different place. Where all the laws she knew didn't apply.

Not necessarily bad. Just so powerful and so different that it was scary. Good can be scary, too.

That's the *real* gateway, she thought. Go through that door and you don't come back. And even though part of her longed desperately to see what was behind it, she was still so frightened that she felt dizzy.

'The thing is, it wasn't *actually* your time,' the guy with the golden-blond hair said quietly.

Oh, yes, I should have known. That's the cliché, Gillian thought. But she thought it weakly. Looking at that door, she didn't have room left inside for cute remarks.

She swallowed, blinking to clear her eyes.

'But here you are. A mistake, but one we have to deal with. In these cases, we usually leave the decision up to the individual.'

'You're saying I can choose whether or not I die.'

'To put it sort of loosely.'

'It's just up to *me*?'

'That's right.' He tilted his head slightly. 'You might want to think your life over at this point.'

Gillian blinked. Then she took a few steps away from him and stared across the supernaturally green grass. She tried to think about her life.

If you'd asked me this morning if I wanted to stay alive, there would have been no question. But now . . .

Now it felt a little like being rejected. As if she weren't good enough. And besides, seeing that she'd come this far . . . did she really want to go back?

It's not as if I were anybody special there. Not smart like Amy, a straight A student. Not brave. Not talented.

Well, what else is there? What would I be going back *to*?

Her mom – drinking every day, asleep by the time Gillian got home. Her dad and the constant arguments. The loneliness she knew she'd be facing now that Amy had a boyfriend. The longing for things she could never have, like David Blackburn with his quizzical smile. Like popularity and love and acceptance. Like having people think she was interesting and – and mature.

Come on. There's got to be something *good* back there.

'Pot Noodles?' the guy's voice said.

Gillian turned toward him. 'Huh?'

'You like those. Especially on a cold day when you come inside. Cats. The way babies smell. Cinnamon toast with lots of butter, like your mom used to make it when she still got up in the morning. Bad monster movies.'

Gillian choked. She'd never told anyone about most of those things. 'How do you *know* all that?'

He smiled. He really had an extraordinary smile. 'Eh, we see a lot up here.' Then he sobered. 'And don't *you* want to see more? Of life, I mean. Isn't there anything left for you to do?'

Everything was left for her to do. She'd never accomplished anything worthwhile.

But I didn't have much time, a small wimpy voice inside her protested. To be quashed immediately by a stern, steady voice. *You think that's an excuse? Nobody knows how much time they've got. You had plenty of minutes, and you wasted most of them.*

'Then don't you think you'd better go back and try again?' the guy said, in a gentle, prodding voice. 'See if you can do a better job?'

Yes. All at once, Gillian was filled with the same burning she'd felt when she got out of the creek. A sense of revelation and of purpose. She could do that. She could change completely, turn her life in a whole new direction.

Besides, there were her parents to consider. No matter how bad things were between them now, it could only make it worse if their daughter suddenly died. They'd blame each other. And Amy would get one of her guilt complexes for not waiting to drive Gillian home from school . . .

The thought brought a little grim satisfaction. Gillian tried to quell it. She had the feeling the guy was listening.

But she *did* have a new perspective on life. A sudden feeling that it was terribly precious, and that the worst thing you could do was waste it.

She looked at the guy. 'I want to go back.'

He nodded. Gave the smile again. 'I thought maybe you would.' His voice was so warm now. There was a quality in it that was like – what? Pure love? Infinite understanding?

A tone that was to sound what perfect light was to vision.

He held out a hand. 'Time to go, Gillian,' he said gently. His eyes were the deepest violet imaginable.

Gillian hesitated just an instant, then reached toward him.

She never actually touched his hand, not in a physical way. Just as her fingers seemed about to meet his, she felt a tingling shock and there was a flash. Then he was gone and Gillian had several odd impressions all at once.

The first was of being . . . unfixed. Detached from her surroundings. A falling feeling.

The second was of something coming at her.

It was coming very fast from some direction she couldn't point to. A place that wasn't defined by up or down or left or right. And it felt huge and winged, the way a hawk's shadow must feel to a mouse.

Gillian had a wild impulse to duck.

But it wasn't necessary. She was moving herself, falling away. Rushing backward through the tunnel, leaving the meadow – and whatever was coming at her – behind. The huge thing had only registered for an instant on her senses, and now, whizzing back through the darkness, she forgot about it.

Later, she would realize what a mistake this had been.

For now, time seemed compressed. She was alone in the tunnel, being pulled down like water down a drain. She tried to look between her feet to see where she was going, and saw something like a deep well beneath her.

At the bottom of the well was a circle of light, like the view backwards through a telescope. And in the circle, very tiny, was a girl's body lying on the snow.

My body, Gillian thought – and then, before she had time to feel any emotion, the bottom of the well was rushing up toward her. The tiny body was bigger and bigger. She felt a tugging pressure. She was being sucked into it – too fast.

Way too fast. She had no control. She fitted perfectly in the body, like a hand slipping into a mitten, but the jolt knocked her out.

Oooh . . . something hurts.

Gillian opened her eyes – or tried to. It was as hard as doing a chin-up. On the second or third attempt she managed to get them open a crack.

Whiteness everywhere. Dazzling. Blinding.

Where . . .? Is it snow?

What am I doing lying down in the snow?

Images came to her. The creek. Icy water. Climbing out. Falling. Being so cold . . .

After that . . . she couldn't remember. But now she knew what hurt. Everything.

I can't *move*.

Her muscles were clenched tight as steel. But she knew

she couldn't stay here. If she did, she'd . . .

Memory burst through her.

I died already.

Strangely, the realization gave her strength. She actually managed to sit up. As she did, she heard a cracking sound. Her clothes were glazed with solid ice.

Somehow she got to her feet.

She shouldn't have been able to do it. Her body had been cold enough to shut down earlier, and since then she'd been lying in the snow. By all the laws of nature, she should be frozen now.

But she was standing. She could even shuffle a step forward.

Only to realize she had no idea which way to go.

She still didn't know where the road was. Worse, it would be getting dark soon. When that happened, she wouldn't even be able to see her own tracks. She could walk in circles in the woods until her body gave out again.

See that white oak tree? Go around it to the right.

The voice was behind her left ear. Gillian turned that way as sharply as her rigid muscles would allow, even though she knew she wouldn't see anything.

She recognized the voice. But it was so much warmer and gentler now.

'You came back with me.'

Sure. Once again the voice was filled with that impossible warmth, that perfect love. *You don't think I'd just leave you to wander around until you froze again, do you? Now head for that tree, kid.*

After that came a long time of stumbling and staggering, over branches, around trees, on and on. It seemed to last forever, but always there was the voice in Gillian's ear, guiding her, encouraging her. It kept her moving when she thought she couldn't possibly go another step.

And then, at last, the voice said, *Just up this ridge and you'll find the road.*

In a dream-like state, Gillian climbed the ridge.

And there it was. The road. In the last light before darkness, Gillian could see it meandering down a hill.

But it was still almost a mile to her house, and she couldn't go any farther.

You don't have to, the voice said gently. *Look up the road.*

Gillian saw headlights.

Now just get in the middle of the road and wave.

Gillian stumbled out and waved like a mechanical doll. The headlights were coming, blinding her. Then she realized that they were slowing.

'We did it,' she gasped, dimly aware that she was speaking out loud. 'They're stopping!'

Of course they're stopping. You did a great job. You'll be all right now.

There was no mistaking the note of finality.

The car was stopped now. The driver's side door was opening. Gillian could see a dark figure beyond the glare of the headlights. But in that instant what she felt was distress.

'Wait, don't leave me. I don't even know who you are—'

For a brief moment, she was once again enfolded by love and understanding.

Just call me Angel.

Then the voice was gone, and all Gillian could feel was anguish.

'What are you doing out— Hey, are you OK?' The new voice broke through Gillian's emptiness. She had been standing rigidly in the headlights; now she blinked and tried to focus on the figure coming toward her.

'God, of course you're not OK. Look at you. You're Gillian, aren't you? You live on my street.'

It was David Blackburn.

The knowledge surged through her like a shock, and it drove all the strange hallucinations she'd been having out of her mind.

It really *was* David, as close as he'd ever been to her.

Dark hair. A lean face that still had traces of a summer tan. Cheekbones to die for and eyes to drown in. A certain elegance of carriage. And that half-friendly, half-quizzical smile . . .

Except that he wasn't smiling now. He looked shocked and worried.

Gillian couldn't get a single word out. She just stared at him from under the icy curtain of her hair.

'What hap— No, never mind. We've got to get you warm.'

At school he was thought of as a tough guy, an independent rebel. But, now, without any hesitation, the tough guy scooped her up in his arms.

Confusion flashed through Gillian, then embarrassment – but underneath it all was something much stronger. An odd bedrock sense of safety. David was warm and solid and she knew instinctively that she could trust him. She could stop fighting now and relax.

'Put this on . . . watch your head . . . here, use this for your hair.' David was somehow getting everything done at once without hurrying. Capable and kind. Gillian found herself inside the car, wrapped in his sheepskin jacket, with an old towel around her shoulders. Heat blasted from the vents as David gunned the engine.

It was wonderful to be able to rest without being afraid

it would kill her. Bliss not to be surrounded by cold, even if the hot air didn't seem to warm her. The worn beige interior of the Mustang seemed like paradise.

And David – well, no, he didn't look like an angel. More like a knight, especially the kind who went out in disguise and rescued people.

Gillian was beginning to feel very fuzzy.

'I thought I'd take a dip,' she said, between chattering teeth. She was shivering again.

'What?'

'You asked what happened. I was a little hot, so I jumped in the creek.'

He laughed out loud. 'Huh. You're brave.' Then he glanced at her sideways with keen eyes and added, 'What *really* happened?'

He thinks I'm brave! A glow better than the heated air enveloped Gillian.

'I slipped,' she said. 'I went into the woods, and when I got to the creek—' Suddenly, she remembered why she'd gone into the woods. She'd forgotten it since the fall had put her own life in danger, but now she seemed to hear that faint, pathetic cry all over again.

'Oh, my God,' she said, struggling to sit upright. 'Stop the car.'

CHAPTER 4

David went on driving. He didn't even pause. 'We're almost home.'

They were nearing the turn onto Meadowcroft Road. Gillian tried to grab for one of the brown hands on the steering wheel, and then looked at her own hand, perplexed. Her fingers felt like blocks of wood.

'*You have to stop,*' she said, settling for volume. 'There's a kid lost in those woods. That's why I went in; I heard this sound like crying. It was coming from somewhere right near the creek. We've got to go back there. Come on, *stop*!'

'Hey, hey, calm down,' he said. 'You know what I bet you heard? A long-eared owl. They roost around here, and they make this noise like a moan, *oo-oo-oo*.'

Gillian didn't think so. 'I was walking home from school. It wasn't dark enough for an owl to be out.'

'OK, a mourning dove. Goes *oh-ah, whoo, whoo*. Or a cat; they can sound like kids sometimes. Look,' he added almost savagely, as she opened her mouth again, 'when we get you home, we can call the Houghton police, and they can check things out. But I am *not* letting a lit— a girl freeze just because she's got more guts than smarts.'

For a moment, Gillian had an intense longing to let him continue to believe she had either guts *or* smarts. But she said, 'It's not that. It's just – I've already been through so much to try to find that kid. I almost died – I think I *did* die. I mean – well, I didn't die, but I got pretty cold, and – and things happened, and I realized how important life is . . .' She floundered to a shivering stop. What was she *saying*? Now he was going to think she was a nut case. And anyway all that stuff must have been a dream. She couldn't make it seem real while sitting in a Mustang with her head wrapped in a towel.

But David flashed her a glance of startled recognition.

'You almost died?' He looked back at the road, turning the car onto Hazel Street, where they both lived. 'That happened to me once. When I was little, I had to have this operation—'

He broke off as the Mustang skidded on some ice. In a moment he was in control again and turning into Gillian's driveway.

It happened to you, too?

David parked and was out of the car before Gillian could gather herself to speak.

Then he was opening her door, reaching for her.

'Gotta get all this ridiculous stuff out of the way,' he said, pushing her hair back as if it were a curtain of cobwebs. Something about the way he said it made Gillian think he liked her hair.

She peered up at him through a gap in the curtain. His eyes were dark brown and normally looked almost hawkish, but just now, as their gazes met, they changed. They looked startled and wondering. As if he saw something in her eyes that surprised him and struck a chord.

Gillian felt a flutter of wonder herself. I don't think he's really tough at all, she thought, as something like a spark seemed to flash between them. He's not so different from me; he's—

She was wracked by a sudden bout of shivers.

David blinked and shook his head. 'We've got to get you inside,' he muttered.

And then, still shivering, she was in the air. Bobbing, being carried up the path to her house.

'You shouldn't be walking to school in the winter,' David said. 'I'll drive you from now on.'

Gillian was struck speechless. On the one hand, she should probably tell him she didn't walk *every* day. On the other hand, who was she kidding? Just the thought of him giving her a ride was enough to make her heart beat wildly.

Between that and the novel feeling of being carried, it wasn't until he was opening the front door that Gillian remembered her mother.

Then she panicked.

Oh, God, I can't let David see her – but maybe it'll be all right.

If there was a smell of food cooking, that meant it was OK. If not, it was one of Mom's bad days.

There was no smell of food as David stepped into the dim hallway. And no sign of life – all the downstairs lights were off. The house was cold and echoing and Gillian knew she had to get David out.

But how? He was carrying her farther in, asking, 'Your parents aren't home?'

'I guess not. Dad doesn't get home until seven most nights.' It wasn't *exactly* a lie. Gillian just prayed her mom would stay put in the bedroom until David left.

'I'll be OK now,' she said hastily, not even caring if she sounded rude or ungrateful. Anything to make him *go*. 'I can take care of myself, and – and I'm OK.'

'The he . . . eck you are,' David said. It was the longest drawn out 'heck' Gillian had ever heard.

He doesn't want to swear around me. That's cute.

'You need to get thawed out, fast. Where's a bathtub?'

Gillian automatically lifted a stiff arm to point down the side hall, then dropped it. 'Now, wait a minute—'

He was already there. He put her on her feet, then disappeared into the bathroom to turn on the water.

Gillian cast an anguished glance upstairs. Just *stay put*, Mom. Stay asleep.

'You've got to get in there and stay for at least twenty minutes,' David said, reappearing. 'Then we can see if you need to go to the hospital at Houghton.'

That made Gillian remember something. 'The police—'

'Yeah, right, I'll call them. As soon as you're in the tub.' He reached out and plucked at her dripping, ice-crusted sweater. 'Can you get this off OK? Do your fingers work?'

'Um . . .' Her fingers didn't work; they were still blocks of wood. Frost-nipped at least, she thought, peering at them. But there was no way he was going to undress her, and there was also no way she was going to call her mother. 'Um . . .'

'Uh, turn around,' David said. He pulled at her sweater again. 'OK, I've got my eyes shut. Now—'

'No,' Gillian said, holding her elbows firmly against her sides.

They stood, confused and indecisive, until they were saved by an interruption, a voice from the main hallway.

'What are you *doing* to her?' the voice said.

Gillian turned and looked around David. It was Tanya Jun, David's girlfriend.

Tanya was wearing a velveteen cap perched on her glossy dark hair and a Christmas sweater with metallic threads woven in. She had almond-shaped grey eyes and a mouth with firm lips moulded over white teeth. Gillian always thought of her as a future corporate executive.

'I saw your car out there,' the future executive said to David, 'and the front door of the house was open.' She looked level-headed, suspicious, and a little bit as if she doubted David's sanity. David looked back and forth between her and Gillian and fumbled for an explanation.

'There's nothing going on. I picked her up on Hillcrest Road. She was – well, *look* at her. She fell in the creek and she's frozen.'

'I see,' Tanya said, still calmly. She gave Gillian a quick assessing glance, then turned back to David. 'She doesn't look too bad. You go to the kitchen and make some hot chocolate. Or hot water with Jell-O in it, something with sugar. I'll take care of her.'

'And the police,' Gillian called after David's disappearing back. She didn't exactly want to look Tanya in the face.

Tanya was a senior like David, in the class ahead of Gillian at Rachel Carson High School. Gillian feared her, admired her, and hated her, in about that order.

'Into the bathroom,' Tanya said. Once Gillian was in, she helped her undress, stripping off the clinging, icy-wet clothes and dropping them in the sink. Everything she did was brisk and efficient, and Gillian could almost see sparks fly from her fingers.

Gillian was too miserable to protest at being stripped naked by somebody with the bedside manner of a female prison guard or an extremely strict nanny. She huddled, feeling small and shivering in her bare skin, and then lunged for the tub as soon as Tanya was done.

The water felt scalding. Gillian could feel her eyes get huge and she clenched her teeth on a yell. It probably felt so hot because *she* was so cold. Breathing through her nose, she forced herself to submerge to the shoulders.

'All right,' Tanya said on the other side of the coral-coloured shower curtain. 'I'll go up and get you some dry clothes to put on.'

'*No!*' Gillian said, shooting half out of the water. Not upstairs, not where her mom was, not where her *room* was.

But the bathroom door was already shutting with a decisive click. Tanya wasn't the kind of person you said no to.

Gillian sat, immobilized by panic and horror, until a fountain of burning pain drove everything else out of her mind.

It started in her fingers and toes and shot upward, a white-hot searing that meant her frozen flesh was coming back to life. All she could do was sit rigid, breathe raggedly through her nose, and try to endure it.

And eventually, it did get better. Her white, wrinkled skin turned dark blue, and then mottled, and then red. The searing subsided to a tingling. Gillian could move and think again.

She could hear, too. There were voices outside the bathroom in the hallway. The door didn't even muffle them.

Tanya's voice: 'Here, I'll hold it. I'll take it to her in a minute.' In a mutter: 'I'm not sure she can drink and float at the same time.'

David's voice: 'Come on, give her a break. She's just a kid.'

'Oh, really? Just how old do you think she is?'

'Huh? I don't know. Maybe thirteen?'

An explosive snort from Tanya.

'Fourteen? Twelve?'

'David, she goes to our school. She's a junior.'

'Really?' David sounded startled and bewildered. 'Nah, I think she goes to P.B.'

Pearl S. Buck was the junior high. Gillian sat staring at the bathtub faucet without seeing it.

'She's in our *biology* class,' Tanya's voice said, edging toward open impatience. 'She sits at the back and never opens her mouth.' The voice added, 'I can see why you thought she was younger, though. Her bedroom's knee-deep in stuffed animals. And the wallpaper's little flowers. And look at these pyjamas. Little bears.'

Gillian's insides felt hotter than her fingers had been at their most painful. Tanya had seen her room, which was the same as it had been since Gillian was ten years old, because there wasn't money for new curtains and wallpaper and there wasn't any more storage space in the garage to put her beloved animals away. Tanya was making fun of her pyjamas. In front of David.

And David . . . thought she was a little kid. That was why he'd offered to drive her to school. He'd meant the junior high. He'd been nice because he felt *sorry* for her.

Two tears squeezed out of Gillian's eyes. She was trembling inside, boiling with anger and hurt and humiliation . . .

Crinch.

It was a sound as loud as a rifle report, but high and crystalline – and drawn out. Something between a crash and a crunch and the sound of glass splintering under boots.

Gillian jumped as if she'd been shot, sat frozen a moment, then pulled the moisture-beaded shower curtain aside and poked her head out.

At the same instant the bathroom door flew open.

'What was that?' Tanya said sharply.

Gillian shook her head. She wanted to say, 'You tell *me*,' but she was too frightened of Tanya.

Tanya looked around the bathroom, spied the steamed-up mirror, and frowned. She reached across the sink to wipe it with her hand – and yelped.

'Ow!' She cursed, staring at her hand. Gillian could see the brightness of blood.

'What the—?' Tanya picked up a washcloth and swiped the mirror. She did it again. She stepped back and stared.

From the tub, Gillian was staring, too.

The mirror was broken. Or, not broken, cracked. But it wasn't cracked as if something had hit it. There was no point of impact, with lines of shattering running out.

Instead, it was cracked evenly from top to bottom, side to side. Every inch was covered with a lattice of fine lines. It almost looked purposeful, as if it were a frosted-glass design.

'David! Get in here!' Tanya said, ignoring Gillian. After a moment the door stirred and Gillian had a steamy distorted glimpse of David's face in the mirror.

'Do you see this? How can something like this happen?' Tanya was saying.

David grimaced and shrugged. 'Heat? Cold? I don't know.' He glanced hesitantly in Gillian's direction, just long enough to locate her face surrounded by the coral shower curtain.

'You OK?' he said, addressing himself to a white towel rack on the far wall.

Gillian couldn't say anything. Her throat was too tight and tears were welling up again. But when Tanya looked at her, she nodded.

'All right, forget it. Let's get you changed.' Tanya turned away from the mirror. David melted back out of the bathroom.

'Make sure her fingers and everything are working all right,' he said distantly.

'I'm fine,' Gillian said when she was alone with Tanya.

'Everything's fine.' She wiggled her fingers, which were tender but functioning. All she cared about right now was getting Tanya to go away. 'I can dress myself.'

Please don't let me cry in front of her.

She retreated behind the shower curtain again and made a splashing noise. 'You guys can leave now.'

Half a sigh from Tanya, who was undoubtedly thinking Gillian was ungrateful. 'All right,' she said. 'Your clothes and your chocolate are right here. Is there somebody you want me to call—?'

'No! My parents – my dad will be here any minute. I'm *fine*.' Then she shut her eyes and counted, breath held.

And, blessedly, there were the sounds of Tanya moving away. Both Tanya and David calling goodbyes. Then silence.

Stiffly, Gillian pulled herself upright, almost falling down when she tried to step out of the bathtub.

She put on her pyjamas and walked slowly out of the bathroom, moving like an old woman. She didn't even glance at the broken mirror.

She tried to be quiet going up the stairs. But just as she reached her bedroom, the door at the end of the upstairs hall swung open.

Her mother was standing there, a long coat wrapped around her, fuzzy fleece-lined slippers on her feet. Her hair, a darker blonde than Gillian's, was uncombed.

'What's going on? I heard noise. Where's your father?'

Not 'Whass goin' on? Whersh your father?' But close.

'It's not even seven yet, Mom. I got wet coming home. I'm going to bed.' The bare minimum of sentences to communicate the necessary information.

Her mother frowned. 'Honey—'

' 'Night, Mom.'

Gillian hurried into her bedroom before her mother

could ask any more questions.

She fell on her bed and gathered an armful of stuffed animals in the bend of her elbow. They were solid and friendly and filled her arm. Gillian curled herself around them and bit down on plush.

And now, at last, she could cry. All the hurts of her mind and body merged and she sobbed out loud, wet cheek on the velveteen head of her best bear.

She wished she'd never come back. She wanted the bright meadow with the impossibly green grass, even if it had been a dream. She wanted everyone to be sorry because she was dead.

All her realizations about life being important were nonsense. Life was a giant hoax. She *couldn't* change herself and live in a completely new direction. There was no new start. No hope.

And I don't care, she thought. I just want to die. Oh, why did I get *made* if it was just for this? There's got to be someplace I belong, something I'm meant to do that's different. Because I don't fit in this world, in this life. And if there isn't something more, I'd rather be dead. I want to dream something else.

She cried until she was numb and exhausted and fell into a deadly still sleep without knowing it.

When she woke up hours later, there was a strange light in her room.

CHAPTER 5

Actually, it wasn't the light she noticed first. It was an eerie feeling that some . . . presence was in her room with her.

She'd had the feeling before, waking up to feel that *something* had just left, maybe even in the instant it had taken her to open her eyes. And that while asleep, she'd been on the verge of some great discovery about the world, something that was lost as soon as she woke.

But tonight, the feeling *stayed*. And as she stared around the room, feeling dazed and stupid and leaden, she slowly realized that the light was wrong.

She'd forgotten to close the curtains, and moonlight was streaming into the room. It had the thin blue translucence of new snow. But in one corner of Gillian's room, by the gilded Italian chest of drawers, the light seemed to have pooled. Coalesced. Concentrated. As if reflecting off a mirror.

There wasn't any mirror.

Gillian sat up slowly. Her sinuses were stuffed up and her eyes felt like hard-boiled eggs. She breathed through her mouth and tried to make sense of what was in the corner.

It looked like . . . a pillar. A misty pillar of light. And instead of fading as she woke up, it seemed to be getting brighter.

An ache had taken hold of Gillian's throat. The light was so beautiful . . . and almost familiar. It reminded her of the tunnel and the meadow and . . .

Oh.

She knew now.

It was different to be seeing this when she wasn't dead. Then, she'd accepted strange things the way you accept them in dreams, without ordinary logic or disbelief interfering.

But now she stared as the light got brighter and brighter, and felt her whole skin tingling and tears pooling in her eyes. She could hardly breathe. She didn't know what to do.

How do you greet an angel in the ordinary world?

The light continued to get brighter, just as it had in the meadow. And now she could see the shape in it, walking toward her and rushing at the same time. Still brighter – dazzling and pulsating – until she had to shut her eyes and saw red and gold after-images like shooting stars.

When she squinted her eyes back open, he was there.

Awe caught at Gillian's throat again. He was so beautiful that it was frightening. Face pale, with traces of the light still lingering in his features. Hair like filaments of gold. Strong shoulders, tall but graceful body, every line pure and proud and *different* from any human. He looked more different now than he had in the meadow. Against the drab and ordinary background of Gillian's room, he burned like a torch.

Gillian slid off her bed to kneel on the floor. It was an automatic reflex.

'Don't do that.' The voice was like silver fire. And then

– it changed. Became somehow more ordinary, like a normal human voice. 'Here, does this help?'

Gillian, staring at the carpet, saw the light that was glinting off a stray safety pin fade a bit. When she tilted her eyes up, the angel looked more ordinary, too. Not as luminous. More like just an impossibly beautiful teenage guy.

'I don't want to scare you,' he said. He smiled.

'Yeah,' Gillian whispered. It was all she could get out.

'Are you scared?'

'Yeah.'

The angel made a frustrated circling motion with one arm. 'I can go through all the gobbledygook: be not afraid, I mean you no harm, all that – but it's such a waste of time, don't you think?' He peered at her. 'Aw, come on, kid, you died earlier today. Yesterday. This isn't really all that strange in comparison. You can deal.'

'Yeah.' Gillian blinked. 'Yeah,' she said with more conviction, nodding.

'Take a deep breath, get up—'

'Yeah.'

'—say something different . . .'

Gillian got up. She perched on the edge of her bed. He was right, she *could* deal. So it hadn't been a dream. She had really died, and there really were angels, and now one was in the room with her, looking almost solid except at the edges. And he had come to . . .

'Why did you come here?' she said.

He made a noise that, if he hadn't been an angel, Gillian would have called a snort. 'You don't think I ever really left, do you?' he said chidingly. 'I mean, think about it. How did you manage to recover from freezing without even needing to go to the hospital? You were in severe hypothermia, you know. The worst. You were facing pulmonary oedema, ventricular fibrillation, the loss of a few of your bits . . .' He wiggled his fingers and waggled his feet. That was when Gillian realized he was standing several inches off the floor. 'You were in bad shape, kid. But you got out of it without even frostbite.'

Gillian looked down at her own ten pink fingers. They were tinglingly over-sensitive, but she didn't have even one blood blister. 'You saved me.'

He gave a half-grin and looked sheepish. 'Well, it's my job.'

'To help people.'

'To help *you*.'

A barely acknowledged hope was forming in Gillian's mind. He never really left her; it was his job to help her. That sounded like . . . Could he be . . .

Oh, God, no, it was too corny. Not to mention presumptuous.

He was looking sheepish again. 'Yeah. I don't know how to put it, either. But it *is* true, actually. Did you know that most people *think* they have one even when they don't? Somebody did a poll, and "most people have an inner certainty that there is some particular, individual spirit watching over them". The New Agers call us spirit guides. The Hawaiians call us *aumakua*. . . .'

'You're a guardian angel,' Gillian whispered.

'Yeah. *Your* guardian angel. And I'm here to help you find your heart's desire.'

'I—' Gillian's throat closed.

It was too much to believe. She wasn't worthy. She should have been a better person so that she would *deserve* some of the happiness that suddenly spread out in front of her.

But then a cold feeling of reality set in. She *wasn't* a better person, and although she was sure enlightenment and whatever else an angel thought your heart's desire was, was terrific, well . . . in her case . . .

She swallowed. 'Look,' she said grimly. 'The things I need help with – well, they're not exactly the kinds of things angels are likely to know about.'

'Heh.' He grinned. He leaned over in a position that would have unbalanced an ordinary person and waved an imaginary something over her head. 'You *shall* go to the ball, Cinderella.'

A wand. Gillian looked at him. 'Now you're my fairy godmother?'

'Yeah. But watch the sarcasm, kid.' He changed to a floating position, his arms clasping his knees, and looked her dead in the eye. 'How about if I say I know your heart's desire is for David Blackburn to fall madly in love with you and for everyone at school to think you're totally hot?'

Heat swept up Gillian's face. Her heart was beating out the slow, hard thumps of embarrassment – and excitement. When he said it out loud like that, it sounded extremely shallow . . . and extremely, extremely desirable.

'And you could *help* with that?' she choked out.

'Believe it or not, Ripley.'

'But you're an *angel*.'

He templed his fingers. 'The paths to enlightenment are many, Grasshopper. Grasshopper? Maybe I should call you Dragonfly. You *are* sort of iridescent. There're lots of other insects, but Dung-Beetle sounds sort of insulting . . .'

I've got a guardian angel who sounds like Robin Williams, Gillian thought. It was wonderful. She started to giggle uncontrollably, on the edge of tears.

'Of course, there's a condition,' the angel said, dropping his fingers. He looked at her seriously. His eyes were like the violet-blue at the bottom of a flame.

Gillian gulped, took a scared breath. 'What?'

'You have to trust me.'

'That's *it*?'

'Sometimes it won't be so easy.'

'Look.' Gillian laughed, gulped again, steadied herself. She looked away from his eyes, focusing on the graceful body that was floating in mid-air. 'Look, after all I've seen . . . after you saved my life – and my *bits* . . . how could I not trust you?' She said it again quietly. 'How could I ever not trust you?'

He nodded. Winked. 'OK,' he said. 'Let's prove it.'

'Huh?' Slowly the feeling of awed incredulity was fading. It was beginning to seem almost normal to talk to this magical being.

'Let's prove it. Get some scissors.'

'Scissors?'

Gillian stared at the angel. He stared back.

'I don't even know where any scissors are.'

'Drawer to the left of the silverware drawer in the kitchen. A big sharp pair.' He grinned like Little Red Riding Hood's grandmother.

Gillian wasn't afraid. She didn't decide not to be, she simply wasn't.

'OK,' she said and went down to get the scissors. The angel went with her, floating just behind her shoulder. At the bottom of the stairs were two Abyssinian cats, curled up head to toe like the Yin-Yang symbol. They were fast asleep. Gillian nudged one gently with one toe, and it opened sleepy crescents of eyes.

And then it was off like a flash – both cats were. Streaking down the side hall, falling over each other, skidding on the hardwood floor. Gillian watched with her mouth open.

'Balaam's ass,' the angel said wisely.

'I *beg* your pardon?' For a moment Gillian thought she was being insulted.

'I mean, animals can see us.'

'But they were *scared*. All their fur – I've never seen them like that before.'

'Well, they may not understand what I am. It happens sometimes. Come on, let's get the scissors.'

Gillian stared down the side hall for a moment, then obeyed.

'Now what?' she said as she brought the scissors back to her room.

'Go in the bathroom.'

Gillian went into the little bathroom that adjoined her bedroom and flicked on the light. She licked dry lips.

'And now?' she said, trying to sound flippant. 'Do I cut off a finger?'

'No. Just your hair.'

In the mirror over the sink, Gillian saw her own jaw drop. She couldn't see the angel, though, so she turned around.

'Cut my *hair*? *Off*?'

'Off. You hide behind it too much. You have to show the world that you're not hiding anymore.'

'But—' Gillian raised protective hands, looking back in the mirror. She saw herself, pale, delicate boned, with eyes like wood violets – peering out from a curtain of hair.

So maybe he had a point. But to go into the world *naked*, without anything to duck behind, with her face exposed . . .

'You said you trusted me,' the angel said quietly.

Gillian chanced a look at *him*. His face was stern and there was something in his eyes that almost scared her. Something unknowable and cold, as if he were withdrawing from her.

'It's the way to prove yourself,' he said. 'It's like taking a vow. If you can do this part, you're brave enough to do what it takes to get your heart's desire.' He paused deliberately. 'But, of course, if you're not brave enough, if you want me to go away . . .'

'No,' Gillian said. Most of what he was saying made sense, and as for what she didn't understand – well, she would have to have faith.

I can do this.

To show that she was serious, she took the open scissors, bracketed the pale blonde curtain at a level with her ear, and squeezed them shut. Her hair just folded around the scissors.

'OK.' The angel was laughing. 'Hold onto the hair at the bottom and *pull*. And try less hair.'

He sounded like himself again: warm and teasing and loving – helpful. Gillian let out her breath, gave a wobbly smile, and devoted herself to the horrible and fascinating business of cutting off long blonde chunks.

When she was done, she had a silky blonde cap. Short. It was shorter than Amy's hair, almost as short as J.Z. Oberlin's hair, the girl at school who worked as a model and looked like a Calvin Klein ad. It was *really* short.

'Look in the mirror,' the angel said, although Gillian was already looking. 'What do you see?'

'Somebody with a bad haircut?'

'Wrong. You see somebody who's brave. Strong. Out there. Unique. Individualist. And, incidentally, gorgeous.'

'Oh, please.' But she *did* look different. Under the ragged St Joan bob, her cheekbones seemed to stand out more; she looked older, more sophisticated. And there was colour in her cheeks.

'But it's still all uneven.'

'We can get it smoothed out tomorrow. The important thing is that you took the first step yourself. By the way, you'd better learn to stop blushing. A girl as beautiful as you has to get used to compliments.'

'You're a funny kind of angel.'

'I told you, it's part of the job. Now let's see what you've got in your closet.'

An hour later, Gillian was in bed again. This time, under the covers. She was tired, dazed, and very happy.

'Sleep fast,' the angel said. 'You've got a big day tomorrow.'

'Yes. But wait.' Gillian tried to keep her eyes open. 'There were some things I forgot to ask you.'

'Ask.'

'That crying I heard in the woods – the reason I went in. Was it a kid? And are they OK?'

There was a brief pause before he answered. 'That information is classified. But don't worry,' he added. 'Nobody's hurt – now.'

Gillian opened one eye at him, but it was clear he wasn't going to say any more. 'OK,' she said reluctantly. 'And the other thing was – I *still* don't know what to call you.'

'I told you. Angel.'

Gillian smiled, and was immediately struck by a jaw-cracking yawn. 'OK. Angel.' She opened her eyes again. 'Wait. One more thing . . .'

But she couldn't think of it. There had been some other mystery she'd wanted to ask about, something that had to do with Tanya, with Tanya and blood. But she couldn't summon it up.

Oh, well. She'd remember later. 'I just wanted to say – thank you.'

He snorted. 'You can say it anytime. Get this through your head, kid: I'm not going anywhere. I'll be here tomorrow morning.' He began to hum a Blind Melon song. ' "I'll always be there when you wake . . ." Yeah, yeah, yeah.'

Gillian felt warm, protected . . . loved. She fell asleep smiling.

The next morning she woke early and spent a long time in the bathroom. She came down the stairs feeling self-conscious and lightheaded – literally. With her hair gone her neck felt as if it were floating. She braced herself as she walked into the kitchen.

Neither of her parents was there, even though her father was usually having breakfast by now. Instead, a girl with dark hair was sitting at the kitchen table, bent closely over a calculus textbook.

'Amy!'

Amy glanced up and blinked. She squinted, blinked again, then jumped up, standing an inch taller than Gillian. She moved forward, her eyes huge.

Then she screamed.

CHAPTER 6

'Your hair!' Amy screamed. 'Gillian, your *hair*! What did you *do* to it?'

Amy's own hair was short, cropped close in back and full in front. She had large, limpid blue eyes that always looked as if she were about to cry, because she was nearsighted but couldn't wear contacts and wouldn't wear glasses. Her face was sweet and usually anxious; just now it looked more anxious than normal.

Gillian put a self-conscious hand to her head. 'Don't you like it?'

'I don't know! It's gone!'

'This is true.'

'But *why*?'

'Calm down, Amy.' (If this is the way everybody's going to react, I think I'm in trouble.) Gillian had discovered that she could talk to Angel without moving her lips and that he could answer in her head. It was convenient.

(*Tell her you cut it because it froze. That ought to flip her guilt circuits.*) Angel's voice sounded the same as it did when she could see him. Soft, wry, distinctly his. It seemed to be located just behind her left ear.

'I had to cut it because it was frozen,' Gillian said. 'It

broke off,' she added brightly, inspired.

Amy's blue eyes got even wider with horror. She looked stricken. 'Oh, my God, Gillian—' Then she cocked her head and frowned. 'Actually, I don't think that's possible,' she said. 'I think it'd stay pliable even frozen. Unless, like, you dipped it in liquid nitrogen . . .'

'Whatever,' Gillian said grimly. 'I did it, Listen, I've got it slicked back behind my ears right now, but the ends are sort of uneven. Can you smooth them out a little?'

'I can try,' Amy said doubtfully.

Gillian sat down, pulling together the neck of the rose-coloured bathrobe she was wearing over her clothes. She handed Amy the scissors. 'Got a comb?'

'Yes. Oh, Gillian, I was trying to tell you. I'm so sorry about yesterday. I just forgot – but it's all my fault – and you almost *died*!' The comb quivered against the back of Gillian's neck.

'Wait a minute. How did you find out about that?'

'Eugene heard it from Steffi Lockhart's little brother, and I think Steffi heard it from David Blackburn. Did he really save you? That's so incredibly romantic.'

'Yeah, sort of.' (Uh, what do I tell people about that? What do I tell them about the whole thing?)

(*The truth. Up to a point. Just leave me and the near-death stuff out.*)

'I've been thinking all morning,' Amy was saying, 'and I realized that I've been an absolute pig this last week. I don't deserve to be called a best friend. And I want you to know that I'm sorry, and that things are going to be different now. I came to pick *you* up first, and then we're going to get Eugene.'

(Oh, joy.)

(*Be nice, dragonfly. She's trying. Say thank you.*)

Gillian shrugged. It didn't seem to matter much *what*

Amy did, now that she had Angel. But she said, 'Thanks, Amy,' and held still as the cold scissors went *snip* behind her ear.

'You're so sweet,' Amy murmured. 'I thought you'd be all mad. But you're such a good person. I felt so terrible, thinking about you alone out there, freezing, and being so brave, trying to save a little kid—'

'Did they *find* a kid?' Gillian interrupted.

'Huh? No, I don't think so. Nobody was talking about anything like that last night. And I haven't heard about any kid being missing, either.'

(*Told you, dragonfly. Are you satisfied now?*)

(Yes, I am. Sorry.)

'But it was still brave,' Amy said. 'Your mom thinks so, too.'

'My mom's up?'

'She went to the store. She said she'd be back in a few minutes.' Amy stepped back and looked at Gillian, scissors held in the air. 'You know, I'm not sure I should be doing this . . .'

Before Gillian could summon up a reply, she heard the sound of the front door opening and the rustling of paper bags. Then her mother appeared, her cheeks red with cold. She had two grocery bags in her arms.

'Hi, girls,' she began, and broke off. She focused on Gillian's hair. Her mouth fell open.

'Don't drop the bags,' Gillian said. She tried to sound careless, but her stomach was clenched like a fist. Her neck felt stiff and unnatural as she held very still. 'Do you like it?'

'I – I—' Gillian's mother put the bags on the counter. 'Amy . . . did you have to cut it *all*?'

'Amy didn't do it. I did it last night. I just got tired of it long—' (*And getting all wet and icy*) '—and getting all wet and icy. So I cut it. So do you like it, or not?'

'I don't know,' her mother said slowly. 'You look so much older. Like a Parisian model.'

Gillian glowed.

'Well.' Her mother shook her head slightly. 'Now that it's done – here, let me shape it a little. Just touch up the ends.' She took the scissors from Amy.

(I'm going to be bald when this is finished!)

(*No, you're not, kid. She knows what she's doing.*)

And, strangely, there was something comforting about feeling her mother gently wield the scissors. About her mother's scent, which was fresh like lavender soap, without any hint of the terrible alcohol smell. It reminded Gillian of the old days, when her mom taught at the junior college and was up every morning and never had uncombed hair or bloodshot eyes. Before the fights started, before her mom had to go to the hospital.

Her mother seemed to feel it, too. She gave Gillian's shoulder a pat as she whisked a bit of cut hair away. 'I got fresh bread. I'll make cinnamon toast and hot chocolate.' Another pat, and then she spoke with careful calm. 'Are you sure you're all right? You must have been . . . pretty cold last night. We can call Dr Kaczmarek if you want; it wouldn't take a minute.'

'No, I'm fine. Really. But where's Daddy? Did he already go to work?'

There was a pause, then her mother said, still calmly, 'Your father left last night.'

'Dad left?' (Dad *left*?)

(*It happened last night while you were asleep.*)

(A *lot* seems to have happened last night while I was asleep.)

(*The world's kind of that way, dragonfly. It keeps on going even when you're not paying attention.*)

'Anyway, we'll talk about it later,' her mother said. A final pat. 'There, that's perfect. You're beautiful, even if you don't look like my little girl anymore. You'd better bundle up, though; it's pretty cold out this morning.'

'I'm already dressed.' The moment had come, and Gillian didn't really care if she shocked her mother now or not. Her father had left again – and if that wasn't unusual, it was still upsetting. The closeness with her mother had been spoiled, and she didn't want cinnamon toast anymore.

Gillian stepped to the middle of the kitchen and shrugged off the pink bathrobe.

She was wearing black hipsters and a black camisole. Over it was a sheer black shirt, worn loose. She had on flat black boots and a black watch, and that was *all* she had on.

'Gillian.'

Amy and her mother were staring.

Gillian stood defiantly.

'But you never wear black,' her mother said weakly.

Gillian knew. It had taken a long time to cull these things from the forgotten hinterlands of her closet. The camisole was from Great-grandma Elspeth, two Christmases ago, and had still had the price tag attached.

'Didn't you sort of forget to put on a sweater on top?' Amy suggested.

(*Stand your ground, kid. You look terrific.*)

'No, I didn't forget. I'm going to wear a coat outside, of course. How do I *look*?'

Amy swallowed. 'Well – great. Extremely hot. But kind of scary.'

Gillian's mother lifted her hands and dropped them. 'I don't really know you anymore.'

(Hooray!)

(*Yup, kid. Perfect.*)

Gillian was happy enough to give her mother a flying kiss. 'Come on, Amy! We'd better get moving if we're going to pick up Eugene.' She dragged the other girl behind her like the tail of a comet. Her mother followed, calling worriedly about breakfast.

'Give us something to take with us. Where's that old black coat I never wore? The fancy one you got me for church. Never mind, I found it.'

In three minutes she and Amy were on the porch.

'Wait,' Gillian said. She fished through the black canvas bag she was carrying in place of a backpack and came up with a small compact and a tube of lipstick. 'I almost forgot.'

She put on the lipstick. It was red, not orange-red or blue-red, but *red* red, the colour of holly berries or Christmas ribbon. That shiny, too. It made her lips look fuller, somehow, almost pouty. Gillian pursed her lips, considered her image, then kissed the compact mirror lightly and snapped it shut.

Amy was staring again. 'Gillian . . . *what* is going *on*? What's happened to you?'

'Come on, we're going to be late.'

'The outfit just makes you look like you're going out to burgle something, but that lipstick makes you look . . . *bad*. Like a girl with a reputation.'

'Good.'

'Gillian! You're scaring me. There's something—' She caught Gillian's arm and peered into her eyes. 'Something about you – *around* you – oh, I don't know what I'm talking about! But it's different and it's dark and it's *not good*.'

She was so genuinely shaken that for a moment Gillian was frightened herself. A quick stab of fear like the flick of a knife in her stomach. Amy was neurotic, sure, but she wasn't the type to hallucinate. What if—

(Angel—)

A horn honked.

Startled, Gillian turned. Right at the edge of the driveway, behind Amy's Geo, was a somewhat battered but still proud tan Mustang. A dark head was sticking out the window.

'Standing me up?' David Blackburn called.

'What – is – *that*?' Amy breathed.

Gillian waved to David – after a sharp nudge from Angel. 'I think it's called a car,' she said to Amy. 'I forgot. He said he'd drive me to school. So, I guess I should go with him. See you!'

It only made sense to go with David; after all, he *had* asked first. Besides, Amy's driving was life threatening; she sped like a maniac and wove all over the road because she couldn't see without her glasses.

It should have been satisfying. After all, yesterday Amy had stood *her* up for a guy – and a guy like Eugene Elfred. But right this moment Gillian was too scared to be smug.

This was it. David was going to see her new self. And it was all happening too fast.

(Angel, what if I faint? What if I throw up? *That's* going to make a great first impression, isn't it?)

(*Keep breathing, kid. Breathe. Breathe. Not that fast. Now smile.*)

Gillian couldn't quite manage a smile as she opened the car door. Suddenly she felt exposed. What if David thought she was cheap or even freakish? Like a little girl dressed up in her mom's clothes?

And her hair – all at once she remembered how David had touched it yesterday. What if he *hated* it?

Trying to breathe, she slipped into the car. Her coat

came open as she sat down. She could hardly make herself look towards the driver's seat.

But when she did, her breath stopped completely. David was wearing a look that she'd never seen on any guy's face before, at least not directed toward her. She'd seen it, occasionally, when guys were looking at other girls, girls at school like Steffi Lockhart or J.Z. Oberlin. A stricken gaze, a compulsive movement of the throat, an expression that almost made you sorry for them. An 'I'm lying down and I don't care if you walk on me, babe,' expression.

David was looking at *her* that way.

Immediately all her fear, including the little stab induced by Amy, was swept away. Her heart was still pounding and little waves of adrenalin were still going through her, but now what it felt like was excitement. Heady, buoyant anticipation. As if she had started on the roller coaster ride of her life.

David actually had to shake himself before he remembered to put the car in gear. And then he kept sneaking glances at her out of the side of his eye.

'You did something to your . . . and your . . .' He made a vague motion near his own head. Gillian's gaze was caught by his hand, which was strong, brown, long-fingered, and handsome.

'Yeah, I cut my hair,' she said. She meant to sound careless and sophisticated, but it came out shaky, with a little laugh at the end. She tried again. 'I figured I didn't want to look too young.'

'Ouch.' He made a face. 'That's my fault, isn't it? You overheard that stuff yesterday. What Tanya and I said.'

(*Tell him you've been thinking of doing it for a while.*)

'Yeah, but I've been thinking of doing it for a while now,' Gillian said. 'It's no big deal.'

David glanced at her as if to say *he* disagreed with that. But it wasn't a disapproving glance. It was more like electrified awe . . . and a sort of discovery that seemed to grow every time he looked at her.

'And I never saw you at school?' he muttered. 'I must've been blind.'

'Sorry?'

'No, nothing. *I'm* sorry.' He drove in silence for a while. Gillian forced herself to stare out the window and realized they were on Hillcrest Road. Strange how different the landscape looked today. Yesterday it had been lonely and desolate; this morning it seemed harmless, and the snow looked soft and comfortable, like old cushions.

'Listen,' David said abruptly. He broke off and shook his head. And then he did something that absolutely amazed Gillian. He pulled the car to the side of the road – or at least as far to the side as he could get it – they were still in the flow of traffic – and parked it.

'There's something I have to say.'

Gillian's heart now seemed to be beating everywhere, in her throat and her fingertips and her ears. She had a dreamlike sensation that her body wasn't solid anymore, that she was just a floating mass of heartbeat. Her vision shimmered. She was . . . waiting.

But what David said was unexpected. 'Do you remember the first time we met?'

'I – yes.' Of course she did. Four years ago; she'd been twelve and tiny for her age. She'd been lying on the ground beside her house, making snow angels. Kind of childish, sure, but in those days a stretch of new snow had affected her that way. And while she was lying on her back, arms out, making the imprint of the angel's wings, a tree branch above her decided to shrug off its load of snow. Suddenly her face was covered in damp, closely packed coldness and she couldn't breathe. She came up spluttering and gasping.

And found herself steadied. Something was holding her, wiping her face gently. The first thing she saw when she got her vision back was a brown hand and a lean brown wrist. Then a face came into focus: high strong bones and dark, mischievous eyes.

'I'm David Blackburn. I just moved in over there,' the boy said. He was wiping her face with his fingers. 'You'd better be careful, snow princess. Next time I might not be around.'

Looking up at him, Gillian had felt her heart explode and leak out of her chest.

And she'd walked away on air, even though he'd patted her head after releasing her. She was in love.

'Well, back then, I sort of got the wrong impression,' David was saying. 'I thought you were a lot younger and more – well, more *fragile* than you are.' There was a pause, and then he said wonderingly, not quite looking at her, 'But, it's like, there's so much more to you. I started realizing that yesterday.'

Gillian understood. David didn't have a reputation for being wild for nothing. He liked girls who were bold, dashing, out there. If he were a knight, he wouldn't fall in love with the pampered princess back at the castle. He'd fall in love with a female knight, or maybe a robber, somebody who could share the Adventure with him, who'd be just as tough as he was.

Of course he had a strong protective streak. That was why he rescued maidens in distress. But he didn't *go* for the maidens who needed rescuing.

'And now,' David was saying, 'Now, I mean, you're . . .' He held his hands up in a whoa motion. He wasn't looking at her at all.

In a moment of perfect bliss, Gillian thought, I'm cool.

'You're kind of incredible,' David said. 'And I feel *really* stupid for not noticing that before.'

Gillian couldn't breathe. There was something between her and David – a kind of quivering electricity. The air was so thick with it that she felt pressure all over her. She had never been so awake before, but at the same time she felt as if most of the world was insubstantial. Only she and David were real.

And the voice in her head seemed very far away. (*Uh, dragonfly, we've got company. Incoming.*)

Gillian couldn't move. A car drove by, swerving to avoid the Mustang. Gillian couldn't see well through the Mustang's steamed-up windows, but she thought faces were looking at her.

David didn't seem to notice the car at all. He was still staring at the gearshift, and when he spoke his voice was very quiet. 'So I guess what I'm saying is, I'm sorry if anything I said hurt your feelings. And – I see you now.'

He raised his head. And Gillian suddenly realized he was going to kiss her.

CHAPTER 7

Gillian felt triumph, wild excitement – and something deeper. An emotion she couldn't describe because there weren't any ordinary words for it. David was looking at her, and it was almost as if she could see *through* his dark eyes. As if she could see inside him . . . see the way things looked to him . . .

What she felt was a little like discovery and a little like déjà vu and a little like waking up and suddenly realizing it's Christmas. Or like being a kid lost in a strange place, cold and bewildered, and then suddenly hearing your mother's voice. But it really wasn't like any of those things; it was *more*. Unexpected welcome . . . strange recognition . . . the shock of belonging . . .

She couldn't quite put it all together, because there was nothing like it in her experience. She'd never *heard* of anything like this. But she had the feeling that when David kissed her, she'd figure it all out and it would be the revelation of her life.

It was going to happen – now. He was moving closer to her, not fast, but as if slowly compelled by something he couldn't control. Gillian had to look down, but she didn't move back or turn her face away. He was close enough now that she could hear his breath and feel him. Her eyes shut of their own accord.

She waited to feel the touch of warmth on her lips . . .

And then something in her mind stirred. A tiny whisper, so far back that she could barely hear it, and she couldn't tell where it came from.

Tanya.

The shock went through Gillian like ice on bare skin. Part of her tried to ignore it, but she was already pulling away, putting a hand up, turning to stare at the window.

Not *out* the window. It was too steamed up now to see anything outside. They were in their own cocoon of whiteness.

Gillian said, 'I *can't*. I mean, not like this. I mean – it isn't fair, because you already – and you haven't . . . I mean . . . *Tanya*.'

'I know.' David sounded as if *he'd* been hit with ice on bare skin, or as if he'd come up from deep water and was looking around dazedly. 'I mean, you're right. I don't know what I was . . . It just – it was like I forgot . . . Look, I'm sure that sounds stupid. You don't believe me.'

'I do believe you.' At least he sounded as incoherent as she did. He wouldn't think she was a total fool; her facade wasn't broken.

'I'm not that kind of guy. I mean, it looks like I am, right here, it looks exactly like I am. But I'm *not*. I mean I never – I'm not like Bruce Faber. I don't do that. I made a promise to Tanya and . . .'

Oh, God, Gillian thought. And then a sort of inward scream: (Help!)

(*I was wondering when you'd remember me.*)

(He made her a promise!)

(*I'm sure he did. They've been going together a while.*)

(But that's *terrible!*)

(*No, it's admirable. What a guy. Now say you've got to get to school.*)

(I can't. I can't *think*. How are we going to—)

(*School first.*)

Dully, Gillian said, 'I guess we'd better get moving.'

'Yeah.' There was a pause, and then David put the car in gear.

They drove in silencc, and Gillian sank deeper and deeper into depression. She'd thought it would be so easy – just show David her new self and everything would fall into place. But it wasn't like that. He couldn't just dump Tanya.

(*Don't worry about it, kid. I have a cunning plan.*)

(But *what?*)

(*I'll tell you when it's time.*)

(Angel, are you *mad* at me? Because I forgot about you?)

(*Of course not. I'm here to arrange things so you can forget me.*)

(Then – because I forgot about Tanya for a while? I don't want to do anything that's wrong . . .)

(*I'm not mad! Heads up. You're there.*)

Gillian couldn't push away the feeling that he *was* mad, though. Or at least surprised. As if something unexpected had happened.

But she didn't have time to dwell on it. She had to get out of David's car and gather herself and face the high school.

'I guess – I'll see you later,' David said as she reached for the door handle. His voice made it a question.

'Yeah. Later,' Gillian said. She didn't have the energy for anything more. She glanced back – once – to see him staring at the steering wheel.

She could see people staring at *her* as she walked to the

school building. It was a new sensation and it gave her a spasm of anxiety.

Were they laughing at her? Did she look silly, was she walking *wrong* somehow?

(*Just breathe and walk.*) Angel's voice sounded amused. (*Breathe – walk – head up – breathe . . .*)

Gillian somehow got through halls and up stairs to her U.S. history class without meeting another student's eyes once.

There, arriving just as the bell rang, she realized she had a problem. Her history textbook, along with all her notes, was floating somewhere down toward West Virginia.

With relief, she caught Amy's eye and headed toward the back of the classroom.

'Can I share your book? My whole backpack went in the creek.' She was a little afraid Amy might be miffed or jealous at the way she'd run off with David, but Amy didn't seem to be either. She seemed more – awed – as if Gillian were some force like a tornado that you might fear, but that you couldn't get mad at.

'Sure.' Amy waited until Gillian had scooted her desk closer, then whispered, 'How come it took you so long to get to school? What were you and David *doing*?'

Gillian rummaged for a pen. 'How do you know we weren't picking up Tanya?'

'Because Tanya was here at school looking for *David*.'

Gillian's heart flip-flopped. She pretended to be very interested in history.

But she gradually noticed that some of the other students were looking at her. Especially the boys. It was the sort of look she'd never imagined getting from a boy.

But these were all juniors, and none of them was in the really popular clique. All that would change in Gillian's next class, biology. Half a dozen of the most popular kids would be there. David would be there – and Tanya.

Gillian felt, with a sudden chill, that she might not really care anymore. What did it matter what other people thought of her if she couldn't have David? But she had a fundamental faith in Angel. Somehow things *had to* work out – if she just stayed calm and played her part.

When the bell rang, she hurried away from Amy's questioning eyes and into the bathroom. She needed a moment to herself.

(*Do something to your lipstick. It seems to have gone away somehow.*) Angel sounded as puzzled as any human boy.

Gillian fixed the lipstick. She ran a comb through her hair. She was somewhat reassured by the sight of herself in the mirror. The girl there wasn't Gillian at all, but a slender, insubstantial femme fatale sheathed like a dagger in black. The girl's hair was silky, the palest of all possible golds. Her violet eyes were subtly shadowed so they looked mysterious, haunting. Her mouth was soft, red, and full: perfect, like the mouth of a model in a lipstick commercial. Against the stark black of her clothing, her skin had the slightly translucent look of apple blossoms.

She's beautiful, Gillian thought. And then to Angel: (I mean, I am. But I need . . . a Look, don't you think? An expression for when people are staring at me. Like, am I Bored or Slightly Amused or Aloof or Completely Oblivious or what?)

(*How about Thoughtful? As if you've got your own inner world to pay attention to. It's true, you know. You do.*)

Gillian was pleased. Thoughtful, absorbed in herself, listening to the music of the spheres – or the music of Angel's voice. She could do that. She settled the canvas bag on her shoulder and started toward her locker.

(*Uh, where are you going?*)

(To get my biology book. I still have that.)

(*No, you don't.*)

Gillian maintained her Thoughtful expression, while noting that heads turned as she walked down the hall. (Yes, I do.)

(No, you don't. Due to circumstances entirely beyond your control, you lost your biology book and all your notes. You need to sit with somebody else and share *his*.)

Gillian blinked. (I – *oh*. Oh, yeah, you're right. I lost my biology book.)

The door of the biology lab loomed like the gate to hell, and Gillian had trouble keeping Thoughtful pinned to her face. But she managed to walk through it and into the quiet buzz that was a class before a bell was about to ring.

(*OK, kid. Go up front and tell Mr Wizard you need a new book. He'll take care of the rest.*)

Gillian did as Angel said. As she stood beside Mr Leveret and told her story she sensed a new quietness in the classroom behind her. She didn't look back and she didn't raise her voice. By the time she was done, Mr Leveret's pouchy, pleasantly ugly face had gone from a startled 'Who are you?' expression (he had to look in the class register to make sure of her name) to one of pained sympathy.

'I've got an extra textbook,' he said. 'And some outlines of my lectures on transparencies. But as for notes—'

He turned to the class at large. 'OK, people. Jill – uh, Gillian – needs a little help. She needs somebody who's willing to share their notes, maybe photocopy them—'

Before he could finish his sentence, hands went up all over the room.

Somehow that brought everything into focus for

Gillian. She was standing in front of a classroom with everyone staring at her – that in itself would have been enough to terrify her in the old days. And sitting there in front was David, wearing an unreadable expression, and Tanya, looking rigidly shocked. And other people who'd never looked directly at her before, and who were now waving their hands enthusiastically.

All boys.

She recognized Bruce Faber, who she'd always thought of as Bruce the Athlete, with his tawny hair and his blue-grey eyes and his tall football build. Normally he looked as if he were acknowledging the applause of a crowd. Just now he looked as if he were graciously extending an invitation to Gillian.

And Macon Kingsley, who she called Macon the Wallet because he was so rich. His hair was brown and styled, his eyes hooded, and there was something cruel to the sensual droop of his mouth. But he wore a Rolex and had a new sports car and right now he was looking at Gillian as if he'd pay a lot of money for her.

And Cory Zablinski – who was Cory the Party Guy because he constantly seemed to be arranging, going to, or just recovering from parties. Cory was wiry and hyper, with foxy brown hair and darting fox-coloured eyes. He had more personality than looks, but he was always in the middle of things, and at this moment he was waving madly at Gillian.

Even Amy's new boyfriend Eugene, who didn't have looks *or* personality in Gillian's opinion, was wiggling his fingers eagerly.

David had his hand up, too, despite Tanya's cold expression. He looked polite and stubborn. Gillian wondered if he'd told Tanya he was just trying to help a poor junior out.

(*Pick . . . Macon.*) The ghostly voice in Gillian's ear was thoughtful.

(Macon? I thought maybe Cory.) She couldn't pick David, of course, not with Tanya looking daggers at her. And she felt uncomfortable about picking Bruce for the same reason – his girlfriend Amanda Spengler was sitting right beside him. Cory was friendly and, well, accessible. Macon, on the other hand, was vaguely creepy.

This time the voice in her head was patient. (*Have I ever steered you wrong? Macon.*)

(Cory's the one who always knows about parties . . .) But Gillian was already moving toward Macon. The most important thing in life, she was discovering quickly, was to trust Angel absolutely.

'Thanks,' she said softly to Macon as she perched on an empty stool behind him. She repeated after Angel: 'I'll bet you take good notes. You seem like a good observer.'

Macon the Wallet barely inclined his head. She noticed that his hooded eyes were moss green, an unusual, almost disturbing colour.

But he was nice to her all period. He promised to have his father's secretary photocopy the thick sheaf of biology notes in his spiral-bound notebook. He lent her a highlighter. And he kept looking at her as if she were some interesting piece of art.

That wasn't all. Cory the Party Guy dropped a ball of paper on the lab table as he walked past to get rid of his gum in the trash can. When Gillian unfolded it she found a Hershey's kiss and a questionnaire: *R U new? Do U like music? What's yr phone #?* And Bruce the Athlete tried to catch her eye whenever she glanced in his direction.

A warm and heady glow was starting somewhere inside Gillian.

But the most amazing part was yet to come. Mr

Leveret, pacing in the front, asked for somebody to review the five kingdoms used to categorize living things.

(*Raise your hand, kid.*)

(But I don't remember—)

(*Trust me.*)

Gillian's hand went up. The warm feeling had changed to a sense of dread. She *never* answered questions in class. She almost hoped Mr Leveret wouldn't see her, but he spotted her right away and nodded.

'Gillian?'

(*Now just say after me . . .*) The soft voice in her head went on.

'OK, the five classes would be, from most advanced to most primitive, Animalia, Plantae, Fungi, Protista . . . and Eugene.' Gillian ticked them off on her fingers and glanced sideways at Eugene as she finished.

(But that's not *nice*. I mean—)

She never got to what she meant. The entire class was roaring with laughter. Even Mr Leveret rolled his eyes at the ceiling and shook his head tolerantly.

They thought she was hysterical. Witty. One of those types who could break up a whole classroom.

(But Eugene—)

(*Look at him.*)

Eugene was blushing pink, ducking his head. Grinning. He didn't look embarrassed or hurt; he actually looked pleased at the attention.

It's still wrong, a tiny voice that wasn't Angel's seemed to whisper. But it was drowned out by the laughter and the rising warmth inside Gillian. She'd never felt so accepted, so *included*. She had the feeling that now people would laugh whenever she said something even marginally funny. Because they *wanted* to laugh; they wanted to be pleased by her – and to please her.

(*Rule One, dragonfly. A beautiful girl can tease any guy and make him like it. No matter what the joke is. Am I right or am I right?*)

(Angel, you're always right.) She meant it with all her heart. She had never imagined that guardian angels could be like this, but she was glad beyond words that they were and that she had one on her side.

At break the miracles continued. Instead of hurrying out the door as she normally did, she found herself walking slowly and lingering in the hall. She couldn't help it, both Macon and Cory were in front of her, talking to her.

'I can have the notes ready for you this weekend,' Macon the Wallet was saying. 'Maybe I should drop them by your house.' His heavy-lidded eyes seemed to bore into her and the sensual droop to his mouth became more pronounced.

'No, I've got a better idea,' Cory was saying, almost dancing around the two of them. 'Mac, m'man, don't you think it's about time you had another party? I mean, it's been weeks, and you've got that big house . . . How about Saturday, and I'll round up a keg and we can all get to know Jill better.' He gestured expansively.

'Good idea,' Bruce the Athlete said cheerfully from behind Gillian. 'I'm free Saturday. What about you, Jill?' He draped a casual arm around her shoulder.

'Ask me Friday,' Gillian said with a smile, repeating the whispered words in her mind. She shrugged off the arm on her own volition. Bruce belonged to Amanda.

A party for me, Gillian thought dazedly. All she'd wanted was to get *invited* to a party given by these kids – she'd never imagined being the focus of one. She felt a stinging in her nose and eyes and a sort of desperation in her stomach. Things were happening almost too fast.

Other people were gathering around curiously.

Incredibly, she was at the centre of a crowd and everyone seemed to be either talking to her or about her.

'Hey, are you new?'

'That's Gillian Lennox. She's been here for years.'

'I never saw her before.'

'You just never *noticed* her before.'

'Hey, Jill, how come you lost your biology book?'

'Didn't you hear? She fell in a creek trying to save some kid. Almost drowned.'

'I heard David Blackburn pulled her out and had to give her artificial respiration.'

'*I* heard they were parked on Hillcrest Road this morning.'

It was intoxicating, exhilarating. And it wasn't just guys who were gathered around her. She would have thought that the girls would be jealous, spiteful, that they'd glare at her or even all walk away from her in one mass snub.

But there was Kimberlee Cherry, Kim the Gymnast, the bubbly, sparkly little dynamo with her sun-blonde curls and her baby-blue eyes. She was laughing and chattering. And there was Steffi Lockhart the Singer, with her café au lait skin and her soulful amber eyes, waving an expressive hand and beaming.

Even Amanda the Cheerleader, Bruce Faber's girlfriend, was in the group. She was flashing her healthy, wide smile and tossing her shiny brown hair, her fresh face glowing.

Gillian understood suddenly. The girls couldn't hate her, or couldn't show it if they did. Because Gillian had *status*, the instant and unassailable status that came from being beautiful and having guys fall all over themselves for her. She was a rising star, a force, a power to be reckoned with. And any girl who snubbed her was risking a nick in her own popularity if Gillian should decide to retaliate. They were *afraid* not to be nice to her.

It was dizzying, all right. Gillian felt as beautiful as an angel and as dangerous as a serpent. She was riding on waves of energy and adulation.

But then she saw something that made her feel as if she had suddenly stepped off a cliff.

Tanya had David by the arm and they were walking away down the hall.

CHAPTER 8

Gillian stood perfectly still and watched David disappear around a corner.

(*It's not time for the plan yet, kid. Now buck up. A cheery face is worth diamonds.*)

Gillian tried to put on a cheery face.

The strange day continued. In each class, Gillian appealed to the teacher for a new book. In each class, she was bombarded with offers of notes and other help. And through it all Angel whispered in her ear, always suggesting just the right thing to say to each person. He was witty, irreverent, occasionally cutting – and so was Gillian.

She had an advantage, she realized. Since nobody had ever noticed her before, it was almost like being a new girl. She could be anything she wanted to be, present herself as anyone, and be believed.

(*Like Cinderella at the ball. The mystery princess.*) Angel's voice was amused but tender.

In journalism class, Gillian found herself beside Daryl Novak, a languid girl with sloe eyes and drooping contemptuous lashes. Daryl the Rich Girl, Daryl the World-weary World Traveller. She talked to Gillian as if Gillian knew all about Paris and Rome and California.

At lunch, Gillian hesitated as she walked into the cafeteria. Usually she sat with Amy in an obscure corner at the back. But recently Eugene had been sitting with Amy, and up front she could see a group that included Amanda the Cheerleader, Kim the Gymnast, and others from The Clique. David and Tanya were at the edge.

(Do I sit with them? Nobody asked me.)

(*Not with them, my little rutabaga. But near them. Sit at the end of that table just beside them. Don't look at them as you walk by. Look at your lunch. Start eating it.*)

Gillian had never eaten her lunch alone before – or at least not in a public place. On days Amy was absent, if she couldn't find one of the few other juniors she felt comfortable with, she snuck into the library and ate there.

In the old days she would have felt horribly exposed, but now she wasn't really alone; she had Angel cracking jokes in her ear. And she had a new confidence. She could almost see herself eating, calm and indifferent to stares, thoughtful to the point of being dreamy. She tried to make her movements a little languid, like Daryl the Rich Girl's.

(And I hope Amy doesn't think I'm snubbing her. I mean, it's not as if she's back there alone. She's got Eugene.)

(*Yeah. We're gonna have to talk about Amy sometime, kid. But right now you're being paged. Smile and be gracious.*)

'Jill! Earth to Jill!'

'Hey, Jill, c'mon over.'

They wanted her. She was moving her lunch over to their table, and she wasn't spilling anything and she wasn't falling as she slid in. She was little and graceful, thistledown light in her movements, and they were surging around her to form a warm and friendly bulwark.

And she wasn't afraid of them. That was the most wonderful thing of all. These kids who'd seemed to her like stars in some TV show about teenagers, were real people who got crumbs on themselves and made jokes she could understand.

Gillian had always wondered what they found so *funny* when they were laughing together. But now she knew it was just the heady atmosphere, the knowledge that they were special. It made it easy to laugh at everything. She knew David, sitting quietly there with Tanya, could see her laughing.

She could hear other voices occasionally, from people on the fringes of her group, people on the outside looking in. Mostly bright chatter and murmurs of admiration. She thought she heard her name mentioned . . .

And then she focused on the words.

'I heard her mom's a drunk.'

They sounded horribly loud and clear to Gillian, standing out against the background noise. She could feel her whole skin tingling with shock and she lost track of the story Kim the Gymnast was telling.

(Angel, who said that? Was it about me – my mom?) She didn't dare look behind her.

'—started drinking a few years ago and having these hallucinations—'

This time the voice was so loud that it cut through the banter of Gillian's group. Kim stopped in mid-sentence. Bruce the Athlete's smile faltered. An awkward silence fell.

Gillian felt a wave of anger that made her dizzy. (Who said that? I'll kill them—)

(*Calm down! Calm* down. *That's not the way to handle it at all.*)

(But—)

(*I said, calm down. Look at your lunch. No, at your lunch. Now say – and make your voice absolutely cool – 'I really hate rumours, don't you? I don't know what kind of people start them.'*)

Gillian breathed twice and obeyed, although her voice wasn't absolutely cool. It had a little tremor.

'I don't know either,' a new voice said. Gillian glanced up to see that David was on his feet, his face hard as he surveyed the table behind her as if looking for the person who'd spoken. 'But I think they're pretty sick and they should get a life.'

There was the cold glint in his eyes that had given him his reputation as a tough guy. Gillian felt as if a hand had steadied her. Gratitude rushed through her – and a longing that made her bite down on her lip.

'I hate rumours, too,' J.Z. Oberlin said in her absent voice. J.Z. the Model was the one who looked like a Calvin Klein ad, breathlessly sexy and rather blank, but right now she seemed oddly focused. 'Somebody was putting around the rumour last year that I tried to kill myself. I never did find out who started it.' Her hazy blue-green eyes were narrowed.

And then everyone was talking about rumours, and people who spread rumours, and what scum they were. The group was rallying around Gillian.

But it was David who stood up for me first, she thought.

She had just looked over at him, trying to catch his eye, when she heard the tinkling noise.

It was almost musical, but the kind of sound that draws attention immediately in a cafeteria. Somebody had broken a glass. Gillian, along with everyone else, glanced around to see who'd done it.

She couldn't see anybody. No one had the right expression of dismay, no one was focused on anything definite. Everybody was looking around in search mode.

Then she heard it again, and two people standing near

the cafeteria doors looked down and then up.

Above the doors, far above, was a semi-circular window in the red brick. As Gillian stared at the window she realized that light was reflecting off it oddly, almost prismatically. There seemed to be crazy rainbows in the glass . . .

And something was sparkling down, falling like a few specks of snow. It hit thc ground and tinkled, and the people by the door stared at it on the cafeteria floor. They looked puzzled.

Realization flashed on Gillian. She was on her feet, but the only words that she could find were, 'Oh, my God!'

'Get out! It's all going to go! Get out of there!' It was David, waving at the people under the window. He was running toward them, which was *stupid*, Gillian thought numbly, her heart seeming to stop.

Other people were shouting. Cory and Amanda and Bruce – and Tanya. Kim the Gymnast was shrieking. And then the window *was* going, chunks of it falling almost poetically, raining and crumbling, shining and crashing. It fell and fell and fell. Gillian felt as if she were watching an avalanche in slow motion.

At last it was over, and the window was just an arch-shaped hole with jagged teeth clinging to the edges. Glass had flown and bounced and skittered all over the cafeteria, where it lay like hailstones. And people from tables amazingly distant were examining cuts from ricocheting bits.

But nobody had been directly underneath, and nobody seemed seriously hurt.

(Thanks to David.) Gillian was still numb, but now with relief. (He got them all out of the way in time. Oh, God, *he* isn't hurt, is he?)

(*He's fine. And what makes you think he did it all alone?*

Maybe I had some part. I can do that, you know – put it into people's heads to do things. And they never even know I'm doing it.) Angel's voice sounded almost – well – piqued.

(Huh? You did that? Well, that was really nice of you.) Gillian was watching David across the room, watching Tanya examine his arm, nod, shrug, look around.

He's *not* hurt. Thank heaven. Gillian felt so relieved it was almost painful.

It was then that it occurred to her to wonder what had happened.

That window – before the glass fell it had looked just like the mirror in her bathroom. Evenly shattered from side to side, spidery cracks over every inch of the surface.

The bathroom mirror had cracked while Tanya was being catty about Gillian's room. *Now* Gillian remembered the last thing she'd wanted to ask Angel last night. It had been about how the mirror came to do that.

This window . . . it had started falling a few minutes after someone insulted Gillian's mother. Nobody had heard it actually break, but it couldn't have happened too long ago.

The small hairs on the back of Gillian's neck stirred and she felt a fluttering inside.

It couldn't be. Angel hadn't even appeared to her yet . . .

But he'd said he was always with her . . .

An angel wouldn't *destroy* things . . .

But Angel was a different kind of angel.

(*Ah, excuse me. Hello? Do you want to share some thoughts with me?*)

(Angel!) For the first time since his soft voice had sounded in her ear, Gillian felt a sense of – overcrowdedness. Of her own lack of privacy. The uneasy fluttering inside her increased. (Angel, I was just – just wondering . . .) And then the silent words burst out. (Angel, you *wouldn't* – would you? You didn't do those things for my sake – break the mirror and that window—?)

A pause. And then, in her head, riotous laughter. *Genuine* laughter. Angel was whooping.

Finally, the sounds died to mental hiccups. *(Me?)*

Gillian was embarrassed. (I shouldn't have asked. It was just so weird . . .)

(*Yeah, wasn't it.*) This time Angel sounded grimly amused. (*Well, never mind; you're already late for class. The bell rang five minutes ago.*)

Gillian coasted through her last two classes in a daze. So much had happened today – she felt as if she'd led a full life between waking up and now.

But the day wasn't over yet.

In her last class, studio art, she once again found herself talking to Daryl the Rich Girl. Daryl was the only one of that crowd that took art or journalism. And in the last minutes before school ended, she regarded Gillian from under drooping eyelashes.

'You know, there are other rumours going around about you. That you and Davey-boy have something going behind Tanya's back. That you meet secretly in the mornings and . . .' Daryl shrugged, pushing back frosted hair with a hand dripping with rings.

Gillian felt jolted awake. 'So?'

'So you really should do something about it. Rumours spread fast, and they grow. I know. You want to either deny them, or' – Daryl's lips quirked in a smile – 'disarm them.'

(Oh, yeah? And just how do I do that?)

(*Shut up and listen to her, kid. This is one smart cookie.*)

'If there're parts that are true, it's usually best to admit those in public. That takes some of the punch out. And it's *always* helpful to track down the person starting the rumours – if you can.'

(*Tell her you know that. And that you're going to see Tanya after school.*)

(*Tanya?* You mean—?)

(*Just tell her.*)

Somehow Gillian gathered herself enough to repeat Angel's words.

Daryl the Rich Girl looked at her with a new expression of respect. 'You're sharper than I thought. Maybe you didn't need my help after all.'

'No,' Gillian said without Angel's prompting. 'I'm always glad for help. It's – it's a rough world.'

'Isn't it, though?' Daryl said and raised already arched eyebrows.

(So it was Tanya who spread that stuff about my mom.) Gillian almost stumbled as she trudged out of art class. She was tired and bewildered. Somehow, she'd have thought Tanya was above that.

(*She had help. It takes a really efficient system to get a rumour to peak circulation that fast. But she was the instigator. Turn left here.*)

(Where am I going?)

(*You're gonna catch her coming out of marketing education. She's alone in there right now. The teacher asked to see her after class, then unexpectedly had to run to the bathroom.*)

Gillian felt distantly amused. She sensed Angel's hand in these arrangements.

And when she poked her head inside the marketing ed. room, she saw that Tanya was indeed alone. The tall girl was standing by a cloudy green blackboard.

'Tanya, we need to talk.'

Tanya's shoulders stiffened. Then she ran a hand across her already perfect dark hair and turned. She looked more like a future executive than ever, with her face set in cool lines and her exotic grey eyes running over Gillian in appraisal. Without Angel, Gillian would have dried up and withered away under that scrutiny.

Tanya said one word. 'Talk.'

What followed was more like a play than a conversation for Gillian. She repeated what Angel whispered to her, but she never had any idea what was coming. The only way to survive was to give herself up completely to his direction.

'Look, I know you're upset with me, Tanya. But I'd like to deal with this with a little maturity, OK?' She followed Angel's instructions over to a desk and brushed absent fingers over its imitation-wood top. 'I don't think there's any need for us to act like children.'

'And *I* don't think I know what you're talking about.'

'Oh, really?' Gillian turned and looked Tanya in the face. 'I think you know exactly what I'm talking about.' (Angel, I feel just like one of those people in a soap opera—)

'Well, you're wrong. And, as a matter of fact, I happen to be busy—'

'I'm talking about the rumours, Tanya. I'm talking about the stories about my mom. And I'm talking about David.'

Tanya stood perfectly still. For a moment she seemed surprised that Gillian was taking such a direct approach. Then her grey eyes hardened with the clear light of battle.

'All right, let's talk about David,' she said in a pleasant voice, moving tigerishly toward Gillian. 'I don't know about any rumours, but I'd like to hear what you and David were doing this morning. Care to tell me?'

(Angel, she's actually *enjoying* this, Look at her! And she's *bigger* than me.)

(*Trust me, kid.*)

'We weren't doing anything,' Gillian said. She had to tip her chin up to look Tanya in the face. Then she looked aside and shook her head. 'All right. I'll be honest about that. I like David, Tanya. I have ever since he moved in. He's good and he's noble and he's honest and he's sweet. But that doesn't mean I want to take him away from you, In fact, it's just the opposite.'

She turned and walked away, looking into the distance. 'I think David deserves the best. And I know he really cares about you. And *that's* what happened this morning – he told me you guys had made a promise to each other. So you see, you've got no reason to be suspicious.'

Tanya's eyes were glittering. 'Don't try to pull that. All this . . .' She waved a hand to indicate Gillian's dress and hair. 'In one day you turn from Little Miss Invisible to *this*. And you start prancing around the school like you own it. You can't pretend you're not trying to get him.'

'Tanya, the way I dress has nothing at all to do with David.' Gillian told the lie calmly, facing the chalk-misted blackboard again. 'It's just – something I needed to do. I was tired of being invisible.' She turned her head slightly, not enough to see Tanya. 'But that's beside the point. The real issue here is what's best for David. And I think *you're* best for him – as long as you treat him fairly.'

'And what is *that* supposed to mean?' Tanya was losing her legendary cool. She sounded venomous, almost shrill.

'It means no more fooling around with Bruce Faber.' (*Oh, my God,* Angel! Bruce Faber? Bruce the Athlete? She's been fooling around with *Bruce Faber*?)

Tanya's voice cracked like a whip. 'What are you talking about? What do you know?'

'I'm talking about those nights at the pool parties last summer in Macon's cabana. While David was up north at his grandma's. I'm talking about what happened in Bruce's car after the Halloween dance.' (In a *cabana*?)

There was a silence. When Tanya spoke again, her voice was a sort of icy explosion. 'How did you find out?'

Gillian shrugged. 'People who're good at spreading rumours can be a two-edged sword.'

'I thought so. That *brat* Kim! Her and her mouth . . .' Then Tanya's voice changed. It became a voice with claws and Gillian could tell she was moving closer. 'I suppose you're planning to tell David about this?'

'Huh?' For a moment Gillian was too confused to follow Angel's directions. Then she got hold of herself. 'Oh, of course I'm not going to tell David. That's why I'm telling *you*. I just want you to promise that you're not going to do anything like that anymore. And I'd appreciate it if you'd stop telling people things about my mom—'

'I'll do worse than that!' Suddenly Tanya was standing right behind Gillian. Her voice was a yelling hiss. 'You have no *idea* what I'll do if you try to mess with me, you snotty little midget. You are going to be so sorry—'

'No, I think you've done plenty already.'

The voice came from the door. Gillian heard it, and in that instant she understood everything.

CHAPTER 9

It was David, of course.

Gillian turned around and stared at him, blinking. He was standing just inside the doorway, his jacket slung over one shoulder, the other hand in his pocket. His jaw was tight, his eyes dark. He was looking at Tanya.

There was a silence.

(How long? How long has he been there, Angel?)

(*Uhhh, I'd say since round about . . . the beginning.*)

(Oh, my.) So that's why Gillian had been so low key and noble and let Tanya do all the yelling and threatening. They must have come off like Dorothy and the Wicked Witch.

A sense of justice stirred inside Gillian. She made a hesitant move toward David.

'David – you don't understand—'

David shook his head. 'I understand just fine. Don't try to cover for her. It's better for me to find out.'

(*Yeah, shut up, mini-brain! Now look mildly distressed, slightly awkward. You guess they want to be alone now.*)

'Uh, I guess you guys want to be alone now.'

(*Anyway, you have to hurry to get your ride.*)

'Anyway, I have to hurry to get my ride.'

(*These aren't the droids you're looking for.*)

'These aren't—' (I'm going to *kill* you, Angel!) Flustered, Gillian made one last gesture of apology and almost ran for the door.

Outside, she walked blindly. (Angel!)

(*Sorry, I couldn't resist. But look at you, kid! Do you know what you've done?*)

(I guess . . . I got rid of Tanya.) As the adrenalin of battle faded, the truth of this was slowly beginning to dawn on her. It brought a hint of glorious warmth, a sparkling promise of future happiness.

(*Smart kid!*)

(And – I did it fairly. It *was* all true, wasn't it, Angel? She's really been messing around with Bruce?)

(*Everybody's been messing around with Bruce. Yes, it was all true.*)

(And what about Kim? Is she the one who spreads rumours about people?)

(*Like butter on Eggos.*)

(I just – she seemed so *sweet.* When we talked about rumours in the cafeteria she patted my hand.)

(*Sure, she's sweet – to your face. Turn left here.*)

Gillian found herself emerging from the school building. As she went down the steps she saw three or four cars parked casually in the roundabout. Macon's BMW convertible was one. He looked up at her and gave an inviting nod toward the car.

Other people shouted. 'Hey, Jill, need a ride?' 'We wouldn't want you to get lost in the woods again!'

Gillian stood, feeling like a southern belle. So many people wanting her – it made her giddy. Angel was grandly indifferent (*Pick anybody!*) and she could see Amy's Geo a little distance away. Amy and Eugene were standing by it, looking up at her. But getting in a car with

Eugene Elfred would be disastrous to her new status.

She picked Cory the Party Guy, and the ride home was filled with his non-stop talk about Macon's party on Saturday. She had trouble getting rid of him at the door. Once she did, she walked up to her bedroom and fell on her bed, arms out. She started at the ceiling.

(Phew!)

It had been the most incredible day of her life.

She lay and listened to the quiet house and tried to gather her thoughts.

The warmth was still percolating inside her, although it was mixed with a certain amount of anxiety. She wanted to see David again. She wanted to know how things had turned out with Tanya. She couldn't let herself feel happy until she was sure . . .

'Relax, would you?'

Gillian sat up. The voice wasn't in her ear, it was beside the bed. Angel was sitting there.

The sight hit her like a physical blow.

She hadn't seen him since that morning and she'd forgotten how beautiful he was.

His hair was dark golden with paler gold lights shimmering in it. His face was, well, classic perfection. Absolutely pure, defined like a sculpture in marble. His eyes were a violet so glorious it actually hurt to look at it. His expression was rapt and uplifted . . . until he winked. Then it dissolved into mischief.

'Uh, hi,' Gillian whispered huskily.

'Hi, kid. Tired?'

'Yeah. I feel . . . used up.'

'Well, take a nap, why don't you? I've got places to go anyway.'

Gillian blinked. Places? 'Angel . . . I never asked you. What's heaven like? I mean, with angels like you, it's got to be different from most people's idea. That meadow I saw – that wasn't it, was it?'

'No, that wasn't it. Heaven, well, it's hard to explain. It's all in the oscillation of the spatial-temporal harmonics, you know – what you'd call the inherent vibration of the plane. At a higher vibration everything assumes a much more complicated harmonic theme . . .'

'You're making this up, aren't you?'

'Yeah. Actually it's classified. Why don't you get some sleep?'

Gillian already had her eyes shut.

She was happy when she woke up to smell dinner. But when she got downstairs, she found only her mother.

'Dad's not home?'

'No. He called, honey, and left a message for you. He'll be out of town on business for a while.'

'But he'll be back for Christmas. Won't he?'

'I'm sure he will.'

Gillian didn't say anything else. She ate the hamburger casserole her mother served – and noticed that her mother didn't eat. Afterward, she sat in the kitchen and played with a fork.

(*You OK?*)

The voice in her ear was a welcome relief. (Angel. Yeah, I'm all right. I was just thinking . . . about how everything started with Mom. It wasn't always like this. She was a teacher at the junior college . . .)

(*I know.*)

(And then, I think it was about five years ago, things just started happening. She started acting crazy. And then she was seeing things – what did I know about drinking then? I just thought she was nuts. It wasn't until Dad started finding empty bottles . . .)

(*I know.*)

(I just wish . . . that things could be different.) A pause. (Angel? Do you think maybe they could be?)

Another pause. Then Angel's voice was quiet. (*I'll work on it, kid. But, yeah, I think maybe they could be.*)

Gillian shut her eyes.

After a moment she opened them again. (Angel, how can I thank you? The things you're doing for me . . . I can't even start to tell you . . .)

(*Don't mention it. And don't cry. A cheery face is worth triple A bonds. Besides, you have to answer the phone.*)

(What phone?)

The phone rang.

(*That phone.*)

Gillian blew her nose and said a practice 'Hello' to make sure her voice wasn't shaky. Then she took a deep breath and picked up the receiver.

'Gillian?'

Her fingers clenched on the phone. 'Hi, David.'

'Look, I just wanted to make sure you were OK. I didn't even ask you that when – you know, this afternoon.'

'Sure, I'm OK.' Gillian didn't need Angel to tell her what to say to this. 'I can handle myself, you know.'

'Yeah. But Tanya can be pretty intense sometimes. After you left she was – well, forget that.'

He doesn't want to say anything bad about her, Gillian thought. She said, 'I'm fine.'

'It's just—' She could almost feel the frustration building on the other side of the line. And then David burst out as if something had snapped, 'I didn't know!'

'What?'

'I didn't know she was – like that! I mean, she runs the teen helpline and she's on the Centralia relief committee and the Food Cupboard project and . . . Anyway, I thought she was different. A good person.'

Conscience twinged. 'David, I think she *is* some of the things you thought. She's brave. When that window—'

'Quit it, Gillian. *You're* those things. *You're* brave and funny and – well, too honourable for your own good. You tried to give Tanya another chance.' He let out a breath. 'But, anyway; you might have guessed, we're finished. I told Tanya that. And now . . .' His voice changed. Suddenly he laughed, sounding as if some burden had fallen off him. 'Well, would you like me to drive you to the party Saturday night?'

Gillian laughed, too. 'I'd like it. I'd love it.' (Oh, Angel – *thank you*!)

She was very happy.

The rest of the week was wonderful. Every day she wore something daring and flattering scavenged from the depths of her closet. Every day she seemed to get more popular. People looked up when she walked into a room, not just meeting her eyes, but trying to catch her eye. They waved to her from a distance. They said hello up and down the halls. Everyone seemed glad to talk to her, and pleased if she wanted to talk to them. It was like being on a skyrocket, going higher and higher.

And, always; her guide and protector was with her. Angel had come to seem like a part of her, the most savvy and ingenious part. He provided quips, smoothed over awkward situations, gave advice about who to tolerate and who to snub. Gillian was developing an instinct for this, too. She was gaining confidence in herself, finding new skills every day. She was literally becoming a new person.

She didn't see much of Amy now. But Amy had Eugene, after all. And Gillian was so busy that she never even got to see David alone.

The day of the party she went to Houghton with Amanda the Cheerleader and Steffi the Singer. They laughed a lot, got whistled at everywhere, and shopped until they were dizzy. Gillian bought a dress and ankle boots – both approved by Angel.

When David picked her up that night, he let out a soft whistle himself.

'I look OK?'

'You look . . .' He shook his head. 'Illegal, but also sort of spiritual. How do you *do* that?'

Gillian smiled.

Macon the Wallet's house was the house of a rich guy. A fleet of artsy reindeer made out of some kind of white twigs and glowing with tiny lights graced the lawn. Inside, it was all high ceilings and track lighting, oriental rugs, old china, silver. Gillian was dazzled.

(My first *real* party! I mean, my first Popular Party. And it's even kind of, sort of for *me*.)

(*Your first real party, and it's all for you. The world is your oyster, kid. Go out and crack it.*)

Macon was coming toward her. Other people were looking. Gillian paused in the doorway of the room for effect, aware that she was making an entrance – and loving it.

Her outfit was designer casual. A black mini-dress with a pattern of purple flowers so dark it could hardly be distinguished. The soft, crepey material clung to her like a second skin. Matte black tights. And of course the ankle boots. Not much makeup; she'd decided on the fresh, soft look for her face. She'd darkened her lashes just enough to make the violet of her eyes a startling contrast.

She looked stunning . . . and effortless. And she knew it very well.

Macon's hooded eyes roved over her with something

like suppressed hunger. 'How's it going? You're looking good.'

'We feel good,' Gillian said, squeezing David's arm.

Macon's eyes darkened. He looked at the intersection of Gillian's hand and David's arm as if it offended him.

David looked back dispassionately, but a sort of wordless menace exuded from him. Macon actually took a step back. But all he said was, 'Well, my parents are gone for the weekend, so make yourself at home. There should be food somewhere.'

There was food everywhere. Every kind of munchy thing. Music blasted from the den, echoing all over the house. As they walked in, Cory greeted them with, 'Hey, guys! Grab a glass, it's going fast.'

When he'd said that he would round up a keg last week, Gillian had foolishly misheard it as 'a cake'. Now she understood. It was a keg of beer and everybody was drinking.

And not just beer. There were hard liquor bottles around. One guy was lying on a table with his mouth open while a girl poured something from a rectangular bottle into it.

'Hey, Jill, this is for you.' Cory was trying to give her a plastic glass with foam overflowing the top.

Gillian looked at him with open scorn. She didn't need Angel's help for this.

'Thanks, but I happen to *like* my brain cells. Maybe if you had more respect for yours you wouldn't be flunking biology.'

There was laughter. Even Cory laughed and winced.

'Right on,' Daryl the Rich Girl said, raising a can of diet Barq's root beer to Gillian in salute. And David waved Cory away and reached for a Coke.

Nobody tried to pressure them and the guy on the table

even looked a little embarrassed. Gillian had learned that you could pull anything off if you were cool enough, composed enough, and if you didn't back down. The feeling of success was much more intoxicating than liquor could have been.

(How about that? Pretty good, huh? Huh? Huh?)

(*Oh . . . oh, yeah, fine.*) Angel seemed to deliberate. (*Of course, it does say, 'Wine maketh the heart of man glad . . .'*)

(Oh, Angel, you're so silly. You sound like Cory!) Gillian almost laughed out loud.

Everything was exciting. The music, the huge house with its opulent Christmas decorations. The people. All the girls threw their arms around Gillian and kissed her as if they hadn't seen her in weeks. Some of the boys tried, but David warned them off with a look.

That was exciting, too. Having everyone know she was together with David Blackburn, that he was *hers*. It put her status through the ceiling.

'Want to look around?' David was saying. 'I can show you the upstairs; Macon doesn't care.'

Gillian looked at him. 'Bored?'

He grinned. 'No. But I wouldn't mind seeing you alone for a few minutes.'

They went up a long carpeted staircase lined with oil paintings. The rooms upstairs were just as beautiful as downstairs: palatial and almost awe inspiring.

It put Gillian in a quiet mood. The music wasn't as loud up here, and the cool marble gave her the feeling of being in a museum.

She looked out a window to see velvet darkness punctuated by little twinkling lights.

'You know, I'm glad you didn't want to drink back there.' David's voice behind her was quiet.

She turned, trying to read his face. 'But . . . you were surprised?'

'Well, it's just sometimes now you seem *so* adult. Sort of worldly.'

'Me? I mean – I mean *you're* the one who seems like that.' And that's what you like in girls, she thought.

He looked away and laughed. 'Oh, yeah. The tough guy. The wild guy. Tanya and I used to party pretty hard.' He shrugged. 'I'm not tough. I'm just a small-town guy trying to get through life. I don't look for trouble. I try to run from it if I can.'

Gillian had to laugh herself at that. But there was something serious in David's dark eyes.

'I admit, it sort of had a way of finding me in the past,' he said slowly. 'And I've done some things that I'm not proud of. But, you know . . . I'd like to change that – if it's possible.'

'Sort of like a whole new side of you that wants to come out.'

He looked startled. Then he glanced up and down her and grinned. 'Yeah. Sort of like that.'

Gillian felt suddenly inspired, hopeful. 'I think,' she said slowly, trying to put her ideas together, 'that sometimes people need to – to express both sides of themselves. And then they can be . . . well, whole.'

'Yeah. If that's possible.' He hesitated. Gillian didn't say anything, because she had the feeling that he was trying to. That there was some reason he'd brought her up to talk to her alone.

'Well. You know something weird?' he said after a moment. 'I *don't* feel exactly whole. And the truth is –' He looked around the darkened room. Gillian could only see his profile. He shook his head, then took a deep breath. 'OK, this is going to sound even dumber than I thought, but I've got to say it. I can't help it.'

He turned back toward her and said with a mixture of determination and apology, 'And since that day when I found you out there in the snow, I have this feeling that I won't be, without . . .' He trailed off and shrugged. 'Well – you,' he said finally, helplessly.

The universe was one enormous heartbeat. Gillian could feel her body echoing it. She said slowly, 'I . . .'

'I know. I *know* how it sounds. I'm sorry.'

'No,' Gillian whispered. 'That wasn't what I was going to say.'

He'd turned sharply away to glare at the window. Now he turned halfway back and she saw the glimmer of hope in his face.

'I was going to say, I understand.'

He looked as if he were afraid to believe. 'Yeah, but do you *really*?'

'I think I do – really.'

And then he was moving toward her and Gillian was holding up her arms. Literally as if drawn to do it – but not just by physical attraction. It sounded crazy, Gillian thought, but it wasn't physical so much as . . . well, spiritual. They seemed to *belong* together.

David was holding her. It felt incredibly strange and at the same time perfectly natural. He was warm and solid and Gillian felt her eyes shutting, her head drifting to his shoulder. Such a simple embrace, but it seemed to mean everything.

The feelings inside Gillian were like a wonderful discovery. And she had the sense that she was on the verge of some other discovery, that if she just opened her eyes and looked into David's at this moment, somehow it would mean a change in the world . . .

(*Kid?*) The voice in Gillian's ear was quiet. (*I* really *hate to say it, but I have to break this up. You have to sidle down to the master bedroom.*)

Gillian scarcely heard and couldn't pay attention.

(*Gillian! I mean it, kid. There's something going on that you have to know about.*)

(Angel?)

(*Tell him you'll be back in a few minutes. This is important!*)

There was no way to ignore that tone of urgency. Gillian stirred. 'David, I have to go for a sec. Be right back.'

David just nodded. 'Sure.' It was Gillian who had trouble letting go of his hand, and when she did she still seemed to feel his grip.

(This had better be good, Angel.) She blinked in the light of the hallway.

(*Go down to the end of the hall. That's the master bedroom. Go on in. Don't turn on the light.*)

The master bedroom was cavernous and dark and filled with large dim shapes like sleeping elephants. Gillian walked in and immediately banged into a piece of heavy furniture.

(*Be careful! See that light over there?*)

Light was showing around the edges of double doors on the other side of the room. The doors were closed.

(*And locked. That's the bathroom. Now, here's what I want you to do. Walk carefully over to the right of the bathroom and you'll find another door. It's the closet. I want you to quietly open that door and get in it.*)

(What?)

Angel's voice was elaborately patient. (*Get in the closet and put your ear against the wall.*)

Gillian shut her eyes. Then, feeling exactly like a burglar, she slowly turned the handle of the closet door and slipped inside.

It was a walk-in closet, very long but stuffy because of the clothes bristling from both sides. Gillian had a profound feeling of intrusion, of being an invader of privacy. She seemed to walk a long way in before Angel stopped her.

(*OK. Here. Now put your ear against the left wall.*)

Eyes still shut, it seemed to make the absolute darkness more bearable – Gillian burrowed between something long sheathed in plastic and something heavy and velvety. With the clothes embracing her on either side, she leaned her head until her bare ear touched wood.

(Angel, I can't believe I'm doing this. I feel really stupid, and I'm scared, and if anybody finds me—)

(*Just* listen, *will you?*)

At first Gillian's heart seemed to drown out all other sounds. But then, faint but clear, she heard two voices she recognized.

CHAPTER 10

'... But only if you absolutely *swear* to me you didn't do it.'

'Oh, how many times? I've been telling you all week I didn't. I never said a *word* to her. I swear.'

The first voice, which sounded taut and a little unbalanced, was Tanya's. The second was Kim the Gymnast's. Despite her brave words, Kim sounded scared.

(Angel? What's going on?)

(*Trouble*.)

'OK,' Tanya's voice was saying. 'Then this is your chance to prove it by helping me.'

'Tan, look. Look. I'm sorry about you and David breaking up. But maybe it's not Gillian's fault—'

'It's *completely* her fault. The stuff with Bruce was over. You know that. There was no reason for David to ever find out – until *she* opened her mouth. And as for how she found out—'

'Not again!' Kim the Gymnast sounded ready to scream. '*I didn't do it.*'

'All right. I believe you.' Tanya's voice was calmer. 'So in that case there's no reason for us to fight. We've got to stick together. Hand me that brush, will you?' There was silence for a moment, and Gillian could imagine Tanya brushing her dark hair to a higher gloss, looking in a mirror approvingly.

'So what are you going to do?' Kim's voice asked.

'Get both of them. In a way, I hate him more. I promised he'd be sorry if he dumped me, and I always keep my promises.'

Squashed between the heavy, swaying clothes on her right and left, Gillian had a wild and almost fatal impulse to giggle.

She knew what was going on. It was just such a . . . a *sitcom* situation that she had a hard time making herself believe in it. Here she was, listening to two people who were actually *plotting against her.* She was overhearing their plans to get her. It was . . . absurd. Bad mystery novel stuff.

And it was happening anyway.

She made a feeble attempt to get back to reality, straightening up slightly.

(Angel, people don't really do these revenge things. Right? They're just talking. And, I mean, I can't even believe I'm hearing all this. It's so . . . so *ridiculous* . . .)

(*You're overhearing it because I brought you here. You have an invisible friend who can lead you to the right place at the right time. And you'd better believe that people carry out these 'revenge things'. Tanya's never made a plan that she hasn't carried through.*)

(The future executive.) Gillian thought it faintly.

(*Future CEO. She's deadly serious, kid. And she's smart. She can make things happen.*)

Gillian no longer felt like giggling.

When she pressed her ear against the wall again, it was clear she'd missed some of the conversation.

'. . . David first?' Kim the Gymnast was saying.

'Because I know what to do with him. He wants to get into Ohio University, you know? He sent the application in October. It was already going to be a little hard because his grades aren't great, but he scored really high on the SATs. It was hard, but I'm going to make it . . .' There was a pause and Tanya's voice seemed to mellow and sweeten. 'Absolutely impossible.'

'How?' Kim sounded shaken.

'By writing to the university. And to our principal and to Ms Renquist, the English lit. teacher, and to David's grandpa, who's supposed to be giving him money to go to college.'

'But why? I mean, if you say something nasty, they'll just think it's sour grapes—'

'I'm going to tell them he passed English lit. last year by cheating. We had to turn in a term paper. But he didn't write the paper he turned in. It was *bought*. From a college guy in Philadelphia.'

Kim's breath whooshed out so loudly that Gillian could hear it. 'How do you know?'

'Because I arranged it, of course. I wanted him to bring his grades up, to get into a university. To *make* something of himself. But of course he can never prove all that. He's the one that paid for it.'

A silence. Then Kim said, with what sounded like forced lightness, 'But, Tan, you could ruin his whole life . . .'

'I know.' Tanya's voice was serene. Satisfied.

'But . . . well, what do you want *me* to do?'

'Be ready to spread the word. That's what you do best, isn't it? I'll get the letters written by Monday. And then on Monday you can start telling people – because I want *everyone* to know. Prime that grapevine!' Tanya was laughing.

'OK. Sure. Consider it done.' Kim sounded more scared

than ever. 'Uh, look, I'd better get back downstairs now – can I use the brush a second?'

'Here.' A clatter. 'And, Kim? Be ready to help me with Gillian, too. I'll let you know what I've got in mind for her.'

Kim said, 'Sure,' faintly. Then there were a few more clatters and the sound of a door rattling open and shut. Then silence.

Gillian stood in the stuffy closet.

She felt physically sick. As if she'd found something loathsome and slimy and unclean writhing under her bed. Tanya was *crazy* – and evil. Gillian had just seen into a mind utterly twisted with hatred.

And smart. Angel had said it.

(Angel, what do I *do*? She really means it, doesn't she? She's going to *destroy* him. And there isn't anything I can do about it.)

(*There may be something.*)

(She's not going to listen to reason. I *know* she's not. Nobody's going to be able to talk her out of it. And threats aren't any good—)

(*I said, there may be something you can do.*)

Gillian came back to herself. (What?)

(*It's a little complicated. And . . . well, the truth is, you may not* want *to do it, kid.*)

(I would do anything for David.) Gillian's response was instant and absolute. Strange, how there were some things you were so sure of.

(*OK. Well, hold that thought. I'll explain everything when we get home – which we should do* fast. *But first I want you to get something from that bathroom.*)

Gillian felt calm and alert, like a young soldier on her first mission in enemy territory. Angel had an idea. As long as she did exactly what Angel said, things were going to turn out all right.

She went into the bathroom and followed Angel's instructions precisely without asking why. Then she went to get David to take her home from the party.

'I'm ready. Now tell me what I can do.'

Gillian was sitting on her bed, wearing the pyjamas with little bears on them. It was well after midnight and the house was quiet and dark except for the lamp on her night stand.

'You know, I think you *are* ready.'

The voice was quiet and thoughtful – and outside her head. In the air about two feet away from the bed, a light began to grow.

And then it was Angel, sitting lotus style, with his hands on his knees. Floating lotus style. He was about level with Gillian's bed and he was looking at her searchingly. His face was earnest and calm, and all around him was a pale, changing light like the aurora borealis.

As always, Gillian felt a physical reaction at the first sight of him. A sort of shock. He was so beautiful, so unearthly, so unlike anyone else.

And right now his eyes were more intense than she had ever seen them.

It scared her a little, but she pushed that, and the physical reaction away. She had to think of David. David, who'd so trustingly taken her home when she 'got sick' an hour ago, and who right now had absolutely no idea what was in store for him on Monday.

'Just tell me what to do,' she said to Angel.

She was braced. She had no idea what it would take to stop Tanya, but it couldn't be anything pleasant – or legal. Didn't matter. She was ready.

So Angel's words were something of a let-down.

'You know you're special, don't you?'

'Huh?'

'You've always been special. And underneath, you've always known it.'

Gillian wasn't sure what to say. Because it sounded terribly cliché – but it was true. She *was* special. She'd had a near-death experience. She'd come back with an angel. Surely only special people did that. And her popularity at school – everyone there certainly thought she was special. But her own inner feeling had started long before that, sometime in childhood. She'd just imagined that everybody felt that way . . . that they were different from others, maybe better, but certainly *different*.

'Well, everybody *does* feel that way, actually,' Angel said, and Gillian felt a little jolt. She always felt it when she suddenly remembered her thoughts weren't private anymore.

Angel was going on. 'But for you it happens to be true. Listen, what do you know about your Great-grandma Elspeth?'

'*What?*' Gillian was lost. 'She's an old lady. And, um, she lives in England and always sends me Christmas presents . . .' She had a vague memory of a photograph showing a woman with white hair and white glasses, a tweed skirt and sensible shoes. The woman held a Pekingese in a little red jacket.

'She grew up in England, but she was born American. She was only a year old when she was separated from her big sister Edith, who was raising her. It happened during World War One. Everyone thought she had no family, so she was given to an English couple to raise.'

'Oh, really? How interesting.' Gillian was not only bewildered but exasperated. 'But what on *earth*—'

'Here's what it's got to do with David. Your great-grandma didn't grow up with her real sister, with her real family. If she had, she'd have known her real heritage. She'd have known . . .'

'Yes?'

'That she was born a witch.'

There was a long, long silence. It shouldn't have been so long. After the first second Gillian thought of things to say, but somehow she couldn't get them past the tightness of her throat.

She ought to laugh. That was *funny,* the idea of Great-grandma, with her sensible shoes, being a witch. And besides, witches didn't exist. They were just *stories*—

—like angels—

—or examples of New Age grown-ups acting silly.

'Angels,' Gillian gasped in a strangled voice. She was beginning to feel wild inside. As if rules were breaking loose.

Because angels were true. She was looking at one. He was floating about two and a half feet off the floor. There was absolutely nothing under him and he could hear her thoughts and disappear and he was *real.* And if angels could be real . . .

Magic happens. She'd seen that on a bumper sticker somewhere. Now she clapped both hands to her mouth. There was something boiling up inside her and she wasn't sure if it was a scream or a giggle.

'My great-grandma is a *witch*?'

'Well, not exactly. She would be if she knew about her family. That's the key, you see, you have to know. Your great-grandma has the blood, and so does your grandma, and so does your mom. And so do you, Gillian. And now . . . you know.' The last words were very gentle, very deliberate. As if Angel were delicately putting into place the last piece of a puzzle.

Gillian's laughter had faded. She felt dizzy, as if she had unexpectedly come to the edge of a cliff and looked over. 'I'm . . . I've got the blood, too.'

'Don't be afraid to say it. You're a witch.'

'Angel . . .' Gillian's heart was beating very hard suddenly. Hard and slow. 'Please . . . I don't really understand any of this. And . . . well, I'm *not*.'

'A witch? You don't know how to be, yet. But as a matter of fact, kid, you're already showing the signs. Do you remember when that mirror broke in the downstairs bathroom?'

'I—'

'And when the window broke in the cafeteria. You asked me if *I* did those things. I didn't. You did. You were angry and you lashed out with your power . . . but you didn't realize it.'

'Oh, God,' Gillian whispered.

'It's a frightening thing, that power. When you don't know how to use it, it can cause all kinds of damage. To other people – and to you. Oh, kid, don't you understand? Look at what's happened to your mother.'

'What about my mother?'

'She . . . is . . . a . . . witch. A lost witch, like you. She's got powers, but she doesn't know how to channel them, she doesn't understand them, and they terrify her. When she started seeing visions –'

'Visions!' Gillian sat straight up. It was as if a light had suddenly gone on in her head, illuminating five years of her life.

'Yeah.' Angel's violet eyes were steady, his face grim. 'The hallucinations came before the drinking, not after. And they were psychic visions, images of things that were going to happen, or that might have happened, or that happened a long time ago. But of course she didn't understand that.'

'Oh, God. Oh, my God.' Electricity was running up and down Gillian's body, setting her whole skin tingling. Tears stung in her eyes – not tears of sadness, but of pure, shocking revelation. 'That's it. That's it. Oh, God, we've got to *help* her. We've got to *tell* her—'

'I agree. But first we have to get *you* under control. And it's not exactly a thing you can just spring on her without any warning. You could do more harm than good that way. We've got to build up to it.'

'Yes. Yes, I see that. You're right.' Gillian blinked rapidly. She tried to calm her breathing, to *think*.

'And just at the moment, she's stable. A little depressed, but stable. She'll wait until after Monday. But Tanya won't.'

'Tanya?' Gillian had nearly forgotten the original discussion. 'Oh, yeah, Tanya. Tanya.' *David*, she thought.

'There is something very practical you can do about Tanya – now that you know what you are.'

'Yes. All right.' Gillian wet her lips. 'Do you think Dad will come back if Mom realizes what she is and gets it all together?'

'I think there's a good possibility. But *listen* to me. To take care of Tanya—'

'Angel.' A show coil of anxiety was unrolling in Gillian's stomach. 'Now that I think about it . . . I mean, aren't witches *bad*? Shouldn't you, well, *disapprove* of this?'

Angel put his golden head in his hands. 'If I thought it was bad would I be here guiding you through it?'

Gillian almost laughed. It was so incongruous – the pale northern lights aura around him and the sound of him talking through clenched teeth.

Then a thought struck her. She spoke hesitantly and wonderingly. 'Did you *come* here to guide me through it?'

He lifted his head and looked at her with those unearthly eyes. 'What do you think?'

Gillian thought that the world wasn't exactly what she had thought. And neither were angels.

The next morning she stood and looked at herself in the mirror. She'd done this after Angel had first come to her and made her cut her hair – she'd wanted to look at her new self. Now she wanted to look at Gillian the witch.

There wasn't anything overtly different about her. But now that she *knew* she seemed to see things she hadn't noticed before. Something in the eyes – some ancient glimmer of knowledge in their depths. Something elfin in the face, in the slant of the cheekbones. A remnant of faery.

'Stop gazing and come shopping,' Angel said, and light coalesced beside her.

'Right,' Gillian said soberly. Then she tried to wiggle her nose.

Downstairs, she borrowed the keys to her mother's station wagon and bundled up. It was an icy-fresh day and the whole world sparkled under a light dusting of new snow. The air filled Gillian's lungs like some strange potion.

(I feel very witchy.) She backed the car out. (Now where do we go? Houghton?)

(*Hardly. This isn't the kind of shopping you do at a mall. Northward, ho! We're going to Woodbridge.*)

Gillian tried to remember Woodbridge. It was a little town like Somerset, but smaller. She'd undoubtedly driven through it at some point in her life.

(We need to go shopping in Woodbridge to take care of Tanya?)

(*Just drive, dragonfly.*)

* * *

Woodbridge's main street ended in a town square bordered by dozens of decorated trees. The stores were trimmed with Christmas lights. It was a postcard scene.

(*OK. Park here.*)

Gillian followed Angel's directions and found herself in the Woodbridge Five and Ten, an old-style variety store, complete with creaking wooden floorboards. She had the terrifying feeling that time had gone back about fifty years. The aisles were tight and the shelves were jammed with baskets full of goods. There was a musty smell.

Beyond asking questions, she stared dreamily at a jar of penny candy.

(*Head on to the back. All the way. Open that door and go through to the back room.*)

Gillian nervously opened the rickety door and peered into the room beyond. But it was just another store. It had an even stranger smell, partly delicious, partly medicinal, and it was rather dimly lit.

'Uh, hello?' she said, in response to Angel's urging. And then she noticed movement behind a counter.

A girl was sitting there. She was maybe nineteen and had dark brown hair and an interesting face. It was quite ordinary in shape and structure – a country girl sort of face – but the eyes were unusually vivid and intense.

'Um, do you mind if I look around?' Gillian said, again in response to Angel.

'Go right ahead,' the girl said. 'I'm Melusine.'

She watched with a perfectly friendly and open curiosity as Gillian moseyed around the shelves, trying to look as if she knew what she was looking for. Everything she saw was strange and unfamiliar, rocks and herby-looking things and different coloured candles.

(*It's not here.*) Angel's voice was resigned. (*We're going to have to ask her.*)

'Excuse me,' Gillian said a moment later, approaching the girl diffidently from the other side. 'But do you have any Dragon's Blood? The – *activated* kind?'

The girl's face changed. She looked at Gillian very sharply. Then she said, 'I'm afraid I've never heard of anything like that. And I wonder what makes you ask.'

Gooseflesh blossomed on Gillian's arms. She had the sudden, distinct feeling that she was in danger.

CHAPTER 11

Angel's voice was taut but calm. (*Pick up a pen from the counter. The black one's fine. Now – let go. Just relax and let me move it.*)

Gillian let go. It was a process she couldn't have described in words if she'd tried. But she watched, with a sort of fascinated horror, as her own hand began to draw on a small white invoice slip.

It drew across the lines, in some kind of pattern. Unfortunately the pen seemed to be out of ink, so all Gillian could see was a faint scribble.

(*Show her the carbon copy.*)

Gillian peeled off the first sheet of paper. Underneath, in carbon, was her design. It looked like a flower – a dahlia. It was crudely coloured in, as if it were meant to be dark.

(What is it, Angel?)

(*A sort of password. Unless you know it, she's not going to let you buy what you need.*)

Melusine's face had changed. She was looking at Gillian with startled interest.

'Unity,' she said. 'I *wondered* about you when you came in. You've got the look – but I've never seen you before. Did you just move here?'

(*Say 'Unity.' It's their greeting. And tell her that you're just passing through.*)

(Angel, is *she* a witch? Are there other witches around here? And how come I have to lie—)

(*She's getting suspicious!*)

The girl *was* looking at Gillian rather oddly. Like someone trying to catch a conversation. It scared Gillian.

'Unity. No, I'm just visiting,' she said hastily. 'And,' she added as Angel whispered, 'I need the Dragon's Blood and, um, two wax figures. Female. And do you have any charged Selket powder?'

Melusine settled back a little. 'You belong to Circle Midnight.' She said it flatly.

(Whaaaat? What's Circle Midnight? And how come she doesn't like me anymore?)

(*It's a sort of witch organization. Like a club. It's the one that does the kind of spells that you need to do right now.*)

(Aha. Bad spells, you mean.)

(*Powerful spells. In your case, necessary spells.*)

Melusine was scooting her chair behind the counter. For a moment Gillian wondered why she didn't get up, and then, as Melusine reached the edge of the counter, she understood. The chair was a wheelchair and Melusine's right leg was missing from the knee down.

It didn't seem to hinder her, though. In a moment, she was scooting back with a couple of packets and a box in her lap. She put the box on the counter and took out two dolls made of dull rose-coloured wax. One of the packets held chunks of what looked like dark red chalk, the other a peacock-green powder.

She didn't look up as Gillian paid for the items. Gillian felt snubbed.

'Unity,' she said formally, as she put her wallet away

and gathered up her purchases. She figured if you said it for hello, you could say it for goodbye.

Melusine's dark eyes flashed up at her intently and almost quizzically. Then she said slowly, 'Merry part . . . and merry meet again.' It almost sounded like an invitation.

(Well, I'm lost.)

(*Just say 'Merry part' and get out of here, kid.*)

Outside, Gillian looked at the town square with new eyes. (The Witches of Woodbridge. So, are they, like, all over here? Do they own the Creamery and the hardware store, too?)

(*You're closer than you think. But we don't have time to stand around. You've got some spells to cast.*)

Gillian took one more look around the quiet tree-lined square, feeling herself standing in the bright air with her packages of spell ingredients. Then she shook her head. She turned to the car.

Sitting in the middle of her bed with the bedroom door locked, Gillian contemplated her materials. The plastic bags of rock and powder, the dolls, and the hair she'd gathered from the brush in Macon's bathroom last night.

Two or three strands of sun blonde curls. Three or four long black glossy hairs.

'And you don't need to tell me what *they're* for,' she said, looking at the air beside her. 'It's voodoo time, huh?'

'Smart girl.' Angel shimmered into being. 'The hair is to personalize the dolls, to link them magically to their human counterparts. You've got to wind a hair around each doll, and name it out loud. Call it Tanya or Kimberlee.'

Gillian didn't move. 'Angel, look. When I got that hair, I had no idea why I was doing it. But when I saw those little wax figures, well, then I realized. And the way that girl Melusine looked at me . . .'

'She has no idea what you're up against. Forget her.'

'I'm just trying to get things straight, all right?' Hands clasped tightly in her lap, she looked at him. 'I've never wanted to hurt people – well, all right, yes, I have. I've had those – those images or whatever at night, like seeing a giant foot splat down on my geometry teacher. But I don't *really* want to hurt people.'

Angel looked patient. 'Who said you were going to hurt them?'

'Well, what's all this *for*?'

'It's for whatever you want it to be for. Gillian, dragonfly, all these materials are just aids for a witch's natural powers. They're a way of focusing the power, directing it to a particular purpose. But what actually happens to Tanya and Kim depends on *you*. You don't have to hurt them. You just have to stop them.'

'I just have to stop them from doing what they're planning to do.' Gillian's mind was already sparking into action. 'And Tanya's planning to write letters. And Kim's planning to spread the word . . .'

'So what if Tanya can't write letters? And if Kimberlee can't talk? It would be sort of . . . poetic justice.' Angel's face was grave, but his eyes were glinting with mischief.

Gillian bit her lip. 'I think it would kill Kim not to talk!'

'Oh, I bet she could live through it.' They were both laughing now. 'So if she had, say, a bad sore throat . . . and if Tanya's arm were paralyzed . . .'

Gillian sobered. 'Not paralyzed.'

'I meant temporarily. Not even temporarily? All right, what about something else that could keep her from typing or holding a pen? How about a bad rash?'

'A rash?'

'Sure. An infection. One she'd have to keep bandaged up so she couldn't use her fingers. That would stop her for a while, until we can think of something else.'

'A rash . . . Yeah, that could work. That would be good.' Gillian took a quick breath and looked down at her materials. 'OK, tell me how to do it!'

And Angel walked her through the strange process. She wound the dolls with hair and named them aloud. She rubbed them with crumbled Dragon's Blood, the dark red chalky stuff. Then she dabbed the hand of one and the throat of the other with the iridescent green Selket powder.

'Now . . . may I be given the power of the words of Hecate. It is not I who utter them, it is not I who repeat them; it is Hecate who utters them, it is she who repeats them.'

(And who the heck's Hecate?) She sent the thought to Angel wordlessly, in case speaking aloud would ruin the spell.

(*Be quiet. Now concentrate. Pick up the Tanya doll and think* Streptococcus pyogenes. *That's a bacteria that'll give her a rash. Picture it in your mind. See the rash on the real Tanya.*)

There was a certain satisfaction in doing it. Gillian couldn't deny that, even to herself. She pictured Tanya's slim olive-skinned right hand, poised to sign a letter that would destroy David's future. Then she pictured itchy red bumps appearing, another hand scratching. Redness spreading across the skin. More itching. More scratching . . .

(Hey, this is fun!)

Then she took care of the Kim doll.

When she was finished, she put both dolls in a shoe box and put the shoe box under her bed. Then she stood up, flushed and triumphant.

'It's over? I did it?'

'You did it. You're a full-fledged witch now. Hecate's the Queen of the Witches, incidentally. Their ancient ruler. And she's special to you – you're descended in a direct line from her daughter Hellewise.'

'I am?' Gillian stood a little straighter. She seemed to feel power tingling through her, a sparkling energy, a sense that she could reach out and mould the world. She felt as if she ought to have an aura. 'Really?'

'Your Great-grandmother Elspeth was one of the Harmans, the Hearth-Women, the line that came from Hellewise. Elspeth's older sister Edgith became a big witch leader.'

How could Gillian have ever thought she was ordinary, less than ordinary? You couldn't argue with facts like these. She was from a line of important witches. She was part of an ancient tradition. She was *special*.

She felt very, very powerful.

That night, her father called. He wanted to know if she was OK, and to let her know he loved her. All Gillian wanted to know was whether he'd be home for Christmas.

'Of course I'll be home. I love you.'

'Love you.'

But she wasn't happy when she hung up. (Angel, we've got to figure things out. Is there a spell I should do on *him*?)

(*I'll think about it.*)

The next morning she sailed into school cheerfully and looked around for someone who would talk. She spotted the cropped red head of J.Z. the Model and waved hello.

'What's up, J.Z.?'

J.Z. turned hazy blue-green eyes on her and fell into step. 'Did you hear about Tanya?'

Gillian's heart skipped a beat. 'No,' she said, with perfect truth.

'She's got some awful rash or infection or something. Like poison ivy. They say it's driving her crazy.' As always, J.Z. spoke slowly and with an almost vacant air. But Gillian thought there was a gleam of satisfaction under the blank look.

She shot J.Z. a sharp glance. 'Well, that's too bad.'

'Sure is,' J.Z. murmured, smiling absently.

'I sure hope nobody else catches it.' She was hoping to hear something about Kim.

But J.Z. just said, 'Well, at least we know David won't.' Then she wandered off.

(Angel, that girl doesn't like Tanya.)

(*A lot of people don't like Tanya.*)

(It's weird. I used to think being popular meant everybody likes you. Now I think it's more like everybody's afraid *not* to like you.)

(*Right. Let them hate you as long as they fear you. But, you see, you've done a public service, putting Tanya out of commission.*)

In biology class, Gillian found out that Kim was absent and had cancelled gymnastics practice for the day. She had something like strep throat and couldn't even talk. Nobody seemed heart-broken over this, either.

(Being popular means everybody's glad when something bad happens to you.)

(*It's a dog-eat-dog world, kid.*) Angel chuckled.

Gillian smiled.

She had protected David. It gave her a wonderful feeling to be able to protect him, to take care of him. Not that she exactly approved of what he'd done. Buying an English paper and turning it in as your own – that was pretty bad. Not just wrong, but petty somehow.

(But I think he was sorry. I think that was maybe one of the things he was saying he wasn't proud of. And maybe there's some way he can make up for it. Like if he wrote another paper and turned it in, and explained to Ms Renquist. Don't you think, Angel?)

(*Hm? Oh, sure. Good idea.*)

(Because sometimes being sorry isn't enough, you know? You've got to *do* something. Angel? Angel?)

(*I'm here. Just thinking about your next class. And your powers and things. Did you know there's a spell to bring in money?*)

(There *is*? Now, that's really interesting. I mean, I don't care about *money* money, but I'd really love a car . . .)

That night Gillian lay in bed, head propped on pillows, legs curled under a throw, and thought about how lucky she was.

Angel seemed to be gone for the moment; she could neither see him nor hear his voice. But it was Angel she was thinking about.

He had brought her so much – and he'd brought her *himself*, which she sometimes thought was the greatest gift of all. What other girl could have *two* gorgeous guys without being unfaithful to either of them, or making either of them jealous? What other girl could have two great loves at once, without doing wrong?

Because that was how she'd come to think of Angel. As a great love. He wasn't a pillar of light to her anymore, or a terrifyingly beautiful apparition with a voice like silver fire. He was almost like an ordinary guy, only impossibly handsome, devastatingly witty, and incidentally supernatural. Since learning she was supernatural herself, Gillian felt he was somehow more accessible.

And he understood her. Nobody had ever known her,

or could ever know her, the way he did. He knew all her deepest secrets and most carefully hidden fears – and he still loved her. The love was obvious every time he spoke to her, every time he appeared and looked at her with those startling eyes.

I'm in love with him, too, Gillian thought. She felt quite calm about it. It was different from the way she loved David. In a way, it was more powerful, because nobody could ever be as close to her as Angel was, but there was no physical aspect to it. Angel was a part of her on a level nothing human could touch. Their relationship was separate from the human world. It was unique.

'Tie me kangaroo down, mate!' A light was appearing beside the bed.

'Where've you been, Australia?'

'Checking on Tanya and Kim the Gym, actually. Tanya's bandaged from shoulder to fingers and she's not thinking about writing *anything*. Kim's sucking a popsicle and moaning. Inaudibly.'

'Good.' Gillian felt a triumphant glow. Which was wrong, of course; she shouldn't *enjoy* other people's pain. But she couldn't hide it from Angel – and those girls deserved it. They would be sorry, sorry, sorry they had ever tangled with Gillian Lennox.

'But we've got to work out a more permanent solution,' she said. 'And figure things out about my parents.'

'I'm working on all of it.' Angel was gazing at her with a kind of dreamy intentness.

'What?'

'Nothing. Just looking at you. You look particularly beautiful tonight, which is absurd considering you're wearing flannel pyjamas with bears on them.'

Gillian felt a quick sweet throb. She looked down. 'These are cats. But the bears are my favourite, actually.'

She looked back up and grinned wickedly. 'I'll bet I could start a little bears fashion at school. You can do anything with enough guts.'

'*You* can do anything, that's for sure. Sweet dreams, beautiful.'

'Silly. Stop it.' Gillian waved a hand at him. But she was still blushing when she lay down and shut her eyes. She felt absurdly happy and complimented. And beautiful. And powerful. And special.

'Hear about Tanya?' Amanda the Cheerleader said at lunch break the next day. She and Gillian were in the girls' bathroom.

Gillian eyed herself in the mirror. A touch with the comb . . . perfect. And maybe a little more lipstick. She was doing the glamour thing today. Dark, mesmerizing eyes and bold, laughing red mouth. Or maybe she should pout instead of laugh. She pursed her lips at herself and said absently, 'Old news.'

'No, I mean the new stuff. She's got complications, apparently.'

Gillian stopped applying lipstick. 'What kind of complications?'

'I don't know. Fever, I think. And her whole arm's turning purple.'

(Angel? *Purple?*)

(*Well, I'd say more mauve myself. Relax, kid. Fever's a natural side effect of a bad rash. Just like poison ivy.*)

(But—)

(*Look at Amanda.* She's *not too upset.*)

(No, 'cause she probably knows Tanya was messing with her boyfriend. Or she has some other reason not to like her. But, I mean, I don't want Tanya *really* hurt.)

(*Don't you? Be honest.*)

(Well, I mean, not really, *really* hurt, you know? Medium hurt. That's all.)

(*I don't think she's going to drop dead this minute.*) Angel said it patiently.

(OK. Good.) Gillian felt a little embarrassed for making a big deal – and at the same time she had a fleeting impulse to go check on Tanya herself. But the impulse was easily quashed. Tanya was getting what she deserved. It was only a rash. How bad could that be?

Besides, Angel was looking after things. And she trusted Angel.

She added the last dab of lipstick and smiled at herself in the mirror. Definitely she was one hot witch.

In sixth period, messengers brought candy canes that people had ordered last week from the Vocal Jazz Club. You could send the candy canes, which came with a ribbon and a note, to anyone you wanted.

Gillian got a pile so large that everyone laughed, and Seth Pyles ran over and snapped a picture of it for the yearbook. After school David came and rummaged through the pile, looking at the messages and shaking his fist, pretending to be jealous.

It was a very good day.

'Happy?' Angel asked that afternoon. David's mother had recruited him for heavy-duty Christmas housecleaning, so Gillian was alone in her bedroom – which meant it was just her and Angel. She was folding socks and humming her favourite carol, 'O Come All Ye Faithful.'

'Can't you tell?'

'Not with all that noise you're making. Are you really happy?'

She looked up. 'Of course I am. I mean, except for the stuff with my parents. I'm totally happy.'

'And being popular is all you expected it to be.'

'Well . . .' Gillian paused in bewilderment. 'It's – it's a little *different* from what I expected. It's not the be-all and the end-all I'd have thought. But then *I'm* different from what I thought.'

'You're a witch. And you want more than just candy canes and parties.'

She looked at him curiously. 'What are you trying to say? That I should do some more spells?'

'I'm saying that there's more to being a witch than doing spells. I can show you, if you trust me.'

CHAPTER 12

'Yes,' Gillian said simply. Her heart rate had picked up a little, but with anticipation rather than fear. Angel was looking very mysterious.

He struck a looking-into-the-distance pose, then said, 'Have you ever had the feeling that you don't really know reality?'

'Frequently,' Gillian said dryly. 'Ever since I met you.'

He grinned. 'I mean even before that. Someone wrote about the "inconsolable secret" that's in each of us. The desire for our own far-off country, for something we've never actually experienced. About how we all long "to bridge some chasm that yawns between us and reality . . . to be reunited with something in the universe from which we now feel cut off . . ." '

Gillian sat bolt upright. '*Yes*. I never heard anybody say it that well before. About the chasm – you always feel that there's something else, *somewhere*, and that you're being left out. I thought it was something the popular people would be in on – but it hasn't got anything to do with them at all.'

'As if the world has some secret, if you could only get on the inside.'

'Yes. Yes.' She looked at him in fascination. 'This is about being a witch, isn't it? You're saying that I've always felt that way because it's *true*. Because for me there is a different reality . . .'

'Nah.' Angel grimaced. 'Actually everybody feels exactly the same. Doesn't mean a thing.'

Gillian collapsed. '*What?*'

'For them. For them, there is no secret place. As for you . . . well, it's not what you're thinking; it's not some higher reality of astral planes or anything. It's as real as those socks. As real as that girl, Melusine, in the store in Woodbridge. And it's where you were meant to be. A place where you'll be welcomed into the heart of things.'

Gillian's heart was racing wildly. 'Where is it?'

'It's called the Night World.'

Grey-blue shadows were gliding up the hills. Gillian drove in the twilight, heading toward the darkness in the east.

'Explain again,' she said, and she said it out loud, even though she couldn't see Angel. There was a slight disturbance of air above the seat to her right, a hint of mist, but that was all. 'You're saying it's not just witches.'

'Not by a long shot. Witches are just one race; there are all sorts of other creatures of the night. All the sorts that you've been taught to think are legends.'

'And they're *real*. And they're just living alongside normal humans. And they always have been.'

'Yes. But it's easy, you see. They look like humans, at least at first glance. As much as *you* look like a human.'

'But I *am* a human. I mean, mostly, right? My great-grandma was a witch, but she married a human and so did my grandma and my mom. So I'm all . . . diluted.'

'It doesn't matter to them. You can claim witch blood. And your powers are beyond dispute. Trust me, they'll welcome you.'

'Besides, I've got *you,*' Gillian said cheerfully. 'I mean, ordinary humans don't have their own invisible guardians, do they?'

'Well.' Angel seemed to coalesce dimly beside her. From what she could see of his face, he was frowning. 'You can't actually tell them about me. Don't ask why; I'm not allowed to explain. But I'll be with you, the way I always am. I'll help you out with what to say. Don't worry; you'll do fine.'

Gillian wasn't worried. She felt steeped in mystery and a sort of forbidden excitement. The whole world seemed magical and unfamiliar.

Even the snow looked different, blue and almost phosphorescent. As Gillian drove through rolling farmlands, a glow appeared above the eastern hills, and then the full moon rose, huge and throbbing with light.

Deeper and deeper, she thought. She seemed to have left everything ordinary behind and to be sliding more and more quickly into an enchanted place where anything – anything at all – could happen.

She wouldn't have been surprised if Angel had directed her to pull off into some snowy clearing and look for a fairy ring. But when he said, 'Turn here,' it was at a main road that led to the straggling outskirts of a town.

'Where are we?'

'Sterback. Little hole-in-the-wall place – except for where we're going. Stop here.'

'Here' was a nondescript building, which looked as if it had originally been Victorian. It wasn't in very good repair.

Gillian got out and looked at the moon shining on the windows. The building might have been a lodge. It was set apart from the rest of the dark and silent town. A wind had started up and she shivered.

(Uh, it doesn't look like anybody's in there.)

(*Go to the door.*) Angel's voice in her mind was comforting, as always.

There was no sign at the door, nothing to indicate that this was a public building. But the stained-glass window above the door was faintly illuminated from the inside. The pattern seemed to be a flower. A black iris.

(*The Black Iris is the name of this place. It's a club—*)

Angel was interrupted by a sudden explosion. That was Gillian's impression. For the first instant she had no idea what it was – just a dark shape flying at her and a violent noise – and she almost fell off the porch. Then she realized that the noise was barking. A chained dog was yammering and foaming, trying to get at her.

(*I'll take care of it.*) Angel sounded grim, and an instant later Gillian felt something like a wave in the air. The dog dropped flat as if it had been shot. It rolled its eyes.

The porch was dead silent again. Everything was silent. Gillian stood and breathed, feeling adrenaline run through her. But before she could say anything, the door opened behind her.

A face looked out of the dimness inside the house. Gillian couldn't make out the features, but she could see the gleam of eyes.

'Who're you?' The voice was slow and flat, not friendly. 'What do you want?'

Gillian followed Angel's whispered words. 'I'm Gillian of the Harman clan, and I want *in*. It's *cold* out here.'

'A Harman?'

'I'm a Hearth-Woman, a daughter of Hellewise, and if you don't let me in, you stupid werewolf, I'm going to do to you what I did to your cousin there.' She stuck out a gloved finger toward the cringing dog. (Werewolf? Angel, there are real werewolves?)

(*I told you. All the legendary creatures.*)

Gillian felt an odd sinking. She had no idea why, and she continued to do just as Angel said. But somehow her stomach was knotting tighter and tighter.

The door opened slowly. Gillian stepped into a dim hall and the door slammed shut again with a curiously final sound.

'Didn't recognize you,' the figure beside her said. 'Thought you might be vermin.'

'I forgive you,' Gillian said, and pulled off her gloves at Angel's direction. 'Downstairs?'

He nodded and she followed him to a door which led to a stairway. As soon as the door opened, Gillian heard music.

She descended, feeling extremely . . . subterranean. The basement was deeper than most basements. And bigger. It was like a whole new world down there.

It wasn't much brighter than upstairs, and there were no windows. It seemed like an *old* place; there was a shuffleboard pattern on the cold tile floor and a faint smell of mildew and moisture. But it was alive with people. There were figures sitting on chairs clumped around the borders of the room and more gathered around a pool table at one end. There were figures in front of a couple of ancient looking pinball machines and figures clustered at what looked like a home bar.

Gillian headed for the bar. She could feel eyes on her every step of the way.

She felt too small and too young as she perched precariously on one of the bar stools. She rested her elbows on the counter and tried to slow her heart down.

The figure behind the bar turned toward her. It was a guy, maybe in his twenties. He stepped forward and Gillian saw his face.

Shock rippled through her. There was something . . . *wrong* with him. Not that he was hideously ugly or that he would have caused a commotion if he got on a bus. Maybe it was something Gillian sensed through her new powers and not through her eyes at all. But the impression she got was that his face looked *wrong*. Tainted by cold dark thoughts that made Tanya's scheming mind look like a sunlit garden.

Gillian couldn't help her recoil. And the bar guy saw it.

'You're new,' he said. The dark and cold seemed to grow in him and she realized he was enjoying her fear. 'Where are you from?'

Angel was shouting instructions at her. 'I'm a Harman,' Gillian said as steadily as she could. 'And – you're right. I'm new.'

(*Good, kid. Don't let him bully you! Now you're going to explain to them just exactly who you are—*)

(In a minute, Angel. Just let me get – settled.) The truth was that Gillian was completely unsettled. The sense of dread that had been growing ever since she walked in was reaching an unbearable pitch. This place was . . . she groped for adjectives. Unwholesome. Corrupt. Scary.

And then she realized something else. Up until now she hadn't been able to make out the faces of the other figures properly. Only eyes and the occasional flash of teeth.

But now – they were moving in around her. It reminded her of sharks, swimming almost aimlessly but ending up in a purposeful gathering. There were people directly behind her – she could feel that with the back of her neck – and there were people on either side of her. When she looked, she could see their faces.

Cold – dark – wrong. Not just wrong, but almost diabolic. These were people who might do anything and enjoy it. Their eyes glittered at her. More than glittered. Some of the eyes were *shining* . . . like an animal's at night . . . and now they were smiling and she could see *teeth*. Long delicate canine teeth that came to a point. *Fangs* . . .

All the legendary creatures . . .

Sheer panic surged through her. And at the same instant, she felt strong hands on her elbows.

'Why don't you come outside with me?' a voice behind her said.

Then things were confused. Angel was yelling again, but Gillian couldn't really hear him over the pounding of her own heart. The hands were exerting pressure, forcing her away from the bar. And the figures with their diabolical faces were settling back, most of them wearing conspiratorial grins.

'Have fun,' somebody called.

Gillian was being hurried up the stairs, whisked through the dim building. A blast of cold air hit her as the door opened and she suddenly felt clearer. She tried to break out of the iron grip that was holding her. It didn't do any good.

She was out in the snow, leaving the house behind. The street was completely deserted.

'Is that your car?'

The hands on her arms eased their pressure. Gillian gave one desperate wrench and turned around.

Moonlight was shining on the snow around her, giving it the texture of white satin. Every shadow was like an indigo stain on the sparkling coverlet.

The person who'd been holding her was a boy a few years older than Gillian. He was lanky and elegant, with ash-blond hair and slightly tilted eyes. Something about the way he held himself made her think of lazy predatory animals.

But his face wasn't *wrong*, the way the other faces had

been. It was set and grim, maybe even a little scary, but it wasn't evil.

'Now, look,' he said, and his voice wasn't evil, either, just rapid and short. 'I don't know who you are, or how you managed to get in there, but you'd better turn around and go home right now. Because whatever you are, you're not a Harman.'

'How do you know?' Gillian blurted before Angel could tell her what to say.

'Because I'm related to the Harmans. I'm Ash Redfern. You don't even know what that means, do you? If you *were* a Harman you'd know that our families are kin.'

(*You* are *a Harman, and you* are *a witch!*) Angel was actually raging. (*Tell him! Tell him!*)

But the ash-blond boy was going on. 'They'll eat you alive in there if they find out for sure. They're not as – tolerant – of humans as I am. So my advice is, get in your car, drive away, and never come back. And never mention this place to anybody else.'

(*You're a lost witch! You're not a human. Tell him!*)

'How come *you're* so tolerant?' Gillian was staring at the boy. His eyes . . . she'd thought they were amber coloured originally, like Steffi's, but now they were emerald green.

He gave her an odd look. Then he smiled. It was a lazy smile, but with something heart-wrenching behind it.

'I met a human girl last summer,' he said quietly, and that seemed to explain everything.

Then he nodded at her car. 'Get out of here. Never come back. I'm just passing through; I won't be around to save you again.'

(*Don't get in the car. Don't go. Tell him. You're a witch; you belong to Circle Midnight.* Don't go!)

For the first time, Gillian deliberately disobeyed an

order of Angel's. She unlocked the car with shaky hands. As she got in, she looked back at the boy. Ash.

'Thank you,' she said.

'Bye.' He wiggled his fingers. He watched as she drove away.

(*Go back there right now! You* belong *there, just as much as any of them. You're one of them. They can't keep you out. Turn around and go back!*)

'Angel, stop it!' She said it out loud. 'I can't! Don't you see that? I *can't*. They were *horrible*. They were – *evil.*'

Now that she was alone, reaction was setting in. Her whole body began to shake. She was suddenly blind with tears, her breath catching in her throat.

'Not evil!' Angel shimmered into the seat beside her. He had never sounded so agitated. 'Just powerful—'

'They were *evil*. They wanted to hurt me. I saw their eyes!' She was lapsing into hysteria. 'Why did you *take* me there? When you wouldn't even let me talk to Melusine? Melusine wasn't like *them.*'

A violent shiver overtook her. The car veered and she struggled with it, barely getting control. All at once everything seemed alien and terrifying; she was out on a long and lonely road, and it was night, and there was an uncanny *being* in the seat beside her.

She didn't know who he was anymore. All she knew was that he wasn't any kind of an angel. The logical alternative sprang immediately to her mind. She was alone in the middle of nowhere *with a demon* . . .

'Gillian, stop it!'

'Who are you? What are you, really? *Who are you?*'

'What do you mean? You know who I am.'

'No, I don't!' She was screaming it. 'I don't know anything about you! Why did you take me there? Why did you want them to hurt me? Why?'

'Gillian, stop the car. *Stop. The. Car.*'

His voice was so commanding, so urgent and imperative, that she actually obeyed. She was sobbing anyway. She couldn't drive or see. She felt, literally and honestly, that she was losing her mind at that exact moment.

'Now look at me. Wipe your face off and look at me.'

After a moment she managed. He was shining. Light seemed to radiate from every inch of him, from the gold filaments of his hair, to his classic features, to the lines of his perfect body. And he'd calmed down. His expression was rapt and uplifted, the serenity only marred by what looked like concern for her.

'Now,' he said. 'I'm sorry if all this scared you. New things are like that sometimes – they seem repulsive just because they're different. But we won't talk about that now,' he added, as Gillian caught a shuddering breath. 'The important thing is that I wasn't trying to hurt you.' His eyes seemed to grow even more intense, pure violet flame.

Gillian hiccupped. 'But – you—'

'I *could* never hurt you, Gillian. Because, you see, we're soulmates.'

He said it with the weight of a monumental revelation. And although Gillian had no idea what it meant, she felt an odd quiver inside, almost of recognition.

'What's that?'

'It's something that happens with people who belong to the Night World. It means that there's only one love for everyone who exists. And when you meet that love, you know them. You know you were meant to be together, and nothing can keep you apart.'

It was true. Every word seemed to resonate inside Gillian, touching off ancient, hidden memories. This was something her ancestors had known.

Her cheeks had dried. Her hysteria was gone. But she felt very tired and very bewildered.

'But . . . if that's true . . .' She couldn't put the thought together.

'Don't worry about it right now.' Angel's voice was soothing. 'We'll talk about it later. I'll explain what it all means. I just wanted you to know that I would never hurt you. I love you, Gillian. Don't you realize that?'

'Yes,' Gillian whispered. Everything was very foggy. She didn't want to think, didn't want to consider the implications of what Angel was saying.

She just wanted to get home.

'Relax and I'll help you drive,' Angel said. 'Don't worry about anything. It's all going to be all right.'

CHAPTER 13

The next day, Gillian tried to concentrate on normal things.

She hurried to school, feeling unrested – had she had nightmares? – and desperately in need of distraction. All day at school, she threw herself into activities, chattering and laughing and keeping people around her, talking about Christmas and parties and finals.

It worked. Angel was very gentle, keeping quietly in the background. All the other students were hyperactive with the thought of only two more days of school. And by the afternoon Gillian had become caught up in her own frantic good spirits.

'We don't even have a tree,' she said to David. 'And it's five days to Christmas Eve. I have to drag my mom out and buy one.'

'Don't buy one,' David said, smiling at her with his dark eyes. 'I'll take you out tonight to a place I know. It's beautiful, and the trees are free.' He winked.

'I'll bring the station wagon,' Gillian said. 'Lots of room. I like *big* trees.'

At home, she stayed busy, prodding her mother to wrap packages and dust off the plastic Christmas flower arrangements. There was no talk with Angel about how to tell her mother about witches.

She was still happy when she picked David up after dinner. He seemed a little subdued, but she wasn't in the mood to ask questions. Instead, she talked about the party Steffi Lockhart was giving on Friday night.

It was a long drive, and she was running out of speculations about Steffi's party when David finally said, 'Somewhere along here, I think.'

'OK. I'll take one of those.' Gillian pointed at the sixty-foot-tall pine trees that lined the road.

David smiled. 'There are some smaller ones farther in.'

There were so many that Gillian had a hard time choosing. At last, she settled on a balsam fir with a perfect silhouette, like a plump lady holding out her skirts. It was wonderfully aromatic as she and David chopped it down and half dragged, half carried it to the car.

'I just love that smell,' she said. 'And I don't even care that my gloves are ruined.'

David didn't answer. He was quiet as he tied the back of the station wagon closed around the tree. He was quiet as they got in the car and Gillian began to drive.

And Gillian couldn't stand it anymore. Little waves of acid were lapping in her stomach. 'What's wrong? You haven't been talking all night.'

'I'm sorry.' He let out his breath, looking out the window. 'I guess . . . I was just thinking about Tanya.'

Gillian blinked. 'Tanya? Should I be jealous?'

He glanced at her. 'No, I mean – her arm.'

A strange sort of prickling cascaded over Gillian, and in that moment everything changed forever. She seemed to ask the next question in a huge, quivering stillness. 'What about her arm?'

'You didn't hear? I thought somebody would've called

you. They took her to the hospital this afternoon.'

'Oh, my God.'

'Yeah, but it's worse. That thing they thought was a rash was necrotizing something-or-other . . . you know, that flesh-eating bacteria.'

Gillian opened her mouth, but no sound came out. The road in front of her seemed very dim.

'Cory said she can't have any visitors – her arm swelled up to three times its normal size. They had to cut it open all the way from her shoulder to her finger to drain it. They think she might lose her finger—'

'Stop it!' A suppressed scream.

David looked at her quickly. 'I'm sorry—'

'No! Just don't talk!' Gillian's automatic reflexes had taken over driving the car. She was hardly aware of anything outside her own body. All her concentration was fixed on the drama inside her own mind.

(Angel! Did you hear that? What is going *on?*)

(*Of course I heard it.*) The voice was slow and thoughtful.

(Well, is it true? Is it?)

(*Look, let's talk about this later, all right, kid? Let's wait—*)

(No! Everything with you is 'Wait' or 'We'll talk about it later.' I want to know *right now:* is it true?)

(*Is what true?*)

(*Is Tanya that sick?* Is she about to lose her *finger?*)

(*It's just an infection, Gillian.* Streptococcus pyogenes. *You were the one who put it there.*)

(You're saying it *is* true. It's true. I did it with *my* spell. I gave her flesh-eating bacteria.) Gillian threw the thoughts out wildly, disjointedly. She couldn't really grasp what it all meant yet.

(*Gillian, we had to stop her from destroying David. It was necessary.*)

(No! No! You knew I didn't really want to hurt her.

What are you *talking* about? How can you even *say* that?) Gillian was in hysteria again, a strange hysteria of the mind. She was vaguely aware that she was still driving, that fences and trees were flying by. Her body was sitting in the car, breathing quickly, speeding, but her real self seemed to be in another place.

(You lied to me. You told me she was all right. Why did you do that?)

(*Calm down, dragonfly—*)

(*Don't call me that!* How can you just – just sit there . . . and not care? What kind of person *are* you?)

And then, Angel's voice changed. He didn't get hysterical or agitated; it was much worse. His voice became calmer. More melodious. Pleasant.

(*I'm just dispensing justice. It's what angels do, you know.*)

Icy horror swept over Gillian.

He sounded insane.

'Oh, God,' she said, and she said it out loud. David looked at her.

'Hey – are you OK?'

She scarcely heard him. She was thinking with fevered intensity: (I don't know *what* you are, but you are *not* an angel.)

(*Gillian, listen to me. We don't have to fight. I* love *you—*)

(Then tell me how to fix Tanya!)

Silence.

(I'll find out myself. I'll go back to Melusine—)

(*No!*)

(Then tell me! Or heal Tanya yourself if you're a real angel!)

A pause. Then: (*Gillian, I've got an idea. A way to make David love you more.*)

(What are you *talking* about?)

(*We need to give him a near-death experience. Then he'll be able to truly understand you. We need to make him die.*)

Everything blurred. Gillian knew they were nearing Somerset, they were on familiar streets. But for a moment her vision went completely grey and sparkling.

'Gillian!' A hand was on hers, a real hand, steadying the wheel. 'Are you all right? Do you want me to drive?'

'I'm OK.' Her vision had cleared. She just wanted to get home. She had to get to that shoe box and fix the spell on Tanya somehow. She had to get home . . . to safety . . .

But nowhere was safe.

(*Don't you understand?*) The voice was soft and insidious in her ear. (*David can never really be like you until he's died the way you have. We have to make him die—*)

'No!' She realized she was speaking aloud again. 'Stop talking to me! Go away!'

David was staring at her. 'Gillian—'

(*I don't want to hurt you, Gillian. Only him. And he'll come back, I promise. He might be a little different. But he'll still love you.*)

Different . . . *David's body*. Angel wanted David's body. As David left, Angel would take possession . . .

They were almost home. But she couldn't get away from the voice. How do you get away from something that's *in your own mind*? She couldn't shut it out . . .

(*Just let go, Gillian. Let me take over. I'll drive for you. I love you, Gillian.*)

'No!' She was panting, her hands gripping the steering wheel so hard it hurt. The word came out jerkily. 'David! You have to drive. I can't—'

(*Relax, Gillian. You won't be harmed. I promise.*)

And she couldn't let go of the steering wheel. The voice seemed to be inside her body, diffusing through her muscles. She couldn't take her foot off the accelerator.

'Gillian, slow down!' David was yelling now. 'Look out!'

(*It will only take a second . . .*)

Gillian's world had been switched into an old-time movie. The flickering black-and-white kind. With each frame, the telephone pole in front of her got bigger and bigger. It was happening very slowly, but at the same time with utter inevitability. They were rushing oh-so-slowly toward that pole, and they were going to hit. On the right side of the car, where David was sitting.

(No! I'll hate you *forever* . . .)

She screamed it in her mind and the last word seemed to echo endlessly. There was time for that.

And then there was a loud sound and darkness.

'Can I see him?'

'Not yet, honey.' Her mother scooted the plastic chair closer to the emergency room bed. 'Probably not tonight.'

'But I *have* to.'

'Gillian, he's unconscious. He wouldn't even know you were there.'

'But I have to *see* him.' Gillian felt the hysteria swelling again, and she clamped her mouth shut. She didn't want a shot, which is what the nurses had said they were going to give her when she started screaming earlier.

She had been here for hours. Ever since the cars with the flashing lights came and pried the station wagon door open and pulled her out. They'd pulled David out, too. But while she had been completely unhurt – 'A miracle! Not even a scratch!' the paramedic had said to her mother – David had been unconscious. And had stayed that way ever since.

The emergency room was cold and it didn't seem to matter how many heated blankets they wrapped around her. Gillian kept shivering. Her hands were blue-white and pinched looking.

'Daddy's coming home,' her mother said, stroking her

arm. 'He's taking the first plane he could get. You'll see him tomorrow morning.'

Gillian shivered. 'Is this the same hospital where Tanya Jun is? No, don't ask. I don't really want to know.' She stuck her hands under her armpits. 'I'm so cold . . .'

And alone. There was no soft voice in her head. And that was *good*, because, God, the last thing she wanted was Angel – or rather that *thing*, whatever it was, that monster that had called itself an angel. But it was strange after so long. To be all alone . . . and not know where *he* might be lurking. He could be listening to her thoughts right now . . .

'I'll get another blanket.' The nurse had shown her mother the heated closet. 'If you could just lie down, honey, maybe you'd feel like sleeping a little.'

'I can't sleep! I have to go see David.'

'Hon, I already told you. You're not going to see him tonight.'

'You said I *might* not get to see him. You didn't say I *wouldn't*! You only said *probably*!' Gillian's voice was rising, getting more shrill, and there was nothing she could do about it. The tears were coming, too, flooding down uncontrollably. She was choking on them.

A nurse came hurrying in, the white curtains around the bed swirling. 'It's all right; it's natural,' she said softly to Gillian's mother. And to Gillian: 'Now, just lean over a little – hold still. A little pinch. This is something to help you relax.'

Gillian felt a sting at her hip. A short time later everything got blurry and the tears stopped.

She woke up in her own bed.

It was morning. Pale sunlight was shining full in the window.

Last night . . . oh, yes. She could vaguely remember her mom and Mrs Beeler, their next-door neighbour, leading her from the hospital to Mrs Beeler's car. She remembered them taking her upstairs and undressing her and putting her to bed. After that she'd had hours of wonderful not-thinking.

And now she was awake and rested and her head was clear. She knew exactly what she had to do even before she swung her legs out from under the covers.

She glanced at the ancient Snoopy clock on her nightstand and got a shock. Twelve thirty-five. No wonder she was rested.

Efficiently, without making a sound, she put on Levis and a grey sweatshirt. No makeup. She ran a comb once through her hair.

She paused, then, to listen. Not just to the house, but to herself. To the world inside her own brain.

Dead quiet. Not a creature stirring. Not that that meant a thing, of course.

Gillian knelt and pulled the shoe box out from under her bed. The wax dolls were garish, red and green, like a hideous parody of Christmas. Her first impulse at the sight of that poisonous green was to get rid of it. Snap off one doll's hand and the other's head.

But what that would do to Tanya and Kim, she didn't want to think. Instead, she forced herself to get a Q-tip from the bathroom, soak it in water, and dab the iridescent green powder away.

She cried as she did it. She tried to concentrate as she had when she'd done the spell, seeing the real Tanya's hand, seeing it heal and become whole.

'Now may I be given the power of the words of Hecate,' she whispered. 'It is not I who utter them, it is not I who repeat them; it is Hecate who utters them, it is she who repeats them.'

When the powder was off, she put the dolls back in the box. Then she blew her nose and rummaged through the pile on her desk until she found a small pink-flowered address book.

She sat on the floor cross-legged, dragged the phone close, and thumbed through the book.

There.

Daryl Novak's cell phone number.

She dialled quickly and shut her eyes. Answer. Answer.

'Hello,' a languid voice said.

Her eyes flew open. 'Daryl, this is Gillian. I need you to do me an enormous favour, and I need you to do it *now*. And I can't even explain why—'

'Gillian, are you OK? Everybody's been worried about you.'

'I'm fine, but I can't talk. I need you to go find Amy Nowick; she's got' – Gillian thought frantically – 'uh, honours chemistry this period. I need you to tell her to drive to the corner of Hazel and Applebutter Street and wait for me there.'

'You want her to leave school?'

'Right now. Tell her I know it's a lot to ask, but I *need* this. It's really important.'

She expected questions. But instead, all Daryl said was, 'Leave it to me. I'll find her.'

'Thanks, Daryl. You're a lifesaver.'

Gillian hung up and found her ski jacket. Tucking the shoe box under her arm, she walked very quietly downstairs.

She could hear voices from the kitchen. A low voice – her dad's. Part of her wanted to run to him.

But what would her parents do if they saw her? Keep her safe and bundled up, keep her *here*. They wouldn't understand what she had to do.

There was no question of telling them the truth, of course. That would just get her another shot. And, eventually, maybe a visit to the mental hospital where her mother had stayed. Everyone would think delusions ran in the family.

She moved stealthily to the front door, quietly opened it, slipped out.

Sometime during the night it had rained and then frozen. Ice hung like dewdrops from the twigs of the hickory tree in the yard.

Gillian ducked her head and hurried down the street. She hoped no one was watching, but she had the feeling of eyes staring from between bare branches and out of shadows.

At the corner of Hazel and Applebutter she stood with her arms wrapped around the box, hopping a little to keep warm.

It's a lot to ask . . .

It *was* a lot to ask, especially considering the way she'd treated Amy recently. And it was funny, considering all the new friends she'd made, that it was Amy she turned to instinctively when she was in trouble.

But . . . there was something solid and genuine and *good* in Amy. And Gillian knew that she would show up.

The Geo swung around the corner and skidded to a stop. Typical Amy-without-glasses driving. Then Amy was jumping out, her face turned anxiously toward Gillian's. Her blue eyes were huge and seemed luminous with tears.

And then they were hugging and crying. Both of them.

'I'm so sorry. I've been so rotten this last week—'

'But I was rotten to you before that—'

'I feel *awful*. You have every right to be mad at me—'

'Ever since I heard about the accident, I've been so *worried.*'

Gillian pulled back. 'I can't stay. I don't have time. And I know how this sounds coming from somebody who hit a pole last night . . . but I need your car. For one thing, I've got to go see David.'

Amy nodded, blotting her eyes. 'Say no more.'

'I can drop you off at home—'

'It's the wrong way. It won't hurt me to walk. I *want* to walk.'

Gillian almost laughed. The sight of Amy dabbing her face with her muffler and stamping her foot on the icy sidewalk, determined to walk, warmed her heart.

She hugged her again, fast. 'Thank you. I'll never forget it. And I'll never be the terrible person I've been to you again, at least—'

She broke off and got in the car. She'd been about to finish the sentence '—at least, if I live through this.'

Because she wasn't at all sure that she would.

But the first thing was to get to David.

She had to see him with her own eyes. To make sure he was all right . . . and that he was himself.

She gunned the motor and set out for Houghton.

CHAPTER 14

She got David's room number from a receptionist at the front desk. She didn't ask if she was allowed to visit.

All Gillian could think as she walked down the hall was, *Please*. Please, if David was only all right, there was a chance that everything could work out.

At the door she stopped and held her breath.

Her mind was showing her all sorts of pictures. David in a coma, hooked up to so many tubes and wires that he was unrecognizable. Worse, David alive and awake and smiling . . . and looking at her with violet eyes.

She knew what Angel's plan had been. At least, she thought she knew. The only question was, had he succeeded?

Still holding her breath, she looked around the door.

David was sitting up in bed. The only thing he was hooked up to was an IV of clear fluid. There was another bed in the room, empty.

He looked toward the door and saw her.

Gillian walked toward him slowly. She kept her face absolutely expressionless, her eyes on him.

Dark hair. A lean face that still had traces of a summer tan. Cheekbones to die for and eyes to drown in . . .

But no half-quizzical, half-friendly smile. He was

looking back at her as soberly as she was looking at him, a book slipping unnoticed from his lap.

Gillian reached the foot of the hospital bed. They stared at each other.

What do I *say*? David, is it really you? I can't. It's too stupid, and what's he going to say back? No, dragonfly, it's not him, it's me?

The silence stretched on. At last, very quietly, the guy on the bed said, 'Are you OK?'

'Yeah.' The word came out clipped and dispassionate. 'Are *you* OK?'

'Yeah, pretty much. I was lucky.' He was watching her. 'You look – kind of different.'

'And you're kind of quiet.'

Something like puzzlement flashed in his eyes. Then something like hurt. 'I was . . . well, you walked in here looking so deadpan, and you sound so . . . cold . . .' He shook his head slightly, his eyes fixed on hers. 'Gillian, did I do something to make you want to hit that pole?'

'I didn't do it on purpose!' She found herself lunging forward, reaching for his hands.

He looked startled. 'OK . . .'

'David, I *didn't*. I was doing everything I could *not* to. I would never want to hurt you. Don't you know that?'

His face cleared. His eyes were very dark but very calm. 'Yes, I do,' he said simply. 'I believe you.'

Strangely, she knew he did. In spite of all the evidence to the contrary, he believed her.

Gillian's hands tightened on his. Their eyes were locked together. It was as if they were getting closer, although neither of them moved physically.

And then it was all happening, what had started to happen at least twice before. Feelings so sweet and strong she could hardly bear it. Strange recognition, unexpected belonging . . . impossible knowing . . .

Gillian's eyes seemed to shut of their own accord. And then somehow they were kissing. She felt the warmth of David's lips. And everything was warm and wonderful . . . but there was more.

It was as if the normal veil that separated two people had melted.

Gillian felt a shock of revelation. *This* was what it meant, what Angel had spoken to her about. She knew it intuitively even though she'd never spoken the word before.

Soulmates.

She'd found hers. The one love for her on this earth. The person she was *meant* to be with, that no one could keep her from. And it wasn't Angel. It was David.

That was the other thing she knew, and knew with a bedrock certainty that nothing could touch. *This* was David, the true David. He was holding her in his arms, kissing her. Her, the ordinary Gillian, who was wearing an old grey sweatshirt and no makeup.

It was absurd that she'd ever believed things like makeup mattered.

David was alive, *that* was what mattered. Gillian didn't have his death on her conscience. And if they could somehow live through the rest of what had to be done, they just might be happier than she had ever imagined.

How weird that she could still think. But they didn't seem to be kissing anymore; they were just holding each other now. And that was almost as good, just feeling his body against hers.

Gillian pulled away.

'David—'

His eyes were full of wonder. 'You know what? I love you.'

'I know.' Gillian realized she was being less than

romantic. She couldn't help it. This was the time for action. 'David, I have to tell you some things, and I don't know if you can believe me. But you've got to try.'

'Gillian, I said I love you. I *mean* that. We—' Then he stopped and searched her face. He seemed to see something that changed his mind. 'I love you,' he said in a different tone. 'So I'll believe you.'

'The first thing is that I'm not anything like what you think. I'm not brave, or noble, or witty in the face of danger or – or *anything* like that. It's all been – a sort of set-up. And here's how it happened.'

And then she told him.

Everything. From the beginning, from the afternoon when she'd heard the crying in the woods and followed it and died and found an angel.

She told him the whole story, about how Angel had appeared in her room that night and how he'd changed her whole life. About the whispering that had guided her ever since.

And about the *very* bad things. Her witch heritage. The spell she'd put on Tanya. The Night World. All the way up to the accident last night.

When she was done, she sat back and looked at him. 'Well?'

'Well, I probably ought to think you're crazy. But I don't. Maybe I'm crazy, too. Or maybe it's because I died once, myself . . .'

'You started to tell me that, that first night – and then the car skidded. What happened?'

'When I was seven my appendix burst. I died on the operating table – and I went to a place like that meadow. I'll tell you the funny thing, though. I felt that rushing thing come at me too – that huge thing you said came at you in the end. Only it actually reached me. And it wasn't dark or scary. It was white – beautiful light – and it had wonderful wings.'

Gillian was staring. 'Then what?'

'It sent me back. I didn't have any choice. It loved me, but I had to go back anyway. So – zoom – back down the tunnel, and pop, back into the body. I've never forgotten it. And, it's hard to explain, but I know it was *real*. I guess that's why I believe you.'

'Then maybe you understand what I've got to do. I don't know what Angel really is . . . I think he may be some kind of demon. But I've got to stop him. Exorcize him or whatever.'

David took her by the arms. 'You can't. You don't know how.'

'But maybe Melusine does. It's either her or that guy Ash at the club. He seemed all right. The only down side is that I think he was a vampire.'

David had stiffened. 'I vote for the witch—'

'Me, too.'

'—but I want you to wait for me. They'll let me out later this afternoon.'

'I *can't*. David, it's for Tanya and Kim, too. Melusine might know how to cure them. Anyway, I'm certainly going to ask her. And I can't let any more time go by.'

David pulled at his hair with the hand that wasn't hooked to the IV. 'OK. All right, give me five minutes, and we'll go together now.'

'No.'

He was looking at the IV as if figuring out how to undo it. 'Yes. Just wait for me—'

Gillian blew him a kiss from the door and ran before he looked up.

He couldn't help her. You couldn't fight Angel in ordinary ways. All David would be was leverage in Angel's hands – a hostage – something to threaten to harm.

Gillian jogged out of the hospital and through the parking lot. She found the Geo.

OK, now if Melusine would just be at the store . . .

(*You don't really want to do this, you know.*)

Gillian slammed the car door closed. She sat up very straight, looking at nothing, as she fastened her seatbelt and started the car.

(*Listen, kid. You ain't never had a friend like me.*)

Gillian pulled out of the parking lot.

(*Come on, give me a break. We can at least talk about this, can't we? There are some things you don't understand.*)

She couldn't listen to him. She didn't dare answer him. The last time, he'd hypnotized her somehow, made her relax and give up control to him. That couldn't happen again.

But she couldn't shut his voice out. She couldn't get away from it.

(*And you can't love* him. *There are rules against it. I'm serious. You belong to the Night World now – you're not* allowed *to love a human. If they find out, they'll kill you both.*)

(And what were you trying to do to us?) Damn, she'd answered him back. She wouldn't do that again.

(*Not hurt you. It was only him I wanted. I could have slipped in as he slipped out . . .*)

Don't listen, Gillian told herself. There must be some way of blocking him, of keeping him out of her mind . . .

She began to sing.

'DECK the halls with boughs of HOL-ly! Fa la la la la . . .'

He hadn't been able to hear her thoughts when she hummed before. It seemed to work, now, as long as she kept her mind on the lyrics. She sang Christmas carols. Loudly. The fast ones, like 'God Rest Ye Merry, Gentlemen' and 'Joy to the World,' were best.

'The Twelve Days of Christmas' got her the last few miles to Woodbridge.

Please be there . . .

'FIVE gold-en rings,' she carolled, hurrying into the Woodbridge Five and Ten with the shoe box under her arm. She didn't care who thought she was crazy. *'FOUR calling birds. THREE French hens . . .'*

She was at the door to the back room.

'TWO turtle doves . . .'

A very startled Melusine looked up from behind the counter.

'And a . . . please, you've got to help me! I've got this Angel who's trying to kill people!' She broke off the song and rushed to Melusine.

'You've . . . what?'

'I've got this – angel thing. And I can't stop him from talking to me . . .' Gillian suddenly realized that Angel *had* stopped talking. 'Maybe he got scared when I came in here. But I still need your help. Please.' Suddenly her eyes were stinging with tears again.

Melusine leaned both elbows on the counter and rested her chin on her hands. She looked surprised, but willing. 'Why don't you tell me about it?'

For the second time that day, Gillian told her story. All of it. She hoped that by telling everything, she could make Melusine understand her urgency. And her lack of experience.

'So I'm not even a real witch,' she said at the end.

'Oh, you're a witch, all right,' Melusine said. There was colour in her cheeks and a look of fascination in her dark eyes. 'He told you the truth about that. Everybody knows about the lost Harman babies. Little Elspeth, the records say that she died in England. But obviously she didn't. And you're her descendant.'

'Which means it's OK for me to do spells?'

Melusine laughed. 'It's OK for anyone to do spells who *can* do spells. In my opinion. Some people don't feel the same way—'

'But can you help me take the spells *off*?' Gillian opened the shoe box. She felt ashamed to show the dolls to Melusine – even though she'd bought them here. 'I wouldn't have done it if I'd known,' she murmured feebly, as Melusine looked at the dolls.

'I know.' Melusine gestured at her to be quiet. Gillian watched tensely and waited for the verdict.

'OK, it looks as if you've started the process already. But I think . . . maybe some healing salve . . . and blessed thistle . . .'

She bustled around, almost flying in her chair. She applied things to the dolls. She asked Gillian to concentrate with her, and she said words Gillian didn't recognize.

Finally, she wrapped the wax dolls in what looked like white silk, and put them back in the box.

'Is that all? It's done?'

'Well, I think it's a good idea to keep the dolls, just in case we need to do more healing. Then, after that, we can unname them and get rid of them.'

'But now Tanya and Kim will be OK?' Gillian was anxious for reassurance, and she couldn't help the quick glance of doubt she cast at Melusine's missing leg.

Melusine was direct. 'If they've had anything amputated, it won't cure them. We can't grow new limbs.' She touched her leg. '*This* happened in a boating accident. But otherwise, yes, they should get better.'

Gillian let out a breath she seemed to have been holding for hours. She shut her eyes. 'Thanks. Thank you, Melusine. You don't know how good it feels to *not* feel like you're maiming somebody.'

Then she opened her eyes. 'But the hard part's still to come.'

'Angel.'

'Yes.'

'Well, I think you're right about it being hard.' She looked Gillian straight in the eye. 'And dangerous.'

'I know that already.' Gillian turned and took a quick pace around the room. 'He can get into my mind and make me do things—'

'Not just your mind. Anyone's.'

'And I'm pretty sure he can move objects by himself. Make cars skid. And he sees *everything*.' She came back to the counter. 'Melusine, what *is* he? And why's he doing all this? And why to *me*?'

'Well, the last question's the easiest. Because you died.' Melusine wheeled quickly to a bookshelf at the end of the counter. She pulled down a volume.

'He must have caught you in the between-place, the place between Earth and the Other Side. The place where *he* was,' she said, wheeling back. 'He pretended to be the welcomer, the one who guides you to the Other Side. That thing rushing at you at the end, that was probably the *real* welcomer. But this "Angel" got you out of the between-place before it could reach you.'

Gillian spoke flatly. 'He's not a real angel, is he?'

'No.'

Gillian braced herself. 'Is he a devil?'

'I don't think so.' Melusine's voice was gentle. She opened the book, flipping pages. 'From the way you brought him back with you, I think he must be a spirit. There are two ways of getting spirits from the between-place: you can summon them or you can go fetch them yourself. You did it the hard way.'

'Wait a minute. You're saying I *brought* him?'

'Well, not consciously. I'm sure you didn't mean to. It sounds like he just sort of grabbed on and whooshed down the tunnel – what we call the narrow path – right along with you. Spirits in the between-place can watch us, sometimes talk to us, but they can't really interact with us. When you brought him to Earth, you set him free to interact.'

'Oh, wonderful,' Gillian whispered. 'So on top of everything, it's my fault from the beginning.' She looked around dazedly, then back at Melusine. 'But what *is* a spirit, really? A dead person?'

'An unhappy dead person.' Melusine turned pages. ' "An earthbound spirit is a damaged soul . . ." ' She shut the book. 'Look, it's actually simple. When a spirit is *really* unhappy – when they've done something awful, or they've died with unfinished business, then they don't go on to the Other Side. They get stuck in – well, the book calls it "the astral planes near Earth." *We* call it the between-place.'

'Stuck.'

'They won't go on. They're too angry and hopeless to even want to be healed. And they can do awful things to living people if they get down here, just out of general miserableness.'

'But how do you get *rid* of them?'

Melusine drew a breath. 'Well, that's the hard part. You can send them back to the between-place – *if* you have some blood and hair from their physical body. And *if* you have all sorts of special ingredients, which I can't get. And *if* you have the right spell, which I don't know.'

'I see.'

'And in any case, that only traps him in the between-place again. It doesn't heal him. But, Gillian, there's something I've got to tell you.' Melusine's face was very serious, and she spoke almost formally. 'You may not need to rely on me.'

'What do you mean?'

'Gillian . . . I don't think you really understand who you are. Did he – this spirit – explain to you just *how* important the Harmans are?'

'He said Elspeth's sister was some big witch leader.'

'The biggest. She's *the* Crone, the leader of all the witches. And the Harmans are, well, they're sort of like the royal family to us.'

Gillian smiled bleakly. 'So I'm a witch princess?'

'You told me that Elspeth is your mother's mother's mother. You're descended entirely through the female line from her. But that's extraordinary. There are almost no Harman girls left. There were only *two* in the world, and now there's you. Don't you see, if you let the Night World know about this, they'll flock to help you. *They'll* take care of Angel.'

Gillian was unimpressed. 'And how long will that take?'

'For them to gather and everything . . . check out your family, make all the preparations . . . I don't know. It could probably be done in a matter of weeks.'

'Too long. *Way* too long. You don't know what Angel can do in a few weeks.'

'Then you can try to do it yourself.'

'But how?'

'Well, you'd have to find out who he was as a person and what business he left unfinished. Then you'd have to finish it. And finally, you'd have to convince him to go on. To be willing to leave the between-place for the Other Side.' She glanced wryly at Gillian. 'I told you it would be hard.'

'And I don't think he'd be very cooperative. He wouldn't *like* it.'

'No. He could hurt you, Gillian.'

Gillian nodded. 'It doesn't matter. It's what I've got to do.'

CHAPTER 15

Melusine was watching her. 'You're strong. I think you can do it, daughter of Hellewise.'

'I'm not strong. I'm *scared.*'

'I think it may be possible to be both,' Melusine said wryly. 'But, Gillian? If you do get through it, please come back. I want to talk to you about some things. About the Night World, and about something called Circle Daybreak.'

The way she said it alarmed Gillian. 'Is it important?'

'It could be very important to you, a witch with human ancestors and surrounded by humans.'

'OK. I'll come back – if.' Gillian glanced once around the shop. Maybe there was some sort of talisman or something she should take . . .

But she knew she was just stalling. If there were anything helpful, Melusine would have already given it to her.

There was nothing left to do now but *go*.

'Good luck,' Melusine said, and Gillian marched to the door. Not that she had any particular idea where she was going.

She was almost at the creaky front door of the Five and Ten when she heard Melusine calling.

'I forgot to mention one thing. Whoever your "Angel"

was, he was probably from this general area. Earthbound spirits usually hang around the place they died. Although that's probably not much help.'

Gillian stood still, blinking. 'No . . . no, it *is* helpful. It's great. It's given me an idea.'

She turned and went through the door without really seeing it, stepped out into the square without really hearing the piped-in Christmas music.

At least I've got a place to go now, she thought.

She drove south, back toward Somerset, then took a winding road eastward into the hills. As she rounded a gentle curve she saw the cemetery spread out beneath her.

It was a very old graveyard, but still popular. Steeped in tradition, but with plenty of room. Grandpa Trevor was buried in the newer section, but there were ancient tombstones on the wooded hill.

If she had a chance of finding Angel, it might be here.

The only way to the older section was up a wooden staircase held in place by railway ties. Gillian climbed it cautiously, holding the handrail. Then she stood at the top and looked around, trying not to shiver.

She was among tall sycamores and oaks which seemed to stretch black bony fingers in every direction. The sun was falling lower in the sky and long shadows tinged with lavender were reaching out from the trees.

Gillian braced herself. And then, as loudly as she could, she yelled.

'Come on, you! You know what I want!'

Silence.

Gillian refused to feel foolish. Gloved hands tucked under her arms, she shouted into the stillness.

'I know you can hear me! I know you're out there! The question is, are you in here?' She kicked a foot toward a snow-covered sandstone marker.

Because of course there was nothing she could do here on her own. The only way to get the information she needed, about who Angel had been in his earthly life and what he'd done or left undone, was from Angel himself.

Nobody else could tell her.

'Is this you?' Gillian scraped snow from a granite gravestone and read the words. ' "Thomas Ewing, 1775, Who bled and Dy'd for Liberty." Were you Thomas Ewing?'

The ice-coated twigs of the tree above her clashed together in the rising wind. It made a sound like a crystal chandelier.

'No, he sounds too brave. And you're obviously just a coward.' She scraped some other stones. 'Hey, maybe you were William Case. "Cut down in the flower of Youth by falling from the Stagecoach." That sounds more like you. Were you William Case?'

(*Are you all finished singing?*)

Gillian froze.

(*Because I've got one for you.*) The voice in her head began to sing raucously. Eerily. (*The Pha-a-antom of the Opera is here, inside your mind . . .*)

'Oh, come on, Angel. You can do better than that. And why aren't you letting me see you? Too scared to meet me face to face?'

A light shimmered over the snow – a beautiful pale golden light that rippled like silk. It grew, it took on a shape.

And then Angel was standing there. Not floating. His feet actually seemed to touch the snow.

He looked terrific. Haunting and beautiful in the gathering twilight. But his beauty was only frightening now. Gillian knew what was underneath it.

'Hi there,' she almost whispered. 'I guess you know what I'm here to talk about.'

'Don't know and don't care. Should you be out here

alone, anyway? Does anybody know where you are?'

Gillian positioned herself in front of him. She looked directly into eyes that were as violet and darkly luminous as the sky.

'I know what you are,' she said, holding those eyes, giving every word equal weight. 'Not an angel. Not a devil. You're just a person. Just like me.'

'Wrong.'

'You've got the same feelings as any other person. And you *can't* be happy being where you are. Nobody could. You can't *want* to be stuck there. If I were dead, I'd *hate* it.'

The last words came out with a force that surprised even Gillian. Angel looked away.

An advantage. Gillian leaped in. 'Hate it,' she repeated. 'Just *hanging* around, getting stagnant, watching other people living their lives. Being *nothing*, doing *nothing* – unless it's to make a little trouble for people on earth. What kind of a life is tha—' She broke off, realizing her mistake.

He was grinning maliciously, recovering. 'No life!'

'All right, what kind of existence, then,' Gillian said coldly. 'You know what I mean. It stinks, Angel. It's putrid. It's disgusting.'

A spasm crossed Angel's face. He whirled away from her. And for the first time since Gillian had seen him, she *saw* agitation in him. He was actually pacing, moving like a caged animal. And his hair – it seemed to be ruffled by some unseen wind.

Gillian pressed her advantage. 'It's about as good as being under *there*.' She kicked at the dead weeds over a grave.

He whirled back, and his eyes were unnaturally bright. 'But I *am* under there, Gillian.'

For a moment, her skin prickled so that she couldn't speak. She had to force herself to say steadily, 'Under that one?'

'No. But I'll show you where. Would you like that?' He made a grand gesture, inviting her down the stairs. Gillian hesitated, then went, knowing he was behind her.

Her heart was pumping wildly. This was almost like a physical contest between them, a contest to see who could upset the other more.

But she had to do it. She had to make a *connection* with him. To reach into his anger and frustration and despair and somehow drag answers out of it.

And it *was* a contest. A contest of wills. Who could shout louder, who could be more merciless. Who could hold on.

The prize was Angel's soul.

She nearly tripped at the bottom of the stairs. It was too dark to see her footing. She noticed, almost absently, that it was getting very cold.

Something like an icy wind went past her – and there was light in front of her. Angel was walking there, not leaving any footprints in the snow. Gillian staggered after him.

They were heading for the newer section of the cemetery. Past it. Into the *very* new section.

'Here,' Angel said. He turned. His eyes were glittering. He was standing behind a gravestone and his own light illuminated it.

Chills washed over Gillian.

This was what she had asked for, it was exactly what she had asked for. But it still made the hair on her neck stand on end.

He was under here. Right here. Beneath the ground. The body of the person she'd loved and trusted . . . whose voice had been the last thing she'd heard at night and the first thing each morning.

He was under here in some kind of box, unless maybe

that had rotted. And he wasn't smiling and golden-haired and handsome. And she was going to find out his name from a stone.

'I'm here, Gillian,' Angel said ghoulishly, leaning over the granite marker, resting his elbows on it. 'Come up and say hello.' He was smiling, but his eyes looked as if he hated her. Wild and reckless and bitter. Capable of anything.

And somehow, the sick horror that had been sweeping through Gillian disappeared.

Her eyes were full, spilling over. The tears froze on her cheeks. She brushed at them absently and knelt beside the grave, not on it. She didn't look at Angel.

She put her hands together for just a moment and bent her head. It was a wordless prayer to whatever Power might be out there.

Then she took off her glove and gently scraped snow away from the marker with her bare hand.

It was a simple granite headstone with a scrolled top. It read 'In loving memory. Our son. Gary Fargeon.'

'Gary Fargeon,' Gillian said softly. She looked up at the figure leaning over the stone. 'Gary.'

He gave a mocking laugh, but it sounded forced. 'Nice to meet you. I was from Sterback; we were practically neighbours.'

Gillian looked back down. The date of birth was eighteen years ago. And the date of death was the previous year.

'You died last year. And you were only seventeen.'

'I had a little car crash,' he said. 'I was extremely drunk.' He laughed again, wildly.

Gillian sat back on her heels. 'Oh, really. Well, that was brilliant,' she whispered.

'What's life?' He bared his teeth. ' "Out, out, brief

candle" – or something like that.'

Gillian refused to be distracted. 'Is *that* what you did?' she asked quietly. 'Got yourself killed? Is that unfinished business somehow?'

'Wouldn't you like to know?' he said.

OK, retreat. He wasn't ready yet. Maybe try some feminine wiles. 'I just thought you trusted me – Angel. I thought we were supposed to be soulmates . . .'

'But by now you know we aren't, don't you? Because you found your real love – that jerk.' Gary turned up the brilliance of his smile. 'But even if we're not soulmates, we *are* connected, you know. We're cousins. Distant, but the bond is there.'

Gillian's hands fell to her sides. She stared up at him. Lights were going on in her brain, but she wasn't quite sure what they illuminated yet.

The strangest thing was that she wasn't entirely surprised.

'Didn't you ever wonder why we both have the same colour eyes?' He stared down at her. Although everything was dark around him, his eyes were like violet flame. 'I mean it isn't exactly common. Your Great-grandmother Elspeth had these eyes. So did her twin brother, Emmeth.'

Twins.

Of course. The lost Harman *babies*, Melusine had said. Elspeth and Emmeth. 'And you're . . .'

He smirked. 'I'm Emmeth's great-grandson.'

Now Gillian could see what her mind was trying to illuminate. Her thoughts were racing. 'You're a witch, too. That was why you knew how to do the spells and things. But how did you figure out what you were?'

'Some idiots from Circle Daybreak came,' Gary said. 'They were looking for lost witches. They'd managed to track Emmeth's descendants down. They told me enough that I understood what kind of powers I had. And then – I told them to get lost themselves.'

'*Why?*'

'They were jerks. All they care about is getting humans and Night People together. But I knew the Night World was the place for me. Humans deserve what they get.'

Gillian stood. Her fingers were getting red and swollen. She tried to pull her glove back on. 'Gary, you *are* a human. At least part. Just like I am.'

'No. We're superior to them. We're special—'

'We are *not* special. We're no better than anyone else!'

Gary was grinning unpleasantly, breathing quickly. 'You're wrong there. The Night People are supposed to be *hunters*. There are even laws that say so.'

A chill that had nothing to do with the wind went through Gillian. 'Oh, really?' Then she had another thought. 'Is *that* why you made me go to that club? So they could hunt *me*?'

'No, you idiot!' Gary's eyes flashed. 'I told you – you're one of them. I just wanted you to *realize* that. You could have stayed, been part of them—'

'But *why*?'

'So you would be like *me*!' The wind was gusting wildly again. Frozen tree branches creaked like creatures in pain.

'*But why?*'

'So you could come be *with* me. So we could be together. Forever. If you joined them, you wouldn't have gone on to the Other Side—'

'When I died! You wanted me dead.'

Gary looked confused. 'That was just at first—'

Gillian was angry now. Yelling. 'You planned the whole thing! You *lured* me. Didn't you? Didn't you? That crying I heard in the woods – that was you, wasn't it?'

'I—'

'Everything you did was designed to kill me! Just so you'd have company!'

'I was lonely!' The words seemed to hang and echo. Then Gary's eyes darkened and he turned away.

'I was so lonely,' he said again, and there was something so hopeless in his voice that Gillian stepped toward him.

'Anyway, I didn't do it,' he said over his shoulder. 'I changed my mind. I thought I could come live with you here—'

'By killing David and taking his body. Yeah. Great plan.'

He didn't move. Helplessly, Gillian reached out a hand. It passed right through his shoulder.

She looked at the hand, then said quietly, 'Gary, tell me what you did. What the unfinished business is.'

'So you can try to send me on.'

'Yes.'

'But what if I don't want to *go* on?'

'You have to!' Gillian clenched her teeth. 'You don't *belong* here, Gary! This isn't your place anymore! And there's nothing you can do here, except . . . except *evil.*' She stopped, breathing hard.

He turned, and she saw the wild look again. 'Maybe that's what I *like* to do.'

'You don't understand. *I'm not going to let you.* I'm not going to stop or give up. I'll do whatever it takes to make you move on.'

'But maybe you won't have the chance.'

A blast of wind. And something else. Stinging granules that struck Gillian's face like tiny needles.

'What if there's a blizzard tonight?'

'Gary, stop it!' The gale buffeted her.

'A freak storm. Something nobody expected.'

'Gary . . .' It was very dark, the moon and stars had

been blotted out. But Gillian could see a driving, swirling whiteness. Her teeth were chattering and her face was numb.

'And what if Amy's car won't start? If something went wrong with the engine . . .'

'Don't do this! Gary!' She couldn't see him now. His light was gone, swallowed in the storm. Snow slashed her face.

'Nobody knows where you are, do they? That wasn't very smart, dragonfly. Maybe you need somebody to look after you, after all.'

Gillian gasped, open-mouthed, for breath. She tried to take a step and the wind thrust her against something hard. A tombstone.

This was what she'd been afraid of. That her angel would turn against her, try to destroy her. But now that it was happening, she found that she knew what to do.

Gary's voice came out of the gale. 'What if I just go away and leave you for a little while?'

Gillian's eyes were watering, the tears freezing on her lashes. It was hard to get a breath. But she gathered herself, hanging on to the tombstone, and yelled.

'You won't! You *know* you won't—'

'How can I know?'

She answered with a question, shouting over the wind. 'Why didn't you kill David?'

Her only answer was the howling gale.

Gillian's sight was dimming. The cold *hurt*. She tried to cling on to the tombstone, but her hands were numb. 'You couldn't do it, Gary! You couldn't kill someone! When it came right down to it, you couldn't! And that's how I know.'

She waited. At first she thought that she'd been wrong. That he'd left her alone in the storm.

Then she realized the wind was dying. The curtains of snow were thinning. Stopping. A light formed in the empty air.

Angel – no, Gary – was standing there. She could see him clearly. She could even see what was in his eyes.

Bitterness. Anger. But something like a plea, too.

'But I did, Gillian. That's exactly what I did. I killed someone.'

Gillian took a breath that started out quick and ended long. Oh. Oh . . . that was bad.

But there might have been some justification. A fight. Self-defence.

She said quietly, 'Who?'

'Can't you guess? Paula Belizer.'

CHAPTER 16

Gillian stood as if her snow-powdered body had been turned to ice. Because it was the worst, the absolute worst that she could possibly have imagined.

He killed a kid.

'The little girl who disappeared a year ago,' she whispered. 'On Hillcrest Road.' The one she'd thought of – completely irrationally – when she'd heard the crying.

'I was doing a spell,' Gary said. 'A strong one; I was a quick learner. It was a fire elemental spell – so I was out in the woods. In the snow, where nothing would burn. And then she showed up chasing her dog.'

He was staring into the distance, his face dead white. Looking not haunting, but haunted. And Gillian knew he wasn't with her at that moment; he was far away, with Paula.

'They broke the circle. It all happened so fast. The fire was everywhere – just one white flash, like lightning. And then it was gone.' He paused. 'The dog got away. But not her.'

Gillian shut her eyes, trying not to imagine it. 'Oh, God.' And then, as something twisted inside her, 'Oh, Gary . . .'

'I put her body in my car. I was going to take her to the hospital. But she was *dead*. And I was – confused. So finally I stopped the car. And I buried her in the snow.'

'Gary . . .'

'I went home. Then I went to a party. That was the kind of guy I was, you see. A partyin' guy. Everything was about good times and me, me, me. That was even what being a witch was about.' For the first time there was emotion in his voice, and Gillian recognized it. Self-hatred.

'And at the party, I got really, really drunk.'

Oh. Suddenly Gillian understood. 'You never told anybody.'

'On the way back home I wrapped my car around a tree. And that was it.' He laughed, but it wasn't a laugh. 'Suddenly I'm in Neverland. Can't talk to anybody, can't touch anybody, but sure can see *everything*. I watched the search for her, you know. They passed about a foot away from her body.'

Gillian gulped and looked away. Something had twisted and broken inside her, some idea of justice that would never be put back together. But this was no time to think about that.

It hadn't really been his fault . . . but what did that matter? You played the hand you got dealt. And Gary had played his badly. He'd started out with everything – good looks, obvious brains, and witch power enough to choke a horse, and he'd blown it.

Didn't matter. They had to go on from here.

She looked up at him. 'Gary, you have to tell me where she is.'

Silence.

'Gary, don't you see? That's your unfinished business. Her family doesn't know . . .' Gillian stopped and swallowed. When she went on, her voice wobbled.

'Whether she's alive or dead. Don't you think they ought to *know* that?'

A long pause. Then he said, like a stubborn child, 'I don't want to go anywhere.'

Like a frightened child, Gillian thought. But she didn't look away from him. 'Gary, they deserve to know,' she said softly. 'Once they're at peace—'

He almost shouted, 'What if there isn't any peace for *me*?'

Not frightened, terrified.

'What if there isn't anywhere for me to go? What if they won't *take* me?'

Gillian shook her head. Her tears overflowed again. And she didn't have any answers for him. 'I don't know. But it doesn't change what we've got to do. I'll stay with you, though, if you want. I'm your cousin, Gary.' Then, very quietly, she said, 'Take me to her.'

He stood for a long moment – the longest of Gillian's life. He was looking at something in the night sky that she couldn't see, and his eyes were utterly bleak.

Then he looked at her and slowly nodded.

'Here?' David bent and touched the snow. He looked up at Gillian. His dark eyes were young – a little scared. But his jaw was set.

'Yes. Right there.'

'It's a pretty strange place to do it.'

'I know. But we don't have any choice.'

David got to work with the shovel. Gillian pushed and mounded snow into walls. She tried to think only of how she'd done this in childhood, about how easy and interesting it had been then. She kept at it until David said, 'I found her.'

Gillian stepped back, brushing off her sleeves and mittens.

It was a clear day, and the afternoon sun was brilliant in a cold blue sky. The small clearing was peaceful, almost a haven. Untouched except for a welt in the snow where a ground mouse had tunnelled.

Gillian took a couple of deep breaths, fists clenched, and then she turned to look.

David hadn't uncovered much. A scrap of charred red wool muffler. He was kneeling beside the shallow trench he'd made.

Gillian was crying again. She ignored it. She said, 'It was the last day before Christmas vacation, so we took the day off from school. We were playing hooky in the woods. We decided to make a snow fort . . .'

'And then we found the body.' David got up and gently put a hand on her elbow. 'It's a weird story, but it's better than the truth.'

'And what can they suspect us of? We never even knew Paula Belizer. They'll know she was murdered because she was buried. But they won't know how she died. They'll think somebody tried to burn the body to get rid of it.'

David put his arm around her waist, and she leaned into him. They stood that way for a few minutes, steadying each other.

It was strange how natural that was, now. David had agreed to help her with all this without a moment's hesitation . . . and Gillian hadn't been surprised. She'd expected it. He was her soulmate. They stood together.

At last, he said quietly, 'Ready?'

'Yes.'

As they left the clearing, David added even more quietly, 'Is he here?'

'No. I haven't seen him since he showed me the place. He just – disappeared. He won't talk to me either.'

David held her tighter.

* * *

Mr Belizer came at dusk, after most of the police had left.

It was almost too dark to see. David had been urging Gillian away for an hour. So had Gillian's parents. They were there, both of them, huddling close and touching her whenever they could. David's father and step-mother were on the other side of David.

Yeah, Gillian thought. It's been a rough last few days on everybody.

But here they all were: David, pale but calm; Gillian, shaky but standing; the parents, bewildered but trying to cope. Not comprehending how their kids could have found so much trouble in such a short time.

At least nobody seemed to suspect them of having hurt Paula Belizer.

And now, here was Paula's dad. Alone. Come to look at the last resting place of his daughter – even though the coroner had already taken his daughter away.

The police let him go up to the clearing with a flashlight.

Gillian tugged at David's hand.

He resisted a second, then let her tow him. Gillian heard murmurs as they went. What are you doing, following that poor man. My God, that's – ghoulish. But none of the parents actually grabbed them to stop them.

They ended up a little distance behind Mr Belizer. Gillian moved to see his face.

Now here was the thing. She didn't know about spirits. She wasn't sure *what* needed to be done to release Gary from the between-place. Did she need to talk to Paula's dad? Explain that she had the feeling whoever had done it was sorry, even if they could never tell him themselves?

It might get her locked up. Showing too much interest in a crime, too much knowledge. But, strangely, that didn't scare her as much as she'd have thought. She was Gary's cousin, and his debts were hers somehow. And things had to be put right.

As she stood hesitating, Mr Belizer fell to his knees in the trampled snow.

Oh, God. That hurt. If strong arms hadn't been holding Gillian up, she might have fallen, too.

David held her and pressed his face into her hair. But Gillian kept looking at the kneeling man.

He was crying. She'd never seen a man his age cry, and it hurt in a way that was *scary*. But there was something else in his face. Something like relief . . . peace.

Kneeling there, with his overcoat spread around him, Mr Belizer said, 'I know my daughter is in a better place. Whoever did this, I forgive them.'

A shock like cold lightning went through Gillian, and then a spreading warmth. She was crying suddenly. Hard. Tears falling straight down from her eyes. But she was filled with a hope that seemed to lift her whole body.

And then David drew in his breath sharply, and she realized he'd raised his head. He was staring at something above Mr Belizer.

Gary Fargeon was hovering there. Like an Angel.

He was crying. And saying something over and over. Gillian caught '—sorry, I'm so sorry . . .'

Forgiveness asked for and given. If not exactly in that order.

That's it, Gillian thought. Her knees began to tremble.

David whispered huskily, 'Can you see that, too?'

'Yes. Can you?'

Nobody else seemed to see it. Mr Belizer was getting up now. He was walking past them, away.

David was still staring. 'So that's what he looks like. No wonder you thought—'

He didn't finish, but Gillian knew. Thought he was an angel.

But . . . why was Gary still here? Wasn't the forgiveness enough to release him? Or was there something else that needed to be done?

Gary turned his head and looked at her. His cheeks were wet. 'Come in a little farther,' he said. 'I have to say something.'

Gillian untangled from David, and then pulled at him. He came, jaw still sagging. They followed Gary past a thicket and into another clearing. As the trees and the darkness closed around them, they seemed suddenly far away from the police noise and bustle.

Gillian guessed even as Gary sank down to face them. But she let him say it.

'You have to forgive me, too.'

'I forgive you,' Gillian said.

'You have to be sure. I did some terrible things to you. I tried to warp you, damage your soul.'

'I know,' Gillian said steadily. 'But you did some good things, too. You helped me – grow up.'

He'd helped her conquer her fears. Gain self-confidence. Discover her heritage. And find her soulmate.

And he'd been close to her in a way that she would probably never be with anyone else ever again.

'You know what?' Gillian was on the verge of tears again. 'I'm going to miss you.'

He stood facing her. He was shining just dimly. His eyes were dark and bruised looking, but his lips were smiling. And he was more beautiful than she had ever seen him.

'Things are going to work out, you know,' he said softly. 'For you. Your mom's going to get better.'

Gillian nodded. 'I think so, too.'

'And I checked on Tanya and Kim. They're going to be

all right. Tanya's still got all her fingers.'

'I know.'

'You should go see Melusine. You could help them a lot with Circle Daybreak. And they can help you deal with the Night World.'

'Yes. All right.'

'And you might want to talk to Daryl at school. She's got a secret that Kim was spreading rumours about last year. It's that—'

'Ang— Gary!' Gillian held up her hand. 'I don't want to know. Someday, if Daryl wants to tell me her secret, she can do it herself. But if not – OK. I have to deal on my own, now.'

She'd already thought about school, all last night while she'd been lying alone in her room. Things were going to change, obviously. It was surprisingly easy to sort out which friends mattered.

Amanda the Cheerleader and Steffi the Singer and J.Z. the Model were all right. No better and no worse than any of the less popular girls. She wouldn't mind if they still liked her.

Daryl, who was not Daryl the Rich Girl anymore, but just Daryl, was better than all right. The sort that might turn out to be a real friend. And of course there was Amy. She owed Amy a lot.

As for the others – Tanya and Kim and Cory and Bruce and Macon – Gillian didn't really *want* to know them. If she never went to another Popular Party, that was fine.

'And I don't want to know if J.Z. really tried to kill herself, either,' she said now.

Gary shut his mouth. Then his eyes actually seemed to twinkle. 'You're going to do all right.' And then, for the first time, he looked at David.

They stared at each other for a moment. Not hostile. Just looking.

When Gary turned back to Gillian he said very quietly, 'One last thing. I didn't change my mind about killing him because I couldn't go through with it. I did it because I didn't want you to hate me forever.'

Oh.

Gillian put out her hand. So did he. Their fingers were close together, blurring into each other . . . but they couldn't touch. They never would.

And then suddenly, Gary looked startled. He turned to look up and behind him.

At the dark, starlit sky.

Gillian couldn't see anything. But she could *feel* something. A sort of rushing. Something was coming.

And Gary was lifted toward it like a leaf on the wind.

His hand was still stretched toward her, but he was in the air. Weightless. Bobbing. And as Gillian watched, his startled expression melted into something like awe.

And then joy. Joy and . . . recognition.

'I've got to go,' he said wonderingly.

Gillian was staring at the sky. She still couldn't see anything. Not the tunnel, not the meadow. Did he mean he had to go to the between-place?

And then she saw the light.

It was the colour of sunlight on snow. That brilliant, but not painful to look at. It seemed to shimmer with every colour in the universe, but all together the colours made white.

'Gary—'

But something was happening. He was moving without moving. Rushing away in some direction she couldn't point to. Getting smaller. Fading. She was losing him.

'Goodbye, Gary,' she whispered.

And the light was going, too. But just before it went, it seemed to take on a shape. It looked something like huge white wings enfolding him.

For the briefest instant, Gillian felt enfolded, too. By power and peace . . . and love.

And then the light was gone. Gary was gone. And everything was still.

'Did you see that?' Gillian whispered through the ache in her throat.

'I think so.' David was staring, his eyes big with awe and wonder.

'Maybe . . . some angels are real.'

He was still staring upward. Then he drew in his breath. 'Look! The stars—'

But it wasn't stars, although it looked like stardust. Crystalline points of light, frozen beauty sifting down. The air was full of it.

'But there aren't any clouds . . .'

'There are now,' David said. Even as he said it, the stars were covered. Gillian felt a cool touch on her cheek.

Like a kiss.

And it was ordinary snow, just an ordinary miracle. She and David stood hand in hand, watching it fall like a blessing in the night.

THE
CHOSEN

For Lolly Carter

CHAPTER 1

It happened at Rashel's birthday party, the day she turned five years old.

'Can we go in the tubes?' She was having her birthday at a carnival and it had the biggest climbing structure of tubes and slides she had ever seen.

Her mother smiled. 'OK kitten, but take care of Timmy. He's not as fast as you are.'

They were the last words her mother ever said to her.

Rashel didn't have to be told, though. She always took care of Timmy: he was a whole month younger than she was, and he wasn't even going to kindergarten next year. He had silky black hair, blue eyes, and a very sweet smile. Rashel had dark hair, too, but her eyes were green – green as emeralds, Mommy always said. Green as a cat's.

As they climbed through the tubes she kept glancing back at him, and when they got to a long row of vinyl-padded stairs – slippery and easy to slide off of – she held out a hand to help him up.

Timmy beamed at her, his tilted blue eyes shining with adoration. When they had both crawled to the top of the stairs, Rashel let go of his hand.

She was heading toward the spider web, a big room

made entirely of rope and net. Every so often she glanced through a fish-bowl window in one of the tubes and saw her mother waving at her from below. But then another mother came to talk to hers and Rashel stopped looking out. Parents never seemed to be able to talk and wave at the same time.

She concentrated on getting through the tubes, which smelled like plastic with a hint of old socks. She pretended she was a rabbit in a tunnel. And she kept an eye on Timmy – until they got to the base of the spider web.

It was far in the back of the climbing structure. There were no other kids around, big or little, and almost no noise. A white rope with knots at regular intervals stretched above Rashel, higher and higher, leading to the web itself.

'OK, you stay here, and I'll go up and see how you do it,' she said to Timmy. This was a sort of fib. The truth was that she didn't think Timmy could make it, and if she waited for him, neither of them would get up.

'No, I don't want you to go without me,' Timmy said. There was a touch of anxiety in his voice.

'It's only going to take a second,' Rashel said. She knew what he was afraid of, and she added, 'No big kids are going to come and push you.'

Timmy still looked doubtful. Rashel said thoughtfully, 'Don't you want ice cream cake when we get back to my house?'

It wasn't even a veiled threat. Timmy looked confused, then sighed heavily and nodded. 'OK I'll wait.'

And those were the last words Rashel heard *him* say.

She climbed the rope. It was even harder than she'd thought it would be, but when she got to the top it was wonderful. The whole world was a squiggly moving mass of netting. She had to hang on with both hands to keep her balance and try to curl her feet around the rough quivering lengths of cable. She could feel the air and sunlight. She laughed with exhilaration and bounced, looking at the coloured plastic tubes all around her.

When she looked back down for Timmy, he was gone.

Rashel's stomach tensed. He *had* to be there. He'd promised to wait.

But he wasn't. She could see the entire padded room below the spider web from here, and it was empty.

OK, he must have gone back through the tubes. Rashel made her way, staggering and swaying, from one handhold to another until she got to the rope. Then she climbed down quickly and stuck her head in a tube, blinking in the dimness.

'Timmy?' Her voice was a muffled echo. There was no answer and what she could see of the tube was empty. 'Timmy!'

Rashel was getting a very bad feeling in her stomach. In her head, she kept hearing her mother say, *Take care of Timmy*. But she hadn't taken care of him. And he could be anywhere by now, lost in the giant structure, maybe crying, maybe getting shoved around by big kids. Maybe even going to tell her mother.

That was when she saw the gap in the padded room.

It was just big enough for a four-year-old or a very slim five-year-old to get through. A space between two cushiony walls that led to the outside. And Rashel knew immediately that it was where Timmy had gone. It was like him to take the quickest way out. He was probably on his way to her mother right now.

Rashel was a very slim five-year-old. She wiggled through the gap, only sticking once. Then she was outside, breathless in the dusty shade.

She was about to head toward the front of the climbing

structure when she noticed the tent flap fluttering.

The tent was made of shiny vinyl and its red and yellow stripes were much brighter than the plastic tubes. The loose flap moved in the breeze and Rashel saw that anyone could just lift it and walk inside.

Timmy wouldn't have gone in *there*, she thought. It wouldn't be like him at all. But somehow Rashel had an odd feeling.

She stared at the flap, hesitating, smelling dust and popcorn in the air. I'm brave, she told herself, and sidled forward. She pushed on the tent beside the flap to widen the gap, and she stretched her neck and peered inside.

It was too dark to see anything, but the smell of popcorn was stronger. Rashel moved farther and farther until she was actually in the tent. And then her eyes adjusted and she realized that she wasn't alone.

There was a tall man in the tent. He was wearing a long light-coloured trench coat, even though it was warm outside. He didn't seem to notice Rashel because he had something in his arms, and his head was bent down to it, and he was doing something to it.

And then Rashel saw what he was doing and she knew that the grown-ups had lied when they said ogres and monsters and the things in fairy-tale books weren't real.

Because the tall man had Timmy, and he was *eating* him.

CHAPTER

2

Eating him or doing something with his teeth. Tearing and sucking. Making noises like Pal did when he ate his dog food.

For a moment Rashel was frozen. The whole world had changed and everything seemed like a dream. Then she heard somebody screaming and her throat hurt and she knew it was her.

And then the tall man *looked* at her.

He lifted his head and looked. And she knew that his face alone was going to give her nightmares forever.

Not that he was ugly. But he had hair as red as blood and eyes that shone gold, like an animal's. There was a light in them that was like nothing she had ever seen.

She ran then. It was wrong to leave Timmy, but she was too scared to stay. She wasn't brave; she was a baby, but she couldn't help it. She was still screaming as she turned around and darted through the flap in the tent.

Almost darted through. Her head and shoulders got outside and she saw the red plastic tubes rising above her – and then a hand clamped on the back of her Gymboree shirt. A big strong hand that stopped her in midflight. Rashel was as helpless as a baby kitten against it.

But just as she was dragged back into the tent, she saw something. *Her mother.* Her mother was coming around the corner of the climbing structure. She'd heard Rashel screaming.

Her mother's eyes were big and her mouth was open, and she was moving fast. She was coming to save Rashel.

'Mommyyyyy!' Rashel screamed, and then she was back inside the tent. The man threw her to one side the way a kid at preschool would throw a piece of crumpled paper. Rashel landed hard and felt a pain in her leg that normally would have made her cry. Now she hardly noticed it. She was staring at Timmy, who was lying on the ground near her.

Timmy looked strange. His body was like a rag doll's – arms and legs flopped out. His skin was white. His eyes were staring straight up at the top of the tent.

There were two big holes in his throat, with blood all around them.

Rashel whimpered. She was too frightened to scream anymore. But just then she saw white daylight, and a figure in front of it. Mommy. Mommy was pulling the tent flap open. Mommy was inside, looking around for Rashel.

That was when the worst thing happened. The worst and the strangest, the thing the police never believed when Rashel told them later.

Rashel saw her mother's mouth open, saw her mother looking at her, about to say something. And then she heard a voice – but it wasn't Mommy's voice.

And it wasn't an out-loud voice. It was inside her head.

Wait! There's nothing wrong here. But you need to stand very, very still.

Rashel looked at the tall man. His mouth wasn't moving, but the voice was his. Her mother was looking at him, too, and her expression was changing, becoming relaxed and . . . stupid. Mommy was standing very, very still.

Then the tall man hit Mommy once on the side of the neck and she fell over and her head flopped the wrong way like a broken doll. Her dark hair was lying in the dirt.

Rashel saw that and then everything was even more like a dream. Her mother was dead. Timmy was dead. And the man was looking at her.

You're not upset, came the voice in her head. *You're not frightened. You want to come right here.*

Rashel could feel the pull of the voice. It was drawing her closer and closer. It was making her still and not afraid, making her forget her mother. But then she saw the tall man's golden eyes and they were *hungry*. And all of a sudden she remembered what he wanted to do to her.

Not me!

She jerked away from the voice and dove for the tent flap again.

This time she got all the way outside. And she threw herself straight at the gap in the climbing structure.

She was thinking in a different way than she had ever thought before. The Rashel that had watched Mommy fall was locked away in a little room inside her, crying. It was a new Rashel who wiggled desperately through the gap in the padded room, a smart Rashel who knew that there was no point in crying because there was nobody who cared anymore. Mommy couldn't save her, so she had to save herself.

She felt a hand grab her ankle, hard enough almost to crush her bones. It yanked, trying to drag her back through the gap. Rashel kicked backward with all her strength and then twisted, and her sock came off and she pulled her leg into the padded room.

Come back! You need to come back right now!

The voice was like a teacher's voice. It was hard not to listen. But Rashel was already scrambling into the plastic tube in front of her. She went faster than she ever had before, hurting her knees, propelling herself with her bare foot.

When she got to the first fish-bowl window, though, she saw a face looking in at her.

It was the tall man. He was staring at her. He banged on the plastic as she went by.

Fear cracked in Rashel like a belt. She scrambled faster, and the knocks on the tube followed her.

He was underneath her now. Keeping up with her. Rashel passed another window and looked down. She could see his hair shining in the sunlight. She could see his pale face looking up at her.

And his eyes.

Come down, came the voice and it wasn't stern anymore. It was sweet. *Come down and we'll go get some ice cream. What kind of ice cream do you like best?*

Rashel knew then that this was how he'd gotten Timmy into the tent. She didn't even pause in her scrambling.

But she couldn't get away from him. He was travelling with her, just under her, waiting for her to come out or get to a place where he could reach in and grab her.

Higher. I need to get higher, she thought.

She moved instinctively, as if some sixth sense was telling her which way to turn each time she had a choice. She went through angled tubes, straight tubes, tubes that weren't solid at all, but made of woven canvas strips. And finally she got to a place where she couldn't go any higher.

It was a square room with a padded floor and netting sides. She was at the front of the climbing structure; she could see mothers and fathers standing and sitting in little groups. She could feel the wind.

Below her, looking up, was the tall man.

Chocolate brownie? Mint chip? Bubble gum?

The voice was putting pictures in her mind. Tastes. Rashel looked around frantically.

There was so much noise – every kid in the climbing structure was yelling. Who would even notice her if she shouted? They'd think she was joking around.

All you have to do is come down. You know you have to come down sometime.

Rashel looked into the pale face turned up to her. The eyes were like dark holes. Hungry. Patient. Certain.

He knew he was going to get her.

He was going to win. She had no way to fight him.

And then something tore inside Rashel and she did the only thing a five-year-old could do against an adult.

She shoved her hand between the rough cords that made the netting, scraping off skin. She pushed her whole small arm through and she pointed down at the tall man.

And she screamed in a way she'd never screamed before. Piercing shrieks that cut through the happy noise of the other kids. She screamed the way Ms Bruce at preschool had taught her to do if any stranger ever bothered her.

'Help meeee! Help meeee! That man tried to touch me!'

She kept screaming it, kept pointing. And she saw people look at her.

But they didn't do anything. They just stared. Lots of faces, looking up at her. Nobody moving.

In a way, it was even worse than anything that had happened before. They could hear her, but nobody was going to help her.

And then she saw somebody moving.

It was a big boy, not quite a grown-up man. He was

wearing a uniform like the one Rashel's father used to wear before he died. That meant he was a Marine.

He was going towards the tall man, and his face was dark and angry. And now, as if they had only needed this example, other people were moving, too. Several men who looked like fathers. A woman with a cell phone.

The tall man turned and ran.

He ducked under the climbing structure, heading toward the back, toward the tent where Rashel's mother was. He moved very fast, much faster than any of the people in the crowd.

But he sent words to Rashel's mind before he disappeared completely.

See you later.

When he was definitely gone, Rashel slumped against the netting, feeling the rough cord bite into her cheek. People down below were calling to her; kids just behind her were whispering. None of it really mattered.

She could cry now; it would be OK, but she didn't seem to have any tears.

The police were no good. There were two officers, a man and a woman. The woman believed Rashel a little. But every time her eyes would start to believe, she'd shake her head and say, 'But what was the man *really* doing to Timmy? Baby-doll, sweetie, I know it's awful, but just *try* to remember.'

The man didn't believe even a little. Rashel would have traded them both for the Marine back at the carnival.

All they'd found in the tent was her mother with a broken neck. No Timmy. Rashel wasn't sure but she thought the man had probably taken him.

She didn't want to think about why.

Eventually the police drove her to her Aunt Corinne's,

who was the only family she had left now. Aunt Corinne was old and her bony hands hurt Rashel's arms when she clutched her and cried.

She put Rashel in a bedroom full of strange smells and tried to give her medicine to make her sleep. It was like cough syrup, but it made her tongue numb. Rashel waited until Aunt Corinne was gone, then she spat it into her hand and wiped her hand on the sheets, way down at the foot of the bed where the blankets tucked in.

And then she put her arms around her hunched-up knees and sat staring into the darkness.

She was too little, too helpless. That was the problem. She wasn't going to be able to do anything against him when he came back.

Because of course he was coming back.

She knew what the man was, even if the adults didn't believe her. He was a vampire, just like on TV. A monster that drank blood. And he knew she knew.

That was why he'd promised to see her later.

At last, when Aunt Corinne's house was quiet, Rashel tiptoed to the closet and slid it open. She climbed the shoe rack and squirmed and kicked until she was on the top shelf above the clothes. It was narrow, but wide enough for her. That was one good thing about being little.

She had to use every advantage she had.

With her toe, she slid the closet door back shut. Then she piled sweaters and other folded things from the shelf on top of herself, covering even her head. And finally she curled up on the hard bare wood and shut her eyes.

Sometime in the night she smelled smoke. She got down from the shelf – falling more than climbing – and saw flames in her bedroom.

She never knew exactly how she managed to run through them and get out of the house. The whole night was like one long blurred nightmare.

Because Aunt Corinne didn't get out. When the fire trucks came with their sirens and their flashing lights, it was already too late.

And even though Rashel knew that *he* had set the fire – the vampire – the police didn't believe her. They didn't understand why he had to kill her.

In the morning they took her to a foster home, which would be the first of many. The people there were nice, but Rashel wouldn't let them hold her or comfort her.

She already knew what she had to do.

If she was going to survive, she had to make herself hard and strong. She couldn't care about anybody else, or trust anybody, or rely on anybody. Nobody could protect her. Not even Mommy had been able to do that.

She had to protect herself. She had to learn to fight.

CHAPTER 3

God, it *stank.*

Rashel Jordan had seen a lot of vampire lairs in her seventeen years, but this was probably the most disgusting. She held her breath as she stirred the nest of tattered cloth with the toe of one boot. She could read the story of this collection of garbage as easily as if the inhabitant had written out a full confession, signed it, and posted it on the wall.

One vampire. A rogue, an outcast who lived on the fringe of both the human world and the Night World. He probably moved to a new city every few weeks to avoid getting caught. And he undoubtedly looked like any other homeless guy, except that none of the human homeless would be hanging around a Boston dock on a Tuesday night in early March.

He brings his victims here, Rashel thought. The pier's deserted, it's private, he can take his time with them. And of course he can't resist keeping a few trophies.

Her foot stirred them gently. A pink-and-blue knit baby jacket, a plaid sash from a school uniform, a Spiderman tennis shoe. All bloodstained. All very small.

There had been a rash of missing children lately. The

Boston police would never discover where they had gone – but now Rashel knew. She felt her lips draw back slightly from her teeth in something that wasn't really a smile.

She was aware of everything around her: the soft splash of water against the wooden pier, the rank coppery smell that was almost a taste, the darkness of a night lit only by a half moon. Even the light moisture of the cold breeze against her skin. She was aware of all of it without being preoccupied with any of it – and when the tiny scratch sounded behind her, she moved as smoothly and gracefully as if she were taking her turn in a dance.

She pivoted on her left foot, drawing her *bokken* in the same motion, and without a break in the movement, she stabbed straight to the vampire's chest. She drove the blow from her hips, exhaling in a hiss as she did it, putting all her strength behind it.

'Gotta be faster than that,' she said.

The vampire, skewered like a hot dog, waved his arms and gibbered. He was dressed in filthy clothing and his hair was a bushy tangle. His eyes were wide, full of surprise and hatred, shining as silver as an animal's in the faint light. His teeth weren't so much fangs as tusks: fully extended, they reached almost to his chin.

'I know,' Rashel said. 'You really, really wanted to kill me. Life's tough, isn't it?'

The vampire snarled one more time and then the silver went out of his eyes, leaving only the look of astonishment. His body stiffened and slumped backward. It lay still on the ground.

Grimacing, Rashel pulled her wooden sword out of the chest. She started to wipe the blade on the vampire's pants, then hesitated, peering at them more closely. Yes, those were definitely little crawly things. And the blankets were just as repulsive.

Oh, well. Use your own jeans. It won't be the first time.

She carefully wiped the *bokken* clean. It was two and a half feet long and just slightly, gracefully curved, with a narrow, sharp, angled tip. Designed to penetrate a body as efficiently as possible – if that body was susceptible to wood.

The sword slipped back into its sheath with a papery whisper. Then Rashel glanced at the body again.

Mr Vampire was already going mummified. His skin was now yellow and tough; his staring eyes were dried up, his lips shrunken, his tusks collapsed.

Rashel bent over him, reaching into her back pocket. What she pulled out looked like the snapped-off end of a bamboo backscratcher – which was exactly what it was. She'd had it for years.

Very precisely, Rashel drew the five lacquered fingers of the scratcher down the vampire's forehead. On the yellow skin five brown marks appeared, like the marks of a cat's claws. Vampire skin was easy to mark right after death.

'This kitten has claws,' she murmured. It was a ritual sentence; she'd repeated it ever since the night she'd killed her first vampire at the age of twelve. In memory of her mother, who'd always called her kitten. In memory of herself at age five, and all the innocence she'd lost. She'd never be a helpless kitten again.

Besides, it was a little joke. Vampires . . . bats. Herself . . . a cat. Anybody who'd grown up with Batman and Catwoman would get it.

Well. All done. Whistling softly, she rolled the body over and over with her foot to the end of the pier. She didn't feel like carting the mummy all the way out to the fens, the salt marshes where bodies were traditionally left in Boston. With a mental apology to everybody who was trying to clean up the harbour, she gave the corpse a final push and listened for the splash.

She was still whistling as she emerged from the pier onto the street. *Hi-ho, hi-ho, it's off to work we go . . .*

She was in a very good mood.

The only disappointment was the constant one, that it hadn't been *the* vampire, the one she'd been looking for ever since she'd been five years old. It had been a rogue, all right – a depraved monster who killed human kids foolishly close to human habitations. But it hadn't been *the* rogue.

Rashel would never forget *his* face. And she knew that someday she would see it again. Meanwhile, there was nothing to do but shish-kebab as many of the parasites as possible.

She scanned the streets as she walked, alert for any sign of Night People. All she saw were quiet brick buildings and streetlights shining pale gold.

And that was a shame, because she was in terrific form tonight; she could feel it. She was every blood-sucking leech's worst enemy. She could stake six of them before breakfast and still be fresh for chemistry first period at Wassaguscus High.

Rashel stopped suddenly, absent-mindedly melting into a shadow as a police car cruised silently down the cross-street ahead. *I* know, she thought. I'll go see what the Lancers are up to. If anybody knows where vampires are, they do.

She headed for the North End. Half an hour later she was standing in front of a brownstone apartment building, ringing the buzzer.

'Who's there?'

Instead of answering, Rashel said, 'The night has a thousand eyes.'

'And the day only one,' came the reply from the intercom. 'Hey there, girl. Come on up.'

Inside, Rashel climbed a dark and narrow stairway to a scarred wooden door. There was a peephole in the door. Rashel faced it squarely, then pulled off the scarf she'd been wearing. It was black, silky, and very long. She wore it wrapped around her head and face like a veil, so that only her eyes showed, and even they were in shadow.

She shook out her hair, knowing what the person on the other side could see. A tall girl dressed like a ninja, all in black, with black hair falling loose around her shoulders and green eyes blazing. She hadn't changed much since she was five, except in height. Right now she made a barbaric face at the peephole and heard the sound of laughter behind the door as bolts were drawn.

She waited until the door was shut behind her again before she said, 'Hi, Elliot.'

Elliot was a few years older than she was, and thin, with intense eyes and little shiny glasses that were always slipping off his nose. Some people would have dismissed him as a geek. But Rashel had once seen him stand up to two werewolves while she got a human girl out a window, and she knew that he had practically singlehandedly started the Lancers – one of the most successful organisations of vampire hunters on the east coast.

'What's up, Rashel? It's been a while.'

'I've been busy. But now I'm bored. I came to see if you guys had anything going.' As Rashel spoke, she was looking at the other people in the room. A brown-haired girl was kneeling, loading objects from boxes into a dark green backpack. Another girl and a boy were sitting on the couch. Rashel recognized the boy from other Lancers meetings, but neither of the girls were familiar.

'Lucky you,' Elliot said. 'This is Vicky, my new second-in-command.' He nodded at the girl on the floor. 'She just moved to Boston; she was the leader of a group on the south shore. And tonight she's taking a little expedition out to some warehouses in Mission Hill. We got a lead that there's been some activity out there.'

'What kind of activity? Leeches, puppies?'

Elliot shrugged. 'Vampires definitely. Werewolves maybe. There's been a rumour about teenage girls getting kidnapped and stashed somewhere around there. The problem is we don't know exactly where, or why.' He tilted his head, his eyes twinkling. 'You want to go?'

'Isn't anybody going to ask *me*?' Vicky said, straightening up from her backpack. Her pale blue eyes were fixed on Rashel. 'I've never even seen this girl before. She could be one of *them*.'

Elliot pushed his glasses higher on his nose. He looked amused. 'You wouldn't say that if you knew, Vicky. Rashel's the best.'

'At what?'

'At everything. When you were going to your fancy prep school, she was out in the Chicago slums staking vampires. She's been in L.A., New York, New Orleans . . . even Vegas. She's wiped out more parasites than the rest of us put together.' Elliot glanced mischievously at Rashel, then leaned toward Vicki.

'Ever heard of the Cat?' he said.

Vicki's head snapped up. She stared at Rashel. 'The Cat? The one all the Night People are afraid of? The one they're offering a reward for? The one who leaves a mark—?'

Rashel shot Elliot a warning look. 'Never mind,' she said. She wasn't sure she trusted these new people. Vicky was right about one thing: you couldn't be too careful.

And she didn't like Vicky much, but she could hardly

turn down such a good opportunity for vampire hunting. Not tonight, when she was in such terrific form.

'I'll go with you – if you'll have me,' she said.

Vicky's pale blue eyes bored into Rashel's a moment, then she nodded. 'Just remember I'm in charge.'

'Sure,' Rashel murmured. She could see Elliot's grin out of the corner of her eye.

'You know Steve, and that's Nyala.' Elliot indicated the boy and girl on the couch. Steve had blond hair, muscular shoulders, and a steady expression; Nyala had skin like cocoa and a faraway look in her eyes, as if she were sleepwalking. 'Nyala's new. She just lost her sister a month ago,' Elliot added in a gentle voice. He didn't need to say *how* the sister had been lost.

Rashel nodded at the girl. She sympathized. There was nothing quite like the shock of first discovering the Night World, when you realized that things like vampires and witches and werewolves were real, and that they were *everywhere*, joined in one giant secret organization. That anybody could be one, and you'd never know until it was too late.

'Everybody ready? Then let's go,' Vicky said, and Steve and Nyala got up. Elliot showed them to the door.

'Good luck,' he said.

Outside, Vicky led the way to a dark blue car with mud strategically caked on the licence plates.

'We'll drive to the warehouse area,' she said.

Rashel was relieved. She was used to walking the city streets at night without being seen – important when you were carrying a rather unconcealable sword – but she wasn't sure that these other three could manage. It took practice.

The drive was silent except for the murmur of Steve's voice occasionally helping Vicky with directions. They passed through respectable neighbourhoods and venerable areas with handsome old buildings until they got to a street where everything changed suddenly. All at once, as if they had crossed some invisible dividing line, the gutters were full of soggy trash and the fences were topped with razor wire. The buildings were government housing projects, dark warehouses, or rowdy bars.

Vicky pulled into a parking lot and stopped the car away from the security lights. Then she led them through the knee-high dead weeds of a vacant lot to a street that was poorly lighted and utterly silent.

'This is the observation post,' Vicky whispered, as they reached a squat brick building, a part of the housing project that had been abandoned. Following her, they zigzagged through debris and scrap metal to get to a side door, and then they climbed a dark staircase covered with graffiti to the third floor. Their flashlights provided the only illumination.

'Nice place,' Nyala whispered, looking around. She had obviously never seen anything like it before. 'Don't you think – there may be other people here besides vampires?'

Steve gave her a reassuring pat. 'No, it's OK.'

'Yeah, it looks like even the junkies have abandoned it,' Rashel said, grimly amused.

'You can see the whole street from the window,' Vicky put in shortly. 'Elliot and I were here yesterday watching those warehouses across the street. And last night we saw a guy at the end of the street who looked a lot like a vampire. You know the signs.'

Nyala opened her mouth as if to say *she* didn't know the signs, but Rashel was already speaking. 'Did you test him?'

'We didn't want to get that close. We'll do it tonight if he shows up again.'

'How do you test them?' Nyala asked.

Vicky didn't answer. She and Steve had pushed aside a couple of rat-chewed mattresses and were unloading the bags and backpacks they'd brought.

Rashel said, 'One way is to shine a flashlight in their eyes. Usually you get eyeshine back – like an animal's.'

'There are other ways, too,' Vicky said, setting the things she was unloading on the bare boards of the floor. There were ski masks, knives made of both metal and wood, a number of stakes of various sizes, and a mallet. Steve added two clubs made of white oak to the pile.

'Wood hurts them more than metal,' Vicky said to Nyala. 'If you cut them with a steel knife they heal right before your eyes – but cut them with wood and they keep bleeding.'

Rashel didn't quite like the way she said it. And she didn't like the last thing Vicky was pulling out of her backpack. It was a wooden device that looked a bit like a miniature stock. Two hinged blocks of wood that fit snugly around a person's wrists and closed with a lock.

'Vampire handcuffs,' Vicky said proudly, seeing her look. 'Made of white oak. Guaranteed to hold any parasite. I brought them from down south.'

'But hold them for what? And what do you need all those little knives and stakes for? It would take hours to kill a vampire with those.'

Vicky smiled fiercely. 'I know.'

Oh. Rashel's heart seemed to thump and then sink, and she looked away to control her reaction. She understood what Vicky had in mind now.

Torture.

'A quick death's too good for them,' Vicky said, still smiling. 'They deserve to suffer – the way they make *our* people suffer. Besides, we might get some information. We need to know where they're keeping the girls they kidnap, and what they're doing with them.'

'Vicky.' Rashel spoke earnestly. 'It's practically impossible to make vampires talk. They're stubborn. When they're hurt they just get angry – like animals.'

Vicky smirked. 'I've made some talk. It just depends on what you do, and how long you make it last. Anyway, there's no harm in trying.'

'Does Elliot know about this?'

Vicky lifted a shoulder defensively. 'Elliot lets me do things my way. I don't have to tell him every little detail. I was a leader myself, you know.'

Helplessly, Rashel looked at Nyala and Steve. And saw that for the first time Nyala's eyes had lost their sleepwalking expression. Now she looked awake – and savagely glad.

'*Yes,*' she said. 'We should try to make the vampire talk. And if he suffers – well, my sister suffered. When I found her, she was almost dead but she could still talk. She told me what it felt like, having all the blood drained out of her body while she was still conscious. She said it hurt. She said . . .' Nyala stopped, swallowed, and looked at Vicky. 'I want to help do it,' she said thickly.

Steve didn't say anything, but then from what Rashel knew of him, that was typical. He was a guy of few words. Anyway, he didn't protest.

Rashel felt odd, as if she were seeing the very worst of herself reflected in a mirror. It made her . . . ashamed. It left her shaken.

But who am I to judge? she thought, turning away. It's true that the parasites are evil, all of them. The whole race needs to be wiped out. And Vicky's right, why should they have a clean death, when they usually don't give their victims one? Nyala deserves to avenge her sister.

'Unless you *object* or something,' Vicky said heavily, and Rashel could feel those pale blue eyes on her. 'Unless you're some kind of vampire sympathizer.'

Rashel might have laughed at that, but she wasn't in a laughing mood. She took a breath, then said without turning around, 'It's your show. I agreed that you were in charge.'

'Good,' Vicky said, and returned to her work.

But the sick feeling in the pit of Rashel's stomach didn't go away. She almost hoped that the vampire wouldn't come.

CHAPTER 4

Quinn was cold.

Not physically, of course. That was impossible. The icy March air had no effect on him; his body was impervious to little things like weather. No, this cold was inside him.

He stood looking at the bay and the thriving city across it. Boston by starlight. It had taken him a long time to come back to Boston after . . . the change.

He'd lived there once, when he'd been human. But in those days Boston was nothing but three hills, one beacon, and a handful of houses with thatched roofs. The place where he was standing now had been clean beach surrounded by salt meadows and dense forest.

The year had been 1639.

Boston had grown since then, but Quinn hadn't. He was still eighteen, still the young man who'd loved the sunny pastures and the clear blue water of the wilderness. Who had lived simply, feeling grateful when there was enough food for supper on his mother's table, and who had dreamed of someday having his own fishing schooner and marrying pretty Dove Redfern.

That was how it had all started, with Dove. Pretty Dove and her soft brown hair . . . sweet Dove, who had a secret a simple boy like Quinn could never have imagined.

Well. Quinn felt his lip curl. That was all in the past. Dove had been dead for centuries, and if her screams still haunted him every night, no one knew but himself.

Because he might not be any older than he had been in the days of the colonies, but he had learned a few tricks. Like how to wrap ice around his heart so that nothing in the world could hurt him. And how to put ice in his gaze, so that whoever looked into his black eyes saw only an endless glacial dark. He'd gotten very good at that. Some people actually went pale and backed away when he turned his eyes on them.

The tricks had worked for years, allowing him not just to survive as a vampire, but to be brilliantly successful at it. He was Quinn, pitiless as a snake, whose blood ran like ice water, whose soft voice pronounced doom on anybody who got in his way. Quinn, the essence of darkness, who struck fear into the hearts of humans and Night People alike.

And just at the moment, he was tired.

Tired and cold. There was a kind of bleakness inside him, like a winter that would never change into spring.

He had no idea what to do about it – although it had occurred to him that if he were to jump into the bay and let those dark waters close over his head, and then *stay* down there for a few days without feeding . . . well, all his problems would be solved, wouldn't they?

But that was ridiculous. He was Quinn. Nothing could touch him. The bleak feeling would go away eventually.

He pulled himself out of his reverie, turning away from the shimmering blackness of the bay. Maybe he should go to the warehouse in Mission Hill, check on its inhabitants. He needed something to *do,* to keep him from thinking.

Quinn smiled, knowing it was a smile to frighten children. He set off for Boston.

Rashel sat by the window, but not the way ordinary people sit. She was kneeling in a sort of crouch, weight resting on her left leg, right leg bent and pointing forward. It was a position that allowed for swift and unrestricted movement in any direction. Her *bokken* was beside her; she could spring and draw at a second's notice.

The abandoned building was quiet. Steve and Vicky were outside, scouting the street. Nyala seemed lost in her own thoughts.

Suddenly Nyala reached out and touched the *bokken*'s sheath. 'What's this?'

'Hm? Oh, it's a kind of Japanese sword. They use wooden swords for fencing practice because steel would be too dangerous. But it can actually be lethal even to humans. It's weighted and balanced just like a steel sword.' She pulled the sword out of the sheath and turned the flashlight on it so Nyala could see the satiny green-black wood.

Nyala drew in her breath and touched the graceful curve lightly. 'It's beautiful.'

'It's made of lignum vitae: the Wood of Life. That's the hardest and heaviest wood there is – it's as dense as iron. I had it carved specially, just for me.'

'And you use it to kill vampires.'

'Yes.'

'And you've killed a lot.'

'Yes.' Rashel slid the sword back into its sheath.

'Good,' Nyala said with a throb in her voice. She turned to stare at the street. She had a small queenly head, with hair piled on the back like Nefertiti's crown. When she turned back to Rashel, her voice was quiet. 'How did you get into all this in the first place? I mean, you seem to know so much. How did you learn it all?'

Rashel laughed. 'Bit by bit,' she said briefly. She didn't like to talk about it. 'But I started like you. I saw one of *them* kill my mom when I was five. After that, I tried to learn everything I could about vampires, so I could fight them. And I told the story at every foster home I lived in, and finally I found some people who believed me. They were vampire hunters. They taught me a lot.'

Nyala looked ashamed and disgusted. 'I'm so stupid – I haven't done anything like that. I wouldn't even have known about the Lancers if Elliot hadn't called me. He saw the article in the paper about my sister and guessed it might have been a vampire killing. But I'd never have found them on my own.'

'You just didn't have enough time.'

'No. I think it takes a special kind of person. But now that I know how to fight them, I'm going to do it.' Her voice was tight and shaky, and Rashel glanced at her quickly. There was something unstable just under the surface of this girl. 'Nobody knows which of them killed my sister, so I just figure I'll get as many of them as I can. I want to—'

'Quiet!' Rashel hissed the word and put a hand over Nyala's mouth at the same instant. Nyala froze.

Rashel sat tensely, listening, then got up like a spring uncoiling and put her head out the window. She listened for another moment, then caught up her scarf and veiled her face with practiced movements. 'Grab your ski mask and come on.'

'What is it?'

'You're going to get your wish – right now. There's a fight down there. Stay behind me . . . and don't forget your mask.'

Nyala didn't need to ask about *that*, she noticed. It was

the first thing any vampire hunter learned. If you were recognized and the vampire got away . . . well, it was all over. The Night People would search until they found you, then strike when you least expected it.

With Nyala behind her, Rashel ran lightly down the stairs and around to the street.

The sounds were coming from a pool of darkness beside one of the warehouses, far from the nearest streetlight. As Rashel reached the place, she could make out the forms of Steve and Vicky, their faces masked, their clubs in their hands. They were struggling with another form.

Oh, for God's sake, Rashel thought, stopping dead.

One other form. The two of them, armed with wood and lying in ambush, couldn't handle one little vampire by themselves? From the racket, she'd thought they must have been surprised by a whole army.

But this vampire seemed to be putting up quite a fight – in fact, he was clearly winning. Throwing his attackers around with supernatural strength, just as if they were ordinary humans and not fearless vampire slayers. He seemed to be enjoying it.

'We've got to help them!' Nyala hissed in Rashel's ear.

'Yeah,' Rashel said joylessly. She sighed. 'Wait here; I'm going to bonk him on the head.'

It wasn't quite that easy. Rashel got behind the vampire without trouble; he was preoccupied with the other two and arrogant enough to be careless. But then she had a problem.

Her *bokken*, the honourable sword of a warrior, had one purpose: to deliver a clean blow capable of killing instantly. She couldn't bring herself to whack somebody unconscious with it.

It wasn't that she didn't have other weapons. She had plenty – back at home in Marblehead. All the tools of a ninja, and some the ninja had never heard of. And she knew some extremely dirty methods of fighting. She could break bones and crush tendons; she could peel an enemy's trachea out of his neck with her bare hands or drive his ribs into his lungs with her feet.

But those were desperate measures, to be used as a last resort when her own life was at stake and the opposition was overwhelming. She simply couldn't do that to a single enemy when she had the jump on him.

Just then the single enemy threw Steve into a wall, where he landed with a muffled 'oof'. Rashel felt sorry for him, but it solved her dilemma. She grabbed the oak club Steve had been holding as it rolled across the concrete. Then she circled nimbly as the vampire turned, trying to face her. At that instant Nyala threw herself into the fight, creating a distraction, and Rashel did what she'd said she would. She bonked the vampire on the head, driving the club like a home runner's swing with the force of her hips.

The vampire cried out and fell down motionless.

Rashel raised the club again, watching him. Then she lowered it, looking at Steve and Vicky. 'You guys OK?'

Vicky nodded stiffly. She was trying to get her breath. 'He surprised us,' she said.

Rashel didn't answer. She was very unhappy, and her feeling of being in top form tonight had completely evaporated. This had been the most undignified fight she'd seen in a long while, and . . .

. . . and it bothered her, the way the vampire had cried out as he fell. She couldn't explain why, but it had.

Steve picked himself up. 'He shouldn't have been *able* to surprise us,' he said. 'That was our fault.'

Rashel glanced at him. It was true. In this business, you were either ready all the time, expecting the unexpected at any moment, or you were dead.

'He was just good,' Vicky said shortly. 'Come on, let's get him out of here before somebody sees us. There's a cellar in the other building.'

Rashel took hold of the vampire's feet while Steve grabbed his shoulders. He wasn't very big, about Rashel's height and compact. He looked young, about Rashel's age.

Which meant nothing, she reminded herself. A parasite could be a thousand and still look young. They gained eternal life from other people's blood.

She and Steve carried their burden down the stairs into a large dank room that smelled of damp rot and mildew. They dropped him on the cold concrete floor and Rashel straightened to ease her back.

'OK. Now let's see what he looks like,' Vicky said, and turned her flashlight on him.

The vampire was pale, and his black hair looked even blacker against his white skin. His eyelashes were dark on his cheek. A little blood matted his hair in the back.

'I don't think he's the same one Elliot and I saw last night. That one looked bigger,' Vicky said.

Nyala pressed forward, staring at her very first captive vampire. 'What difference does it make? He's one of them, right? Nobody human could have thrown Steve like that. He might even be the one who killed my sister. And he's ours now.' She smiled down, looking almost like someone in love. 'You're ours,' she said to the unconscious boy on the floor. 'Just you wait.'

Steve rubbed his shoulder where it had hit the wall. All he said was 'Yeah,' but his smile wasn't nice.

'I only hope he doesn't die soon,' Vicky said, examining the pale face critically. 'You hit him pretty hard.'

'He's not going to die,' Rashel said. 'In fact, he'll probably wake up in a few minutes. And we'd better hope he's not one of the really powerful telepaths.'

Nyala looked up sharply. 'What?'

'Oh – all vampires are telepathic,' Rashel said absently. 'But there's a big range as to how powerful they are. Most of them can only communicate over a short distance – like within the same house, say. But a few are a lot stronger.'

'Even if he *is* strong, it won't matter unless there are other vampires around,' Vicky said.

'Which there may be, if you and Elliot saw another one last night.'

'Well . . .' Vicky hesitated, then said, 'We can check outside, make sure he doesn't have any friends hiding around that warehouse.'

Steve was nodding, and Nyala was listening intently. Rashel started to say that from what she'd seen, they couldn't find a vampire in hiding to save their lives – but then she changed her mind.

'Good idea,' she said. 'You take Nyala and do that. It's better to have three people than two. I'll tie him up before he comes around. I've got bast cord.'

Vicky glanced over quickly, but her hostility seemed to have faded since Rashel had knocked the vampire over the head. 'OK, but let's use the handcuffs. Nyala, run up and get them.'

Nyala did, and she and Vicky fixed the wooden stocks on the vampire's wrists. Then they left with Steve.

Rashel sat on the floor.

She didn't know what she was doing, or why she'd sent Nyala away. All she knew was that she wanted to be alone, and that she felt . . . rotten.

It wasn't that she didn't have anger. There were times when she got so angry at the universe that it was actually like a little voice inside her whispering, *Kill, kill, kill*. Times when she wanted to strike out blindly, without caring who she hurt.

But just now the little voice was silent, and Rashel felt sick.

To keep herself busy, she tied his feet with bast, a cord made from the inner bark of trees. It was as good for holding a vampire as Vicky's ridiculous handcuffs.

When it was done, she turned the flashlight on him again.

He was good-looking. Clean features that were strongly chiselled but almost delicate. A mouth that at the moment looked rather innocent, but which might be sensuous if he were awake. A body that was lithe and flat-muscled, if not very tall.

All of which had no effect on Rashel. She'd seen attractive vampires before – in fact, an inordinate number of them seemed to be really beautiful. It didn't mean anything. It only stood as a contrast to what they were like inside.

The tall man who'd killed her mother had been handsome. She could still see his face, his golden eyes.

Filthy parasites. Night World scum. They weren't really people. They were monsters.

But they could still feel pain, just like any human. She'd hurt this one when she hit him.

Rashel jumped up and started to pace the cellar.

All right. This vampire deserved to die. They all did. But that didn't mean she had to wait for Vicky to come back and poke him with pointy sticks.

Rashel knew now why she'd sent Nyala away. So she could give the vampire a clean death. Maybe he didn't deserve it, but she couldn't stand around and watch Vicky kill him slowly. She *couldn't*.

She stopped pacing and went to the unconscious boy.

The flashlight on the floor was still pointing at him, so she could see him clearly. He was wearing a lightweight black shirt – no sweater or coat. Vampires didn't need protection from the cold. Rashel unbuttoned the shirt, exposing his chest. Although the angled tip of her *bokken* could pierce clothing, it was easier to drive it straight into vampire flesh without any barrier in between.

Standing with one foot on either side of the vampire's waist, she drew the heavy wooden sword. She held it with both hands, one near the guard, the other near the knob on the end of the hilt.

She positioned the end exactly over the vampire's heart.

'This kitten has claws,' she whispered, hardly aware she was saying it.

Then she took a deep breath, eyes shut. She needed to work to focus, because she'd never done anything like this before. The vampires she'd killed had usually been caught in the middle of some despicable act – and they'd *all* been fighting at the end. She'd never staked one that was lying still.

Concentrate, she thought. You need *zanshin*, continuing mind, awareness of everything without fixing on anything.

She felt her feet becoming part of the cold concrete beneath them, her muscles and bones becoming extensions of the ground. The strike would carry the energy of the earth itself.

Her hands brought the sword up. She was ready for the kill. She opened her eyes to perfect her aim.

And then she saw that the vampire was awake. His eyes were open and he was looking at her.

CHAPTER 5

Rashel froze. Her sword remained in the air, poised over the vampire's heart.

'Well, what are you waiting for?' the vampire said. 'Go on and do it.'

Rashel didn't know what she was waiting for. The vampire was in a position to block her sword with his wooden handcuffs, but he didn't do any such thing. She could tell by his body language that he wasn't going to, either. Instead he just lay there, looking up at her with eyes that were as dark and empty as the depths of space.

His hair was tousled on his forehead and his mouth was a bleak line. He didn't seem afraid. He just went on staring with those fathomless eyes.

All right, Rashel thought. Do it. Even the leech is telling you do. Do it fast – now.

But instead she found herself pivoting and stepping slowly away from him.

'Sorry,' she said out loud. 'I don't take orders from parasites.'

She kept her sword at the ready in case he made any sudden moves. But all he did was glance down at the wooden handcuffs, wiggle his wrists in them, and then lie back.

'I see,' he said with a strange smile. 'So it's torture this time, right? Well, that should be amusing for you.'

Stake him, dummy, came the little voice in Rashel's head. Don't talk to him. It's dangerous to get in a conversation with his kind.

But she couldn't refocus herself. In a minute, she told the voice. First I have to get my own control back.

She knelt in her ready-for-action crouch and picked up the flashlight, turning it full on his face. He blinked and looked away, squinting.

There. Now she could see him, but he couldn't see her. Vampire eyes were hypersensitive to light. And even if he did manage to get a glimpse of her, she was wearing her scarf. She had all the advantages, and it made her feel more in command of the situation.

'Why would you think we want to torture you?' she said.

He smiled at the ceiling, not trying to look at her. 'Because I'm still alive.' He raised the handcuffs. 'And aren't these traditional? A few vampires from the south shore have turned up mutilated with stocks like these on. It seemed to have been done for fun.' Smile.

Vicky's work, Rashel thought. She wished he would stop smiling. It was such a disturbing smile, beautiful and a little mad.

'Unless,' the vampire was going on, 'it's information you want.'

Rashel snorted. 'Would I be likely to get information from you if I *did* want it?'

'Well.' Smile. 'Not likely.'

'I didn't think so,' Rashel said dryly.

He laughed out loud.

Oh, God, Rashel thought. *Stake* him.

She didn't know what was wrong with her. OK, he was

charming – in a weird way. But she'd known other charming vampires – smooth, practiced flatterers who tried to sweet-talk or cajole their way out of being staked. Some had tried to seduce her. Almost all had tried mind control. It was only because Rashel had the will to resist telepathy that she was alive today.

But this vampire wasn't doing any of the ordinary things – and when he laughed, it made Rashel's heart thump oddly. His whole face changed when he laughed. A sort of light shone in it.

Girl, you are in *trouble*. Kill him quick.

'Look,' she said, and she was surprised to find her voice a little shaky. 'This isn't personal. And you probably don't care, but I'm not the one who was going to torture you. This is business, and it's what I have to do.' She took a deep breath and reached for the sword by her knee.

He turned his face to the light. He wasn't smiling now and there was no amusement in his voice when he said, 'I understand. You've got . . . honour.' Looking back at the ceiling, he added, 'And you're right, this is the way it always has to end when our two races meet. It's kill or be killed. The law of nature.'

He was speaking to her as one warrior to another. Suddenly Rashel felt something she'd never felt for a vampire before. Respect. A strange wish that they weren't on opposite sides in this war. A regret that they could never be anything but deadly enemies.

He's somebody I could talk to, she thought. An odd loneliness had taken hold of her. She hadn't realized she cared about having anyone to talk to.

She found herself saying awkwardly, 'Is there anybody you want notified – afterward? I mean, do you have any family? I could make sure the news gets around, so they'd know what had happened to you.'

She didn't expect him to actually give her any names. That would be crazy. In this game knowledge was power, with each side trying to find out who the players on the other side were. If you could identify someone as a vampire – or a vampire hunter – you knew who to kill.

It was Batman and Catwoman all over. The important thing was to preserve your secret identity.

But this vampire, who was obviously a lunatic, said thoughtfully, 'Well, you *could* send a note to my adopted father. He's Hunter Redfern. Sorry I can't give you an address, but he should be somewhere down east.' Another smile. 'I forgot to tell you my name. It's Quinn.'

Rashel felt as if she'd been hit with an oak club.

Quinn.

One of the most dangerous vampires in all the Night World. Maybe *the* most dangerous of the made vampires, the ones who'd started out human. She knew him by reputation – every vampire hunter did. He was supposed to be a deadly fighter and a brilliant strategist; clever, resourceful . . . and cold as ice. He despised humans, held them in utter contempt. He wanted the Night World to wipe them out, except for a few to be used for food.

I was wrong, Rashel thought dazedly. I should have let Vicky torture him. I'm sure he deserves it, if any of them do. God only knows what he's done in his time.

Quinn had turned his head toward her again, looking straight into the flashlight even though it must be hurting his eyes.

'So you see, you'd better kill me fast,' he said in a voice soft as snow falling. 'Because that's certainly what I'm going to do to *you* if I get loose.'

Rashel gave a strained laugh. 'Am I supposed to be scared?'

'Only if you have the brains to know who I am.'

Now he sounded tired and scornful. 'Which obviously you don't.'

'Well, let me see. I seem to remember *something* about the Redferns . . . Aren't they the family who controls the vampire part of the Night World Council? The most important family of all the lamia, the born vampires. Descended directly from Maya, the legendary first vampire. And Hunter Redfern is their leader, the upholder of Night World law, the one who colonized America with vampires back in the sixteen hundreds. Tell me if I'm getting any of this wrong.'

He gave her a cold glance.

'You see, we have our sources. And I seem to remember them mentioning *your* name, too. You were made a vampire by Hunter . . . and since his own children were all daughters, you're also his heir.'

Quinn laughed sourly. 'Yes, well, that's an on-again, off-again thing. You might say I have a love-hate relationship with the Redferns. We spend most of the time wishing each other at the bottom of the Atlantic.'

'Tch, vampire family infighting,' Rashel said. 'Why is it always so hard to get along with your folks?' Despite her light words, she had to focus to keep control of her breathing.

It wasn't fear. She truly wasn't scared of him. It was something like confusion. Clearly, she should be killing him at this moment instead of chatting with him. She couldn't understand why she wasn't doing it.

The only excuse she had was that it seemed to make him even more confused and angry than it did her.

'I don't think you've heard *enough* about me,' he said, showing his teeth. 'I'm your worst nightmare, human. I even shock other vampires. Like old Hunter . . . he has certain ideas about propriety. How you kill, and who. If he knew some of the things I do, he'd fall down dead himself.'

Good old Hunter, Rashel thought. The stiff moral patriarch of the Redfern clan, still caught up in the seventeenth century. He might be a vampire, but he was definitely a New Englander.

'Maybe I should find a way to tell him,' she said whimsically.

Quinn gave her another cold look, this time tempered with respect. 'If I thought you could *find* him, I'd worry.'

Rashel was suddenly struck by something. 'You know, I don't think I've ever heard anyone say your first name. I mean, I presume you have one.'

He blinked. Then, as if he were surprised himself, he said, 'John.'

'John Quinn. John.'

'I didn't invite you to *call* me it.'

'All right, whatever.' She said it absently, deep in thought. John Quinn. Such a normal name, a *Boston* name. The name of a real person. It made her think of him as a person, instead of as Quinn the dreadful.

'Look,' Rashel said, and then she asked him something she'd never asked a Night Person before. She said, 'Did you *want* Hunter Redfern to make you a vampire?'

There was a long pause. Then Quinn said expressionlessly, 'As a matter of fact, I wanted to kill him for it.'

'I see.' I'd want to do the same, Rashel thought. She didn't mean to ask any more questions, but she found herself saying, 'Then why did he do it? I mean, why pick you?'

Another pause. Just when she was sure he wouldn't answer, he said, 'I was – I wanted to marry one of his daughters. Her name was Dove.'

'You wanted to marry a vampire?'

'I didn't know she was a vampire!' This time Quinn's voice was quick and impatient. 'Hunter Redfern was accepted in Charlestown. Granted, a few people said his wife had been a witch, but in those days people said that if you smiled in church.'

'So he just lived there and nobody knew,' Rashel said.

'Most people accepted him.' A faint mocking smile curved Quinn's lips. 'My own father accepted him, and he was the minister.'

Despite herself, Rashel was fascinated. 'And you had to be a vampire to marry her? Dove, I mean.'

'I didn't get to marry her,' Quinn said tonelessly. He seemed as surprised as she was that he was telling her these things. But he went on, seeming to speak almost to himself. 'Hunter wanted me to marry one of his other daughters. I said I'd rather marry a pig. Garnet – that's the oldest – was about as interesting as a stick of wood. And Lily, the middle one, was evil. I could see that in her eyes. I only wanted Dove.'

'And you told him that?'

'Of course. He agreed to it finally – and then he told me his family's secret. Well.' Quinn laughed bitterly. 'He didn't *tell* me, actually. It was more of a demonstration. When I woke up, I was dead and a vampire. It was quite an experience.'

Rashel opened her mouth and then shut it again, trying to imagine the horror of it. Finally she just said, 'I bet.'

They sat for a moment in silence. Rashel had never felt so . . . close to a vampire. Instead of disgust and hatred, she felt pity.

'But what happened to Dove?'

Quinn seemed to tense all over. 'She died,' he said nastily. It was clear that his confidences were over.

'How?'

'None of your business!'

Rashel tilted her head and looked at him soberly. 'How, John Quinn? You know, there are some things you really ought to tell other people. It might help.'

'I don't need a damn psychoanalyst,' he spat. He was furious now, and there was a dark light in his eyes that ought to have frightened Rashel. He looked as wild as she felt sometimes, when she didn't care who she hurt.

She wasn't frightened. She was strangely calm, the kind of calm she felt when her breathing exercises made her feel one with the earth and absolutely sure of her path.

'Look, Quinn—'

'I really think you'd better kill me now,' he said tightly. 'Unless you're too stupid or too scared. This wood won't hold forever, you know. And when I get out, I'm going to use that sword on *you*.'

Startled, Rashel looked down at Vicky's handcuffs. They were bent. Not the oak, of course – it was the metal hinges that were coming apart. Soon he'd have enough room to slip them off.

He was very strong, even for a vampire.

And then, with the same odd calm, she realized what she was going to do.

'Yes, that's a good idea,' she said. 'Keep bending them. I can say that's how you got out.'

'What are you talking about?'

Rashel got up and searched for a steel knife to cut the cords on his feet. 'I'm letting you go, John Quinn,' she said.

He paused in his wrenching of the handcuffs. 'You're insane,' he said, as if he'd just discovered this.

'You may be right.' Rashel found the knife and slit

through the bast cords.

He gave the handcuffs a twist. 'If,' he said deliberately, 'you think that because I was a human once, I have any pity on them, you are very, very wrong. I hate humans more than I hate the Redferns.'

'Why?'

He bared his teeth. 'No, thank you. I don't have to explain anything to you. Just take my word for it.'

She believed him. He looked as angry and as dangerous as an animal in a trap. 'All right,' she said, stepping back and putting her hand on the hilt of her *bokken*. 'Take your best shot. But remember, I beat you once. I was the one who knocked you out.'

He blinked. Then he shook his head in disbelief. 'You little *idiot,*' he said. 'I wasn't paying attention. I thought you were another of those jerks falling over their own feet. And I wasn't even fighting *them* seriously.' He sat up in one fluid motion that showed the strength he had, and the control of his own body.

'You don't have a chance,' he said softly, turning those dark eyes on her. Now that he wasn't looking into the flashlight, his pupils were huge. 'You're dead already.'

Rashel had a sinking feeling that was telling her the same thing.

'I'm faster than any human,' the soft voice went on. 'I'm stronger than any human. I can see better in the dark. And I'm much, much nastier.'

Panic exploded inside Rashel.

All at once, she believed him absolutely. She couldn't seem to get her breath, and a void had opened in her stomach. She lost any vestige of her previous calm.

He's right – you were an idiot, she told herself wildly. You had every chance to stop him and you blew it. And why? Because you were sorry for him? Sorry for a deranged monster who's going to tear you limb from limb now? Anyone as stupid as that *deserves* what they get.

She felt as if she were falling, unable to get hold of anything . . .

And then suddenly she did seem to catch something. Something that she clung to desperately, trying to resist the fear that wanted to suck her into darkness.

You couldn't have done anything else.

It was the little voice in her mind, being helpful for once. And, strangely, Rashel knew it was true. She *couldn't* have killed him when he was tied up and helpless, not without becoming a monster herself. And after hearing his story, she couldn't have ignored the pity she felt.

I'm probably going to die now, she thought. And I'm still scared. But I'd do it over again. It was right.

She hung on to that as she let the last seconds tick away, the last window of opportunity to stake him while the cuffs still held. She knew they were ticking away, and she knew Quinn knew.

'What a shame to rip your throat out,' he said.

Rashel held her ground.

Quinn gave the handcuffs a final wrench, and the metal hinges squealed. Then the stocks clattered onto the concrete and he stood up, free. Rashel couldn't see his face anymore; it was above the reach of the flashlight.

'Well,' he said evenly.

Rashel whispered, 'Well.'

They stood facing each other.

Rashel was waiting for the tiny involuntary body movements that would give away which direction he was going to lunge. But he was more still than any enemy she'd ever seen. He kept his tension inside, ready to explode only when he directed it. His control seemed to be complete.

He's got *zanshin*, she thought.

'You're very good,' she said softly.

'Thanks. So are you.'

'Thanks.'

'But it isn't going to matter in the end.'

Rashel started to say, 'We'll see' – and he lunged.

She had an instant's warning. A barely perceptible movement of his leg told her he was going to spring to his right, her left. Her body reacted without her direction, moving smoothly . . . and she didn't realize until she was doing it that she wasn't using the sword.

She had stepped forward, inside his attack, and deflected it with a mirror palm block, striking the inner side of his arm with her left arm. Hitting the nerves to try and numb the limb.

But not cutting him. She realized with a dizzy sense of horror that she didn't *want* to use the sword on him.

'You are going to *die*, idiot,' he told her, and for an instant she wasn't sure if it was him saying it or the voice in her head.

She tried to push him away. All she could think was that she needed time, time to get her survival reflexes back. She shoved at him—

—and then her bare hand brushed his, and something happened that was completely beyond her experience.

CHAPTER 6

What she felt was a shivering jolt that began in her palm and ran up her arm like electricity. It left tingling in its wake. But the real shock was in her head.

Her mind exploded. That was the only way she could describe it. A noiseless, heatless explosion that shattered her completely. All at once, Rashel couldn't support her own weight anymore. She could feel Quinn's arms supporting her.

She had no sense of the room around her. She was floating in a white light and the only solid thing to hang on to was Quinn. It was something like the terror she'd felt before . . . but it wasn't just terror. Impossibly, what she felt was more like wild elation.

She realized that Quinn was holding her so tightly that it hurt. But even stronger than the sensation of his arms was the sense she had of his *mind*. A direct conduit seemed to have opened between them. She could feel his astonishment, his shock, his wonder. And she knew he could feel hers.

It's telepathy, some distant part of herself said, trying desperately to get control again. It's some new vampire trick.

But she knew it wasn't a trick. Quinn was as astounded

as she was – she could *feel* that. Maybe he was even worse off. He was breathing rapidly and shallowly and a fine trembling seemed to have taken over his body.

Rashel held on to him, thinking crazy things. She wanted to comfort him. She could sense, probably better than he could himself, how frighteningly vulnerable he was under that frozen exterior.

Like me, I suppose, Rashel thought giddily. And then she suddenly realized that *he* was feeling *her* vulnerability just as she had felt his. Fear welled up in her so sharply that she panicked.

She tried to find a way to shut him out, to resist the way she resisted mind control – but she knew it was useless. He had gotten past her guard already. He was *inside*.

'It's all right,' Quinn said, and she realized that he had stopped trembling. His voice was almost dispassionate, and at the same time madly gentle. Rashel had the feeling that he'd decided that since he couldn't fight this thing, he might as well be as insane as possible.

Strangest of all, she found his words reassuring.

And there was fire under the ice that seemed to encase him. She could feel that now, and she had the dizzy sense that she was the first one to discover it.

They had fallen to the floor somehow, and they were sitting just at the edge of the light. Quinn was holding her by the shoulders, precisely, and Rashel was astonished at her own response to the clinical grip. It stopped her breath, held her absolutely motionless.

Then, just as precisely, every movement deliberate, Quinn found the end of her scarf and began to unwind it.

He was still filled with that mad gentleness, that lunatic calm. And she wasn't stopping him. He was going to expose her face, and she wasn't doing a thing about it.

She *wanted* him to. In spite of her terror, she wanted him to see her, to know who she was. She wanted to be face to face with him in that strange light that had enveloped both their minds. It didn't seem to matter what happened afterward.

She said, 'John.'

He unwound another length of the scarf, preoccupied and intent as if he were making some archaeological discovery. 'You didn't tell me your name.' It was a statement. He wasn't pushing her.

She might as well write it out on a death warrant and hand it to him. Quinn could reveal himself to humans – but then Quinn could disappear completely if he wanted, hole up in some hidden vampire enclave where no human could search him out. Rashel couldn't. He knew she was a vampire hunter. If he knew her name and her face, he'd have every power to destroy her.

And the scariest thing of all was that some part of her didn't care.

He was down to the last turn of the scarf. In a moment her face would be exposed to the air . . . and to vampire eyes that could see in this darkness.

I'm Rashel, Rashel thought. She couldn't quite get the words to her lips. She took a deep breath.

And at the same instant a light blazed into her eyes.

Not the ghostly light that had been in her mind. Real light, the beams from several high-power flashlights, harsh and horribly bright. They cut through the dark cellar and threw Rashel and Quinn into stark illumination.

Rashel gasped. One hand instinctively flew to her scarf to keep it over her face. She felt as if she had been caught naked.

And she was horrified to realize that she hadn't heard

anyone come into the cellar. She had been completely absorbed, oblivious to her surroundings. What had happened to all her training? What was *wrong* with her?

She couldn't see anything beyond the light. Her first thought was that it was Quinn's vampire friends come to save him. He seemed to think it might be, too; at least he was standing shoulder to shoulder with her, even trying to push her back a little.

With an odd pang, Rashel realized she could only guess what he was thinking now. The connection between them had been cleanly severed.

Then a voice came from beyond the terrible brightness, a sharp voice filled with outrage. 'How did he get loose? What are you two *doing*?'

Vicky. I'm going insane, Rashel thought. I completely forgot about her and the others coming back. No, I forgot about their existence.

But there were more than three flashlights on the stairs.

'The Big E sent us some backup,' Vicky was saying, and Rashel felt a surge of fear. She counted five flashlights, and in the edges of beams she caught the figures of a couple of sturdy-looking guys. Lancers.

Rashel tried desperately to gather her wits.

She knew what had to be done, at least. She nudged Quinn with her shoulder and whispered, 'Get out of here. There should be another stairway on the other side of the room. When you run for it, I'll get in their way.' She pitched her voice so low that only vampire ears could hear it. The good thing about having her face veiled was that nobody could read her lips.

But Quinn wasn't going. He looked as if he'd just been awakened with a bucketful of ice water. Shocked, angry, and still a little dazed. He stood where he was, staring into all the flashlights like an animal at bay.

The lights were advancing. Rashel could make out Vicky's figure now at the front. There was going to be a fight, and people were going to get killed.

Steve's voice said, 'What did he do to you?'

'What's she been doing with *him*, that's the question,' Vicky snapped back. Then she said clearly, 'Remember, everybody, we want him alive.'

Rashel gave Quinn a harder shove. '*Go*.' When he just glared, she hissed, 'Don't you realize what they want to do to you?'

Quinn turned so that the advancing party couldn't see his face. He snarled, 'They're not exactly overjoyed with *you* either.'

'I can take care of myself.' Rashel was shaking with frustration. 'Just leave. Go!'

Quinn looked as angry with her as he was with the hunters. He didn't want her help, she realized. He wasn't used to taking anything from anyone, and to be forced to do it made him furious.

But there wasn't any other choice. And Quinn finally seemed to recognize that. With one last glare at her, he broke and headed for the darkness at the other side of the cellar.

The flashlights swung in confusion. Rashel, glad to be able to *move*, sprang between the vampire hunters and the stairway.

And then there was a lot of fumbling and crashing, with people running into each other and swearing and yelling. Rashel enjoyed the chance to work off her frustration. She got in everyone's way long enough for a very fast vampire to disappear.

After which it was just her and the vampire hunters. Five flashlights turned on her and seven amazed and angry people staring.

Rashel got up and brushed herself off. Time to face the consequences. She stood, head high, looking at all of them.

'What happened?' Steve said. 'Did he hypnotize you?'

Good old Steve. Rashel felt a rush of warmth toward him. But she couldn't use the out he was offering her. She said, 'I don't know what happened.'

And *that* was true. She couldn't even begin to explain to herself what had gone on between her and the vampire. She'd never heard of anything like it.

'I think you let him get away on purpose,' Vicky said. Rashel couldn't see Vicky's pale blue eyes, but she sensed that they were as hard as marbles. 'I think you planned it from the beginning – that's why you told us to go up to the street.'

'Is that true?' One of the flashlights swung down and suddenly Nyala was in front of Rashel, her body tense, her voice almost pleading. Her eyes were fixed on Rashel's, begging Rashel to say it wasn't so. 'Did you do it on purpose?'

All at once Rashel felt very tired. Nyala was fragile and unstable, and in her own mind she'd made Rashel into a hero. Now that image was being shattered.

For Nyala's sake, Rashel almost wished she could lie. But that would be worse in the end. She said expressionlessly, 'Yes. I did it on purpose.'

Nyala recoiled as if Rashel had slapped her.

I don't blame you, Rashel thought. I think it's crazy, too.

The truth was that the farther away she got from Quinn's presence, the less she could understand what she'd done. It was beginning to seem like a dream, and not a very clear dream at that.

'But *why*?' one of the Lancer boys at the back asked.

The Lancers knew Rashel, knew her reputation. They didn't want to think the worst of her. Like Nyala, they desperately wanted an excuse.

'I don't know why,' Rashel said, looking away. 'But he wasn't controlling my mind.'

Nyala exploded.

'I *hate* you,' she burst out. She was trembling with fury, spitting out sentences at Rashel like poison darts. 'That vampire could have been the one who killed my sister. Or he could have known who did it. I was going to ask him that, but now I'll never get the chance. Because of *you*. You let him go. We had him and you let him go!'

'It's more than that,' Vicky put in, her voice cold and contemptuous. 'We were going to ask him about those teenage girls getting kidnapped. Now we can't. So it's going to keep happening, and it's all going to be your fault.'

And they were right. Even Nyala was right. How did Rashel know that Quinn hadn't killed Nyala's sister?

'You're a vampire lover,' Vicky was saying. 'I could tell from the beginning. I don't know, maybe you're one of those damned Daybreakers who wants us all to get along, but you're not on *our* side.'

A couple of the Lancers started to protest at this, but Nyala's voice cut through them. 'She's on *their* side?' She stared from Vicky to Rashel, her body rigid. 'You just wait. Just wait until I tell people that Rashel is the Cat and that she's really on the Night World side. *You just wait.*'

She's hysterical, Rashel realized. Even Vicky was looking surprised at this, as if she were uneasy at what she'd started.

'Nyala, listen—' Rashel began.

But Nyala seemed to have reached some peak of fury at which nothing from outside could touch her. 'I'll tell everybody in Boston! You'll see!' She whirled around and plunged toward the stairway as if she were going to start doing it right now.

Rashel stared after her. Then she said to Vicky, 'You'd better send a couple of the guys to catch up to her. She's not safe alone in this neighbourhood.'

Vicky gave her a look that was half angry and half shaken. 'Yeah. OK, everybody but Steve go after her. You guys take her home.'

They left, not without a few backward glances at Rashel.

'We'll drive you back,' Vicky said. Her voice wasn't warm, but it wasn't as hostile as it had been.

'I'll walk to my own car,' Rashel said flatly.

'Fine.' Vicky hesitated, then blurted, 'She probably won't do what she said. She's just upset.'

Rashel said nothing. Nyala had sounded – and looked – as if she meant to do *exactly* what she said. And if she did . . .

Well, it would be an interesting question as to who would kill Rashel first, the vampires or the vampire hunters.

Wednesday morning dawned with grey skies and icy rain. Rashel trudged from class to class at Wassaguscus High, lost in thought. At home, her latest foster family left her alone – they were used to her going her own way. She sat in her small bedroom in the townhouse with the lights dimmed, thinking.

She still couldn't understand what had happened to her, but with every hour the memory of it was fading steadily. It was too *strange* to fit into the reality of life, and it became more and more like a dream. One of those dreams in which you do things you would never ordinarily do, and are ashamed of when you wake up in the morning.

All that warmth and closeness – she'd felt that for a *vampire*? She'd been excited by a parasite's touch? She'd wanted to comfort a leech?

And not just any leech, either. The infamous Quinn. The legendary human hater. How could she have let him go? How many people would suffer because of her lapse in sanity?

Who knows, she decided finally, maybe it *had* been some kind of mind control. She certainly couldn't make any sense of it otherwise.

By Thursday, one thing at least was clear in her mind. Vicky had been right about the consequences of what she'd done. Rashel hadn't thought about that at the time, but now she had to face it. She had to make it right.

She had to find the kidnapped girls on her own – if girls *were* getting kidnapped. There was nothing about missing teenagers in the *Globe*. But if it was happening, Rashel had to find out about it and stop it . . . if she could.

OK. So she'd go back to Mission Hill tonight and start investigating. Check the warehouse area again – this time, her way.

There was one other thing that was clear to her, that became obvious as she got her priorities straight. Something she had to do, not for Nyala, or for Vicky, or for the Lancers, but just for herself. For her own honour, and for everybody who lived in the world of sunlight.

The next time she saw Quinn, she had to kill him.

Rashel moved along the deserted street, keeping to the shadows, moving silently. Not easy when the ground was wet and strewn with broken glass. There were no sidewalks, no grass, no plant life of any kind except the dead weeds in the abandoned lots. Just soggy trash and shattered bottles.

A grim place. It fit Rashel's mood as she made her way stealthily toward the abandoned project building where Vicky had brought them Tuesday night.

From its front door, she surveyed the rest of the street. Lots of warehouses. Several of them were protected with high chain-link fences topped with barbed wire. All of them had barred windows – or no windows – and metal freight doors.

The security precautions didn't bother Rashel. She knew how to cut chain-link and pick locks. What bothered her was that she didn't know where to start.

The Night People could be using any of the warehouses. Even knowing where Steve and Vicky had fought Quinn didn't help, because *he* had jumped *them*. He'd obviously seen them lying in ambush and deliberately gone after them. Which meant his real destination could have been any of the buildings on this street – or none of them.

All right. Patience was indicated here. She'd just have to start at one end . . .

Rashel lost her thought and leaped back into the shadows before she consciously realized why she was doing it. Her ears had picked up a sound – a low rumbling coming from somewhere across the street.

She flattened herself against the brick wall behind her, then kept her body absolutely immobile. Her eyes darted from building to building and she held her breath to hear better.

There. It was coming from inside *that* warehouse, the one down at the far end of the street. And she could identify it now – the sound of an engine.

As she watched, the freight door in the front of the warehouse went sliding up. Headlights pierced the night from behind it. A truck was pulling out onto the street.

Not a very big truck. A U-Haul. It cleared the doors and stopped. A figure was pulling the sliding metal door down. Now it was making its way to the cab of the U-Haul, climbing in.

Rashel strained her eyes, trying to make out any signs of vampirism in the figure's movements. She thought she could detect a certain telltale fluidity to the walk, but it was too far away to be sure. And there was nothing else to give her a clue about what was going on.

It could be a human, she thought. Some warehouse owner going home after a night of balancing books.

But her instinct told her differently. The hair at the back of her neck was standing on end.

And then, as the truck began to cruise off, something happened that settled her doubts and sent her flying down the street.

The back doors of the U-Haul opened just a bit, and a girl fell out. She was slender, and a streetlight caught her blonde hair. She landed on the rubble-strewn road and lay there for an instant as if dazed. Then she jumped up, looked around wildly, and started running in Rashel's direction.

CHAPTER 7

By the time Rashel intercepted the girl, the truck was already braking to turn around. Someone was shouting, 'She's out! We lost one!'

'This way!' Rashel said, reaching toward the girl with one hand and gesturing with the other.

Up close, she could see that the girl was small, with dishevelled blonde hair falling over her forehead. Her chest was heaving. Instead of looking grateful, she seemed terrified by Rashel's arrival. She stared at Rashel a moment, then she tried to dart away.

Rashel snagged her in midlunge. 'I'm your friend! Come on! We've got to go *between* streets, where the truck can't follow us.'

The truck was finishing its turn. Headlights swept toward them. Rashel looped an arm around the girl's waist and took off at a dead run.

The blonde girl was carried along. She whimpered but she ran, too.

Rashel was heading for the area between two of the warehouses. She knew that if there really were vampires in that truck, her only chance was to get herself and the blonde girl to her car. The vampires could run much faster than any human.

She'd picked these two warehouses because the chain-link fence behind them wasn't too high and had no barbed wire at the top. As they reached it, Rashel gave the girl a little shove. 'Climb!'

'I can't!' The girl was trembling and gasping. Rashel looked her over and realized that it was probably the literal truth. The girl didn't look as if she'd ever climbed anything in her life. She was wearing what seemed to be party clothes and high heels.

Rashel saw the truck's headlights in the street and heard the engine slowing.

'You have to!' she said. 'Unless you want to go back with *them*.' She interlocked her fingers, making a step with her hands. 'Here! Put your foot here and then just try to grab on when I bounce you up.'

The girl looked too scared not to try. She put her foot in Rashel's hand – just as the headlights switched off.

It was what Rashel had expected. The darkness was an advantage to the vampires; they could see much better in it than humans. They were going to follow on foot.

Rashel took a breath, then heaved upward explosively as she exhaled. The blonde girl went sailing toward the top of the fence with a shriek.

A bare instant later, Rashel launched herself at the top of the fence, grabbed it, and swung her legs over. She dropped to the ground almost noiselessly and held her arms up to the blonde girl.

'Let go! I'll catch you.'

The girl, who was clambering awkwardly over the top, looked over her shoulder. 'I can't—'

'*Do it!*'

The girl dropped. Rashel broke her fall, set her on her feet, and grabbed her arm above the elbow. 'Come on!'

As they ran, Rashel scanned the buildings around them. She needed a corner, someplace where she could get the girl behind her and safe. She could defend a corner – if there weren't more than two or three vampires.

'How many of them are there?' she asked the girl.

'Huh?' The girl was gasping.

'How – many – are – there?'

'I don't know, and I can't run anymore!' The girl staggered to a halt and bent double, hands on her knees, trying to get her breath back. 'My legs . . . are just like jelly.'

It was no use, Rashel realized in dismay. She couldn't expect this bit of blonde fluff to outsprint a vampire. But if they stopped here in the open, they were dead. She cast a desperate look around.

Then she saw it. A Bostonian tradition – an abandoned car. In this city, if you got tired of your car you just junked it on the nearest embankment. Rashel blessed the unknown benefactor who'd left this one. Now, if only they could get in . . .

'This way!' She didn't wait for the girl to protest, but grabbed her and dragged her. 'Come on, you can do it! Make it to that car and you don't have to run anymore.'

The words seemed to inspire the girl into a last effort. They reached the car and Rashel saw that one of the back windows was broken out cleanly.

'In!'

The girl was small-boned and went through the window easily. Rashel dove after her. Then she shoved her down into the leg space in front of the seat and hissed, 'Don't make a sound.'

She lay tensely, listening. She barely had time to breathe twice before she heard footsteps.

Soft footsteps, stealthy as a prowling tiger's. Vampire

footsteps. Rashel held her breath and waited.

Closer, closer . . . Rashel could feel the other girl shaking. She watched the dark ceiling of the car and tried to plan a defence if they were caught.

The footsteps were right outside now. She heard the grate of glass not ten feet from the car door.

Just please don't let them have a werewolf with them, she thought. Vampires might see and hear better than humans, but a werewolf could sniff its prey out. It couldn't possibly miss the smell of humans in the car.

Outside, the footsteps paused, and Rashel's heart sank. Eyes open, she silently put her hand on her sword.

And then she heard the footsteps moving quickly – away. She listened as they faded, keeping utterly still. Then she kept still some more, while she counted to two hundred.

Then, very carefully, she sat up and looked around.

No sight or sound of vampires.

'Can I *please* get up now?' came a small whimpering voice from the floor.

'If you keep quiet,' Rashel whispered. 'They still may be somewhere nearby. We're going to have to get to my car without them catching us.'

'Anything, as long as I don't have to *run*,' the girl said plaintively, emerging from the floor more dishevelled than ever. 'Have you ever tried to run in four-inch heels?'

'I never wear heels,' Rashel murmured, scanning up and down the street. 'OK, I'll get out first, then you come through.'

She slid out the window feet-first. The girl stuck her head through. 'Don't you ever use *doors*?'

'Sh. Come on,' Rashel whispered. She led the way through the dark streets, moving from shadow to shadow. At least the girl could walk softly, she thought. And she had a sense of humour even in danger. That was rare.

Rashel drew a breath of relief when they reached the narrow twisting alley where her Saturn was parked. They weren't safe yet, though. She wanted to get the blonde girl out of Mission Hill.

'Where do you live?' she said, as she started the engine. When there was no answer, she turned. The girl was staring at her with open uneasiness.

'Uh, how come you're dressed like that? And who are you, anyway? I mean, I'm glad you saved me – but I don't understand *anything*.'

Rashel hesitated. She needed information from this girl, and that was going to take time – and trust. With sudden decision she unwound her scarf, one-handed, until her face was exposed. 'Like I said, I'm a friend. But first just tell me: do you know what kind of people had you in that truck?'

The girl turned away. She was already shivering with cold; now she shivered harder. 'They weren't people. They were . . . ugh.'

'Then you do know. Well, I'm one of the people that hunts down *that* kind of people.'

The girl looked from Rashel's face to the sheathed sword that rested between them. Her jaw dropped. 'Oh, my God! You're Buffy the Vampire Slayer!'

'Huh? Oh.' Rashel had missed the series. 'Right. Actually, you can call me Rashel. And you're . . . ?'

'Daphne Childs. And I live in Somerville, but I don't want to go home.'

'Well, that's fine, because I want to talk to you. Let's find a Dunkin' Donuts.'

Rashel found one outside of Boston, a safe one she knew had no Night World connections. She pulled a coat on over her black ninja outfit and lent Daphne a spare sweater from the trunk of her car. Then they went inside and ordered jelly sticks and hot chocolate.

'Now,' Rashel said. 'Tell me what happened. How did you end up in that truck?'

Daphne cupped her hands around her hot chocolate. 'It was all so *horrible* . . .'

'I know.' Rashel tried to make her voice soothing. She hadn't had much practice at it. 'Try to tell me anyway. Start at the beginning.'

'OK, well, it started at the Crypt.'

'Uh, as in "Tales from the . . ."? Or as in the Old Burial Ground?'

'As in the club on Prentiss Street. It's this underground club, and I mean *really* underground. I mean, nobody seems to know about it except the people who go there, and they're all our age. Sixteen or seventeen. I never see any adults, not even DJs.'

'Go on.' Rashel was listening intently. The Night People had clubs, usually carefully hidden from humans. Could Daphne have wandered into one?

'Well. It's *extremely* and seriously cool, or at least that's what I thought. They have some amazing music. I mean, it's beyond doom, it's beyond goth, it's sort of like *void* rock. Just listening to it makes you go all weird and bodiless. And the whole place is decorated like this post-apocalypse wasteland. Or maybe like the underworld . . .' Daphne stared off into the distance. Her eyes, a very deep cornflower blue under heavy lashes, looked wistful and almost hypnotized.

Rashel poked her and chocolate slopped onto the table. 'Reminisce about it later. What kind of people were in the club? Vampires?'

'Oh, no.' Daphne looked shocked. 'Just regular kids. I know some from my school. And there's lots of runaways,

I guess. Street kids, you know.'

Rashel blinked. 'Runaways . . .'

'Yeah. They're mostly very cool, except the ones who do drugs. Those are spooky.'

An illegal club full of runaway kids, some of whom would probably do anything for drugs. Rashel could feel her skin tingling.

I think I've stumbled onto something big.

'Anyway,' Daphne was going on, 'I'd been going there for about three weeks, you know, whenever I could get away from home—'

'You didn't tell your parents about it,' Rashel guessed flatly.

'Are you joking? It's not a place you tell *parents* about. Anyway, my family doesn't care where I go. I've got four sisters and two brothers and my mom and my stepdad are getting divorced . . . they don't even notice when I'm gone.'

'Go on,' Rashel said grimly.

'Well, there was this guy.' Daphne's cornflower eyes looked wistful again. 'This guy who was really gorgeous, and really mysterious, and really just – just *different* from anybody I ever met. And I thought he was maybe interested in me, because I saw him looking at me once or twice, so I sort of joined the girls who were always hanging around him. We used to talk about weird things.'

'Like?'

'Oh, like surrendering yourself to the darkness and stuff. It was like the music, you know – we were all really into death. Like what would be the most horrible way to die, what would be the most awful torture you could live through, what you look like when you're in your grave. Stuff like that.'

'For God's sake, *why*?' Rashel couldn't disguise her revulsion.

'I don't know.' All at once, Daphne looked small and sad. 'I guess because most of us felt life was pretty rotten. So you kind of face things, you know, to try to get used to them. You probably don't understand,' she added, grimacing.

Rashel did understand. With a sudden shock, she understood completely. These kids were scared and depressed and worried about the future. They had to do something to deaden the pain . . . even if that meant embracing pain. They escaped one darkness by going into another.

And am I any different? I mean, this obsession I've got with vampires . . . it's not exactly what you'd call normal and healthy. I spend my whole life dealing with death.

'I'm sorry,' she said, and her voice came out more gentle than when she'd been trying to soothe Daphne before. Awkwardly, she patted the other girl's arm once. 'I shouldn't have yelled. And I do understand, actually. Please go on.'

'Well.' Daphne still looked defensive. 'Some of the girls would write poetry about dying . . . and some of them would prick themselves with pins and lick the blood off. They said they were vampires, you know. Just pretending.' She glanced warily at Rashel.

Rashel simply nodded.

'And so I talked the same way, and did the same stuff. And this guy Quinn just seemed to love it – hey, look out!' Daphne jerked back to avoid a wave of hot chocolate. Rashel's sudden movement had knocked her cup over.

Oh, God, what is *wrong* with me? Rashel thought. She said, 'Sorry,' through her teeth, grabbing for a wad of napkins.

She should have been expecting it. She *had* been

expecting it; she knew that Quinn must be involved in this. But somehow the mention of his name had knocked the props from under her. She hadn't been able to control her reaction.

'So,' she said, still through her teeth, 'the gorgeous mysterious guy was named Quinn.'

'Yeah.' Daphne wiped chocolate off her arm. 'And I was starting to think he really liked me. He told me to come to the club last Sunday and to meet him alone in the parking lot.'

'And you did.' Oh, I am going to kill him so dead, Rashel thought.

'Sure. I dressed up . . .' Daphne looked down at her bedraggled outfit. 'Well, this *did* look terrific once. So I met him and we went to his car. And then he told me that he'd chosen me. I was so happy I almost fainted. I thought he meant for his girlfriend. And then . . .' Daphne trailed off again. For the first time since she'd begun the story, she looked frightened. 'Then he asked me if I really wanted to surrender to the darkness. He made it sound so romantic.'

'I bet,' Rashel said. She rested her head on her hand. She could see it all now, and it was the perfect scam. Quinn checked the girls out, discovered which would be missed and which wouldn't. He kidnapped them from the parking lot so that no one saw them, no one even connected them with the Crypt. Who would notice or care that certain girls stopped showing up? Girls would always be coming and going.

And there had been nothing in the newspaper because the daylight world didn't realize that girls were being taken. There probably wasn't even a struggle during the abduction, because these girls were *willing* to go – in the beginning.

'It must have been a shock,' Rashel said dryly, 'to find

out that there really *was* a darkness to surrender to.'

'Uh, yeah. Yeah, it was. But I didn't actually find that out then. I just said, sure, I wanted to. I mean, I'd have said the same thing if he asked me did I really want to watch Lawrence Welk reruns with him. He was that gorgeous. And he was looking at me in this totally *soulful* way, and I thought he was going to kiss me. And then . . . I fell asleep.' Daphne frowned at her paper cup.

'No, you didn't.'

'I *did*. I know it sounds crazy, but I fell asleep and when I woke up I was in this place, this little office in this warehouse. And I was on this iron cot with this pathetic lumpy mattress, and I was *chained down*. I had *chains* on my ankles, just like people in jail. And Quinn was gone, and there were two other girls chained to other cots.' Without warning, Daphne began to cry.

Rashel handed her a napkin, feeling uncomfortable. 'Were the girls from the Crypt, too?'

Daphne sniffed. 'I don't know. They might have been. But they wouldn't *talk* to me. They were, like, in a trance. They just lay there and stared at the ceiling.'

'But you weren't in a trance,' Rashel said thoughtfully. 'Somehow you woke up from the mind control. You must be resistant like me.'

'I don't know anything about mind control. But I was so scared I pretended to be like the other girls when this guy came to bring us food and take us to the bathroom. I just stared straight ahead like them. I thought maybe that way I would get a chance to escape.'

'*Smart* girl,' Rashel said. 'And the guy – was it Quinn?'

'No. I never saw Quinn again. It was this blond guy named Ivan from the club; I called him Ivan the Terrible. And there was a girl who brought us food sometimes – I don't know her name, but I used to see her at the club, too. They were like Quinn; they each had their own little group, you know.'

At least two others besides Quinn, Rashel thought. Probably more.

'They didn't hurt us or anything, and the office was heated, and the food was OK – but I was so *scared,*' Daphne said. 'I didn't understand what was going on at all. I didn't know where Quinn was, or how I'd gotten there, or what they were going to do with us.' She swallowed.

Rashel didn't understand that last either. What *were* the vampires doing with the girls in the warehouse? Obviously not killing them out of hand.

'And then last night . . .' Daphne's voice wobbled and she stopped to breathe. 'Last night Ivan brought this new girl in. He carried her in and put her on a cot. And . . . and . . . then he bit her. He bit her on the neck. But it wasn't a game.' The cornflower-blue eyes stared into the distance, wide with remembered horror. 'He *really* bit her. And blood came out and he drank it. And when he lifted his head up I saw his teeth.' She started to hyperventilate.

'It's OK. You're safe now,' Rashel said.

'I didn't *know*! I didn't know those things were real! I thought it was all just . . .' Daphne shook her head. 'I didn't know,' she said softly.

'OK. I know it's a big shock. But you've been dealing with it really well. You managed to get away from the truck, didn't you? Tell me about the truck.'

'Well – that was tonight. I could tell day from night by looking at this little window high up. Ivan and the girl came and took the chains off us and made us all get in the truck. And then I was *really* scared – I didn't know where they were taking us, but I heard something about a boat. And I knew wherever it was, *I didn't want to go.*'

'I think you're right about that.'

Daphne took another breath. 'So I watched the way Ivan shut the door of the truck. He was in back with us. And when he was looking the other way, I sort of jumped at the door and got it open. And then I just fell out. And then I ran – I didn't know which way to go, but I knew I had to get away from them. And then I saw you. And . . . I guess you saved my life.' She considered. 'Uh, I don't know if I remembered to say thank you.'

Rashel made a gesture of dismissal. 'No problem. You saved yourself, really.' She frowned, staring at a drop of chocolate on the plastic table without seeing it.

'Well. I *am* grateful. Whatever they were going to do to me, I think it must have been pretty awful.' A pause, then she said, 'Uh, Rashel? Do *you* know what they were going to do to me?'

'Hm? Oh.' Rashel nodded slowly, looking up from the table. 'Yes, I think so.'

CHAPTER 8

'Well?' Daphne said.

'I think it's the slave trade.'

And, Rashel thought, I think I was right – this is something big.

The Night World slave trade had been banned a long time ago – back in medieval days, if she remembered the stories correctly. The Council apparently had decided that kidnapping humans and selling them to Night People for food or amusement was just too dangerous. But it sounded as if Quinn might be reviving it, probably without the Council's permission. How very enterprising of him.

I was right about killing him, too, Rashel thought. There's no choice now. He's as bad as I imagined – and worse.

Daphne was goggling. 'They were going to make me a *slave*?' she almost yelled.

'Sh.' Rashel glanced at the man behind the doughnut counter. 'I think so. Well – a slave and a sort of perpetual food supply if you were sold to vampires. Probably just dinner if you were going to werewolves.'

Daphne's lips repeated *werewolves* silently. But Rashel was speaking again before she could ask about it.

'Look, Daphne – did you get *any* idea about where you

might be going? You said they mentioned a boat. But a boat to where? What city?'

'I don't *know*. They never talked about any city. They just said the boat was ready . . . and something about an *aunt-clave*.' She pronounced it *ont-clave*. 'The girl said, "When we get to the *aunt-clave* . . ." ' Daphne broke off as Rashel grabbed her wrist.

'An enclave,' Rashel whispered. Thin chills of excitement were running through her. 'They were talking about an enclave.'

Daphne nodded, looking alarmed. 'I guess.'

This was big. This was . . . bigger than big. It was incredible.

A vampire enclave. The kidnapped girls were being taken to one of the hidden enclaves, one of the secret strongholds no vampire hunter had ever managed to penetrate. No human had even discovered the location of one.

If I could get there . . . if I could get in . . .

She could learn enough to destroy a whole town of vampires. Wipe an enclave off the face of the earth. She *knew* she could.

'Uh, Rashel? You're hurting me.'

'Sorry.' Rashel let go of Daphne's arm. 'Now, listen,' she said fiercely. 'I saved your life, right? I mean, they were going to do terrible things to you. So you owe me, right?'

'Yeah, sure; sure, I owe you.' Daphne made pacifying motions with her hands. 'Are you OK?'

'Yes. I'm fine. But I need your help. I want you to tell me everything about that club. *Everything* I need to get in – and get chosen.'

Daphne stared at her. 'I'm sorry; you're crazy.'

'No, no. I know what I'm doing. As long as they don't know I'm a vampire hunter, it'll be OK. I *have* to get to that enclave.'

Daphne slowly shook her blonde head. 'What, you're going to, like, slay them all? By yourself? Can't we just tell the *police*?'

'Not all by myself. I could take a couple of other vampire hunters to help me. And as for the police . . .' Rashel stopped and sighed. 'OK. I guess there are some things I should explain. Then maybe you'll understand better.' She raised her eyes and looked at Daphne steadily. 'First, I should tell you about the Night World. Look, even before you met those vampires, didn't you ever have the feeling that there was something *eerie* going on, right alongside our world and all mixed up in it?'

She made it as simple as she could, and tried to answer Daphne's questions patiently. And at last, Daphne sat back, looking sick and more frightened than Rashel had seen her yet.

'They're *all over*,' Daphne said, as if she still didn't believe it. 'In the police departments. In the government. And nobody's ever been able to do anything about them.'

'The only people who've had any success are the ones who work secretly, in small groups or alone. We stay hidden. We're very careful. And we weed them out, one by one. That's what it means to be a vampire hunter.'

She leaned forward. 'Now do you see why it's so important for me to get to that enclave? It's a chance to get at a whole bunch of them all at once, to wipe out one of their hiding places. Not to mention stopping the slave trade. Don't you think it should be stopped?'

Daphne opened her mouth, shut it again. 'OK,' she said finally, and sighed. 'I'll help. I can tell you what to talk about, how to act. At least what worked for me.' She cocked her head. 'You're going to have to dress differently . . .'

'I'll get a couple of other vampire hunters and we'll meet tomorrow after school. Let's say six-thirty. Right now, I'm taking you home. You need to sleep.' She waited to see if Daphne would object, but the other girl just nodded and sighed again.

'Yeah. You know, after some of the things I've learned, home's starting to look good.'

'Just one more thing,' Rashel said. 'You can't tell anybody about what happened to you. Tell them anything – that you ran away, whatever – but not the truth. OK?'

'OK.'

'And especially don't tell anyone about me. Got it? My life may depend on it.'

'Elliot's not here.' The voice on the telephone was cold and as hostile as Rashel had ever heard it.

'Vicky, I need to talk to him. Or *somebody*. I'm telling you, this is our chance to get to an enclave. The girl from the warehouse *heard* them talking about it.' It was Friday afternoon and Rashel was phoning from a booth near her school.

Vicky was speaking heavily. 'We staked out that street for days and didn't see anything, but *you* just happened to be in the right place at the right time to help a girl escape.'

'Yes. I already told you.'

'Well, that was convenient, wasn't it?'

Rashel gripped the handset more tightly. 'What do you mean?'

'Just that it would be a very dangerous thing, going to a vampire enclave. And that a person would have to really *trust* whoever was giving them the information about it. You'd have to be sure it wasn't a trap.'

Rashel stared at the phone buttons, controlling her breathing. 'I see.'

'Yes, well, you don't have much credibility around here

anymore. Not since letting that vampire get away. And this sounds like just the sort of thing you'd do if you *were* in on it with them.'

Great, Rashel thought. I've managed to convince her that I really am a vampire sympathizer. Aloud she said, 'Is that what Nyala is telling everybody? That I'm working with the Night World?'

'I don't know *what* Nyala is doing.' Vicky sounded waspish and a little uneasy. 'I haven't seen her since Tuesday and nobody answers at her house.'

Rashel tried to make her voice calm and reasonable. 'Will you at least tell Elliot what I'm doing? Then he can call me if he wants to.'

'Don't hold your breath,' Vicky said, and hung up.

Great. Terrific. Rashel replaced the handset wondering if she wasn't supposed to hold her breath until Elliot called, or until Vicky passed on the message.

One thing was clear: she couldn't count on any help from the Lancers. Or any other vampire hunters. Nyala could be spreading any kind of rumours, and Rashel didn't dare even call another group.

There was no choice. She'd have to do it alone.

That night she went to Daphne's house.

'Well, she's grounded,' Mrs Childs said at the door. She was a small woman with a baby in one hand, a Pampers in the other, and a toddler clutching her leg. 'But I guess you can go upstairs.'

Upstairs, Daphne had to chase a younger sister out of the bedroom before Rashel could sit down. 'You see, I don't even have a *room* of my own,' she said.

'And you're grounded. But you're alive,' Rashel said, and raised her eyebrows. 'Hi.'

'Oh. Hi.' Daphne looked embarrassed. Then she smiled,

sitting cross-legged on her bed. 'You're wearing normal clothes.'

Rashel glanced down at her sweater and jeans. 'Yeah, the ninja outfit's just my career uniform.'

Daphne grinned. 'Well, you're still going to have to look different if you're going to get into the club. Should we start now, or do you want to wait for the others?'

Rashel stared at a row of perfume bottles on the dresser across the room. 'There aren't going to be any others.'

'But I thought you said . . .'

'Look. It's hard to explain, but I've had a little problem with the vampire hunters around here. So I'm doing it without them. It's no problem. We can start now.'

'Well . . .' Daphne pursed her lips. She looked different from the dishevelled wild creature Rashel had rescued from the street last night. Her blonde hair was soft and fluffy, her cornflower blue eyes were large and innocent, her face was round and sweet. She was fashionably dressed and she seemed relaxed, in her own element in this normal teenager's room. It was Rashel who felt out of place.

'Well . . . do you want to just take along a friend or something?' Daphne asked.

'I don't have a friend,' Rashel said flatly. 'And I don't want one. Friends are people to worry about, they're *baggage*. I don't like baggage.'

Daphne blinked slowly. 'But at school . . .'

'I don't stay at schools more than one year at a time. I live with foster families, and I usually get myself sent to a new city every year. That way I stay ahead of the vampires. Look, this isn't about me, OK? What I want to know—'

'But . . .' Daphne was staring at the mirror. Rashel followed her gaze to see that the reflecting surface was almost completely covered by pictures. Pictures of Daphne with guys, Daphne with other girls. Daphne counted her friends in droves, apparently. 'But doesn't that get *lonely*?'

'No, it doesn't get lonely,' Rashel said through her teeth. She found herself getting rough with the lacy little throw pillow on her lap. 'I like being on my own. Now are we done with the press conference?'

Looking hurt, Daphne nodded. 'OK. I talked with some people at school and everything at the club is going on the same as usual – except that Quinn hasn't been there since Sunday. Ivan and the girl were there Tuesday and Wednesday, but not Quinn.'

'Oh, really?' That was interesting. Rashel had known from the beginning that her greatest problem was going to be Quinn. The other two vampires hadn't seen her – she didn't think they even realized that Daphne had run off with a vampire hunter last night. But Quinn had spoken to her. Had been . . . very close to her.

Still, what could he have seen in that cellar, even with his vampire vision? Not her face. Not even her hair. Her ninja outfit covered her from neck to wrist to ankle. All he could possibly know was that she was tall. If she changed her voice and kept her eyes down, he shouldn't be able to recognize her.

But it would be easier still if he weren't there in the first place, and Rashel could try her act on Ivan.

'That reminds me,' she said. 'Ivan and the girl – are their little groups into death, too?'

Daphne nodded. 'Everybody in the whole place is, basically. It's that kind of place.'

A perfect place for vampires, in other words. Rashel wondered briefly if the Night People owned the club or if some obliging humans had just constructed the ideal habitat for them. She'd have to check into that.

'Actually,' Daphne was saying, a little shyly, 'I've got a poem here for you. I thought you could say you wrote it.

It would sort of prove you were into the same thing as the other girls.'

Rashel took the piece of notebook paper and read:

There's warmth in ice; there's cooling peace in fire,
And midnight light to show us all the way.
The dancing flame becomes a funeral pyre;
The Dark was more enticing than the Day.

She looked up at Daphne sharply. 'You wrote this before you knew about the Night World?'

Daphne nodded. 'It's the kind of thing Quinn liked. He used to say he was the darkness and the silence and things like that.'

Rashel wished she had Quinn right there in the room, along with a large stake. These young girls were like moths to his flame, and he was taking advantage of their innocence. He wasn't even *pretending* to be harmless; instead he was encouraging them to love their own destruction. Making them think it was their idea.

'About your clothes,' Daphne was going on. 'My friend Marnie is about your size and she lent me this stuff. Try it on and we'll see if it looks right.' She tossed Rashel a bundle.

Rashel unfolded it, examined it doubtfully. A few minutes later she was examining herself even more doubtfully in the mirror.

She was wearing a velvety black jumpsuit which clung to her like a second skin. It was cut in a very low V in front, but the sleeves reached down in Gothic points on the backs of her hands almost to the middle finger. Around her neck was a black leather choker that looked to her like a dog collar.

She said, 'I don't know . . .'

'No, no, you look great. Sort of like a Betsey Johnson

ultra model. Walk a little . . . turn around . . . OK, yeah. Now all we have to do is paint your fingernails black, add a little makeup, and—' Daphne stopped and frowned.

'What's wrong?'

'It's the way you walk. You walk like, well, like *them*, actually. Like the vampires. As if you're stalking something. And you don't ever make a noise. They're going to know you're a vampire hunter from the way you move.'

It was a good point, but Rashel didn't know what to do about it. 'Um . . .'

'I've got it,' Daphne said brightly. 'We'll put you in heels.'

'*Oh*, no,' Rashel said. 'There is absolutely no way I'm going to wear those things.'

'But it'll be perfect, see? You won't be *able* to walk normally.'

'No, and I won't be able to run, either.'

'But you aren't going there to run. You're going to talk and dance and stuff.' Hands on her hips, she shook her head. 'I don't know, Rashel, you really need somebody to go there with you, to help you with this stuff . . .'

Daphne stopped and her eyes narrowed. She stared at the mirror for a moment, then she nodded. 'Yeah. That's it. There's no other choice,' she said, expelling her breath. She turned to face Rashel squarely. 'I'll just have to go with you myself.'

'*What?*'

'You *need* somebody with you; you can't do this all alone. And there's nobody better than me. I'll go with you and this time we'll both get chosen.'

Rashel sat on the bed. 'I'm sorry; this time *you're* crazy. You're the last person the vampires would ever choose. You know all about them.'

'But they don't know that,' Daphne said serenely. 'I

told everybody at school today that I didn't remember anything that happened from Sunday on. I had to tell them something, you know. So I said that I never got to meet Quinn; that I didn't know what happened to me, but I woke up last night alone on this street in Mission Hill.'

Rashel tried to think. Would any of the vampires believe this story?

The answer surprised her. They just might. If Daphne had begun to come out of the mind control while she was in the truck . . . if she had jumped out and started running, only to become fully conscious a little while later . . . Yes. It could work. The vampires would assume that she'd have amnesia for the whole period she was in a trance, and maybe for a little before. It *could* work . . .

'But it's too dangerous,' she said. 'Even if I let you go to the club with me, I could never let you get chosen.'

'Why not? You already said I must be resistant to their mind-control thingy, right?' Daphne's blue eyes were sparking with energy and her cheeks were flushed. 'So that makes me perfect for the job. I can do it. I know I can help you.'

Rashel stood helplessly. Take this fluffy bunny of a girl to a vampire enclave? Let her get sold as a slave to bloodsucking monsters? Ask her to fight ruthless snakes like Quinn?

'I like to work alone,' she said in a hard voice.

Daphne folded her arms over her chest, refusing to be intimidated. 'Well, maybe it's time you tried something different. Look, I've never met anyone like you. You're so independent, so adventurous, so – *amazing*. But even you can't do everything by yourself. I know I'm not a vampire hunter, but I'd like to be your friend. Maybe you should try trusting a friend this time.'

Her eyes met Rashel's, and at that moment she didn't

look like a fluffy bunny, but like a small, confident, and intelligent young woman.

'Besides, it was me who got kidnapped,' Daphne said, shrugging. 'Don't you think I should get to pay them back a little?'

Rashel caught herself almost grinning. She couldn't help liking this girl, or feeling a glow of warmth at her praise. But still . . . She drew in a careful breath and watched Daphne closely. 'And you're not scared?'

'Of *course* I'm scared. I'd be stupid not to be. But I'm not so scared I can't go.'

It was the right answer. Rashel looked around the cluttered lacy room and nodded slowly. At last she said, 'OK, you're in. Tomorrow's Saturday. We'll do it tomorrow night.'

CHAPTER 9

How long since he'd identified with humans?

That had all stopped the day he stopped being human himself. Not at the *moment* he'd stopped being human, though. At first all his anger had been for Hunter Redfern . . .

Waking up from the dead was an experience you don't forget. For Quinn, it happened in the Redfern cabin on a husk mattress in front of the fire.

He opened his eyes to see three beautiful girls leaning over him. Garnet, with her wine-coloured hair shining in the ruby light, Lily with her black hair and her eyes like topaz, and Dove, his own Dove, brown-haired and gentle, with anxious love in her face.

That was when Hunter informed him that he'd been dead for three days.

'I told your father you'd gone to Plymouth; don't tell him otherwise. And don't try to move yet; you're too weak. We'll bring in something soon and you can feed.' He stood behind his daughters, his arms around them, all of them looking down at Quinn. 'Be happy. You're one of us now.'

But all Quinn felt was horror – and pain. When he put his thumbs to his teeth, he found the source of the pain. His canine teeth were as long as a wildcat's and they throbbed at the slightest touch.

He was a monster. An unholy creature who needed blood to survive. Hunter Redfern had been telling the truth about his family, and he'd changed Quinn into one of them.

Insane with fury, Quinn jumped up and tried to get his hands around Hunter's throat.

And Hunter just laughed, fending off the attack easily. The next thing Quinn knew, he was running down the blazed trail in the forest, heading for his father's house. Staggering and stumbling down the trail, rather. He was almost too weak to walk.

Then suddenly Dove was beside him. Little Dove who looked as if she couldn't outrun a flower. She steadied him, held him up, and tried to convince him to go back.

But Quinn could only think of one thing: getting to his father. His father was a minister; his father would know what to do. His father would help.

And Dove, at last, agreed to go with him.

Later Quinn would realize that of course he should have known better.

They reached Quinn's home. At that point, if Quinn was afraid of anything, it was that his father wouldn't believe this wild story of bloodthirst and death. But one look at Quinn's new teeth convinced his father of everything.

He could recognize a devil when he saw one, he said.

And he knew his duty. Like every Puritan's, it was to cast out sin and evil wherever he found it.

With that, his father picked up a brand from the fire – a good piece of seasoned pine – and then grabbed Dove by the hair.

It was around this time that the screaming started, the screaming Quinn would be able to hear forever after if he listened. Dove was too gentle to put up much of a fight. And Quinn himself was too weak to save her.

He tried. He threw himself on top of Dove to shield her from the stake. He would always have the scar on his side to prove it. But the wood that nicked him pierced Dove to the heart. She died looking up at him, the light in her brown eyes going out.

Then everything was confusion, with his father chasing him, crying, brandishing the bloody stake pulled from Dove's body. It ended when Hunter Redfern appeared at the door with Lily and Garnet. They took Quinn and Dove home with them, while Quinn's father went running to the neighbours for help. He wanted help burning the Redfern cabin down.

That was when Hunter said it, the thing that severed Quinn's ties with his old world. He looked down at his dead daughter and said, 'She was too gentle to live in a world full of humans. Do you think you can do any better?'

And Quinn, dazed and starving, so frightened and full of horror that he couldn't talk, decided then that he would. Humans were the enemy. No matter what he did, they would never accept him. He had become something they could only hate – so he might as well become it thoroughly.

'You see, you don't have a family anymore,' Hunter mused. 'Unless it's the Redferns.'

Since then, Quinn had thought of himself only as a vampire.

He shook his head, feeling clearer than he had for days.

The girl had disturbed him. The girl in the cellar, the girl whose face he had never seen. For two days after that night, all he could think of was somehow finding her.

What had happened between them . . . well, he still

didn't understand that. If she had been a witch, he'd have thought she bewitched him. But she was human. And she'd made him doubt everything he knew about humans.

She'd awakened feelings that had been sleeping since Dove died in his arms.

But now . . . now he thought it was just as well he hadn't been able to find her. Because the cellar girl wasn't just human, she was a vampire hunter. Like his father. His father, who, wild-eyed and sobbing, had driven the stake through Dove's heart.

As always, Quinn felt himself losing his grip on sanity as he remembered it.

What a pity that he'd have to kill the cellar girl the next time he saw her.

But there was no help for it. Vampire hunters were worse than the ordinary human vermin, who were just stupid. Vampire hunters were the sin and the evil that had to be cast out. The Night World was the only world.

And I haven't been to the club in a week, Quinn thought, showing his teeth. He laughed out loud, a strange and brittle sound. Well, I guess I'd better go tonight.

It's all part of the great dance, you see, he thought to the cellar girl, who of course couldn't hear him. The dance of life and death. The dance that's going on right this minute all over the world, in African savannas and Arctic snowfields and the bushes in Boston Common.

Killing and eating. Hunting and dying. A spider snags a bluebottle fly; a polar bear grabs a seal. A coyote springs on a rabbit. It's the way the world has always been.

Humans were part of it, too, except that they let slaughterhouses do the killing for them and received their prey in the form of McDonald's hamburgers.

There was an order to things. The dance required that someone be the hunter and someone else be the hunted.

With all those young girls longing to offer themselves to the darkness, it would be *cruel* of Quinn not to provide a darkness to oblige them.

They were all only playing their parts.

Quinn headed for the club, laughing in a way that scared even him.

The club was only a few streets away from the warehouse, Rashel noted. Made sense. Everything about this operation had the stamp of efficiency, and she sensed Quinn's hand in that.

I wonder what he's getting paid to provide the girls for sale? she thought. She'd heard that Quinn liked money.

'Remember, once we get inside, you don't know me,' she said to Daphne. 'It's safer for both of us that way. They might suspect something if they knew that first you escaped and now you're turning up with a stranger.'

'Got it.' Daphne looked excited and a little scared. Under her coat, she was wearing a slinky black top and a brief skirt, and her black-stockinged legs twinkled as she ran toward the club door.

Under Rashel's coat, hidden in the lining, was a knife. Like her sword, it was made of lignum vitae, the hardest wood on earth. The sheath had several interesting secret compartments.

It was the knife of a ninja, and Sensei, who had taught Rashel the martial arts, wouldn't have approved at all. He wouldn't have approved of Rashel dressing like a ninja, either. His own family had been samurai, and he'd taught her to fight with honour.

But then Sensei hadn't understood about vampires . . . until it was too late. They'd gotten him while he was asleep, after tracking Rashel back from a job.

Sometimes honour just won't cut it, Rashel thought as

she walked toward the club, trying very hard not to fall off her high heels. Sometimes ya gotta fight dirty.

The entrance of the Crypt was a battered green door inset with a narrow cloudy window. The building looked as if it had once been a small factory – there was still an ancient wooden sign on the door that read NO ADMITTANCE. AUTHORIZED PERSONNEL ONLY.

Rashel's lip quirked as she knocked just below the sign.

The next instant she had the feeling that she was being inspected, evaluated. She stood with her hands in her coat pockets, the coat held open to show the velvet jump-suit underneath. She tried to assume a Daphne-like expression.

Light played on the other side of the cloudy window: somber light, deep purples and blues with an occasional flash of sullen red. Rashel gritted her teeth and waited.

Finally the door opened.

'Hi, how're you doing, where'd you hear about us?' the blond boy on the other side of the door said, holding out a hand. He said it all in a mumble, as if by rote, and his body seemed cast in a permanent slouch. But there was something sharp in his eyes, and Rashel had to control her instinct to fall into a fighting stance.

He was a vampire.

No doubt about it. Those silvery-blue eyes belonged to a killer.

Ivan the Terrible, I presume, Rashel thought. She gave him her hand, making it limp and passive. Then she smiled at him.

'A friend of mine said that this place was seriously cool,' she said in her new voice, which was supposed to be light and musical like Daphne's. Instead, she noticed regretfully, it sounded a bit like the light musical purr of a cat to its dinner.

'So I just had to come, and I really like what I see. In fact, I'd like to get to know *you* better.' She stepped closer to Ivan and smiled again. Should she bat her eyelashes?

Ivan looked both interested and slightly alarmed. 'Who's your friend?'

Gazing into his eyes, Rashel said, 'Marnie Emmons.' She knew Marnie wasn't there that night.

Ivan the Terrible nodded and gestured her in. 'Have fun. And, uh, maybe I'll see you sometime later.'

Rashel said, 'Oh, I hope so,' and swept in.

She had passed the first test. She had no doubt that if Ivan hadn't approved of her, she'd be outside on the pavement right now. And since Daphne had made it in, too, her story must have passed inspection. That was a relief.

Inside, the place looked like hell. Not a shambles. It literally looked like Hell. Hades. The Underworld. The lights turned it into a place of infernal fire and twisting purple shadows. The music was weird and dissonant and sounded to Rashel as if it were being played backward.

She caught scraps of conversation as she walked across the floor.

'. . . going out Dumpster diving later . . .'

'. . . no money. So I gotta jack somebody . . .'

'. . . told Mummy I'd be at the key-club meeting . . .'

You get a real cross section here, she thought dryly.

Everybody had one thing in common, though; they were young. Kids. The oldest looked about eighteen. The youngest – well, there were a few girls Rashel would put at twelve. She had an impulse to go back and insert something wooden into Ivan.

A slow fire that had started in her chest when she first heard about the Crypt was burning hotter and hotter with everything she saw here. This entire place is a snare, a gigantic Venus' flytrap, she thought as she took off her coat and added it to a pile on the floor.

But if she wanted to shut it down, she had to stay cool, stick to her plan. Standing by a cast-iron column, she scanned the room for vampires.

And there, standing with a little group that included Daphne, was Quinn.

It gave Rashel an odd shock to see him, and she wanted to look away. She couldn't. He was laughing, and somehow *that* caught hold of her like a fishhook. For a moment the morbid lighting of the room seemed rainbow-coloured in the radiance shed by that laughter.

Appalled, Rashel realized that her face had flushed and her heart was beating fast.

I *hate* him, she thought, and this was true. She did hate him for what he was doing to her. He made her feel unmoored and adrift. Confused. Helpless.

She understood why those girls were clustered around him, longing to fling themselves into his darkness like a bunch of virgin sacrifices jumping into a volcano. I mean, what else do you *do* with a guy like that? she thought.

Kill him. It would be the only solution even if he weren't a vampire, she decided with sudden insane cheer. Because prolonged contact with that smile was obviously going to *annihilate* her.

Rashel blinked rapidly, getting a grip on herself. All right. Concentrate on that, on the job to be done. She was going to have to kill him, but not now; right now she had to get herself chosen.

Walking carefully on her heels, she went over to join Quinn's group.

He didn't see her at first. He was facing Daphne and a couple of other girls, laughing frequently – too frequently. He looked wild and a little feverish to Rashel. A sort of devilish Mad Hatter at an insane tea party.

'. . . and I just felt so totally awful that I didn't get to meet you,' Daphne was saying, 'and I just wish I knew what *happened*, because it was just so seriously weird . . .'

She was telling her story, Rashel realized. At least none of the people listening seemed openly suspicious.

'I haven't seen you here before,' came a voice behind her.

It belonged to a striking girl with dark hair, very pale skin, and eyes like amber or topaz . . . or a hawk's. Rashel froze, every muscle tensing, trying to keep her face expressionless.

Another vampire.

She was sure of it. The camellia-petal skin, the light in the eyes . . . this must be the girl vampire who'd brought Daphne food in the warehouse.

'No, this is my first time,' Rashel said, making her voice light and eager. 'My name's Shelly.' It was close enough to her own name that she would turn automatically if anyone said it.

'I'm Lily.' The girl said it without warmth, and those hawklike eyes continued to bore straight into Rashel's.

Rashel had to struggle to stay on her feet.

It's *Lily Redfern,* she thought, working desperately to keep an idiot smile plastered on her face. I know it is. How many Lilys can there be who'd be working with Quinn?

I've got a Redfern right here in front of me. I've got Hunter Redfern's *daughter* here.

For an instant she was tempted to simply make a dash for her knife. Killing a celebrity like Lily seemed almost worth giving up the enclave.

But on the other hand, Hunter Redfern was a moderate sort of vampire, with a lot of influence on the Night World Council. He helped keep other vampires in line. Striking at him through his daughter would just make him mad, and then he might start listening to the Councilors who wanted to slaughter humans in droves.

And Rashel would lose any hope of getting at the heart of the slave trade, where the real scum were.

I hate politics, Rashel thought. But she was already beaming at Lily, prattling for all she was worth. 'It was my friend Marnie who told me about this place, and I'm really glad I came because it's even better than I thought, and I've got this poem I wrote—'

'Really. Well, I'm dying *not* to hear it,' Lily said. Her hawklike eyes had lost interest. Her face was filled with open contempt – she'd dismissed Rashel as a hopeless fawning idiot. She walked away without glancing back.

Two tests passed. One to go.

'That's what I like about Lily. She's just so absolutely cold,' a girl beside Rashel said. She had wavy bronze hair and bee-stung lips. 'Hi, I'm Juanita,' she added.

And she's serious, Rashel thought as she introduced herself. Quinn's group had noticed her at last, and they all seemed to agree with Juanita. They were fascinated by Lily's cold personality, her lack of feeling. They saw it as strength.

Yeah, because feeling hurts. Maybe I should worship her, too, Rashel thought. She was finding too many things in common with these girls.

'Lily the ice princess,' another girl murmured. 'It's like she's not even really from earth at all. It's like she's from another planet.'

'Hold that thought,' a new voice said, a crisp, laughing, slightly insane voice. The effect it had on Rashel was remarkable. It made her back stiffen and sent tingles up her palms. It closed her throat.

OK, test number three, she thought, drawing on every ounce of discipline she'd learned in the martial arts. Don't lose *zanshin*. Stay loose, stay frosty, and go with it. You can do this.

She turned to meet Quinn's eyes.

CHAPTER 10

Or not to meet them so much as graze past them, before concentrating on his chin. She didn't dare stare directly into them for long.

'Maybe she *is* from another planet,' Quinn was saying to the girl. 'Maybe she's not human. Maybe I'm not, either.'

That's right, Rashel thought. Make fun of them by telling them a truth they won't believe.

But, she noticed, Quinn looked more as if he didn't care what they found out than as if he were mocking them. 'Maybe she's from another *world*. Did you ever think of that?'

Rashel was confused again. Quinn seemed to be trying to get himself killed. He appeared to be verging on telling these girls about the Night World, and under the laws of the Night World, that was punishable by death.

You're really slipping, Rashel thought. First the slave trade, now this. I thought you were supposed to be such a stickler for the law.

'There are darker dimensions,' Quinn was confiding to the group, 'than you have ever imagined. But, you see, it's all part of life's grand design, so *it's all right*. Did you know' – he put his arm around a girl's shoulders, gesturing outward as if inviting her to look at some horizon – 'that there's a certain kind of wasp that lays its eggs in the body of a caterpillar? A live caterpillar. And it stays alive, you see, while the eggs hatch and the little waspettes eat it from the inside out. Now, who do you think invented that?'

Rashel wondered if vampires could get drunk.

'That would probably be the most horrible way to die,' Daphne chimed in, her musical voice ghoulish. 'Being eaten by insects. Or maybe being burned.'

'It would probably depend on how fast you burned,' Quinn said meditatively. 'A flash of fire – high enough temperature – you burn the nerves out in the first few seconds. Slow baking would be different.'

'I'm writing a poem about fire,' Rashel said. She was surprised to find that she was annoyed because Quinn didn't really seem to have noticed her. On second thought, she *should* be annoyed; her plan depended on him not only noticing but choosing her.

She was going to have to capture his attention.

'Do you have it with you?' Daphne was asking helpfully.

'No, but I can tell you the beginning,' Rashel said. She braced herself to look at Quinn as she recited:

'There's warmth in ice; there's cooling peace in fire,
And midnight light to show us all the way.
The dancing flame becomes a funeral pyre;
The Dark was more enticing than the Day.'

Quinn blinked. Then he smiled, and he looked Rashel over, clearly taking notice of the velvet jumpsuit and ending with her face. He looked everywhere . . . except into her eyes.

'That's right; you've got it,' he said with that same

brittle exhilaration. 'And there's plenty of dark out there for *everyone*.'

Rashel's worry that he might look too deep if he met her gaze was groundless. Quinn didn't seem to be really seeing anybody here.

'There *is* plenty of darkness,' Rashel said. She moved toward him, feeling strangely brave. Her instincts sensed a weakness in him, a flaw. 'It's everywhere. It's inescapable. So the only thing we can do is embrace it.' She was standing right in front of him now, looking at his mouth. 'If we hold it close, it won't hurt so much.'

'Well. Exactly.' Quinn showed his teeth, but it wasn't the manic smile. It was a grimace. He didn't look happy anymore; suddenly, for just an instant, he looked tired and sick. He was almost leaning away from Rashel.

'I came here so I could do that,' Rashel said in a sultry voice. She was scaring herself a little. In the name of the charade, she was doing everything she could to seduce him – but it was surprisingly easy and surprisingly enjoyable. There was a sort of tingling all over her body, as if the jumpsuit had picked up a charge.

'I came to look for the darkness,' she said. Softly.

Quinn laughed abruptly. The feverish good humour came flooding back. 'And you found it,' he said. He went on laughing and laughing, and he reached out to touch Rashel's cheek.

Don't let him touch you!

The thought flashed through Rashel's mind and communicated to her muscles in an instant. Without knowing how she knew, she was certain that if he touched her, it would all be over. It was skin-to-skin contact that had nearly fried every circuit in her brain before.

She danced back from his fingertips and smiled teasingly, while her heart tried to pound its way out of her chest.

'This place is so crowded,' she said throatily.

'Huh? Oh. Then why don't we schedule something more private? I could pick you up tomorrow night. Say seven o'clock in the parking lot.'

Bingo.

'But Quinn.' It was Daphne, looking aggrieved. 'You told *me* to meet you tomorrow.' She trembled her chin.

Quinn started at her, and for once, Rashel could read his face easily. He was thinking that anybody *that* stupid deserved it.

'Well, you can both come,' he said expansively. 'Why not? The more the merrier.'

He walked away laughing and laughing.

Rashel watched him go, resisting an impulse to shake her head. She'd done it; she'd passed the last test and been chosen. So why was her heart still pounding?

She glanced out of the side of her eye at Daphne. 'Well, I don't know about anybody else, but I've had enough excitement for tonight.' She went to get her coat, with the rest of Quinn's coterie glaring jealously after her.

She had one enjoyable experience on the way out. Ivan, still slouching, tried to stop her at the door.

'Shelly, hey. I thought we were going to get to know each other better.'

Rashel didn't need him anymore; she had her invitation. 'I'd rather get to know a head louse,' she said in her sweet chatty voice, and she stepped on his foot hard with her high heel.

In the car, she waited a full twenty minutes, watching the front of the club, before Daphne joined her.

'Sorry, but I didn't want anybody to think we were leaving together.'

'You did a great job,' Rashel said, driving away. 'You even managed to get both of us invited to meet Quinn together – that was dangerous, but it worked. The only thing that surprised me is that he invited us in front of everybody. Is that how he did it before?'

'No. Not at all. Last time, he sort of whispered it to me when nobody was around. But, you know, nothing was normal tonight. I mean, he usually asks new girls questions – I guess to figure out if they have families who'll miss them. And he isn't usually that – that . . .'

'Manic?'

'Yeah. I wonder what's going on with him?'

Rashel pressed her lips together and stared straight ahead through the windshield.

'You sure you want to go through with this?'

It was Sunday night and they were nearing the parking lot of the Crypt.

'I've told you and told you,' Daphne said. 'I'm ready. I can do it.'

'OK. But, listen, if there's any trouble, I want you to run. Run away from the club and don't look back for me. All right?'

Daphne nodded. At Rashel's suggestion, she was wearing something more sensible tonight: black pants heavy enough to provide some warmth, a dark sweater, and shoes she could run in. Rashel was dressed the same way, except that she was wearing high boots. The knife was in one.

'You go first,' Rashel said, parking a street away from the club. 'I'll come in a minute.'

She watched Daphne walk away, hoping she wasn't going to get this little blonde bunny killed.

She herself was the danger. Quinn was going to use mind control on them to get them to go to the warehouse quietly. And Rashel wasn't sure what would happen when he did it.

Just don't let him touch you, she told herself. You can carry it off as long as he doesn't touch you.

Five minutes later, she started toward the Crypt.

Quinn was in the dark parking lot, standing by a silvery-grey Lexus. As Rashel reached the car, she saw the pale blob of Daphne's face through the window.

'I almost thought you weren't coming.' There was now a sort of savagery mixed in with Quinn's lunatic good humour. As if he was angry she wasn't smart enough to save herself.

'Oh, I wouldn't miss this for the world.' Rashel kept her eyes on the car. She wanted to get this over with. 'Are we going somewhere?'

There was that tiny hesitation that seemed to come every time she spoke to him, as if it were taking him a minute to focus. Or as if he were trying to figure something out, she thought nervously.

Then he answered smoothly, 'Oh, right, get in.'

Rashel got in. She glanced once at Daphne in the back seat. Daphne said, 'What's up?' in a chirpy voice laced with feminine rivalry.

Good girl.

Quinn was getting in the driver's side. Once the door was shut, he turned the engine on to run the heater. The windows immediately began to fog.

Rashel sat in a state of continuing mind, ready for the unexpected at any moment.

Only the unexpected didn't come. Nothing came. Quinn was just sitting there in the driver's seat.

Watching her.

With a sudden void in her stomach that threatened her *zanshin,* Rashel realized that it was too dark. Too *familiar*. They were sitting here together in silence, so close, visible to each other only in silhouette, just as they had in the cellar. She could almost *feel* Quinn's confusion as he tried to figure out what was bothering him.

And Rashel was afraid to say anything, afraid that her chirpiest voice wouldn't be a good-enough disguise. The horrible feeling of connection was mounting, like some giant green wave looming over them both. In a moment it would break, and Quinn would say, 'I know you,' and switch on the light to see the face without the veil.

Rashel's fingers edged toward her knife.

Then, through the electric buzzing in her ears, she heard Daphne say, 'You know, I just love this car. I bet it goes really fast, too. This is all so exciting – I'm just so glad I *got* here this time. Not like last week.'

She went on, blathering easily, while Rashel sank back lightheaded with relief. The connection was broken; Quinn was now looking at his instrument panel as if trying to escape the chatter. And now Daphne was talking about how exciting it was to ride in the dark.

Smart, smart girl.

Quinn had to interrupt her to say, 'So, you two girls want to surrender to the darkness?' He said it as if he were asking if they wanted to order pizza.

'Yes,' Rashel said.

'Oh, yes,' Daphne said. 'It's just like we always say. I think that would be just the most seriously cool—'

Quinn made a gesture at her as if to say, 'For God's sake, shut up.' Not a rough gesture. It was more like an exasperated choir director trying to get through to some soprano who wouldn't stop at the end of the measure. Stop *here*.

And Daphne shut up.

Like that.

As if he'd turned off a switch in her. Rashel twisted

slightly to look at the backseat and saw that Daphne had slumped to one side, body limp, her breathing peaceful.

Oh, God, Rashel thought. She was used to the kind of mind control other vampires had tried on her. The persuasive, whispery-voice-in-the-head type. And when Quinn hadn't tried to use that, or to call for help in the cellar, she'd assumed he was low on telepathy.

Now she knew the truth. He packed a telepathic punch like a pile driver. No, like a karate blow: swift, precise, and deadly.

He turned to look at her, a dark shape against a lighter darkness. Rashel tried to brace herself.

'And the rest is silence,' Quinn said, and gestured at her.

Rashel fell into a void.

She woke up as she was being carried into the warehouse. She had enough presence of mind not to open her eyes or make any other sign that she was conscious. It was Quinn carrying her; she could tell even with her eyes shut.

When he dumped her on a mattress, she deliberately fell so that her head was turned away from him and her hair was over her face.

She had a moment's fear that he was going to discover the knife in her boot when he shackled her ankles. But he didn't even roll up her pant leg. He seemed to be doing everything as quickly as possible, without really paying attention.

Rashel heard the shackle snap shut. She kept perfectly still.

She lay and listened as he brought Daphne in and chained her. Then she heard voices close by and the sound of other footsteps.

'Put that one down here – what happened to her

purse?' That was Lily.

'It's still in the car.' Ivan.

'OK, bring it in with the other one. I'll do her feet.'

Thump of a body hitting a mattress. Footsteps going away. The metallic clink of chains. Then a sigh from Lily. Rashel could imagine her straightening up and looking around in satisfaction.

'Well, that's it. Ivan's got number twenty-four in the car. I guess we're going to have one very happy client.'

'Joy,' Quinn said flatly.

Twenty-four? One client?

'I'll leave a message that everything's going to be ready for the big day.'

'Do that.'

'You're awfully moody, you know. It's not just me who's noticed it.'

A pause, and Rashel imagined Quinn giving one of his black looks. 'I was just thinking it was ironic. I turned down a job as a slave trader once. That was before. Do you remember before, Lily? When we lived in Charlestown and your sister Dove was still alive. A captain from Marblehead asked if I wanted to ship out to Guinea for some human cargo. Black gold, I think he called it. As I remember, I hit him on the nose. And Fight-the-Good-Fight-for-Faith Johnson reported me for brawling.'

'Quinn, what's wrong with you?'

'Just reminiscing about the old days in the sunlight. Of course, you wouldn't know about that, would you? You're lamia; you were born this way. Technically, I suppose, you were born dead.'

'And technically, *I* suppose, you're going peculiar. My father always said it would happen.'

'Yes, and I wonder what your father would think about all this? His daughter selling humans for money. And to such a client, and for such a reason—'

At that moment, while Rashel was listening desperately, hanging on every word, heavy footsteps interrupted. Ivan had returned. Quinn broke off, and he and Lily remained silent as another body thumped on a bed.

Rashel cursed mentally. *What* client? *What* reason? She'd supposed the girls were being sold as regular house slaves or food supplies. But clearly that wasn't the case.

And then something happened that drove thoughts of the future right out of her mind. She heard footsteps next to her bed, and she was aware of someone leaning close. Not Quinn, the smell was wrong.

Ivan.

A rough hand grabbed her hair and pulled her head back. Another arm slid under her waist, lifting her up.

Panic shot through Rashel, and she tried to push it away. She forced herself to stay limp, eyes shut, arms dangling passively.

I ought to have been prepared for this.

She'd realized from the beginning that playing her part might include allowing herself to get bitten. To feel vampire teeth on her throat, to allow them to spill her blood.

But it had never happened to her before, and it took every ounce of her will to keep from fighting. She was scared. Her arched throat felt exposed and vulnerable, and she could feel a pulse beating in it wildly.

'What are you doing?'

Quinn's voice was sharp as the crack of glacier ice. Rashel felt Ivan go still.

'I've got something to settle with this girl. She's a smartass.'

'Take your hands off her. Before I knock you through the wall.'

'Quinn—' Lily said.

Quinn's voice was painfully distinct. 'Drop her. Now.'

Ivan dropped Rashel.

'He's right,' Lily said coolly. 'They're not for you, Ivan, and they have to be in perfect shape.'

Ivan muttered something sullen and Rashel heard footsteps moving away. She lay and listened to her heart slowly calming.

'I'm going to get some sleep,' Quinn said, sounding flat and dull.

'See you Tuesday,' Lily said.

Tuesday, Rashel thought. Great. It's going to be a very long two days.

They were the most boring two days of her life. She got to know every corner of the small glass-windowed office. The windows were a problem, since she was never absolutely sure if Lily or Ivan were outside one of them, standing in the warehouse proper and looking through. She listened carefully for the warehouse doors, froze instantly at any suspicious sound, and trusted to luck.

Daphne woke up Monday morning. Rashel had her neck twisted sideways and was staring through the office glass up at the one tiny window set high in the warehouse wall. Just as it turned grey with dawn, Daphne sat up and screamed.

'Sh! It's all right! You're here in the warehouse with me.'

'Rashel?'

'Yeah. We made it. And I'm glad you're awake.'

'Are we alone?'

'More or less,' Rashel said. 'There are two other girls, but they're both hypnotized. You'll see when it gets lighter.'

Daphne let out her breath. 'Wow . . . we did it. That's great. So how come I'm so completely and utterly terrified?'

'Because you're a smart girl,' Rashel said grimly. 'Just wait until Tuesday when they take us out.'

'Take us out where?'

'That's the question.'

CHAPTER 11

The U-Haul whirred across smooth resonant pavement and Rashel tried to guess where they were. She had been drawing a map in her mind, trying to imagine each turn they made, each change of the road underneath them.

Ivan sat slouched, blocking the back doors of the truck. His eyes were small and mean, and they flickered over the girls constantly. In his right hand he held a taser, a hand-held electrical stun gun, and Rashel knew he was dying to use it.

But the cargo was being very docile. Daphne was beside Rashel, leaning against her very slightly for comfort, her dark blue eyes fixed vacantly on the far wall. They were shackled together: although both Lily and Ivan had been checking Daphne constantly for signs of waking up, they were clearly taking no chances.

On the opposite side of the truck were the two other girls. One was Juanita, her wavy bronze hair tangled from two days of lying on it, her bee-stung lips parted, her gaze empty. The second girl was a towhead, with flyaway hair and Bambi eyes staring blankly. Ivan called her Missy.

She was about twelve.

Rashel allowed herself to daydream about things to do to Ivan.

Then she focussed. The van was stopping. Ivan jumped up, and a minute later he was opening the back doors. Then he and Lily were unshackling the girls and herding them out, telling them to hurry.

Rashel breathed deeply, grateful for the fresh open air. Salty air. Keeping her gaze aimless and glassy, she looked around. It was twilight and they were on a Charlestown dock.

'Keep moving,' Ivan said, a hand on her shoulder.

Ahead, Rashel saw a sleek thirty-foot power cruiser bobbing gently in a slip. A figure with dark hair was on the deck, doing something with lines. Quinn.

He barely glanced up as Ivan and Lily hustled the girls onto the boat, and he didn't help steady Missy when she almost lost her balance jumping from the dock. His mood had changed again, Rashel realized. He seemed withdrawn, turned inward, brooding.

'Move!' Ivan shoved her, and for an instant, Quinn's attention shifted. He stared at Ivan with eyes like black death, endless and fathomless. He didn't say a word. Ivan's hand dropped from Rashel's back.

Lily led them down a short flight of steps to a cramped but neat little cabin and gestured them to an L-shaped couch behind a dinette table. 'Here. Sit down. You two here. You two there.'

Rashel slipped into her seat and stared vacantly across at the sink in the tiny galley.

'You all stay here,' Lily said. 'Don't move. Stay.'

She would have made a great slave overseer, Rashel thought. Or dog trainer.

When Lily had disappeared up the stairs and the door above had banged shut, Rashel and Daphne simultaneously let out their breath.

'You doing OK?' Rashel whispered.

'Yeah. A little shaky. Where d'you think we're going?'

Rashel just shook her head. Nobody knew where the vampire enclaves were. An idea was beginning to form in her mind, though. There must be a reason they were travelling by boat – it would have been safer and easier to keep the prisoners in the U-Haul. Unless they were going to a place you couldn't get to by U-Haul.

An island. Why shouldn't some of the enclaves be on islands? There were hundreds of them off the eastern coast.

It was a very unsettling thought.

On an island they would be completely isolated. Nowhere to escape to if things got bad. No possible hope of help from outside.

Rashel was beginning to regret that she'd brought Daphne into this. And she had the ominous feeling that when they got to their destination, she was going to regret it even more.

The boat sliced cleanly through the water, heading into darkness. Behind Quinn was the skyline of Boston, the city lights showing where the ocean ended and the land began. But ahead there was no horizon, no difference between sky and sea. There was only formless, endless void.

The inky blackness was dotted with an occasional solitary winking light – herring boats. They only seemed to make the vastness of empty water more lonely.

Quinn ignored Lily and Ivan. He was not in a good mood.

He let the cold air soak into him, permeating his body, mixing with the cold he felt inside. He imagined himself freezing solid – a rather pleasant thought.

Just get to the enclave, he thought emptily. Get it over with.

This last batch of girls had upset him. He didn't know

why, and he didn't want to think about it. They were vermin. All of them. Even the dark-haired one who was so lovely that it was almost too bad she was certifiably insane. The little blonde one was crazy, too. The one who, having had the luck to fall out of the frying pan once, had come right back, coated herself with butter and breadcrumbs, and jumped in again.

Idiot. Someone like that deserved . . .

Quinn's thought broke off. Somewhere deep inside him was a little voice saying that no one, however idiotic, deserved what was going to happen to those girls.

You're the idiot. Just get them to the enclave and then you can forget all this.

The enclave . . . it was Hunter Redfern who had first thought of enclaves on islands. Because of Dove, he'd said.

'We need a place where the Redferns can live safely, without looking over their shoulders for humans with stakes. An island would do.'

Quinn hadn't objected to the classification of himself as a Redfern – although he had no intention of marrying Garnet or Lily. Instead he said, practically, 'Fishermen visit those islands all the time. Humans are settling them. We'd have company soon.'

'There are spells to guard places humans shouldn't go. I know a witch who'll do it, to protect Lily and Garnet.'

'Why?'

Hunter had grinned. 'Because she's their mother.'

And Quinn had said nothing. Later he'd met Maeve Harman, the witch who had mingled her blood with the lamia. She didn't seem to like Hunter much, and she kept their youngest daughter, Roseclear, who was being raised as a witch, away from him. But she did the spell.

And they'd all moved to the island, where Garnet finally gave up on Quinn and married a boy from a nice lamia family. Her children were allowed to carry on the Redfern name. And as time went on, other enclaves had sprung up . . .

But none quite like the one Quinn was heading for now.

He shifted on his seat in the cockpit. Ahead, there was a horizon again. A luminous silver moon was rising above the pond-still dark water. It shone like an enchantment, as if to guide Quinn's way.

Scrrrunch.

Rashel winced as the boat docked. Somebody wasn't being careful. But they'd arrived, and it could only be an island. They'd been heading east for over two hours.

Daphne lifted her head weakly. 'I don't care if they eat us the minute we get off, as long as I get to feel solid ground again.'

'This practically is solid ground,' Rashel whispered. 'It's been dead calm the whole way.'

'Tell that to my stomach.' Daphne moaned, and Rashel poked her. Someone was coming down the stairs.

It was Lily. Ivan waited above with the taser. They herded the girls off the boat and up onto a little dock.

Rashel did her vacant-eyed staring around again, blessing the moonlight that allowed her to see.

It wasn't much of a dock. One wharf with a gas pump and a shack. There were three other powerboats in slips.

And that was all. Rashel couldn't see any sign of life. The boats rode like ghost ships on the water. There was silence except for the slap of the waves.

Private island, Rashel thought.

Something about the place made the hair on the back of her neck rise.

With Lily in front and Ivan in back, the group was herded to a hiking trail that wound up a cliff.

It's just an island, Rashel told herself. You should be dancing with joy. This is the enclave you wanted to get to. There's nothing . . . *uncanny* . . . about this place.

And then, as they reached the top of the cliff, she saw the rocks. *Big* rocks. Monoliths that reminded her eerily of Stonehenge. It looked as if a giant had scattered them around.

And there were houses built among them, perched on the lonely cliff, looking down on the vast dark sea. They all seemed deserted, and somehow they reminded Rashel of gargoyles, hunched and waiting.

Lily was headed for the very last house on the sandy unpaved road.

It was one of those huge 'summer cottages' that was really a mansion. A massive white frame house, two and a half storeys high, with elaborate ornamentation.

Shock coursed through Rashel.

A frame house. *Wood.*

This place wasn't built by vampires.

The lamia built out of brick or fieldstone, not out of the wood that was lethal to them. They must have bought this island from humans.

Rashel was tingling from head to toe. This is definitely not a normal enclave. Where are all the people? Where's the town? What are we *doing* here?

'Move, move.' Lily marched them around the back of the house and inside. And at last, Rashel heard the sounds of other life. Voices from somewhere inside the house.

But she didn't get to see who the voices belonged to. Lily was taking them into a big old-fashioned kitchen, past a pantry with empty shelves.

At the end of the pantry was a heavy wooden door, and on a stool by the door was a boy about Rashel's age. He had bushy brown hair and was wearing cowboy boots.

He was reading a comic book.

'Hey, Rudi,' Lily said crisply. 'How're our guests?'

'Quiet as little lambs.' Rudi's voice was laconic, but he stood up respectfully as Lily went by. His eyes flickered over Rashel and the other girls.

Werewolf.

Rashel's instincts were screaming it. And the name . . . werewolves often had names like Lovell or Felan that meant 'wolf' in their native language.

Rudi meant 'famous wolf' in Hungarian.

Best guards in the world, Rashel thought grimly. Going to be hard to get past him.

Rudi was opening the door. With Lily prodding her from behind, Rashel walked down a narrow, extremely steep staircase. At the base of the stairway was another heavy door. Rudi unlocked it and led the way.

Rashel stepped into the cellar.

What she saw was something she'd never seen before. A large low-ceilinged room. Dimly lit. With two rows of twelve iron beds along opposite walls.

There was a girl in each bed.

Teenage girls. All ages, all sizes, but every one beautiful in her own unique way.

It looked like a hospital ward or a prison. As Rashel walked between the rows, she had to fight to keep her face blank. These girls were chained to the beds, and awake . . . and scared.

Frightened eyes looked at Rashel from every cot, then darted toward the werewolf. Rudi grinned at them, waving and nodding to either side. The girls shrank away.

Only a few seemed brave enough to say anything.

'Please . . .'

'How long do we have to stay here?'

'I want to go home!'

The last two beds in each row were empty. Rashel was put into one. Daphne looked both sick and frightened as the shackles closed over her ankles, but she went on gamely staring straight ahead.

'Sleep tight, girlies,' Rudi said. 'Tomorrow's a big day.'

And then he and Lily and Ivan walked out. The heavy wooden door slammed behind them, echoing in the stone-walled cellar.

Rashel sat up in one motion.

Daphne twisted her head. 'Is it safe to talk?' she whispered.

'I think so,' Rashel said in a normal voice. She was staring with narrowed eyes down the rows of beds. Some of the girls were looking at them, some were crying. Some had their eyes shut.

Daphne burst out with the force of a breaking dam, '*What are they going to do to us?*'

'I don't know,' Rashel said. Her voice was hard and flat, her movements disciplined and precise, as she slid the knife out of her boot. 'But I'm going to find out.'

'What, you're gonna saw through the chains?'

'No.' From a guard on the side of the sheath, Rashel pulled a thin strip of metal. She bared her teeth slightly in a smile. 'I'm going to pick the lock.'

'Oh. OK. Great. But then what? I mean, what's happening here? What kind of place is this? I was expecting some kind of – of Roman slave auction or something, with, like, everybody dressed in togas and vampires waving and bidding—'

'You may still see something like that,' Rashel said. 'I agree, it's weird. This is not a normal enclave. I don't know, maybe it's some kind of holding centre, and they're going to take us someplace else to sell us . . .'

'Actually, I'm afraid not,' a quiet voice to her left said.

Rashel turned. The girl in the bed beside her was sitting up. She had flaming red hair, wistful eyes, and a diffident manner. 'I'm Fayth,' she said.

'Shelly,' Rashel said briefly. She didn't trust anyone here yet. 'That's Daphne. What do you mean, you're afraid not?'

'They're not taking us somewhere else to sell us.' Fayth looked almost apologetic.

'Well, I'd like to know what they're going to do with us *here,*' Rashel said. She sprung one lock on the shackles and jabbed the lockpick into the other. 'Twenty-four girls on an island with one inhabited house? It's insane.'

'It's a bloodfeast.'

Rashel's hand on the lockpick went still.

She looked over a Fayth and said very softly, 'What?'

'They're having a bloodfeast. On the spring equinox, I think. Starting tomorrow night at midnight.'

Daphne was reaching across the gap for Rashel. 'What, what? What's a bloodfeast? *Tell* me.'

'It's . . .' Rashel dragged her attention from Fayth. 'It's a feast for vampires. A big celebration, a banquet. Three courses, you know.' She looked around the room. 'Three girls. And there are twenty-four of us . . .'

'Enough for eight vampires,' Fayth said quietly, looking apologetic.

'So you're saying that they take a little blood from each of three girls.' Daphne was leaning anxiously toward Rashel. 'That's what you're saying, right? Right? A little sip here, a little sip there—' She broke off as Rashel and Fayth both looked at her. 'You're *not* saying that.'

'Daphne, I'm sorry I got you into this.' Rashel took a breath and opened the second lock on her shackles, avoiding Daphne's eyes. 'The idea of a bloodfeast is that you drink the blood of three people in one day. All their blood. You drain them.'

Daphne opened her mouth, shut it, then at last said pathetically, 'And you don't burst?'

Rashel smiled bleakly in spite of herself. 'It's supposed to be the ultimate high or something. You get the power of their blood, the power of their lifeforce, all at once.' She looked at Fayth. 'But it's been illegal for a long time.'

Fayth nodded. 'So's slavery. I think somebody wants it to make a comeback.'

'Any idea who?'

'All I know is that somebody very rich has invited seven of the most powerful made vampires here for the feast. Whoever he is, he really wants to show them a good time.'

'To make an alliance,' Rashel said slowly.

'Maybe.'

'The made vampires ganging up against the lamia.'

'Possibly.'

'And the spring equinox . . . they're celebrating the anniversary of the first made vampire. The day Maya bit Thierry.'

'Definitely.'

'Just wait a minute,' Daphne said. 'Just everybody press pause, OK? How come you know about all this stuff?' She was staring at Fayth. 'Made vampires, this vampires, that vampires, Maya . . . I never heard of any of these people.'

'Maya was the first of the lamia,' Rashel said rapidly, glancing back at her. 'She's the ancestress of all the vampires who can grow up and have children – the *family* vampires. The made vampires are different. They're humans who get made into vampires by being bitten. They can't grow any older or have kids.'

'And Thierry was the first human to get made into a

vampire,' Fayth said. 'Maya bit him on the spring equinox . . . thousands of years ago.'

Rashel was watching Fayth closely. 'So now maybe you'll answer her question,' she said. 'How do you know all this? No humans know about Night World history – except vampire hunters and damned Daybreakers.'

Fayth winced, and then Rashel understood why she seemed so apologetic. 'I'm a damned Daybreaker.'

'Oh, God.'

'What's Daybreaker?' Daphne prompted, poking Rashel.

'Circle Daybreak is a group of witches who're trying to get humans and Night People to . . . I don't know, all dance around and drink Coke together,' Rashel said, nonplussed. She was confused and revolted – this girl had seemed so normal, so sensible.

'To live in harmony, actually,' Fayth said to Daphne. 'To stop hating and killing each other.'

Daphne wrinkled her nose. 'You're a witch?'

'No. I'm human. But I have friends who're witches. I have friends who're vampires. I know lamia and humans who're soulmates—'

'Don't be disgusting!' Rashel almost shouted it. It took her a moment to get hold of herself. Then, breathing carefully, she said, 'Look, just watch it, Daybreaker. I need your information, so I'm willing to work with you – temporarily. But watch the language or I'll leave you here when I get the rest of us out. Then you can live in harmony with eight vampires on your own.'

Despite her effort at control, her voice was shaking. Somehow Fayth's words seemed to keep echoing in her mind, as if they had some strange and terrible importance. The word *soulmates* itself seemed to ricochet around inside her.

And Fayth was acting oddly, too. Instead of getting mad, she just looked at Rashel long and steadily. Then she said softly, 'I see . . .'

Rashel didn't like the way she said it. She turned toward Daphne, who was saying eagerly, 'So we're going to get out of here? Like a prison break?'

'Of course. And we'll have to do it *fast*.' Rashel narrowed her eyes, trying to think. 'I assumed we'd have more time . . . and there's that werewolf to get past. And then once we do get out, we're on an island. That's bad. We can't live long out in the wild – it's too cold and they'd track us. But there has to be a way . . .' She glanced at Fayth. 'I don't suppose there's any chance of other Daybreakers showing up to help.'

Fayth shook her head. 'They don't know I'm here. We'd heard that something was going on in a Boston club, that somebody was gathering girls for a bloodfeast. I came to check it out – and got nabbed before I made my first report.'

'So we're on our own. That's all right.' Rashel's mind was in gear now, humming with ideas. 'OK, first, we'll have to see what these girls can do – which of them can help us—'

Fayth and Daphne were listening intently, when Rashel was interrupted by the last thing she expected to hear in a place like this.

The sound of somebody shouting her name.

'Rashel! Rashel the vampire hunter! Rashel the Cat!'

CHAPTER 12

The voice was shrill, almost hysterical.

Unbalanced, Rashel thought dazedly, looking around. The sound of her secret being yelled out loud stunned her.

But just for an instant. The next moment she was moving swiftly between the rows of girls, looking for . . .

'Nyala!'

'I know why you're here!' Nyala sat up tensely. She looked just as she had when Rashel had seen her last, cocoa skin, queenly head, wide haunted eyes. She was even dressed in the same dark clothes she'd been wearing the night they caught Quinn.

'You're here because you were in on it all along! You pretend to be a vampire hunter—'

'Shut up!' Rashel said desperately. Nyala was shouting loud enough to be heard on the other side of the door. She knelt on Nyala's bed. 'I'm not pretending, Nyala.'

'Then how come you're free and we're all chained up? You're on their side! You call yourself the Cat—'

Rashel clamped a hand over her mouth.

'Listen to me,' she hissed. Her heart was pounding. All the girls around her were staring and she expected to hear the cellar door open at any moment. 'Nyala, *listen*. I know you don't like me or trust me – but you've got to stop yelling that. We may only have one chance to get out of here.'

Nyala's chest was heaving. Her eyes, the colour of dark plums, stared into Rashel's.

'I *am* a vampire hunter,' Rashel whispered, willing Nyala to believe it. 'I made a mistake letting that vampire go that night . . . I admit it. But I've been trying ever since to put things right. I got captured on purpose so I could find out what was going on here – and now I'm going to try to get all these girls free.' She spoke slowly and distinctly, hoping Nyala could sense the truth of her words. 'But, Nyala, if the Night People find out I'm a vampire hunter – much less the Cat – they are going to take me out and kill me right this minute. And then I don't think the rest of you have a chance.'

She stopped to breathe. 'I know it's hard to trust me. But please, please try. Do you think you can do that?'

A long pause. Nyala's eyes searched hers. Then, at last, Nyala nodded.

Rashel took her hand off Nyala's mouth. She sat back on the bed and they stared at each other.

'Thank you,' Rashel said. 'I'm going to need your help.' Then she shook her head. 'But how did *you* get here? How did you find the club?'

'I didn't find any club. I went back to that street with the warehouses on Wednesday. I thought maybe the vampire might come back. And then – somebody grabbed me from behind.'

'Oh, Nyala.' Wednesday night, Rashel thought. The night Daphne saw Ivan carry in a new girl and put her on a cot. That girl was Nyala. Rashel put a hand to her head. 'Nyala – I almost saved you. I was there the next night – when Daphne fell out of the truck. Do you remember that? If I had only known . . .'

Nyala wasn't listening. 'Then there was this whisper in my mind, telling me to sleep. And I couldn't move – I couldn't move my arms or my legs. But I wasn't asleep. And then he carried me into a warehouse and he bit me.' Her voice was detached, almost pleasant. But her eyes froze Rashel in place.

'He bit me in the neck and I knew I was going to die, just like my sister. I could feel the blood coming out. I wanted to scream but I couldn't move. I couldn't do anything.' She smiled oddly at Rashel. 'I'll tell you a secret. It's still there, the bite. You can't see it, but it's still there.' She turned her head to show a smooth unblemished neck.

'Oh, God, Nyala.' Rashel had felt awkward trying to make gestures of comfort with Daphne, but now she didn't think. She just grabbed Nyala and hugged her hard.

'Listen to me,' she said fiercely. 'I know how you feel. I mean – no, I *don't* know, because it hasn't happened to me. But I'm *sorry*. And I know how you felt when you lost your sister.' She leaned back and looked at Nyala, almost shaking her. 'But we have to keep fighting. That's what's important right now. We can't let them win. Right?'

'Yes . . .' Nyala looked slowly around her bed, then up at Rashel. 'Yes, that's right.' Her eyes seemed to sharpen and focus.

'I'm making a plan to get out of here. And you have to stay calm and help me.'

'Yes.' Nyala sounded more definite this time. Then she smiled almost serenely and whispered, 'And we'll get our revenge.'

'Yeah.' Rashel pressed her hand. 'Somehow, we will. I promise you.'

She walked back to her cot feeling eyes on her,

although nobody asked any questions. Her own eyes were stinging.

What had happened to Nyala was her fault. The girl had already been on the edge, and because of Rashel, she'd gotten herself caught and attacked by a vampire. And now . . .

Now Rashel was worried about Nyala's sanity, even if they did manage to get off the island.

She's right about one thing, though, Rashel thought. Revenge. It's the only way to wipe out the things that have been done to these girls.

The fire in her chest was back – as if there were coals where her throat and heart ought to be. She let it harden her and burn away any stray thoughts of mercy for Quinn. Strange how she kept having thoughts of him, long after she'd made the resolution to kill him.

'Is she OK?' Daphne said worriedly. 'I remember her from the warehouse.'

'I know.' Rashel took the lockpick and sat on Daphne's cot. She began to work at Daphne's shackles. 'I don't know if she's OK. The vampires haven't been living in harmony with her.' She glanced bitterly at Fayth, who just looked back gravely and steadily.

'Nobody thinks *all* the Night People are good,' Fayth said. 'Or all the humans. We don't approve of violence. We want to stop it all.'

'Well, sometimes it takes violence to stop violence,' Rashel said shortly. Fayth didn't answer.

'But why was she calling you a cat?' Daphne asked.

Rashel could feel Fayth's gaze on her. '*The* Cat. It's the name of a vampire hunter, one who's killed a lot of vampires.'

Daphne's dark blue eyes widened slightly. 'Is it you?'

Rashel sprung a lock. Somehow, with these two girls

staring at her, she didn't feel quite so brash as she had a moment ago. She didn't feel terribly proud of being the Cat.

Without looking up, she said, 'Yes.' Then she glanced behind her at Fayth.

Fayth said nothing.

'There's going to be more killing before this is all done,' Rashel said. 'And I can't think of anybody who deserves it more than the vampires who brought us here. So you let me take care of that, and we won't argue about it. All right?' She sprung the other lock on Daphne's shackles. Daphne immediately stretched her legs luxuriously, then swung them to the floor. Fayth just nodded slowly.

'All right, then. Listen. The first thing we've got to do is get these girls organized.' Rashel moved to work on Fayth's chains. 'You're both good talkers. I want the two of you to go around and talk to them individually. I want to know who's going to be able to help us and who's still under mind control. I want to know who's going to be a problem. And I especially want to know who has any experience with boats.'

'Boats?' Fayth said.

'No place on this island is safe. We have to get off. There are four boats in the harbour right now – if we can just find somebody to handle them.' She looked from Daphne to Fayth. 'I want you to bring me back at least two sensible girls who have some chance of not sinking a powerboat. Got it?'

Daphne and Fayth glanced at each other. They nodded. 'Right, boss,' Daphne murmured, and they started off.

Rashel sat, weighing a chain in her hand and thinking. There was no need to tell Daphne – yet – that she didn't plan to ship out with the boats.

* * *

Half an hour later Daphne and Fayth stood before her beaming. At least Daphne was beaming; Fayth was wearing that grave smile that was starting to drive Rashel crazy.

'Allow me to introduce Anne-lise,' Daphne said, leading Rashel to a cot. 'Originally a native of Denmark. She's done the race circuit in Antigua – whatever that means. Anyway, she says she can handle a boat.'

The girl in the cot was one of the oldest there, eighteen or nineteen. She was blonde, long-legged, and built like a Valkyrie. Rashel liked her at once.

'And this is Keiko over here,' Fayth said in her simple way. 'She's young, but she says she grew up around boats.'

This one Rashel wasn't so sure about. She was tiny, with hair like black silk and a rosette mouth. She looked like a collector's doll. 'How old are you?'

'Thirteen,' Keiko said softly. 'But I was born on Nantucket. My parents have a Ciera Sunbridge. I think I can do what you're asking – it's just the navigation that worries me.'

'There isn't anybody else,' Daphne stage-whispered in Rashel's ear. 'So my advice is we trust the kid.'

'I think the navigation will be straight west,' Rashel said. She smiled reassuringly at Keiko. 'Anyway, even the open ocean will be safer than here.' She gestured to Daphne and Fayth to come back to their corner.

'OK. Good job. You're right about trusting the kid; I don't think we have any other choice. We definitely need two boats for all these girls. What else did you find out?'

'Well, the ones that are still under mind control are the ones that came with us,' Daphne said. 'Juanita and Missy. And the one that might cause trouble is your buddy Nyala. She's not completely hinged, if you know what I mean.'

Rashel nodded. 'The mind control may be a problem – how long did it take to wear off the others, Fayth?'

'A day or so after they came in. But that's not the only problem, Rashel. Anne-lise and Keiko think they can handle the boats – but not tonight. Not until tomorrow.'

'We can't wait until tomorrow,' Rashel said impatiently. 'That's cutting it way too fine.'

'I don't think we have a choice. Rashel, all these girls are tranquilized. Drugged.'

Rashel blinked. 'How—?' She shut her eyes. 'Oh.'

'The food,' Fayth said, as Rashel nodded in resignation. 'I realized right off that there was something in it. I think most of the girls know – and they'd *rather* be tranquilized than think about what's happening to them.'

Rashel rubbed her forehead wearily. No wonder the girls hadn't asked her any questions. No wonder they weren't all screaming their heads off. They were doped to the gills.

'From now on we've got to keep them from eating,' she said. 'They need clear heads if we're going to escape.' She looked at Fayth. 'OK. We wait. But that's going to make everything more dangerous. How often do they bring food in here?'

'Twice a day. Late morning and around eight at night. And then they take us to the bathroom two by two.'

'Who does it?'

'Rudi. Sometimes he has another werewolf with him.'

Daphne bit her lip anxiously. 'Are we equipped for werewolves?'

Rashel smiled. Holding her knife, she pulled the decorative knob at the end of the sheath. It came off, revealing a metal blade. She reversed the knob and stuck it in the end of the sheath, so the blade stuck out like a bayonet. The hard wooden sheath itself was now a weapon.

'The blade is silver-coated steel,' she said in satisfaction. 'We are equipped for werewolves.'

'You see?' Daphne said to Fayth. 'This girl thinks of everything.'

Rashel put the knife away. 'All right. Let's talk to everybody again. I want to explain my plan. When we do this tomorrow night, it's going to take cooperation and precision.'

And, she thought, a lot of luck.

'Chow time!'

Rudi walked between the rows of cots, tossing packages from a plastic bag to either side of him. He looked, Rashel thought, exactly like a trainer throwing herring to seals.

She scanned the aisle behind him. No other werewolf at the door. Good.

It had been a long night and a longer day. The girls were dizzy from lack of food, keyed up, and getting more tense with each untranquilized hour. A couple of them couldn't seem to shake their first impression of Rashel – which had come from Nyala's yelling.

'Eat up, girlies. Got to keep up your strength.' A slightly warm foil package hit Rashel's lap, another hit the mattress. Same thing as brunch – hot dogs of the kind you get at a convenience store. Smeared with mustard and drugs. The girls had been surviving on the grapefruit juice he'd poured for them.

As Rudi turned to throw a package to Juanita, Rashel rose smoothly from her cot. In one motion she leaped and came down right on target.

'Don't make a sound,' she said in Rudi's ear. 'And don't even *think* about changing.'

She had his arm twisted behind his back and the silver knife to his throat. Rudi didn't seem to know how he'd gotten there. There were hot dogs all over the floor.

'Now,' Rashel said. 'Let's talk about jujitsu. This is what

you call a proper hold. Resistance to it will cause serious pain and quite possibly a fractured joint. Are you getting this, Rudi?' Rudi wiggled a little and Rashel exerted pressure upward on his knuckles. Rudi yelped and danced on his toes.

'Hush! What I want to know is, where is the other werewolf?'

'Guarding the dock.'

'Who else is on the dock?'

'I – nobody.'

'Is there anybody on the stairs or in the kitchen? Don't lie to me, Rudi, or I'll get annoyed.'

'No. They're all in the gathering room.'

Rashel nodded at Daphne. Daphne jumped out of her bed.

'Remember – quick and quiet everybody,' she said, like a cheerleader who'd been promoted to drill sergeant.

Rashel felt Rudi boggle as every girl in the room kicked off her covers and stood up free.

'What the— what the—'

'Now, Rudi.' Keeping his elbow trapped against her, Rashel exerted pressure again, moving him easily in the direction she wanted. 'You go first. You're going to unlock the top door for us.'

'Anne-lise and Keiko in front,' Daphne said. 'Missy right here. Let's go.'

'I can't unlock it. I can't. They'll kill me,' Rudi muttered, as Rashel moved him up the stairs.

'Rudi, look at these young women.' Rashel swung him around so he had a good view of the prisoners behind him. They stood in one tense, clear-eyed, lightly breathing mass. 'Rudi, if you don't unlock that door, I am going to tie you up and leave you alone with them . . . and this silver knife. I promise, whatever the vampires do to you won't be worse.'

Rudi stared at the girls, who stared back at him. All ages, all sizes, united.

'I'll unlock the door.'

'Good boy.'

He fumbled getting the door open. When it was done, Rashel pushed him through first, looking tensely around. If there were vampires here, she had to change tactics fast.

The kitchen was empty – and music was blasting from somewhere inside the house. Rashel gave a quick savage grin. It was a lucky break she wouldn't have dared to pray for. The music might just save these girls' lives.

She pulled Rudi out of the way and nodded to Daphne.

Daphne stood at the head of the stairs, silently waving the girls out. Fayth led the way with the Valkyrie Anne-lise and the tiny Keiko behind her. The other girls hurried past, and Rashel was proud of how quiet they were.

'Now,' she whispered, pushing Rudi back into the stairwell. 'One last question. Who's throwing the bloodfeast?'

Rudi shook his head.

'Who hired you? Who bought the slaves? Who's the client, Rudi?'

'I don't know! I'm telling you! Nobody knows who hired us. It was all done on the phone!'

Rashel hesitated. She wanted to keep questioning him – but right now the important thing was to get the girls off the island.

Daphne was still waiting in the kitchen, watching Rashel.

Rashel looked at her and then helplessly at Rudi's bushy brown head. She should kill him. It was the only smart thing to do, and it was what she'd planned to do. He was a conspirator in the plan to brutally murder twenty-four teenage girls – and he enjoyed it.

But Daphne was watching. And Fayth would give her that *look* if she heard Rashel had done him in.

Rashel let out her breath. 'Sleep tight,' she said, and hit Rudi on the head with the hilt of her knife.

He slumped unconscious and she shut the cellar door on him. She turned quickly to Daphne. 'Let's go.'

Daphne almost skipped ahead of her. They went out the back door and picked up the hiking path.

Rashel moved swiftly, loping across the beaten-down wild grass. She caught up to the string of girls.

'That's it, Missy,' she whispered. 'Nice and quiet. Nyala, you're limping: does your leg hurt? A little faster, everybody.'

She made her way up to the front. 'OK, Anne-lise and Keiko. When we get there, I'll take care of the guard. Then you know what to do.'

'Find which boats we can handle. Destroy whatever we can on the others and set them adrift. Then each take half the girls and head west,' Anne-lise said.

'Right. If you can't make it to land, do your best and then call the Coast Guard.'

'But not right away,' Keiko put in. 'Lots of islanders use ship-to-shore radio instead of telephones. The vampires may be monitoring it.'

Rashel squeezed her shoulder. 'Smart girl. I knew you were right for the job. And remember, if you *do* call the Coast Guard, don't give the right name of the boat and don't mention this island.' It was perfectly possible that there were Night People in the Coast Guard.

They were almost at the bottom of the cliff, and so far no alarms had sounded. Rashel scanned the moving group again, then became aware that Daphne was behind her.

'Everything OK?'

'So far,' Daphne said breathlessly. She added, 'You're good at this, you know. Encouraging them and all.'

Rashel shook her head. 'I'm just trying to keep them together until they're not my problem anymore.'

Daphne smiled. 'I think that's what I just said.'

The wharf was below them, the boats bobbing quietly. The ocean was calm and glassy. Silver moonlight gave the scene a postcard look. Ye Olde Quaint Marina, Rashel thought.

She loped to the front again. 'Stay behind me, all of you.' She added to Daphne, 'I'll show you what I'm good at.'

A few feet of rocks and sand and she was on the wharf. Eyes on the shack, knife ready, she moved silently. She wanted to take care of the werewolf without noise, if possible.

Then a dark shape came hustling out of the shack into the moonlight. It took one look at Rashel and threw back its head to howl.

CHAPTER 13

Rashel knew she had to stop the guard before he could make a sound. The vampires' mansion was on the farther cliffs, overlooking open sea rather than the harbour, and the music ought to help drown outside noises – but the greatest danger was still that they would be heard before the girls could get away.

She launched herself at the werewolf, throwing a front snap kick to his chest. She could hear the air whoosh out as he fell backward. Good. No breath for howling. She landed with both knees on top of him.

'This is silver,' she hissed, pressing the blade against his throat. 'Don't make a noise or I'll use it.'

He glared at her. He had shaggy hair and eyes that were already half-animal.

'Is there anybody on the boats?' When he didn't answer, she pressed the silver knife harder. *'Is there?'*

He snarled a breathless 'No.' His teeth were turning, too, spiking and lengthening.

'Don't change—' Rashel began, but at that moment he decided to throw her off. He heaved once, violently.

A snap of her wrist would have plunged the silver blade into his throat even as she fell. Instead Rashel rolled backward in a somersault, tucking in her head and ending up on her right knee. Then, as the werewolf jumped at her, she slammed the sheathed knife upward against his jaw.

He fell back unconscious.

Too bad, I wanted to ask him about the client. Rashel looked shoreward, to see that Daphne, Anne-lise, and Nyala were on the pier with her. They were each holding a rock or a piece of wood broken from the jagged pilings of the wharf.

They were going to help me, Rashel thought. She felt oddly warmed by it.

'OK,' she said rapidly. 'Anne-lise and Keiko, with me. Everybody else, stay. Daphne, keep watch.'

In a matter of minutes she and the boating girls had checked the boats and found two with features they thought they could handle . . . and with fuel. Anne-lise had removed a couple of crucial engine pieces out of the others.

'Took out the impellers and the solenoids,' she told Rashel mysteriously, holding out a grimy hand.

'Good. Let's set them adrift. Everybody else, get yourself on a boat. Find a place to sit fast and sit *down*.' Rashel moved to the back of the group where Fayth had her arms around a couple of the girls who looked scared of setting out on the dark ocean. 'Come on, people.' She meant to herd them in front of her like chickens.

That was when it happened.

Rashel had an instant's warning – the faint crunch of sand on rock behind her. And then something hit her with incredible force in the middle of the back. It knocked her down and sent her knife flying.

Worse, it sent her mind reeling in shock. *She hadn't been prepared.* That instant's warning hadn't been enough –

because she had already lost *zanshin*.

She no longer had the gift of continuing mind. She had lost her single purpose. In the old days she'd been fixed on one thing – to kill the Night People. There had been no hesitation, no confusion.

But now . . . she'd already faltered twice tonight, knocking the werewolves unconscious instead of killing them. She was confused, uncertain. And, as a result, unprepared.

And now I'm dead, she thought. Her numbed mind was desperately trying to recover and come up with a strategy.

But there was a wild snarling in her ear and a trail of hot pain down her back. Animal claws. There was a wolf on top of her.

Rudi had gotten loose.

Rashel gathered herself and bucked to throw the wolf off. He slipped and she tried to roll out from under him, arms up to keep her throat protected.

The werewolf was too heavy – and too angry. He scrambled over her rolling body like a lumberjack on a log. His snarling muzzle kept darting for her throat in quick lunges. Rashel could see his bushy coat standing on end.

She felt fire across her ribs – his claws had torn through her shirt. She ignored it. Her one thought was to keep him away from her throat. Keeping an elbow up, she reached for the knife with her other hand.

No good. She hadn't rolled far enough. Her fingertips just missed the hilt.

And Rudi the wolf was right in her face. All she could see were sharp wet teeth, black gums, and blazing yellow eyes. Her face was misted with hot canine breath.

Every snap of those jaws made a hollow *glunk*. Rashel only had one option left – to block each lunge as it came. But she couldn't keep that up forever. She was already tiring.

It's over, she thought. The girls who might have helped her – Daphne and Nyala and Anne-lise – were at the far end of the wharf or on the boats. The other girls were undoubtedly too scared even to try. Rashel was alone, and she was going to die very soon.

My own stupid fault, she thought dimly. Her arms were shaking and bloodied. She was getting weaker fast. And the wolf knew.

Even as she thought it, she missed a block.

Her arm slipped sideways. Her throat was exposed. In slow motion she saw the jaws of the wolf opening wide, driving toward her. She saw the triumph in those yellow eyes. She knew, with a curious sense of resignation, that the next thing she would feel was teeth ripping through her flesh. The oldest way to die in the world.

I'm sorry, Daphne, she thought. I'm sorry, Nyala. Please go and be safe.

And then everything seemed to freeze.

The wolf stopped in midlunge, head jerking backward. Its eyes were wide and fixed. Its jaws were open but not moving. It looked as if it might howl.

But it didn't. It collapsed in a hot quivering heap on top of Rashel, legs stiff. Rashel scrambled out from under it automatically.

And saw her knife sticking out of the base of its skull.

Quinn was standing above it.

'Are you all right?'

He was breathing quickly, but he looked calm. Moonlight shone on his black hair.

The entire world was huge and quivering and oddly bright. Rashel still felt as if she were moving in slow motion.

She stared at Quinn, then looked toward the wharf.

Girls were scattered all over, as if frozen in the middle of running in different directions. Some were on the decks of the two remaining boats. Some were heading toward her. Daphne and Nyala were only fifteen feet away, but they were both staring at Quinn and seemed riveted in place. Nyala's expression was one of horror, hate – and recognition.

Waves hissed softly against the dock.

Think. Now *think*, girl, Rashel told herself. She was in a state of the strangest and most expanded consciousness she'd ever felt. Her hands were icy cold and she seemed to be floating – but her mind was clear.

Everything depended on how she handled the next few minutes.

'Why did you do that?' she asked Quinn softly. At the same time she shot Daphne the fastest and the most intense look of her life. It meant *Go now*. She willed Daphne to understand.

'You just lost a guard,' she went on, getting up slowly.

Keep his eyes on you. Keep moving. Make him talk.

'Not a very good one,' Quinn said, looking with fastidious disgust at the heap of fur.

Go, Daphne, *run*, Rashel thought. She knew the girls still had a chance. There were no other vampires coming down the path. That meant that Rudi had either been too angry to give a general alarm or too scared. That was one good thing about were-wolves – they acted on impulse.

Quinn was the danger now.

'Why not a good one?' she asked. 'Because he damaged the merchandise?' She lifted her torn shirt away from her ribs.

Quinn threw back his head and laughed. Something jerked in Rashel's chest, but she used the moment to change her position. She was right by the wolf now, with her left hand at the exact level of the knife.

'That's right,' Quinn said. A wild and bitter smile still played around his lips. 'He was presumptuous. You almost surrendered to the wrong darkness there, Shelly. By the way, where'd you get a silver knife?'

He doesn't know who I am, Rashel thought. She felt both relief and a strange underlying grief. He still thought she was some girl from the club – maybe a vampire hunter, but not *the* vampire hunter. The one he'd admitted was good.

So he's unprepared. He's off his guard.

If I can kill him with one stroke, before he calls to the other vampires, the girls may get away.

She glanced at the wharf again, deliberately, hoping to draw his gaze. But he didn't look behind him, and Daphne and the other stupid girls weren't leaving.

Refusing to go without her. Idiots!

Now or never, Rashel thought.

'Well, anyway,' she said, 'I think you saved my life. Thank you.'

Keeping her eyes down, she held out her hand, her right hand. Quinn looked surprised, then reached out automatically.

With one smooth motion, like a snake uncoiling, Rashel attacked.

Her right hand drove past his hand and clamped on his wrist. Her left hand plunged down to grab the knife. Her fingers closed on the hilt and pulled – and the sheath with its attached silver blade stayed in the werewolf's neck.

Just as she'd planned. The knife itself came free, the real knife, the one made of wood.

And then Quinn tried to throw her and her body responded automatically. She was moving without conscious direction, anticipating his attacks and blocking them even as he started to make them. It transformed the fight into a dance. Faster than thought, graceful as a lioness, she countered every move he made.

Zanshin to the max.

She ended up straddling him with her knife at his throat.

Now. Fast. *End it.*

She didn't move.

You *have* to, she told herself. Quick, before he calls the others. Before he knocks you out telepathically. He can do it, you know that.

Then why isn't he trying?

Quinn lay still, with the point of the wooden knife in the hollow of his throat, just where his dark collar parted. His throat was pale in the moonlight and his hair was black against the sand.

Footsteps sounded behind Rashel. She heard rapid light breathing.

'Daphne, take the boats and go now. Leave me here. Do you understand?' Rashel spoke every word distinctly.

'But Rashel—'

'*Do it now!*' Rashel put a force she hadn't known she had behind the words. She heard the quick intake of Daphne's breath, then footsteps scampering off.

All the while, she hadn't taken her eyes off Quinn.

Like everything else, the green-black blade of her knife was touched with moonlight. It seemed to shimmer almost liquidly. Lignum vitae, the Wood of Life. It would be death for him. One thrust would put it through his throat. The next would stop his heart.

'I'm sorry,' Rashel whispered.

She was. She was truly sorry that this had to be done. But there was no way out. It was for Nyala, for all the girls he'd kidnapped and hunted and lured. It was to keep girls like them safe for the future.

'You're a hunter,' Rashel said softly, trying for steadiness. 'So am I. We both understand. This is the way it goes. It's kill or be killed. It all comes down to that in the end.' She paused to breathe. '*Do* you understand?'

'Yes.'

'If I don't stop you, you'll be a danger forever. And I can't let that happen. I can't let you hurt anyone else.' She was aware that she was shaking her head slightly in her attempt to explain to him. Her lungs ached and there were tears in her eyes. 'I *can't*.'

Quinn didn't speak. His eyes were black and bottomless. His hair was slightly mussed on his forehead, but he didn't show any other sign of just having been in a fight.

He's not going to struggle, Rashel realized.

Then make it quick and merciful. No need for him to feel the pain of wood through his throat. She switched her grip on the knife, raising it over his chest. Holding it with both hands, poised above his heart. One swift downward stroke and it would be over.

For the first time since she had killed a Night Person, she didn't say what she always said. She wasn't the Cat right now; this wasn't revenge for her. It was necessity.

'I'm sorry,' she whispered, and shut her eyes.

He whispered, 'This kitten has claws.'

Rashel's muscles locked.

Her eyes opened.

'Go on,' Quinn said. 'Do it. You should have done it the first time.' His gaze was as steady as Fayth's. She could see moonlight in his eyes.

He didn't look wild, or bitter, or mocking. He only looked serious and a little tired.

'I should have realized it before, that you were the one in the cellar. I knew there was something about you. I just couldn't figure out what. At least now I've seen your face.'

Rashel's arms wouldn't come down.

What was wrong with her? Her resolve was draining away. Her whole body was weak. She felt herself begin to tremble, and realized to her horror she couldn't stop it.

'Everything you said was true,' he said. 'This is how it has to end.'

'Yes.' Something had swollen in Rashel's throat and it hurt.

'The only other possibility is that I kill you. Better this way than that.' He looked exhausted suddenly – or sick. He turned his head and shut his eyes.

'Yes,' Rashel said numbly. He believed that?

'Besides, now that I *have* seen your face, I can't stand the sight of myself in your eyes. I know what you think of me.'

Rashel's arms dropped.

But limply. The blade pointed upward, between her own wrists. She sat there with her knuckles on his chest and stared at a scraggly wild raspberry bush growing out of the cliff.

She had failed Nyala, and Nyala's sister, and countless other people. Other humans. When it really counted, she was letting them all down.

'I can't kill you,' she whispered. 'God help me, I can't.'

He shook his head once, eyes still shut. She was open to attack, but he didn't do anything.

Then he looked at her. 'I told you before. You're an idiot.'

Rashel hit him under the jaw the way she'd hit the guard. The hilt of her dagger caught him squarely. He didn't move to avoid the blow.

It knocked him out cold.

Rashel wiped her cheeks and got up, looking around

for something to tie him with. Her whole life was torn to pieces, falling around her. She didn't understand anything. All she could do was try to finish what she'd come here for.

Action, that was what she needed. Thought could wait. It would have to wait.

Then she glanced at the wharf.

She couldn't believe it. It seemed as if at least a week had passed since she yelled at Daphne, *and they were all still here*.

The boats were here, the girls were here, and Daphne was running toward her.

Rashel strode to meet her. She grabbed Daphne by the shoulders and shook hard.

'Get – out – of – here! Do you *understand*? What do I have to do, throw you in the water?'

Daphne's eyes were huge and blue. Her blonde hair flew like thistledown with the shaking. When Rashel stopped, she gasped, 'But you can come with us now!'

'No, I can't! I still have things to do.'

'Like what?' Then Daphne's eyes darted to the cliff. She stared at Rashel. 'You're going *after* them? You're crazy!' Looking frightened, she grabbed Rashel's hands on her shoulders. 'Rashel, there are supposed to be eight of them, right? Plus Lily and Ivan and who knows what else! You really think you can kill them all? What, are they all just going to line up?'

'No. I don't know. But I don't need to kill them all. If I can get the guy who set this up, the client, it will be worth it.'

Daphne was shaking her head, in tears. 'It won't be worth it! Not if they kill you – which they will. You're already hurt—'

'It'll be worth it if I can stop him from doing this again,'

Rashel said quietly. She couldn't yell anymore. She didn't have the strength. Her voice was quenched, but she held Daphne's eyes. 'Now get somebody to throw me some rope or something to tie these guys with. And then leave. No, give me five minutes to get to the top of the cliff. Six minutes. That way maybe I can surprise them before they realize you're gone.'

Daphne was crying steadily now. Before she could say anything, Rashel went on. 'Daphne, any minute now they *could* realize that. Someone's bound to check the cellar before midnight. Every second we stand here could make the difference. Please, please, don't fight me anymore.'

Daphne opened her mouth, then shut it. Her eyes were desolate. 'Please try to take care of yourself,' she whispered. She let go of Rashel's shoulders and hugged her hard. 'We all know you're doing it for us. I'm proud to be your friend.'

Then she turned and ran, herding the others toward the boats.

A moment later she threw Rashel two pieces of line. Rashel tied up Quinn first, then the werewolf.

'Six minutes,' she said to Daphne. Daphne nodded, trying not to cry.

Rashel wouldn't say goodbye. She hated that. Even though she knew perfectly well that she was never going to see Daphne again.

Without looking back, she loped up the hiking trail.

CHAPTER 14

The first person Rashel met in the mansion was Ivan.

It was sheer dumb luck, the same luck that had helped keep her alive so far tonight. She slipped in the back door, the way she and the girls had gone out. Standing in the huge silent kitchen, she listened for an instant to the music that was still blasting from the inner house.

Then she swivelled to check the cellar – and met Ivan the Terrible running up the stairs.

He had clearly just discovered that his twenty-four valuable slave girls were missing. His blond hair was flying, his eyes were wide with alarm, his mouth was twisted. He had the taser in one hand and a bunch of plastic handcuffs – the kind police use on rioters – in the other.

When Rashel suddenly appeared on the stairway, his eyes flew open even wider. His mouth opened in astonishment – and then Rashel's foot impacted with his forehead. The snap kick knocked him backward, and he tumbled down the stairs to hit the wooden door below.

Rashel leaped after him, making it to the bottom only a second after he did. But he was already out.

'What are these? Were you supposed to take some girls

up?' She kicked at the plastic handcuffs. Ivan the Unconscious didn't answer.

She glanced at her watch. Only a quarter to nine. Maybe he'd been taking the girls to get washed or something. It seemed too early to start the feast.

Running noiselessly back up the stairs, she quietly closed the door. Now she had to follow the music. She needed to see where the vampires were, how they were situated, how she could best get at them. She wondered where Lily was.

The kitchen opened into a grand dining room with an enormous built-in sideboard. It had undoubtedly been made to accommodate whole suckling pigs or something, but Rashel had a dreadful vision of a girl lying on that coffinlike mahogany shelf, hands tied behind her, while vampire after vampire stopped by to have a snack.

She pushed the idea out of her mind and moved silently across the floorboards.

The dining room led to a hall, and it was from the end of the hallway that music was coming. Rashel slipped into the dimly lit hall like a shadow, moving closer and closer to the doors there. The last door was the only one that showed light.

That one, she thought.

Before she could get near it, a figure blocked the light. Instantly Rashel darted through the nearest doorway.

She held her breath, standing in the darkened room, watching the hall. If only one or two vampires came out, she could pick them off.

But nobody came out and she realized it must have just been someone passing in front of the light. At the same moment she realized that the music was very loud.

This wasn't another room, it was the same room. She was in one gigantic double parlour, with a huge wooden screen breaking it up into two separate spaces. The screen was solid, but carved into a lacy pattern that let flickering light through.

Rashel thrust her knife in her waistband, then crept to the screen and applied her eye.

A spacious room, very masculine, panelled like the dining room in mahogany and floored in cherry parquet. Glass brick windows – opaque. All Rashel's worry about somebody looking out had been for nothing. A fire burned in a massive fireplace, the light bringing out the ruddy tones in the wood. The whole room looked red and secret.

And there they were. The vampires for the bloodfeast.

Seven of the most powerful made vampires in the world, Fayth had said. Rashel counted heads swiftly. Yes, seven. No Lily.

'You boys don't look that scary,' she murmured.

That was one thing about made vampires. Unlike the lamia, who could stop aging – or start again – whenever they wanted, made vampires were stuck. And since the process of turning a human body into a vampire body was incredibly difficult, only a young human could survive it.

Try to turn somebody over twenty into a vampire and they would burn out. Fry. Die.

The result was that all made vampires were stuck as teenagers.

What Rashel was looking at could have been the cast for some new TV soap about friends. Seven teenage guys, different sizes different colours, but all Hollywood handsome, and all dressed to kill. They could have been talking and laughing about a fishing trip or a school dance . . . except for their eyes.

That was what gave them away, Rashel thought. The eyes showed a depth no high school guy could ever have. An experience, an intelligence . . . and a coldness.

Some of these teenagers were undoubtedly hundreds of years old, maybe thousands. All of them were absolutely deadly.

Or else they wouldn't be here. They each expected to kill three innocent girls starting at midnight.

These thoughts flashed through Rashel's mind in a matter of seconds. She had already decided on the best way to plunge into the room and start the attack. But one thing kept her from doing it.

There were only seven vampires. And the eighth was the one she wanted. The client. The one who'd hired Quinn and set up the feast.

Maybe it *was* one of these. Maybe that tall one with the dark skin and the look of authority. Or the silvery blond with the odd smile . . .

No. Nobody really looks like a host. I think it's the one who's still missing.

But maybe she couldn't afford to wait. They might hear the powerboats leaving over the steady pounding of the music. Maybe she should just . . .

Something grabbed her from behind.

This time she had no warning. And she wasn't surprised anymore. Her opinion of herself as a warrior had plummeted.

She intended to fight, though. She went limp to loosen the grip, then reached between her own legs to grab her attacker's ankle. A jerk up would throw him off balance . . .

Don't do it. I don't want to have to stun you, but I will.

Quinn.

She recognized the mental voice, and the hand clamped across her mouth. And both the telepathy and the skin contact were having an effect on her.

It wasn't like before; no lightning bolts, no explosions.

But she was overwhelmed with a sense of *Quinn*. She seemed to feel his mind – and the feeling was one of drowning in dark chaos. A storm that seemed just as likely to kill Quinn as anyone else.

He lifted her cleanly and backed out of the room with her, into the hall, then up a flight of stairs. Rashel didn't fight. She tried to clear her head and wait for an opportunity.

By the time he'd pulled her into an upstairs room and shut the door, she realized that there wasn't going to be an opportunity.

He was just too strong, and he could stun her telepathically the instant she moved to get away. The tables had turned. There was nothing to do now but hope that she could face death as calmly as he had. At least, she thought, it would put a stop to her confusion.

He let go of her and she slowly turned to look at him.

What she saw sent chills between her shoulder blades. His eyes were as dark and chaotic as the clouds she'd sensed in his mind. It was scarier than the cold hunger she'd seen in the eyes of the seven guys downstairs.

Then he smiled.

A smile that shed rainbows. Rashel pressed her back against the wall and tried to brace herself.

'Give me the knife.'

She simply looked at him. He pulled it out of her waistband and tossed it on the bed.

'I don't like being knocked out,' he said. 'I don't know why, but something about it really bothers me.'

'Quinn, just get it over with.'

'And it took me a while to get myself untied. Every time I meet you, I seem to end up hog-tied and unconscious. It's getting monotonous.'

'Quinn . . . you're a vampire. I'm a vampire hunter. Do

what you have to.'

'We're also always threatening each other. Have you noticed that? Of course, everything we keep saying is true. It *is* kill or be killed. And you've killed a lot of my people, Rashel the Cat.'

'And you've killed a lot of mine, John Quinn.'

He glanced away, looking into a middle distance. His pupils were enormous. 'Less than you might think, actually. I don't usually kill to feed. But, yes, I've done enough. I said before, I know what you think of me.'

Rashel said nothing. She was frightened and confused and had been under strain for quite a long time. She felt that at any moment she could snap.

'We belong to two different races, races that hate each other. There's no way to get around that.' He turned his dark eyes back on her and gave her a brilliant smile. 'Unless, of course, we *change* it.'

'What are you talking about?'

'I'm going to make you a vampire.'

Something inside Rashel seemed to give way and fall. She felt as if her legs might collapse.

He couldn't mean it, he couldn't be serious. But he was. She could tell. There was a kind of surface serenity pasted over the dark roiling clouds in his eyes.

So this was how he'd solved an unsolvable problem. He *had* snapped.

Rashel whispered, 'You know you can't do that.'

'I know I *can* do that. It's very simple, actually – all we have to do is exchange blood. And it's the only way.' He took hold of her arms just above the elbow. 'Don't you understand? As long as you're human, Night World law says you have to *die* if I love you.'

Rashel stood stricken.

Quinn had stopped short, as if he were startled himself

by what he'd said. Then he gave an odd laugh and shook his head. 'If I love you,' he repeated. 'And that's the problem, of course. I do love you.'

Rashel leaned against the wall for support. She couldn't think anymore. She couldn't even breathe properly. And somewhere deep inside her there was a trembling that wouldn't stop.

'I've loved you from that first night, Rashel the Cat. I didn't want to admit it, but it was true.' He was still gripping her tightly by the arms, leaning close to her, but his eyes were distant, lost in the past.

'I'd never met a human like you,' he said softly, as if remembering. 'You were strong, you weren't weak and pathetic. You weren't looking for your own destruction. But you were going to let me go. Strength *and* compassion. And . . . honour. Of course I loved you.' His dark eyes focussed again. He looked at her sharply. 'I'd have been crazy not to.'

Falling into darkness . . . Rashel had a terrifying desire to simply collapse in his arms. Give in. He was so strangely beautiful, and the power of his personality was overwhelming.

And of course she loved him, too.

That was suddenly excruciatingly clear. Undeniable. From the beginning he had struck a chord in her that no one else had ever touched. He was so much like her – a hunter, a fighter. But he had honour, too. However he might try to deny it or get around it, deep inside him there was still honour.

And like her, he knew the dark side of life, the pain, the violence. They had both seen – and done – things that normal people wouldn't understand.

She was supposed to hate him . . . but from the beginning she'd seen herself in him. She had felt the bond, the connection between them . . .

Rashel shook her head. 'No!' She had to stop thinking these things. She would *not* surrender to the darkness.

'You can't stop me, you know,' Quinn said softly. 'That ought to make things easier for you. You don't even have to make a decision. It's all my fault. I'm very, very bad, and I'm going to make you a vampire.'

Somehow that gave Rashel her voice back. 'How can you do that – to someone you *love*?' she spat.

'Because I don't want you dead! Because as long as you're human, you're going to get yourself killed!' He put his face close to hers, their foreheads almost touching. 'I will *not* let you kill yourself,' he said through his teeth.

'If you make me a vampire, I *will* kill myself,' Rashel said.

Her mind had cleared. However much she wanted to give in, however enticing the darkness might be, it all disappeared when she thought of how it would end. She would be a vampire. She'd be driven by bloodlust to do things that would horrify her right now. And she'd undoubtedly find excuses for doing them. She would become a monster.

Quinn was looking shaken. She'd scared him, she could see it in his eyes.

'You'll feel differently once it's done,' he said.

'No. Listen to me, Quinn.' She kept her eyes on his, looking deep, trying to let him see the truth of what she was saying. 'If you make me a vampire, the moment I wake up I'll stab myself with my own knife. Do you think I'm not brave enough?'

'You're too brave; that's your problem.' He was faltering. The surface serenity was breaking up. But that wasn't really helpful, Rashel realized, because underneath it was an agony of desperate confusion.

Quinn really couldn't see any other solution. Rashel couldn't see any herself – except that she didn't really expect to survive tonight.

Quinn's face hardened, and she could see him pushing away doubts. 'You'll get used to it,' he said harshly, his voice grating. 'You'll see. Let's start now,' he added.

And then he bit her.

He was so fast. Unbelievably fast. He caught her jaw and tilted her head back and to the side – not roughly but with an irresistible control and precision. Then before Rashel had time to scream, she felt a hot sting. She felt teeth, vampire teeth, extended to an impossible delicacy and sharpness, pierce her flesh.

This is it. This is death.

Panic flooded her. But it wasn't death, of course – not yet. She wouldn't even be changed into a vampire by a single exchange of blood. No, instead it would be slow torture . . . days of agony . . . pain . . .

She kept waiting for the pain.

Instead she felt a strange warmth and languor. Was he actually drinking her blood? All she could sense was Quinn's mouth nuzzling at her neck, his arms around her tightly. And . . .

His mind.

It happened all at once. In a sudden silent explosion, white light engulfed her. It burst around her. She was floating in it. Quinn was floating in it. It was shining around them and through them, and she could feel a connection with Quinn that made their last connection seem like a faulty telephone line.

She *knew* him. She could see him, his soul, whatever you wanted to call it, whatever it was that made him John Quinn. They seemed to be floating together in some other space, in a naked white light that revealed everything and mercilessly lit up all the most secret places.

And if anyone had asked her, Rashel would have said that would be horrible, and she would have run for her life to get away from it.

But it wasn't horrible. She could see dreadful dark bits in Quinn's mind, and dreadful dark bits in hers. Tangled, thorny, scary parts, full of anger and hate. But there were so many other parts – some of them almost unused – that were beautiful and strong and whole. There was so much *potential.* Rainbow places that were aching to grow. Other parts that seemed to quiver with light, desperate to be awakened.

We ask so little of ourselves, Rashel thought in wonder. If everybody's like this – we stunt ourselves so badly. We could be so much more . . .

I don't want you to be more. You're amazing enough the way you are.

It was Quinn. Not even his voice, just – Quinn. His thoughts. And Rashel knew her thoughts flowed to him without her even making an effort.

You know what I mean. Isn't this strange? Does this always happen with vampires?

Nothing like this has ever happened to me in my life, Quinn said.

What he felt was even more, and Rashel could sense it directly, in a dizzying sweet wave. There was an understanding between them that ran deeper than any words could convey.

Whatever was happening to them, however they had gotten to this place, one thing was obvious. Under the white light that revealed their inner selves, it was clear that small differences like being vampire or human didn't matter. They were both just people. John Quinn and Rashel Jordan. People who were stumbling through life trying to deal with the hurt.

Because there was hurt. There was pain in the landscape of Quinn's mind. Rashel sensed it without words or even images; she could *feel* the feelings that had scarred Quinn.

Your father did something – he killed Dove? Oh, John. Oh, John, I'm so sorry. I didn't know.

Rainbow lights shimmered when she called him John. It was the part of him that he had repressed the most ruthlessly. The part that she could almost feel growing in her presence.

No wonder you hated humans. After everything you'd been through, to have your own father want you dead . . .

And no wonder you hated vampires. They killed someone close to you – your mother? And you were so young. I'm . . . sorry. He wasn't as easy with words as she was, but here they didn't need words. She could sense his sorrow, his shame, and his fierce protectiveness. And she could sense the emotion behind his next question. *Who did it?*

I don't know. I'll probably never know. Rashel didn't want to pursue it. She didn't want to feed the dark side of Quinn; she wanted to see more of the shimmering light. She wanted to make the light grow until the dark disappeared.

Rashel, that may not be possible. Quinn's thought wasn't bitter; it was serious and gentle. Tinged with infinite regret. *I may not be able to become anything better—*

Of course you can. We all can. Rashel cut him off with absolute determination. She could feel the bone-deep cold that had set into him years ago, that he'd allowed to set in. *I won't* let *you be cold,* she told him, and she went for a romp in his mind, kissing things and blowing warmth into them, thinking sunlight and comfort everywhere.

Please stop; I think you're killing me. Quinn's thought was shaky – half serious and half hysterical, like the helpless gasp of somebody being tickled to death.

Rashel's whole being was singing with elation. She was young – how strange that she had never really *felt* young until now – and she was in love and stronger than she had ever been before. She had John Quinn the vampire squirming and semi-hysterical. She was unstoppable. Anything was possible.

I'll make *everything be right,* she told Quinn, and she was happy to see that she'd driven his doubt and his sadness away, at least for the moment. *Do you really want me to stop?*

No. Quinn sounded dazed now – and bemused. *I've decided I'll enjoy dying this way. But . . .*

Rashel couldn't follow the rest of his thought, but she felt a new coldness, something like a wind from outside.

Outside.

She'd forgotten there was an outside. In here, in the private cocoon of their minds, there was nothing but her and Quinn. It was almost as if nothing else existed.

But . . .

There was a whole world out there. Other people. Things happening. Things Rashel had to stop . . .

'Oh, God, Quinn – the vampires.'

CHAPTER 15

The sound of her own voice sent Rashel spinning out of the light.

It was as if she were emerging from deep water – from one world into another. Or as if she were reentering her own body. For a moment everything was confusion, and Rashel wasn't sure of where she was or how she was positioned . . . and then she felt her arms and legs and saw yellow light. Lamp-light. She was in an upstairs room in a mansion on a private island, and Quinn was holding her.

They had somehow ended up on the floor, half kneeling, half supported by the wall, their arms around each other, Rashel's head on his shoulder. She had no idea when he'd stopped biting her. She also had no idea how much time had passed.

She coughed a little, shaken by what had just happened. That other place, with the light – it still seemed more real than the hard shiny boards of the floor underneath her and the white walls of the room. But it also seemed encased in its own reality. Like a dream. She didn't know if they would ever be able to get back there again.

'Quinn?' He was Quinn again. Not John.

'Yes.'

'Do you know what happened? I mean, do you understand it?'

'I think,' he said, and his voice was gentle and precise, 'that sharing blood can strengthen a telepathic bond. I've always been able to block it out when I fed before, but . . .' He didn't finish.

'But it happened that other time. Or something like it happened. When I first met you.'

'Yes. Well. Well, I think it's . . . there's something called . . .' He gave up and resorted to nonverbal communication. *There's something called the soulmate principle. I've never believed in it. I've laughed at people who talked about it. I would have bet my life that—*

'What *is* it, Quinn?' Rashel had heard of it, too, especially recently. But it wasn't something from her world, and she wanted a Night Person to explain.

It's the idea that everyone has one and just one soulmate in the world, and that if you find them, you recognize them immediately. And . . . well, that's that.

'But it's not supposed to happen between humans and Night People. Right?'

There are some people who think that it is happening – now – for some reason – especially between humans and Night People. The Redferns seem to be getting it in particular. There was a pause, then Quinn said aloud, 'I should probably apologize to some of them, actually.' He sounded bemused.

Rashel sat up, which was difficult. She didn't want to let go of Quinn. He kept hold of her fingers, which helped a little.

He looked more mussed than he had down near the wharf, his neat hair disordered, his eyes large and dark and dazed. She met his gaze directly. 'You think we're soulmates?'

'Well.' He blinked. 'Do you have a better explanation?'

'No.' She took a breath. 'Do you still want to make me a vampire?'

He stared at her, and something flamed and then fell in pain in his eyes. For an instant he looked as if she'd hit him – then all she could see was regret.

'Oh, Rashel.' In one motion he caught her and held her. His face was pressed to her hair. She could feel him breathing like some stricken creature – and then she felt him regain control, grabbing discipline from somewhere, wrapping himself in it. He rested his chin on her head. 'I'm sorry you have to ask that, but I understand. I don't want to make you a vampire. I want—' *I want you to be what you were two minutes ago. That happy, that idealistic . . .*

He sounded as if it were something that had been lost forever.

But Rashel felt a new happiness, and a new confidence. He had changed. She could sense how much he had changed already. They were in the real world, and he wasn't raving about needing to kill her, or her needing to kill him.

'I just wanted to be sure,' she said. She tightened her own arms around him. 'I don't know what's going to happen – but as long as we're right together, I think I can face it.'

I think we live or die together from now on, Quinn said simply.

Yes, Rashel thought. She could still feel lingering sadness in Quinn, and confusion in herself, but they *were* right together. She didn't need to doubt him anymore.

They trusted each other.

'We have to do something about the people downstairs,' she said.

'Yes.'

'But we can't kill them.'

'No. There's been enough killing. It has to stop.' Quinn sounded like a swimmer who'd been tumbling in a riptide, and whose feet had finally found solid ground.

Rashel sat up to look at him. 'But we can't just let them walk out of here. What if they try it again? I mean, whoever set this bloodfeast up . . .' She suddenly realized that she had asked everybody else, but not him. 'Quinn, who *did* set this up?'

He smiled, a faint echo of his old savage smile. Now it was grim and self-mocking. 'I don't know.'

'You don't *know*?'

'Some vampire who wanted to get the made vampires together. But I've never met him. Lily was the go-between, but I'm not sure she knows either. She only spoke to him on the phone. Neither of us asked a lot of questions. We were doing it for the money.' He said it flatly, not sparing himself.

And to be rebellious, Rashel thought. To be as bad and as damned as possible, because you figured you might as well. She said, 'Whoever it is might just go somewhere else and find somebody else to get his slaves for him. Those seven guys could be having a new bloodfeast next month.'

'That has to be stopped, too,' Quinn said. 'How to stop it without violence, that's the question.' His fingers were still tight on Rashel's, but he was staring into the distance, lost in grim and competent thought.

It was a new side of Quinn. Rashel had seen him in almost every mood from despairing to manic, but she had never *worked* with him before. Now she realized that he was going to make a strong and resourceful ally.

Suddenly Quinn seemed to focus.

'I've got it,' he said. He smiled suddenly, mocking but without the bitterness. 'When violence won't work, there's no other choice but to try persuasion.'

'That's not funny.'

'It's not meant to be.'

'You're going to say, "Please don't kill any more young girls"?'

'I'm going to say, "Please don't kill any more young girls or I'll report you to the Joint Council." Listen, Rashel.' He took her by the arms, his eyes flashing with excitement. 'I have some authority in the Night World – I'm the Redfern heir. And Hunter Redfern has more. Between us, we can make all kinds of trouble for these made vampires.'

'But Fayth – a friend of mine – said they were all so powerful.' In the intensity of the moment, Rashel almost missed the fact that she'd just called Fayth her friend.

Quinn was shaking his head. 'No, you have to understand. These aren't rogues, they're Night World citizens. And what they're doing is completely illegal. You can't just kill a bunch of girls from one area without permission. Slavery's illegal, bloodfeasts are illegal. And no matter how powerful they are, they can't stand up against the Night World Council.'

'But—'

'We threaten them with exposure to the Council. With exposure to Hunter Redfern – and to the lamia. The lamia will go crazy at the thought of made vampires getting together in some kind of alliance. They'll take it as a threat of civil war.'

It might work, Rashel was thinking. The made vampires were just individuals – they'd be up against whole lamia families. Especially against the Redfern family, the oldest and most respected clan of vampires.

'Everybody's scared of Hunter Redfern,' she said slowly.

'He's got tremendous influence. He practically owns the Council. He could run them out of the Night World if he wanted. I think they'll listen.'

'You really do think of him as a father, don't you?' Rashel said, her voice soft. She searched Quinn's eyes. 'Whatever you say about hating him – you respect him.'

'He's not as bad as most. He has . . . honour, I guess. Usually.'

And he's a New Englander, Rashel thought. That means he's against vice. She considered another moment, then she nodded. Her heart was beating fast, but she could feel a smile breaking on her face. 'Let's try persuasion.'

They stood – and then they paused a moment, looking at each other. We're strong, Rashel thought. We've got unity. If anyone can do this, we can.

She picked up her knife almost absent-mindedly. It was a piece of art, a valued possession, and she didn't want to lose it.

They walked down the stairs side by side. Music was still blasting from the gathering room at the end of the hall. It hadn't been that long, Rashel realized. The whole world had changed since she'd been in this hallway – but somehow it had all happened in minutes.

Now, Quinn said silently before they went in. *There shouldn't be any danger – I don't think they'll be stupid enough to attack me – but be alert anyway.*

Rashel nodded. She felt cool and business-like, and she thought she was perfectly rational. It was only later that she realized they had walked into the room like little lambs into the tiger's lair, still dizzy and reeling from the discovery of love.

Quinn went in first and she could hear voices stop as he did. Then she was walking through the door, into that ruddy flickering room with shadows dancing on the walls.

And there they were again, those handsome young guys who looked like a TV-series ensemble. They were looking at Quinn with various expressions of interest and surprise. When they saw her, the expressions sharpened to pleasure and inquiry.

'Hey, Quinn!'

'Hi there, Quinn.'

'So you've arrived at last. You've kept us waiting long enough.' That from the dark one who was looking at his watch.

Quinn said, 'Turn off the music.'

Someone went to a built-in mahogany cabinet and turned off an expensive stereo.

Quinn was looking around the room, as if to appraise each of them. 'Campbell,' he said, nodding slightly. 'Radhu. Azarius. Max.'

'So you're the one who brought us here,' Campbell said. He had rusty hair and a sleepy smile. 'We've all been dying to find out.'

'Who's that?' someone else added, peering at Rashel. 'The first course?'

Quinn smiled fractionally, with a look that made the guy who'd asked step backward. 'No, she's not the first course,' he said softly. 'In fact, unfortunately, all the courses have disappeared.'

There was a silence. Everyone stared at him. Then the guy with the silver-blond hair said, *'What?'*

'They've all – *fsst* – disappeared.' Quinn made an expressive gesture. 'Escaped. Vanished.'

Another silence. Rashel didn't like this one. She was beginning to get an odd impression from the group, as if she were in a room, not with people, but with animals that had been kept past their feeding time.

'What the hell are you talking about?' the dark one,

the one Quinn had called Azarius, said tightly.

'What kind of joke is this?' Campbell added.

'It's not a joke. The girls who were brought for the bloodfeast are gone,' Quinn said slowly and distinctly, just in case anybody hadn't gotten it yet. Then he said, 'And as a matter of fact, it's a good thing.'

'A *good* thing? Quinn, we're starving.'

'They can't have gone *too* far,' the silver blond said. 'After all, it's an island. Let's go and—'

'Nobody's going anywhere,' Quinn said. Rashel moved closer to him. She was still nervous. These guys were on the edge of getting out of control.

But she trusted Quinn, and she could tell they were afraid of him. And, she told herself, they'll be even more afraid in a minute.

'Look, Quinn, if you brought us here to—'

'I didn't bring you here. In fact, I don't know *who* brought you here, but it doesn't matter. I've got the same thing to say to all of you. There isn't going to be any bloodfeast, now or ever. And anybody who objects to that can take their problem to the Council.'

That shut everyone up. They simply stared at Quinn. It was clearly the last thing they expected.

'In fact, if you don't want the Council to hear about this, I'd advise everybody to go home quietly and pretend it never happened. And to have a headache the next time anybody asks you to a bloodfeast.'

This silence was broken by somebody muttering, 'You dirty . . .'

Meanwhile, Rashel's mind had begun to tick. Just *how* were these guys going to go home quietly? There weren't any boats. Unless the host brought one when he came – *if* he came. And where was he, anyway? And where was Lily?

'Quinn,' she said softly.

But somebody else was speaking. 'You'd tell the Council?' a lean tough-looking guy with brown hair asked.

'No, I'd let Hunter Redfern tell the Council,' Quinn said. 'And I don't really think you want that. He might put it in a bad light. Raise your hands everybody who thinks Hunter Redfern would approve of this little party.'

'Do I get a vote?'

The voice came from the doorway. It was deeper than the voices of the young guys in the room. Rashel recognized the sound of danger instinctively, and turned. And later it seemed to her that even before she turned, she knew what she would see.

A tall man standing easily, with a girl and a child behind him in the shadows. He was coloured by the flickering ruby light of the fire, but Rashel could still see that his hair was red as blood. And his eyes were golden.

Golden like hawk's eyes, like amber. Like Lily Redfern's eyes. Why hadn't she realized that before?

The face was a face she would never forget. It came to her every night in her dreams. It was the man who'd killed her mother. The man who'd chased her through the climbing structure, promising her ice cream.

All at once, Rashel was five years old again, weak and helpless and terrified.

'Hello, Quinn,' Hunter Redfern said.

Quinn was absolutely still beside Rashel. She had the feeling that he couldn't even think. And she understood why. She'd seen into his mind; she knew what Hunter represented to him. Stern necessity, even ruthlessness, but honour, too. And he was just now finding out that that was all a lie.

'Don't look so upset,' Hunter said. He stepped forward with an amiable smile. His golden eyes were fixed on

Quinn; he hadn't even glanced at Rashel yet. 'There's a reason for all this.' He gestured to the vampires in the room, and his voice was gentle, rational. 'We need allies in the Council; the lamia are getting too lax. Once I've explained it all to you, you'll understand.'

The way he'd made Quinn understand that Quinn had to be a vampire, Rashel thought. The way he'd made Quinn understand that humans were the enemy.

She was shaking all over, but there was a white-hot fire inside her that burned through the fear.

'Was there a reason for killing my mother?' she said.

The golden eyes turned toward her. Hunter looked mildly startled. Beside her, Quinn's head jerked around.

'I was only five, but I remember it all,' Rashel said. She took a step closer to Hunter. 'You killed her just like *that* – snapped her neck. Was there a reason for killing Timmy? He was four years old and you drank his blood. Was there a reason for killing my great-aunt? You set a fire to get me, but it got her.'

She stopped, staring into those predatory golden eyes. She'd searched for this man for twelve years, and now he didn't seem to recognize her. 'What's wrong, did you hunt too many little kids to keep track of?' she said. 'Or are you so crazy you believe your own public image?'

Quinn whispered, 'Rashel . . .'

She turned. 'I'm sure. He was the one.'

In that instant, she saw Quinn's face harden implacably against the man who'd made him a Redfern. His eyes went dark as black holes – no light escaped. Rashel suddenly had the feeling of glacial cold. Look into eyes like that and what you saw alone might kill you, she thought.

But she had her own fire inside her, her own vengeance. The knife was in her waistband. If she could just get close enough . . . She moved toward Hunter

Redfern again. 'You destroyed my life. And you don't even remember, do you?'

'I remember,' the little shadow beside him said.

And then the world flipped and Rashel felt the floor slipping away from her. The child behind Hunter was walking into the light – and suddenly she could smell plastic and old socks, and she could feel vinyl under her hands. Memories were flooding up so quickly that she was drowning in them.

All she could say was 'Oh, Timmy. Oh, God, Timmy.'

He was standing there, just as she'd seen him last, twelve years ago. Shiny dark hair and wide tilted blue eyes. Except that the eyes weren't exactly a child's eyes. They were some strange and terrible combination of child and adult. There was too much knowledge in them.

'You left me,' Timmy said. 'You didn't care about me.'

Rashel sank her teeth into her lip, but tears spilled anyway. 'I'm sorry . . .'

'Nobody cared about me,' Timmy said. He reached up to take Hunter's sleeve. 'No humans, anyway. Humans are vermin.' He smiled his old sweet smile.

Hunter looked down at Timmy, then up at Quinn. 'It's amazing how quickly they learn. You haven't met Timmy, have you? He's been living in Vegas, but I think he can be useful here.' He turned to Rashel and his eyes were pure evil. 'Of course I remember you. It's just that you've changed a little; you've gotten older. You're different from us, you see.'

'You're weak,' Lily put in. She had stepped forward, too, to stand beside her father. Now she linked her arm in his. 'You're short-lived. You're not very bright, and not very important. In a word, you're . . . *dinner*.'

Hunter smiled. 'Well put.' Then he dropped the smile and said to Quinn, 'Step away from her, son.'

Quinn moved slightly, closer to Rashel. 'This is my soulmate,' he said, in his softest and most disturbing voice. 'And we're leaving together.'

Hunter Redfern stared at him for several long moments. Something like disbelief flickered in his eyes. Then he recovered and said quietly, 'What a shame.'

Behind Rashel there were noises of stirring. It was as if a hot wind from the savanna had blown in, and the lions had caught its scent.

'You know, I was already worried about you, Quinn,' Hunter said. 'Last summer you let Ash and his sisters get away with running out on the enclave. Don't think I didn't notice that. You're getting lax, getting soft. There's too much of that going around lately.'

Stand back to back, Quinn told Rashel. She was already moving into position. The vampires were forming a ring, encircling them. She could see smiles on every face.

'And Lily says you've been strange these last few days – moody. She said you seemed preoccupied with a human girl.'

Rashel drew her knife. The vampires were watching her with the fixed attention of big felines watching their prey. Absolute focus.

'But the soulmate idea – that's really the last straw. It's like a disease infecting our people. You understand why I have to stamp it out.' Hunter paused. 'For old time's sake, let's finish this quickly.'

A voice that wasn't Quinn's added in Rashel's mind, *I told you I'd see you later.*

Rashel stood on the balls of her feet, letting Hunter's words slide off her and drip away. She couldn't think about him right now. She had to concentrate on awareness, open her energy, and free her mind. This was going to be the biggest fight of her life, and she needed *zanshin.*

But even as she found it, a small voice inside her was whispering the truth. There were simply too many vampires. She and Quinn couldn't hold them all off at once.

CHAPTER 16

A fighter knows instinctively when there's no chance. But Rashel planned to fight anyway.

And then she noticed something wrong.

The vampires should have caught it first. Their senses were sharper. But their senses were turned inward, focussed on the victims in front of them. Rashel was the only one whose senses were turned outward, alert to everything but focussed on nothing.

There was a smell that was wrong and a sound. The smell was sharp, stinging, and close by. The sound was soft, distant, but recognizable.

Gasoline. She could smell gasoline. And she could hear a faint dull roar that sounded like the fireplace in the gathering room – but was coming from somewhere else in the house.

It didn't make sense. She didn't understand. But she believed it.

'Quinn, get ready to run,' she said, a gasp on a soft breath. Something was about to happen.

No, we have to fight—

His thought to her broke off. Rashel turned to look at the doorway.

Hunter Redfern had moved into the gathering room – but there was *someone* in the hall. Then the someone stepped forward and Rashel could see her face.

Nyala was smiling brilliantly. Her small queenly head was high and her dark eyes were flashing. She was holding a red gasoline can in one hand and a litre of grapefruit juice in the other. The bottle was almost full of liquid and had a burning rag stuffed in the top.

Gas. Gas from the pump on the wharf, Rashel thought. A Generation-X Molotov cocktail.

'It's all over the house,' Nyala said, and her voice was lilting. 'Gallons and gallons. All over the rooms and the doors.'

But she shouldn't be hanging *on* to it, Rashel thought. That bottle is going to explode.

'You see, I *am* a real vampire hunter, Rashel. I figure this way, we get rid of them all at once.'

And the house is already burning . . .

Behind the carved screen on the right side of the room, ruddy light was flickering, growing. The faint roar that had disturbed Rashel was louder now. Closer.

And everything's *wood,* Rashel thought. Wood panelling, wood floors. Frame house. A deathtrap for vampires.

'Get her,' Hunter Redfern said. But none of the vampires charged toward Nyala with her about-to-explode bottle of death and her can of fire accelerant. In fact, they were backing away, moving to the perimeter of the room.

Hunter spun to face Nyala directly. *You need to put that down,* he began in telepathic tones of absolute authority – at the same time Rashel shouted, 'Nyala, *no—*'

The sound of telepathy seemed to set something off in Nyala. Flashing a dazzling savage smile, she smashed the grapefruit juice bottle at his feet.

With almost the same motion, she threw the gasoline can, too. It was flying in a graceful arc toward the fireplace, spinning, spilling liquid, and vampires were scattering to try to get out of the way.

And then everything was exploding – or maybe *erupting* was a better word. It was as if a dragon had breathed suddenly into the room, sending a roaring gale of fire through it.

But Rashel didn't have time to watch – she and Quinn were both diving. Quinn was diving for the floor past Nyala, trying to drag Rashel with him. Rashel was diving for Timmy.

She didn't know why. She didn't think about it consciously. She simply had to do it.

She hit Timmy with the entire force of her body and knocked him to the floor. She covered him as the fire erupted behind her. Then she scrambled to her knees, her arm locked around his chest.

Everything was noise and heat and confusion. Vampires were yelling at each other, running, shoving each other. The ones who'd been splattered with gas were on fire, trying to put it out, getting in one another's way.

'Come on!' Quinn said, pulling Rashel up. 'I know a way outside.'

Rashel looked for Nyala. She didn't see her. As Quinn dragged her into the hall, she saw dark smoke come billowing from the dining-room area. The hall was bathed in reddish light.

'Come on!'

Quinn was pulling her across the hall, through the smoke. Into a room that was full of orange flames.

'Quinn—'

Timmy was kicking and struggling in Rashel's arms. Yelling at her. She kept her grip on him.

And she went with Quinn. She had to trust him. He knew the house.

She hadn't realized how frightening fire was, though. It was like a beast with hot shrivelling breath. It seemed *alive* and it seemed to want to get her, roaring out at her from unexpected places.

And it spread so fast. Rashel would never have believed it could move so quickly through a house, even a house soaked with gasoline. In a matter of minutes the building had become an inferno. Everywhere she looked, there was fire, smoke, and a horrifying reflection of flames.

They were on the other side of the room now, and Quinn was kicking at a door. His sleeve was on fire. Rashel twisted her hand out of his and beat at it to put it out. She almost lost hold of Timmy.

Then the door was swinging outward and cool air was rushing in and the fire was roaring like a crazy thing to meet it. She was simply running, in panic, her only thought to hold on to Timmy and to stay with Quinn.

They were out. But she smelled burning. And now Quinn was grabbing her, rolling her over and over on the sandy unpaved road. Rashel realized, dimly, that her clothes were on fire in back.

Quinn stopped rolling her. Rashel sat up, tried to glance at her own back, then looked for Timmy.

He was crouched on the road, staring at the house. Rashel could see flames coming out of the windows. Smoke was pouring upward and everything seemed as bright as daylight beneath it.

'Are you all right?' Quinn said urgently. He was looking her over.

Rashel's whole body was washed with adrenaline and her heart was pounding insanely. But she couldn't take her eyes off the house.

She stumbled to her feet. 'Nyala's in there! I have to get her.'

Quinn looked at her as if she were raving. Rashel just shook her head and started helplessly toward the house. She didn't want to go anywhere near it. She knew the fire wanted her dead. But she couldn't leave Nyala in there to burn.

Then Quinn was shoving her roughly back. 'You stay here. I'll get her.'

'No! I have to—'

'You have to watch Timmy! Look, he's getting away!'

Rashel whirled. She didn't have any clear idea of where Timmy might be getting away to – but he was on his feet and moving. Toward the house, then away from it. She grabbed for him again. When she turned back toward Quinn, Quinn was gone.

No – there he was, darting into the house. Timmy was screaming again, kicking in her arms.

'I hate you!' he shouted. 'Let go of me! Why did you take me out?'

Rashel stared at the house. Quinn was inside now. In that holocaust of flame. And he'd gone because of her, to save her from going herself.

Please, she thought suddenly and distinctly. Please don't let him die.

The flames were roaring higher. The night was brilliant with them. Fire was raining in little burning bits from the sky, and Rashel's nose and eyes stung. She knew she should get farther back, but she couldn't. She had to watch for Quinn.

'Why? I hate you! Why did you take me out?'

Rashel looked at the strange little creature in her arms, the one that was biting and kicking as if it wanted to go back into the burning house. She didn't know what

Timmy had become – some weird combination of child, adult, and animal, apparently. And she didn't know what kind of future he could possibly have.

But she did know, now, why she'd brought him out.

She looked at the childish face, the angry eyes full of hate. 'Because my mom told me to take care of you,' she whispered.

And then she was crying. She was holding him and sobbing. Timmy didn't try to hold her back, but he didn't bite her anymore either.

Still sobbing, Rashel looked over his head toward the house. Everything was burning. And Quinn was still inside . . .

Then she saw a figure silhouetted against the flames. Two figures. One holding the other, half carrying it.

'Quinn!'

He was running toward her, supporting Nyala. They were both covered with soot. Nyala was swaying, laughing, her eyes huge and distant.

Rashel threw her arms around both of them. The relief that washed over her was almost more painful than the fear. Her legs literally felt as if they had no bones – she was going to collapse at any second. She was tottering.

'You're alive,' she whispered into Quinn's charred collar. 'And you got her.' She could feel Quinn's arm around her, holding hard. Nothing else seemed to matter.

But now Quinn was taking his arm away, pushing her along the road. 'Come on! We've got to get to the wharf before they do.'

In a flash, Rashel understood. She got a new grip on Timmy and turned to run toward the hiking path. Her knees were shaking, but she found she could make them move.

They lurched down the path in the wild grass, Quinn

supporting Nyala, she carrying Timmy. Rashel didn't know how many vampires had made it out of the burning house – she hadn't seen any – but she knew that any who did would head for the dock.

Where she and Anne-lise had disabled the boats.

But as the wharf came into view, Rashel saw something that hadn't been there when she left it. There was a yacht in the harbour, swinging at anchor.

'It's Hunter's,' Quinn said. 'Hurry!'

They were flying down the hill, staggering onto the wharf. Rashel saw no sign of the werewolf she'd tied up earlier, but she saw something else new. An inflatable red dinghy was tied to the pier.

'Quick! You get in first.'

Rashel put Timmy down and got in. Quinn lifted Timmy into her arms, then put Nyala in. Nyala was staring around her now, laughing in spurts, then stopping to breathe hard. Rashel put her free arm around her as Quinn climbed in the dinghy.

Every second, Rashel was expecting to see Hunter Redfern appear, blackened and smouldering, with his arms outstretched like some vengeful demon.

And then the tiny motor was purring and they were moving away from the wharf. They were leaving it behind. They were on the ocean, the cool dark ocean, freeing themselves from land and danger.

Rashel watched as the yacht got bigger and bigger. They were close to it now. They were there.

'Come on. We can climb up the swimming ladder. Come on, *fast,*' Quinn said. He was reaching for her, his face unfamiliar in a mask of soot, his eyes intense. Absolutely focused, absolutely determined.

Thank God he knows what to do on a boat. I wouldn't. She let Quinn help her up the ladder, then helped Timmy and Nyala. Nyala had stopped laughing entirely now. She was simply gasping, looking bewildered.

'What happened? What—?' She stared toward the cliffs where orange flame was shooting into the sky. 'I did that. Did I do that?'

Quinn had pulled up the anchor. He was heading for the cockpit. Timmy was crying.

Kneeling on the deck, Rashel held Nyala. Nyala's eyelashes were burned to crisp curls. There was white ash on the ends. Her mouth was trembling and her body shook as if she were having convulsions.

'I had to do it,' she got out in a thick voice. 'You know I had to, Rashel.'

Timmy sobbed on. A motor roared to life. All at once they were moving swiftly and the island with its burning torch was falling behind.

'I had to,' Nyala said in a choked voice. 'I had to. I had to.'

Rashel leaned to rest her head on Nyala's hair. Wind was whipping around her as they raced away. She held the tiny vampire in one arm and the trembling human girl in the other. And she watched the fire get smaller and smaller until it looked like a star on the ocean.

CHAPTER 17

Hunter's yacht was bigger than the powerboat Quinn had brought to the island. There was a salon down in the cabin and two separate staterooms. Right now, Timmy was in one of them. Nyala was in another. Quinn had put them both to sleep.

Quinn and Rashel were in the cockpit.

'Do you think any of the vampires got out?' Rashel said softly.

'I don't know. Probably.' His voice was as quiet as hers.

He was filthy, covered with sand and soot, burned here and there, and wildly dishevelled. He had never looked more beautiful to Rashel.

'You saved Nyala,' she whispered. 'And I know you did it for me.'

He looked at her and some of the tense focus went out of his eyes. The hardness in his face softened.

Rashel took his hand.

She didn't know how to say the rest of what she meant. That she knew he had changed, that he was changing every minute. She could almost *feel* the new parts of his mind opening and growing – or rather, the old parts, the parts he'd deliberately left behind when he stopped being human.

'Thank you, John Quinn,' she whispered.

He laughed. It wasn't a savage laugh, or a bitter laugh, or even the charming Mad Hatter laugh. It was just a real laugh. Tired and shaky, but happy.

'What else could I do?'

Then he reached for her and they were holding each other. They might look like two refugees from a disaster movie, but all Rashel felt was the singing joy of their closeness. It was such comfort to be able to hold on to Quinn, and such wonder to feel him holding her back.

A feeling of peace stole over her.

There were still problems ahead. She knew that. Her mind was already clicking through them, forming a dim checklist of things to worry about when she regained the ability to worry.

Hunter and the other vampires. They might still be alive. They might come looking for revenge. But even if they did . . . Rashel had spent her whole life fighting the Night World alone. Now she had Quinn beside her, and together they could take on anything.

Daphne and the girls. Rashel felt sure they were safe; she trusted Anne-lise and Keiko. But once they got home, they'd be traumatized. They would need help. And someone would need to figure out what they should tell the rest of the world.

Not that anyone would believe it was real vampires who had kidnapped them if they said so, Rashel thought. The police would pass it off as a cult or something. Still, the girls know the truth. They may be fresh recruits for the fight . . .

Against what? How could she be a vampire hunter now? How could she try to destroy the Night World?

Where could a reformed vampire and a burned-out

vampire hunter go when they fell in love?

The answer, of course, was obvious. Rashel knew even as she formed the question, and she laughed silently into Quinn's shoulder.

Circle Daybreak. They'd become damned Daybreakers.

Granted, they weren't the type to dance in circles with flowers in their hair, singing about love and harmony and all that. But if Circle Daybreak was going to make any headway, it needed something besides love and harmony.

It needed a fighting arm. Somebody to deal with the vampires who were hopelessly evil and bent on destruction. Somebody to save people like Nyala's sister. Somebody to protect kids like Timmy.

Come to think of it, Circle Daybreak was where Nyala and Timmy belonged, too. Right now they need peace and healing, and people who would understand what they'd been through. I don't know, Rashel thought, maybe witches can help.

She hoped so. She thought Nyala would be all right – there was a kind of inner strength to the girl that kept her fighting. She wasn't so sure about Timmy. Trapped in a four-year-old body, his mind twisted by whatever lies Hunter had told him . . . what kind of normal life could he ever have?

But he was alive, and there was a chance. And maybe there were parts of his mind that were bright and warm and aching to grow.

Elliot and Vicky and the other vampire hunters. Rashel would have to talk to them, try to explain what she'd learned. She didn't know if they'd listen. But she would have to try.

'All anybody can do is try,' she said softly.

Quinn stirred. He leaned back to look into her face. 'You're right,' he said, and she realized that he'd been thinking about the same things.

Our minds work alike, she thought. She had found her partner, her equal, the one to work and live and love with her. Her soulmate.

'I love you, John Quinn,' she said.

And then they were kissing each other and she was finding in him a tenderness that even she hadn't suspected. But it made sense. After all, the opposite of absolute ruthlessness is absolute tenderness – and when you ripped the one away, you were left with the other.

I wonder what else I'll find out about him? she thought, dizzy with discovery. Whatever it is, it's sure to be interesting.

'I love you, Rashel Jordan,' he said against her lips.

Not Rashel the Cat. The Cat was dead, and all the old anger and the hate had burned away. It was Rashel Jordan who was starting a new future.

She kissed Quinn again and felt the beauty and the mystery of his thoughts. 'Hold me tighter,' she whispered. 'I'm a little cold.'

'You are? I feel so warm. It's spring tomorrow, you know.'

And then they both were quiet, lost in each other. The boat sped on through the sparkling ocean and into the promise of the moonlit night.

SOULMATE

For Marion Foster Divola

CHAPTER 1

The werewolves broke in while Hannah Snow was in the psychologist's office.

She was there for the obvious reason. 'I think I'm going insane,' she said quietly as soon as she sat down.

'And what makes you think that?' The psychologist's voice was neutral, soothing.

Hannah swallowed.

OK, she thought. Lay it on the line. Skip the paranoid feeling of being followed and the ultraparanoid feeling that someone was trying to kill her, ignore the dreams that woke her up screaming. Go straight to the *really* weird stuff.

'I write notes,' she said flatly.

'Notes.' The therapist nodded, tapping a pencil against his lips. Then as the silence stretched out: 'Uh, and that bothers you?'

'Yes.' She added in a jagged rush, 'Everything used to be so perfect. I mean, I had my whole life under control. I'm a senior at Sacajawea High. I have nice friends; I have good grades. I even have a scholarship from Utah State for next year. And now it's all falling apart . . . because of me. Because I'm going *crazy*.'

'Because you write notes?' the psychologist said, puzzled. 'Um, poison pen letters, compulsive memo taking . . . ?'

'Notes like these.' Hannah leaned forward in her chair and dropped a handful of crumpled scraps of paper on his desk. Then she looked away miserably as he read them.

He seemed like a nice guy – and surprisingly young for a shrink, she thought. His name was Paul Winfield – 'Call me Paul,' he'd said – and he had red hair and analytical blue eyes. He looked as if he might have both a sense of humour and a temper.

And he likes me, Hannah thought. She'd seen the flicker of appreciation in his eyes when he'd opened the front door and found her standing silhouetted against the flaming Montana sunset.

And then she'd seen that appreciation change to utter blankness, startled neutrality, when she stepped inside and her face was revealed.

It didn't matter. People usually gave Hannah two looks, one for the long, straight fair hair and the clear grey eyes . . . and one for the birthmark.

It slanted diagonally beneath her left cheekbone, pale strawberry colour, as if someone had dipped a finger in blusher and then drawn it gently across Hannah's face. It was permanent, the doctors had removed it twice with lasers, and it had come back both times.

Hannah was used to the stares it got her.

Paul cleared his throat suddenly, startling her. She looked back at him.

' "Dead before seventeen," ' he read out loud, thumbing through the scraps of paper. ' "Remember the Three Rivers – DO NOT throw this note away." "The cycle *can* be broken." "It's almost May – you know what happens then." ' He picked up the last scrap. 'And this one just says, "He's coming." '

He smoothed the papers and looked at Hannah. 'What do they mean?'

'I don't know.'

'You don't know?'

'I didn't write them,' Hannah said through her teeth.

Paul blinked and tapped his pencil faster. 'But you said you *did* write them—'

'It's my handwriting. I admit that,' Hannah said. Now that she had gotten started, the words came out in gasping bursts, unstoppable. 'And I find them in places where nobody else could put them . . . in my sock drawer, inside my pillowcase. This morning I woke up and I was holding that last one in my fist. But *I still don't write them.*'

Paul waved his pencil triumphantly. 'I see. You don't *remember* writing them.'

'I don't remember because I didn't *do* it. I would never write things like that. They're all nonsense.'

'Well.' Tap. Tap. 'I guess that depends. "It's almost May" – what happens in May?'

'May first is my birthday.'

'That's, what, a week from now? A week and a day. And you'll be . . . ?'

Hannah let out her breath. 'Seventeen.'

She saw the psychologist pick up one of the scraps, she didn't need to ask which one.

Dead before seventeen, she thought.

'You're young to be graduating,' Paul said.

'Yeah. My mom taught me at home when I was a kid, and they put me in first grade instead of kindergarten.'

Paul nodded, and she thought she could see him thinking *over-achiever*.

'Have you ever' – he paused delicately – 'had any thoughts about suicide?'

'*No*. Never. I would never do anything like that.'

'Hmm . . .' Paul frowned, staring at the notes. There was a long silence and Hannah looked around the room.

It was decorated like a psychologist's office, even though it was just part of a house. Out here in central Montana, with miles between ranches, towns were few and far between. So were psychologists, which was why Hannah was here. Paul Winfield was the only one available.

There were diplomas on the walls; books and impersonal knick-knacks were in the bookcase. A carved wooden elephant. A semi-dead plant. A silver-framed photograph. There was even an official-looking couch. And am I going to lie on that? Hannah thought. I don't *think* so.

Paper rustled as Paul pushed a note aside. Then he said gently, 'Do you feel that someone else is trying to hurt you?'

Hannah shut her eyes.

Of course she felt that someone was trying to hurt her. That was part of being paranoid, wasn't it? It proved she was crazy.

'Sometimes I have the feeling I'm being followed,' she said at last in almost a whisper.

'By . . . ?'

'I don't know.' Then she opened her eyes and said flatly, 'Something weird and supernatural that's out to get me. And I have dreams about the apocalypse.'

Paul blinked. 'The – apoc . . .'

'The end of the world. At least I guess that's what it is. Some huge battle that's coming: some giant horrible *ultimate* fight. Between the forces of . . .' She saw how he was staring at her. She looked away and went on resignedly. 'Good.' She held out one hand. 'And evil.' She held out the other. Then both hands went limp and she put them in her lap. 'So I'm crazy, right?'

'No, no, no.' He fumbled with the pencil, then patted his pocket. 'Do you happen to have a cigarette?'

She glanced at him in disbelief, and he flinched. 'No, of course you don't. What am I saying? It's a filthy habit. I quit last week.'

Hannah opened her mouth, closed it, then spoke slowly. 'Look, Doctor – I mean, Paul. I'm here because I don't *want* to be crazy. I just want to be *me* again. I want to graduate with my class. I want to have a great summer horseback riding with my best friend, Chess. And next year I want to go to Utah State and study dinosaurs and maybe find a duckbill nest site of my own. I want my *life* back. But if you can't help me . . .'

She stopped and gulped. She almost never cried; it was the ultimate loss of control. But now she couldn't help it. She could feel warmth spill out of her eyes and trace down her cheeks to tickle her chin. Humiliated, she wiped away the teardrops as Paul peered around for a tissue. She sniffed.

'I'm sorry,' he said. He'd found a box of Kleenex, but now he left it to come and stand beside her. His eyes weren't analytical now; they were blue and boyish as he tentatively squeezed her hand. 'I'm sorry, Hannah. It sounds awful. But I'm sure I *can* help you. We'll get to the bottom of it. You'll see, by summer-time you'll be graduating with Utah State and riding the duckbills, just like always.' He smiled to show it was a joke. 'All this will be behind you.'

'You really think?'

He nodded. Then he seemed to realize he was standing and holding a patient's hand: not a very professional position. He let go hastily. 'Maybe you've guessed; you're sort of my first client. Not that I'm not trained – I was in the top ten percent of my class. So. Now.' He patted his pockets, came up with the pencil, and stuck it in his mouth. He sat down. 'Let's start with the first time you remember having one of these dreams. When—'

He broke off as chimes sounded somewhere inside the house. The doorbell.

He looked flustered. 'Who would be . . .' He glanced at a clock in the bookcase and shook his head. 'Sorry, this should only take a minute. Just make yourself comfortable until I get back.'

'Don't answer it,' Hannah said.

She didn't know why she said it. All she knew was that the sound of the doorbell had sent chills running through her and that right now her heart was pounding and her hands and feet were tingling.

Paul looked briefly startled, then he gave her a gentle reassuring smile. 'I don't think it's the apocalypse at the door, Hannah. We'll talk about these feelings of apprehension when I get back.' He touched her shoulder lightly as he left the room.

Hannah sat listening. He was right, of course. There was nothing at all menacing about a doorbell. It was her own craziness.

She leaned back in the soft contoured chair and looked around the room again, trying to relax.

It's all in my head. The psychologist is going to help me . . .

At that instant the window across the room exploded.

CHAPTER 2

Hannah found herself on her feet. Her awareness was fragmented and understanding came to her in pieces because she simply couldn't take in the whole situation at once. It was too bizarre.

At first she simply thought of a bomb. The explosion was that loud. Then she realized that something had come *in* the window, that it had come flying through the glass. And that it was in the room with her now, crouching among the broken shards of window pane.

Even then, she couldn't identify it. It was too incongruous; her mind refused to recognize the shape immediately. Something pretty big, something dark, it offered. A body like a dog's but set higher, with longer legs. Yellow eyes.

And then, as if the right lens had suddenly clicked in front of her eyes, she saw it clearly.

A wolf. There was a big black *wolf* in the room with her.

It was a gorgeous animal, rangy and muscular, with ebony-coloured fur and a white streak on its throat like a bolt of lightning. It was looking at her fixedly, with an almost human expression.

Escaped from Yellowstone, Hannah thought dazedly.

The naturalists were reintroducing wolves to the park, weren't they? It couldn't be wild; Ryan Harden's great-grandpa had bragged for years about killing the last wolf in Amador county when he was a boy.

Anyway, she told herself, wolves don't attack people. They never attack people. A single wolf would never attack a full-grown teenager.

And all the time her conscious mind was thinking this, something deeper was making her move.

It made her back up slowly, never taking her eyes off the wolf, until she felt the bookcase behind her.

There's something you need to get, a voice in her mind was whispering to her. It wasn't like the voice of another person, but it wasn't exactly like her own mental voice, either. It was a voice like a dark cool wind: competent and rather bleak. *Something you saw on a shelf earlier,* it said.

In an impossibly graceful motion, from eight feet away, the wolf leaped.

There was no time to be scared. Hannah saw a bushy, flowing black arc coming at her and then she was slammed into the bookcase. For a while after that, everything was simply chaos. Books and knick-knacks were falling around her. She was trying to get her balance, trying to push the heaviness of a furry body away from her. The wolf was falling back, then jumping again as she twisted sideways to get away.

And the strangest thing was that she actually *was* getting away. Or at least evading the worst of the wolf's lunges, which seemed to be aimed at knocking her to the floor. Her body was moving as if this were somehow instinctive to her, as if she knew how to do this.

But I *don't* know this. I never fight . . . and I've certainly never played dodge ball with a wolf before . . .

As she thought it, her movements slowed. She didn't

feel sure and instinctive any longer. She felt confused.

And the wolf seemed to know it. Its eyes glowed eerily yellow in the light of a lamp that was lying on its side. They were such strange eyes, more intense and more savage than any animal's she'd ever seen. She saw it draw its legs beneath it.

Move – now, the mysterious new part of her mind snapped.

Hannah moved. The wolf hit the bookcase with incredible force, and then the bookcase itself was falling. Hannah flung herself sideways in time to avoid being crushed – but the case fell with an unholy noise directly in front of the door.

Trapped, the dark cool voice in Hannah's mind noted analytically. *No exit anymore, except the window.*

'Hannah? Hannah?' It was Paul's voice just outside the room. The door flew open – all of four inches. It jammed against the fallen bookcase. 'God! What's going on in there? Hannah? Hannah!' He sounded panicked now, banging the door uselessly against the blockage.

Don't think about him, the new part of Hannah's mind said sharply, but Hannah couldn't help it. He sounded so desperate. She opened her mouth to shout back to him, her concentration broken.

And the wolf lunged.

This time Hannah didn't move fast enough. A terrible weight smashed into her and she was falling, flying. She landed hard, her head smacking into the floorboards.

It *hurt.*

Even as she felt it, everything greyed out. Her vision went sparkling, her mind soared away from the pain, and a strange thought flickered through her head.

I'm dead now. It's over again. Oh, Isis, Goddess of Life, guide me to the other world . . .

'Hannah! Hannah! What's going on in there?' Paul's frantic voice came to her dimly.

Hannah's vision cleared and the bizarre thoughts vanished. She wasn't soaring in sparkling emptiness and she wasn't dead. She was lying on the floor with a book's sharp corner in the small of her back and a wolf on her chest.

Even in the midst of her terror, she felt a strange appalled fascination. She had never seen a wild animal this close. She could see the white-tipped guard hairs standing erect on its face and neck; she could see saliva glistening on its lolling red tongue. She could smell its breath – humid and hot, vaguely dog-like but much wilder.

And she couldn't move, she realized. The wolf was as long as she was tall, and it weighed more than she did. Pinned underneath it, she was utterly helpless. All she could do was lie there shivering as the narrow, almost delicate muzzle got closer and closer to her face.

Her eyes closed involuntarily as she felt the cold wetness of its nose on her cheek. It wasn't an affectionate gesture. The wolf was nudging at strands of her hair that had fallen across her face. Using its muzzle like a hand to push the hair away.

Oh, God, please make it stop, Hannah thought. But she was the only one who could stop this – and she didn't know how.

Now the cold nose was moving across her cheekbone. Its sniffing was loud in her ear. The wolf seemed to be smelling her, tasting her, and looking at her all at once.

No. Not looking at *me*. Looking at my birthmark.

It was another one of those ridiculous, impossible thoughts – and it snapped into place like the last piece in a puzzle deep inside her. Irrational as it was, Hannah felt absolutely certain it was true. And it set off the cool wind voice in her mind again.

Reach out, the voice whispered, quiet and businesslike. *Feel around you. The weapon has to be there somewhere. You saw it on the bookcase.* Find *it.*

The wolf stopped its explorations, seeming satisfied. It lifted its head . . . and laughed.

Really laughed. It was the eeriest and most frightening thing Hannah had ever seen. The big mouth opened, panting, showing teeth, and the yellow eyes blazed with hot bestial triumph.

Hurry, hurry.

Hannah's eyes were helplessly fixed on the sharp white teeth ten inches away from her face, but her hand was creeping out, feeling along the smooth pine floorboards around her. Her fingers glided over books, over the feathery texture of a fern – and then over something square and cold and faced with glass.

The wolf didn't seem to notice. Its lips were pulling back farther and farther. Not laughing anymore. Hannah could see its short front teeth and its long curving canines. She could see its forehead wrinkling. And she could *feel* its body vibrate in a low and vicious growl.

The sound of absolute savagery.

The cool wind voice had taken over Hannah's mind completely. It was telling her what would happen next. The wolf would sink his teeth into her throat and then shake her, tearing skin and ripping muscles away. Her blood would spray like a fountain. It would fill her severed windpipe and her lungs and her mouth. She would die gasping and choking, maybe drowning before she bled out.

Except . . . that she had silver in her hand. A silver picture frame.

Kill it, the cool voice whispered. *You've got the right weapon. Hit it dead in the eye with a corner. Drive silver into its brain.*

Hannah's ordinary mind didn't even try to figure out how a picture frame could possibly be the right weapon. It didn't object, either. But faint and faraway, there came another voice in her head. Like the cool wind voice, it wasn't hers, but it wasn't someone else's, either. It was a clear crystal voice that seemed to sparkle in jewelled colours as it spoke.

You are not a killer. You don't kill. You have never killed, no matter what happened to you. You do not kill.

I don't kill, Hannah thought slowly, in agreement.

Then you're going to die, the cool wind voice said brutally, much louder than the crystal voice. *Because this animal won't stop until either it's dead or you are. There's no other way to deal with these creatures.*

Then it happened. The wolf's mouth opened. In a lightning-fast move, it darted for her throat.

Hannah didn't think. She brought the picture frame up . . . and slammed it into the side of the wolf's head.

Not into the eye. Into the ear.

She felt the impact – hard metal against sensitive flesh. The wolf gave a yelping squeal and staggered sideways, shaking its head and hitting at its face with a forepaw. Its weight was off her for an instant, and an instant was all Hannah needed.

Her body moved without her conscious direction, sliding out from under the wolf, twisting and jumping to her feet.

She kept her grasp on the picture frame.

Now. Look around! The bookcase – no, you can't move it. The window! Go for the window.

But the wolf had stopped shaking its head. Even as Hannah started across the room, it turned and saw her. In one flowing, bushy leap it put itself between her and the window. Then it stood looking at her, every hair on its body bristling. Its teeth were bared, its ears upright, and its eyes glared with pure hatred and menace.

It's going to spring, Hannah realized.

I am not a killer. I can't kill.

You don't have any choice—

The wolf sprang.

But it never reached her. Something else came soaring through the window and knocked it off course.

This time, Hannah's eyes and brain identified the creature at once. Another wolf. My *God,* what is going on?

The new animal was grey-brown, smaller than the black wolf and not as striking. Its legs were amazingly delicate, twined with veins and sinews like a racehorse's.

A female, something faraway in Hannah's mind said with dreamlike certainty.

Both wolves had recovered their balance now. They were on their feet, bristling. The room smelled like a zoo.

And now I'm really going to die, Hannah thought. I'm going to be torn to pieces by *two* wolves. She was still clutching the picture frame, but she knew there was no chance of fighting them both off at once. They were going to rip her to bits, quarrelling over who got more of her.

Her heart was pounding so hard that it shook her body, and her ears were ringing. The female wolf was staring at her with eyes more amber than yellow, and Hannah stared back, mesmerized, waiting for it to make its move.

The wolf held the gaze for another moment, as if studying Hannah's face, in particular the left side of her face. Her cheek. Then she turned her back to Hannah and faced the black wolf.

And snarled.

Protecting me, Hannah thought, stunned. It was unbelievable – but she was beyond disbelief at this point. She had stepped out of her ordinary life and into a fairy tale full of almost-human wolves. The entire world had gone crazy and all she could do was try to deal with each moment as it came.

They're going to fight, the cool wind voice in her mind told her. *As soon as they're into it, run for the window.*

At that moment everything erupted into bedlam. The grey wolf had launched herself at the black. The room echoed with the sound of snarling, and of teeth clicking together as both wolves snapped again and again.

Hannah couldn't make out what was going on in the fight. It was just a blurred chaos as the wolves circled and darted and leaped and ducked. But it was by far the most terrifying thing she had ever witnessed. Like the worst dog fight imaginable, like the feeding frenzy of sharks. Both animals seemed to have gone berserk.

Suddenly there was a yelp of pain. Blood welled up on the grey female's flank.

She's too small, Hannah thought. Too light. She doesn't have a chance.

Help her, the crystal voice whispered.

It was an insane suggestion. Hannah couldn't even imagine trying to get in the middle of that snarling whirlwind. But somehow she found herself moving anyway. Placing herself behind the grey wolf. It didn't matter that she didn't believe she was doing it, or that she had no idea how to team up with a wolf in fighting another wolf. She was there and she was holding her silver picture frame high.

The black wolf pulled away from the fight to stare at her.

And there they stood, all three of them panting, Hannah with fear and the wolves with exertion. They were frozen like a tableau in the middle of the wrecked office, all looking at each other tensely. The black wolf on one side, his eyes shining with single-minded menace. The grey wolf on the other, blood matting her coat, bits of fur floating away from her. And Hannah right behind her, holding up the picture frame in a shaking hand.

Hannah's ears were filled with the deep reverberating sound of growling.

And then a deafening report that cut through the room like a knife.

A gunshot.

The black wolf yelped and staggered.

Hannah's senses had been focused on what was going on inside the room for so long that it was a shock to realize there was anything *outside* it. She was dimly aware that Paul's yells had stopped some time ago, but she hadn't stopped to consider what that meant.

Now, with adrenalin washing over her, she heard his voice.

'Hannah! Get out of the way!'

The shout was tense, edged with fear and anger – and determination. It came from the opposite side of the room, from the darkness outside the window.

Paul was there at the broken window with a gun. His face was pale and his hand was shaking. He was aiming in the general direction of the wolves. If he fired again he might hit either of them.

'Get into a corner!' The gun bobbed nervously.

Hannah heard herself say, 'Don't shoot!'

Her voice came out hoarse and unused-sounding. She moved to get in between the gun and the wolves.

'Don't shoot,' she said again. 'Don't hit the grey one.'

'Hit the grey one?' Paul's voice rose in something like hysterical laughter. 'I don't even know if I can hit the wall! This is the first time I've ever shot a gun. So just – just try to get out of the way!'

'No!' Hannah moved toward him, holding out her hand. 'I can shoot. Just give it to me—'

'Just move out of the *way*—'

The gun went off.

For an instant Hannah couldn't see where the bullet had gone and she wondered wildly if *she* had been shot. Then she saw that the black wolf was lurching backward. Blood dripped from its neck.

Steel won't kill it, the wind voice hissed. *You're only making it more angry . . .*

But the black wolf was swinging its head to look with blazing eyes from Hannah with her picture frame to Paul with his gun, to the grey wolf with her teeth. The grey wolf snarled just then and Hannah had never seen an animal look closer to being smug.

'One more shot . . .' Paul breathed. 'While it's cornered . . .'

Ears flat, the black wolf turned toward the only other window in the room. It launched into a vaulting leap straight toward the unbroken glass. There was a shattering crash as it went through. Glass fragments flew everywhere, tinkling.

Hannah stared dizzily at the curtains swirling first outside, then inside the room, and then her head snapped around to look at the grey wolf.

Amber eyes met hers directly. It was such a human stare . . . and definitely the look of an equal. Almost the look of a friend.

Then the grey wolf twisted and loped for the newly broken window. Two steps and a leap – she was through.

From somewhere outside there came a long drawn-out howl of anger and defiance. It was fading, as if the wolf was moving away.

Then silence.

Hannah shut her eyes.

Her knees literally felt as if they wanted to buckle. But she made herself move to the window, glass grating under her boots as she stared into the night.

The moon was bright, one day past full. She thought she could just see a dark shape loping toward the open prairie, but it might have been her imagination.

She let out her breath and sagged against the window. The silver picture frame fell to the floor.

'Are you hurt? Are you OK?' Paul was climbing through the other window. He tripped on a wastebasket getting across the room, then he was beside her, grabbing for her shoulders, trying to look her over.

'I think I'm all right.' She was numb, was what she was. She felt dazed and fragmented.

He blinked at her. 'Um . . . you have some particular fondness for grey wolves or something?'

Hannah shook her head. How could she ever explain?

They stared at each other for a moment, and then, simultaneously, they both sank to the floor, squatting among the shards of glass, breathing hard.

Paul's face was white, his red hair dishevelled, his eyes large and stunned. He ran a shaky hand over his forehead, then put the gun down and patted it. He twisted his neck to stare at the wreck of his office, the overturned bookcase, the scattered books and knick-knacks, the two broken windows, the glass fragments, the bullet hole, the flecks of blood, and the tufts of wolf hair that still drifted across the pine floorboards.

Hannah said faintly, 'So who was at the door?'

Paul blinked twice. 'Nobody. Nobody was at the door.' He added almost dreamily, 'I wonder if wolves can ring doorbells?'

'What?'

Paul turned to look straight at her.

'Has it ever occurred to you,' he blurted, 'that you may *not* be paranoid after all? I mean, that something weird and uncanny really *is* out to get you?'

'Very funny,' Hannah whispered

'I mean—' Paul gestured around the room, half laughing. He looked punch-drunk. 'I mean, you *said* something was going to happen – and something did.' He stopped laughing and looked at her with wondering speculation. 'You really did know, didn't you?'

Hannah glared at the man who was supposed to guide her back to sanity. 'Are you *crazy*?'

Paul blinked. He looked shocked and embarrassed, then he glanced away and shook his head. 'God, I don't know. Sorry; that wasn't very professional, was it? But . . .' He stared out the window. 'Well, for a moment it just seemed possible that you've got some kind of secret locked up there in your brain. Something . . . extraordinary.'

Hannah said nothing. She was trying to forget about too many things at once: the new part of her that whispered strategies, the wolves with human eyes, the silver picture frame. She had no idea what all these things added up to, and she didn't want to know. She wanted to force them away from her and go back to the safe ordinary world of Sacajawea High School.

Paul cleared his throat, still looking out the window. His voice was uncertain and almost apologetic. 'It can't be true, of course. There's got to be a rational explanation. But, well, if it were true, it occurs to me that somebody had better unlock that secret. Before something worse happens.'

CHAPTER 3

The sleek white limousine raced through the night like a dolphin underwater, carrying Thierry Descouedres away from the airport. It was taking him to his Las Vegas mansion, white walls and palm trees, limpid blue fountains and tiled terraces. Rooms full of artwork and museum-quality furniture. Everything anyone could ask for.

He shut his eyes and leaned back against the crimson cushions, wishing he were somewhere else.

'How was Hawaii, sir?' The driver's voice came from the front seat.

Thierry opened his eyes. Nilsson was a good driver. He seemed to be about Thierry's own age, around nineteen, with a neat ponytail, dark glasses despite the fact that it was night time, and a discreet expression.

'Wet, Nilsson,' Thierry said softly. He stared out the window. 'Hawaii was very . . . wet.'

'But you didn't find what you were looking for.'

'No. I didn't find what I was looking for . . . again.'

'I'm sorry, sir.'

'Thank you, Nilsson.' Thierry tried to look past his own reflection in the window. It was disturbing, seeing that young man with the white-blond hair and the old, old eyes looking back at him. He had such a pensive expression . . . so lost and so sad.

Like somebody always looking for something he can't find, Thierry thought.

He turned away from the window in determination.

'Everything been going all right while I've been gone?' he asked, picking up his cell phone. Work. Work always helped. Kept you busy, kept your mind off things, kept you away from *yourself*, basically.

'Fine, I think, sir. Mr James and Miss Poppy are back.'

'That's good. They'll make the next Circle Daybreak meeting.' Thierry's finger hovered over a button on the phone, considering whom to call. Whose need might be the most urgent.

But before he could touch it, the phone buzzed.

Thierry pressed SEND and held it to his ear. 'Thierry.'

'Sir? It's me, Lupe. Can you hear me?' The voice was faint and broken by static, but distant as it was, Thierry could hear that the caller sounded weak.

'Lupe? Are you all right?'

'I got in a fight, sir. I'm a little torn up.' She gave a gasping chuckle. 'But you should see the *other* wolf.'

Thierry reached for a leather-bound address book and a gold Mont Blanc pen. 'That's not funny, Lupe. You shouldn't be fighting.'

'I know, sir, but—'

'You've really got to restrain yourself.'

'Yes, sir, but—'

'Tell me where you are, and I'll have somebody pick you up. Get you to a doctor.' Thierry made a practice mark with the pen. No ink came out. He stared at the nib of it in mild disbelief. 'You buy an eight-hundred-dollar pen and then it doesn't write,' he murmured.

'Sir, you're not listening to me. You don't understand. *I've found her.*'

Thierry stopped trying to make the pen write. He stared at it, at his own long fingers holding the chunky, textured gold barrel, knowing that this sight would be impressed on his memory as if burned in with a torch.

'Did you hear me, sir? I've found her.'

When his voice came out at last, it was strangely distant. 'Are you sure?'

'Yes. Yes, sir, I'm sure. She's got the mark and everything. Her name is Hannah Snow.'

Thierry reached over the front seat and grabbed the astonished Nilsson with a hand like iron. He said very quietly in the driver's ear, 'Do you have a pencil?'

'A pencil?'

'Something that writes, Nilsson. An instrument to make marks on paper. Do you *have* one? Quick, because if I lose this connection, you're fired.'

'I've got a pen, sir.' One-handed, Nilsson fished in his pocket and produced a biro.

'Your salary just doubled.' Thierry took the pen and sat back. 'Where are you, Lupe?'

'The Badlands of Montana, sir. Near a town called Medicine Rock. But there's something else, sir.' Lupe's voice seemed less steady all of a sudden. 'The other wolf that fought me – he saw her, too. And he got away.'

Thierry's breath caught. 'I see.'

'I'm sorry.' Lupe was suddenly talking quickly, in a burst of emotion. 'Oh, Thierry, I'm sorry. I tried to stop him. But he got away – and now I'm afraid he's off telling . . . *her*.'

'You couldn't help it, Lupe. And I'll be there myself, soon. I'll be there to take care of – everything.' Thierry looked at the driver. 'We've got to make some stops,

Nilsson. First, the Harman store.'

'The witch place?'

'Exactly. You can triple your salary if you get there fast.'

When Hannah got to Paul Winfield's house the next afternoon, the sheriff was there. Chris Grady was an honest-to-goodness Western sheriff, complete with boots, broad-brimmed hat, and vest. The only thing missing, Hannah thought as she walked around to the back of the house where Paul was hammering boards across the broken windows, was a horse.

'Hi, Chris,' she said.

The sheriff nodded, sun-weathered skin crinkling at the corners of her eyes. She took off her hat and ran a hand through shoulder-length auburn hair. 'I see you found yourself a couple of giant timber wolves, Hannah. You're not hurt, are you?'

Hannah shook her head no. She tried to summon up a smile but failed. 'I think they were maybe wolf-dogs or something. Pure-bred wolves aren't so aggressive.'

'That print wasn't made by any wolf-dog,' Chris said. On the concrete flagstones outside the window there was a paw print made in blood. It was similar to a dog's footprint, with four pads plus claw marks showing. But it was more than six inches long by just over five inches wide.

'Judging from that, it's the biggest wolf ever heard of around here, bigger than the White Wolf of the Judith.' The sheriff's eyes drifted to the empty rectangles of the broken windows. 'Big and mean. You people be careful. Something's going on here that I don't like. I'll let you know if we catch your wolves.'

She nodded to Paul, who was sucking his finger after banging it with the hammer. Then she set her hat back on her head and strode off to her car.

Hannah stared at the paw print silently. Everyone else thought there was something going on. Everyone but her.

Because there can't be, she thought. Because it *has* to all be in my head. It has to be something I can figure out and fix quick . . . something I can control.

'Thanks for seeing me again so soon,' she said to Paul.

'Oh . . .' He gestured, tucking the hammer under his arm. 'It's no trouble. I want to get to the bottom of what's upsetting you as much as you do. And,' he admitted under his breath as he let them in the house, 'I don't actually have any other patients.'

Hannah followed him down a hallway and into his office. It was dim inside, the boards across the windows reducing the late afternoon sunlight to separate oddly-angled shafts.

She sat in the contoured chair. 'The only thing is, how *can* we get to the bottom of it? I don't understand what's upsetting me, either. It's all too strange. I mean, on the one hand, I'm clearly insane.' She spoke flatly as Paul took his seat on the opposite side of the desk. 'I have crazy dreams, I think the world is going to end, I have the feeling I'm being followed, and yesterday I started hearing voices in my head. On the other hand, me being insane doesn't explain wolves jumping through the windows.'

'Voices?' Paul murmured, looking around for a pencil. Then he gave up and faced her. 'Yeah, I know. I understand the temptation. Last night after having those wolves stare at me, I was about ready to believe that there had to be something . . .' He trailed off and shook his head, lifting papers on his desk to glance under them. 'Something . . . really strange going on. But now it's day time, and we're all rational people, and we realize that we have to deal with things rationally. And, actually, you know, I think I may have come up with a rational explanation.' He found a pencil and with an expression of vast relief began to waggle it between his fingers.

Hope stirred inside Hannah. 'An explanation?'

'Yeah. I mean, first of all, it's possible that your premonitions and things are entirely unconnected with the wolves. People never want to believe in coincidence, but it happens. But even if the two things are connected – well, I don't think that means that anybody's after you. It could be that there's some sort of disturbance in this area – something that's stirring up the whole ecosystem, making wolves crazy, doing who knows what to other animals . . . and that you're somehow sensing this. You're *attuned* to it somehow. Maybe it's earthquake weather or – or sunspots or negative ions in the air. But whatever it is, it's causing you to think that some terrible disaster is coming. That the world is ending or that you're about to be killed.'

Hannah felt the hope sink inside her, and it was more painful than not having had it at all. 'I suppose that could happen,' she said. She didn't want to hurt his feelings. 'But how does it explain this?'

She reached into the canvas bag she carried instead of a purse and pulled out a folded slip of paper.

Paul took the paper and read it. ' "They've seen you. They're going to tell him. This is your last chance to get away." ' He stuck the pencil in his mouth. 'Hmmm . . .'

'I found it this morning wrapped around my toothbrush,' Hannah said quietly.

'And it's your handwriting?'

She shut her eyes and nodded.

'And you don't remember writing it.'

'I *didn't* write it. I know I didn't.' She opened her eyes and took a deep breath. 'The notes scare me. Everything that's happening scares me. I don't understand any of it, and I don't see how I'm supposed to *fix* it if I don't understand it.'

Paul considered, chewing on the pencil gently. 'Look, whatever's happening, whoever's writing the notes, I think your subconscious mind is trying to tell you something. The dreams are evidence of that. But it's not telling you enough. There's something I was going to suggest, something I don't exactly believe in, but that we can try anyway. Something to get to your subconscious directly so we can ask it what's going on.'

Get to her subconscious directly . . . Hannah held her breath. 'Hypnosis?'

Paul nodded. 'I'm not a big hypnosis fan. It's not some magical trance like TV and the movies want you to believe. It's just a state of mind where you're a little more relaxed, a little more likely to be able to remember threatening things without choking up. But it's nothing you can't achieve yourself by doing breathing exercises at home.'

Hannah wasn't happy. Hypnosis still seemed to mean giving up control. If not to Paul, then to her own subconscious.

But what else am I supposed to do? She sat and listened to the quiet helplessness in her mind for a moment. Not a peep from the cool wind voice or the crystal voice – and that was *good*, as far as she was concerned. Still, it pointed up the fact that she didn't have an alternative.

She looked at Paul. 'OK. Let's do it.'

'Great.' He stood, then reached for a book on the corner of his desk. 'Always assuming I remember how . . . OK, why don't you lie down on the couch?'

Hannah hesitated, then shrugged. If I'm going to do it, I might as well do it right. She lay down and stared at the dark beams in the ceiling. In spite of how miserable she was feeling, she had an almost irresistible impulse to giggle.

Here she was on a real psychologist's couch, waiting to be hypnotized. Her friends at school would never consider even going to a shrink – out here in Montana craziness was OK. After all, you had to be a little eccentric to be living in this hard land in the first place. What wasn't OK was admitting you couldn't deal with it on your own, paying too much attention to it, asking for help. And allowing yourself to be hypnotized was even worse.

They all think I'm the most independent and together of any of them. If they could see me now.

'OK, I want you to get comfortable and shut your eyes,' Paul said. He was perched with one hip on the edge of his desk, leg swinging, book in hand. His voice was quiet and soothing – the professional voice.

Hannah shut her eyes.

'Now I want you to imagine yourself floating. Just floating and feeling very relaxed. There's nothing you need to think about and nowhere you need to go. And now you're seeing yourself enveloped by a beautiful violet light. It's bathing your entire body and it's making you more and more relaxed . . .'

The couch *was* surprisingly comfortable. Its curves fit under her, supporting her without being intrusive. It was easy to imagine that she was floating, easy to imagine the light around her.

'And now you feel yourself floating down deeper . . . into a deeper state of relaxation . . . and you're surrounded by a deep blue light. The blue light is all around you, shining through you, and it's making you more comfortable, more relaxed . . .'

The soft soothing voice went on, and at its direction Hannah imagined waves of coloured light bathing her body. Deep blue, emerald green, golden yellow, glowing orange. Hannah saw it all. It was amazing and effortless;

her mind just showed her the pictures.

And as the colours came and went she felt herself becoming more and more relaxed, warm and almost weightless. She couldn't feel the couch underneath her any longer. She was floating on light.

'And now you're seeing a ruby red light, very deep, very relaxing. You're so relaxed; you're calm and comfortable, and everything feels safe. Nothing will upset you; you can answer all my questions without ever feeling distressed. Do you understand me?'

'Yes,' Hannah said. She was aware of saying it, but it wasn't exactly as if *she* had said it. She wasn't aware of *planning* to say it. Something within her seemed to be answering Paul using her voice.

But it wasn't frightening. She still felt relaxed, floating in the ruby light.

'All right. I'm now speaking to Hannah's subconscious. You will be able to remember things that Hannah's waking mind isn't aware of, even things that have been repressed. Do you understand?'

'Yes.' Again, the voice seemed to come before Hannah decided to speak.

'Good. Now, I've got this last note here, the one you found wrapped around your toothbrush this morning. Do you remember this note?'

'Yes.' Of course.

'OK, that's good. And now I want you to go back in your mind, back to the time that this note was written.'

This time Hannah was aware of a need to speak. 'But how can I do that? I don't *know* when it was written. I didn't write—'

'Just – just – just let go, Hannah,' Paul said, overriding her. His voice soothing again, he added, 'Feel relaxed, feel yourself becoming very relaxed, and let your conscious mind go. Just tell yourself to go back to the time this note was written. Don't worry about *how*. See the ruby light and think "I will go back". Are you doing that?'

'Yes,' Hannah said. Go back, she told herself gamely. Just relax and go back, OK?

'And now, a picture is beginning to form in your mind. You are seeing something. What are you seeing?'

Hannah felt something inside her give way. She seemed to be falling into the ruby light. Her ordinary mind was suspended; it seemed to have been shuttled off to the side somewhere. In this odd dream-like state, nothing could surprise her.

Paul's voice was gently insistent. 'What are you seeing?'

Hannah saw it.

A tiny picture that seemed to open up, unfold as she stared at it.

'I see myself,' she whispered.

'Where are you?'

'I don't know. Wait, maybe I'm in my room.' She could see herself, wearing something long and white – a nightgown. No, she *was* that self, she was in her bedroom, wearing her nightgown. She was in Paul's office, lying on the couch, but she was in her bedroom at the same time. How strange, she thought dimly.

'All right, now the picture will get clearer. You'll begin to see things around you. Just relax and you'll begin to see them. Now, what are you doing?'

Without feeling anything – except a kind of distant amusement and resignation – Hannah said, 'Writing a note.'

Paul muttered something that sounded like, '*Aha*.' But it might have been, 'Uh-*huh*.' Then he said softly, 'And why are you writing it?'

'I don't know – to warn myself. I have to warn myself.'

'About what?'

Hannah felt herself shake her own head helplessly.

'OK . . . what are you feeling as you write it?'

'Oh . . .' That was easy. Paul was undoubtedly expecting her to say something like 'fear' or 'anxiety.' But that wasn't the strongest thing she was feeling. Not the strongest at all.

'Longing,' Hannah whispered. She moved her head restlessly on the couch. 'Just – longing.'

'I beg your pardon?'

'I want – so much . . . I want . . .'

'What do you want?'

'*Him.*' It came out as a sob. Hannah's ordinary mind watched somewhere in amazement, but Hannah's body was entirely taken over by the feeling, racked with it. 'I know it's impossible. It's danger and death to me. But *I don't care*. I can't help it . . .'

'Whoa, whoa, whoa. I mean, you're feeling very relaxed. You're very calm and you can answer my questions. Who is this person that you're longing for?'

'The one who comes,' Hannah said softly and hopelessly. 'He's wicked and evil . . . I know that. She explained it all to me. And I know he'll kill me. The way he always has. *But I want him.*'

She was trembling. She could feel her own body radiating heat – and she could hear Paul swallow. Somehow in this expanded state of consciousness she seemed to be able to see him, as if she could be everywhere at once. She knew he was sitting there on the edge of the desk, looking at her dazedly, bewildered by the transformation in the young woman on his couch.

She knew he could see *her*, her face pale and glowing from inner heat, her breath coming quickly, her body gripped by a fine muscular tremor. And she knew he was stirred, and frightened.

'Oh, boy.' Paul's breath came out and he shifted on the desk. He bowed his head, then lifted it, looking for a pencil. 'OK, I have to admit, I'm lost. Let's just go back to the beginning here. You feel that somebody is after you, and that he's tried to kill you before? Some old boyfriend who's stalking you, maybe?'

'No. He hasn't tried to kill me. He *has* killed me.'

'He has killed you.' Paul bit his pencil. He muttered, 'I should have known better than to have started this. I don't believe in hypnosis anyway.'

'And he's going to do it again. I'll die before my seventeenth birthday. It's my punishment for loving him. It always happens that way.'

'Right. OK. OK, let's try something *really* basic here . . . Does this mystery guy have a name?'

Hannah lifted a hand and let it drop. 'When?' she whispered.

'What?'

'*When?*'

'When what? What?' Paul shook his head. 'Oh, hell—'

Hannah spoke precisely. 'He's used different names at different times. He's had – hundreds, I guess. But I think of him as Thierry. Thierry Descouedres. Because that's the one he's used for the last couple of lifetimes.'

There was a long silence. Then Paul said, 'The last couple of . . . ?'

'Lifetimes. It may still be his name now. The last time I saw him he said he wouldn't bother to change it anymore. He wouldn't bother to hide any longer.'

Paul said, 'Oh, God.' He stood, walked to the window, and put his head in his hands. Then he turned back to Hannah. 'Are we talking about . . . I mean, tell me we're not talking about . . .' He paused and then his voice came out soft and boneless. 'The Big R? You know . . .' He winced. 'Reincarnation?'

A long silence.

Then Hannah heard her own voice say flatly, 'He hasn't been reincarnated.'

'Oh.' Paul's breath came out in relief. 'Well, thank God. You had me scared there for a minute.'

'He's been alive all this time,' Hannah said. 'He isn't human, you know.'

CHAPTER 4

Thierry knelt by the window, careful not to make a noise or disturb the dry earth beneath him. It was a skill so familiar to his body that he might have been born with it. Darkness was his native environment; he could melt into a shadow at an instant's notice or move more quietly than a stalking cat. But right now he was looking into the light.

He could see her. Just the curve of her shoulder and the spill of her hair, but he knew it was her.

Beside him, Lupe was crouched, her thin body human but quivering with animal alertness and tension. She whispered, softer than a breath, 'All right?'

Thierry tore his gaze from that shoulder to look at her. Lupe's face was bruised, one eye almost closed, lower lip torn. But she was smiling. She'd stuck around Medicine Rock until Thierry had arrived, tailing the girl called Hannah Snow, making sure no harm came to her.

Thierry took Lupe's hand and kissed it. *You're an angel,* he told her, and made even less sound than she had in speaking because he didn't use his vocal chords at all. His voice was telepathic. *And you deserve a long vacation. My limo's at the tourist resort in Clearwater; take it to the airport at Billings.*

'But – you're not planning to stay here alone, are you? You need backup, sir. If *she* comes—'

I can take care of things. I brought something to protect Hannah. Besides she *won't do anything until she talks to me.*

'But—'

Lupe, go. His tone was gentle, but it was unmistakably not the urging of a friend anymore. It was the order of her liege lord, Thierry of the Night World, who was accustomed to being obeyed. Funny, Thierry thought, how you never realized *how* accustomed you were to being obeyed until somebody defied you. Now, he turned away from Lupe and looked through the cracks in the boarded-up window again.

And promptly forgot that Lupe existed. The girl on the couch had turned. He could see her face.

Shock coursed through him.

He had known it was her – but he hadn't known that it would *look* so much like her. Like the way she had looked the first time, the first time she had been born, the first time he had seen her. This was what he thought of as her true face, and though he'd seen various approximations of it through the years, he'd never seen *it* again. Until now.

This was the exact image of the girl he'd fallen in love with.

The same long, straight fair hair, like silk in different shades of wheat colour, spilling over her shoulders. The same wide grey eyes that seemed full of light. The same steady expression, the same tender mouth, upper lip indenting the lower to give her a look of unintentional sensuality. The same fine bone structure, the high cheekbones and graceful line of jaw that made her a sculptor's dream.

The only thing that was different was the birthmark.

The psychic brand.

It was the colour of watered wine held up to the light, of watermelon ice, of a pink tourmaline, the palest of gemstones. Blushing rose. Like one large petal, slantwise beneath her cheekbone. As if she'd laid a rose against her cheek for a moment and it had left its imprint on her flesh.

To Thierry, it was beautiful, because it was part of her. She'd worn it in every lifetime after the first. But at the same time the very sight of it made his throat clamp shut and his fists clench in helpless grief and fury – fury against himself. The mark was *his* shame, his punishment. And his penance was to watch her wear it in her innocence through the years.

He would pour out his blood on the dry Montana dirt right now if it would take the mark away. But nothing in either the Night World or the human world could do that – at least nothing he'd found in uncounted years of searching.

Oh, Goddess, he loved her.

He hadn't allowed himself to *feel* it for so long – because the feeling could drive him insane while he was away from her. But now it came over him in a flood that he couldn't have resisted if he'd tried. It made his heart pound and his body tremble. The sight of her lying there, warm and alive, separated from him by only a few flimsy boards and an equally flimsy human male . . .

He wanted her. He wanted to yank off the boards, step through the window, brush aside the red-haired man, and take her in his arms. He wanted to carry her off into the night, holding her close to his heart, to some secret place where nobody could ever find her to hurt her.

He didn't. He knew . . . from experience . . . that it didn't work. He'd done it once or twice, and he'd paid for it. She had hated him before she died.

He would never risk that again.

And so now, on this spring night near the turn of the millennium in the state of Montana in the United States of America, all Thierry could do was kneel outside a window and watch the newest incarnation of his only love.

He didn't realize at first, though, what his only love was actually doing. Lupe had told him that Hannah Snow was seeing a psychologist. But it was only now, listening to what was going on in the room that Thierry slowly realized exactly what Hannah and the psychologist were up to.

They were trying to recover her memories. Using hypnosis. Breaking into her subconscious as if it were some bank vault.

It was dangerous.

Not just because the guy performing the hypnosis didn't seem to know what he was doing. But because Hannah's memory was a time-bomb, full of trauma for her and deadly knowledge for any human.

They shouldn't be doing this.

Every muscle in Thierry's body was tense. But there was no way he could stop it. He could only listen – and wait.

Paul repeated with slow resignation, 'He's not human.'

'No. He's a Lord of the Night World. He's powerful . . . and evil,' Hannah whispered. 'He's lived for thousands of years.' She added, almost absently, *'I'm* the one who's been reincarnated.'

'Oh, terrific. Well, that's a twist.'

'You don't believe me?'

Paul seemed to suddenly remember that he was talking with a patient, and a hypnotized patient at that. 'No, I – I mean, I don't know what to believe. If it's a fantasy, there's got to be something underneath it, some psychological reason for you to make it all up. And that's what we're looking for. What all this means to *you*.' He hesitated, then said with new determination, 'Let's take you back to the first time you met this guy. OK, I want you to relax in the light; you're feeling very good. And now I want you to go back through time, just like turning back the pages of a book. In your mind, go back . . .'

Hannah's ordinary mind was intruding, waking up, overriding the dreamy part of her that had been answering Paul's questions. 'Wait, I – I don't know if that's a good idea.'

'We can't figure this out until we find out what it all symbolizes; what it means to you.'

Hannah still didn't feel convinced, but she had the feeling she wasn't supposed to argue under hypnosis. Maybe it doesn't matter, though, she thought. I'm waking up now; I probably won't be *able* to go back.

'I want you to see yourself as fifteen years old, see yourself as fifteen. Go back to the time when you were fifteen. And now I want you to see yourself at twelve years old; go in your mind to the time when you are twelve. Now go farther back, see yourself at nine years old, at six years old, at three years old. Now go back and see yourself as a baby, as an infant. Feel very comfortable and see yourself as a tiny baby.'

Hannah couldn't help but listen. She *did* feel comfortable, and her mind did show her pictures as the years seemed to turn back. It was like watching a film of her life running backward, herself getting smaller and smaller, and in the end tiny and bald.

'And now,' the soothing, irresistible voice said, 'I want you to go *farther* back. Back to the time before you were born. The time before you were born as Hannah Snow. You are floating in the red light, you feel very relaxed, and you are going back, back . . . to the time when you *first* met this man you think of as Thierry. Whatever that time might be, go back. Go back to the first time.'

Hannah was being drawn down a tunnel.

She had no control and she was scared. It wasn't like the rumoured near-death tunnel. It was red, with translucent, shining, pulsing walls – something like a womb. And she was being pulled or sucked through it at ever-increasing speed.

No, she thought. But she couldn't say anything. It was all happening too fast and she couldn't make a sound.

'Back to the first time,' Paul intoned, and his words set up a sort of echo in Hannah's head, a whispering of many voices. As if a hundred Hannahs had all gotten together and murmured sibilantly, 'The First Time. The First Time.'

'Go back . . . and you will begin to see pictures. You will see yourself, maybe in a strange place. Go back and see this.'

The First Time . . .

No, Hannah thought again. And something very deep inside her whimpered, 'I don't want to see it.' But she was still being pulled through the soft red tunnel, faster and faster. She had a feeling of unimaginable distance being crossed. And then . . . she had a feeling of some threshold being reached.

The First Time..

She exploded into darkness, squirted out of the tunnel like a watermelon seed between wet fingers.

Silence. Dark. And then – a picture. It opened like a tiny leaf unfolding out of a seed, got bigger until it surrounded her. It was like a scene from a movie, except that it was all around her, she seemed to be floating in the middle of it.

'What do you see?' came Paul's voice softly from very far away.

'I see . . . me,' Hannah said. 'It's me, it looks just like me. Except that I don't have a birthmark.' She was full of wonder.

'Where are you? What do you see yourself doing?'

'I don't know where I am.' Hannah was too amazed to be frightened now. It was so strange . . . she could see this better than any memory of her real life. The scene was incredibly detailed. At the same time, it was completely unfamiliar to her. 'What I'm doing . . . I'm holding . . . something. A rock. And I'm doing something with it to a little tiny . . . something.' She sighed, defeated, then added, 'I'm wearing *animal skins*! It's a sort of shirt and pants all made of skins. It's unbelievably . . . primitive. Paul, there's a cave behind me.'

'Sounds like you're *really* far back.' Paul's voice sounded in stark contrast to Hannah's wonder and excitement. He was clearly bored. Amused, resigned, but bored.

'And – there's a girl beside me and she looks like Chess. Like my best friend, Chess. She's got the same face, the same eyes. She's wearing skins, too . . . some kind of skin dress.'

'Yeah, and it has about the detail of most of the past-life regressions in this book,' Paul said wryly. Hannah could tell he was flipping pages. 'You're doing *something* to *something* with a rock. You're wearing *some kind* of skins. The book's full of descriptions like that. People who want to imagine themselves in the olden days, but who don't know the first thing about them,' he muttered to himself.

Hannah didn't wait for him to remember that he was talking to a hypnotized patient. 'But you didn't tell me to *be* the person back then. You just told me to see it.'

'Huh? Oh. OK, then, *be* that person.' He said it so casually.

Panic spurted through Hannah. 'Wait – I . . .'

But it was happening. She was falling, dissolving, merging into the scene around her. She was becoming the girl in front of the cave.

The First Time . . .

Distantly, she heard her own voice whispering, 'I'm holding a flint burin, a tool for drilling. I'm boring holes in the tooth of an arctic fox.'

'Be that person,' Paul was repeating mechanically, still in the bored voice. Then he said, 'What?'

'Mother's going to be furious – I'm supposed to be sorting fruit we stored last winter for the Spring Gathering. There's not much left and it's mostly rotten. But Ran killed a fox and gave the skull to Ket, and we've spent all morning knocking the teeth out and making them into a necklace for Ket. Ket just *has* to have something new to wear every festival.'

She heard Paul say softly, 'Oh, my God . . .' Then he swallowed and said, 'Wait, you want to be a paleontologist, right? You know about old things . . .'

'I want to be a what? I'm going to be a shaman, like Old Mother. I should get married, but there's nobody I want. Ket keeps telling me I'll meet somebody at a gathering, but I don't think so.' She shivered. 'Weird – I've got chills all of a sudden. Old Mother says she can't see my destiny. She pretends that's nothing to worry about, but I know *she's* worried. That's why she wants me to be a shaman, so I can fight back if the spirits have something rotten in mind for me.'

Paul said, 'Hannah – uh, let's just make sure we can get you out of this, all right? You know, in case that should become necessary. Now, when I clap my hands you're going to awaken completely refreshed. OK? OK?'

'My name's Hana.' It was pronounced slightly differently: *Hah-na*. 'And I'm already awake. Ket is laughing at me. She's threading the teeth on a sinew string. She says I'm daydreaming. She's right; I wrecked the hole for this tooth.'

'When I clap my hands, you're going to wake up. When I clap my hands, you're going to wake up. You will be Hannah Snow in Montana.' A clap. 'Hannah, how do you feel?' Another clap. 'Hannah? Hannah?'

'It's Hana. Hana of the River People. And I don't know what you're talking about; I can't *be* somebody else.' She stiffened. 'Wait – something's happening. There's some kind of commotion from the river. Something's going on.'

The voice was desperate. 'When I clap my hands—'

'*Shh*. Be quiet.' Something was happening and she had to see it, she had to know. She had to stand up . . .

Hana of the Three Rivers stood up.

'Everybody's all excited by the river,' she told Ket.

'Maybe Ran fell in,' Ket said. 'No, that's too much to hope for. Hana, what am I going to do? He wants to mate me, but I just can't picture it. I want somebody *interesting*, somebody *different* . . .' She held up the half-finished necklace. 'So what do you think?'

Hana barely glanced at her. Ket looked wonderful, with her short dark hair, her glowing slanted green eyes, and her mysterious smile. The necklace was attractive; red beads alternated with delicate milky-white teeth. 'Fine, beautiful. You'll break every heart at the gathering. I'm going down to the river.'

Ket put down the necklace. 'Well, if you insist – wait for me.'

The river was broad and fast-flowing, covered with little white-capped waves because it had just been joined by two tributaries. Hana's people had lived in the limestone caves by the three rivers for longer than anyone could remember.

Ket was behind her as Hana made her way through new green cattails to the bend in the river. And then she saw what the fuss was about.

There was a stranger crouching in the reeds. That was exciting enough – strangers didn't come very often. But this stranger was like no man Hana had ever seen.

'It's a demon,' Ket whispered, awed.

It was a young man, a boy a few years older than Hana herself. He might have been handsome in other circumstances. His hair was very light blond, lighter than the dry grass of the steppes. His face was well-made; his tall body was lithe. Hana could see almost all of that body because he was only wearing a brief leather loincloth. That didn't bother her; everybody went naked in the summer when it was hot enough. But this wasn't summer; it was spring and the days could still be chilly. No sane person would go travelling without clothes.

But that wasn't what shocked Hana, what held her standing there rigid with her heart pounding so hard she couldn't breathe. It was the rest of the boy's appearance. Ket was right – he was clearly a demon.

His eyes were wrong. More like the eyes of a lynx or a wolverine than the eyes of a person. They seemed to throw the pale sunlight back at you when you looked into them. But the eyes were nothing compared to the teeth. His canine teeth were long and delicately curved. They came to a sharp and very non-human point.

Almost involuntarily, Hana looked down at the fox tooth she still held in her palm. Yes, they were like that, only bigger.

The boy was filthy, caked with mud from the river, his blond hair ruffled crazily, his eyes staring wildly from side to side. There was blood on his mouth and chin.

'He's a demon, all right,' one of the men said. Five men were standing around the crouching boy, several of them with spears, others with hastily grabbed rocks. 'What else could have a human body with animal eyes and teeth?'

'A spirit?' Hana said. She didn't realize that she was going to say it until the words were out. But then, with everybody looking at her, she drew herself up tall. 'Whether he's a demon or a spirit, you'd better not hurt him. It's Old Mother who should decide what to do with him. This is a matter for shamans.'

'You're not a shaman yet,' another of the men said. It was Arno, a very broad-shouldered man who was the leader of the hunters. Hana didn't like him.

And she wasn't sure why she had spoken up in favour of the stranger. There was something in his eyes, the look of a suffering animal. He seemed so alone, and so frightened – and so much in pain, even though there were no visible wounds on his body.

'She's right, we'd better take him to Old Mother,' one of the hunters said. 'Should we hit him on the head and tie him up, or do you think we can just herd him?'

But at that moment, a high thin sound came to Hana over the rushing of the river. It was a woman screaming.

'Help me! Somebody come help me! Ryl's been attacked!'

CHAPTER 5

Hana turned and hurried up the riverbank. The woman screaming was Sada, her mother's sister, and the girl who was stumbling beside her was Ryl, Hana's little cousin.

Ryl was a pretty girl, ten years old. But right now she looked dazed and almost unconscious. And her neck and the front of her leather tunic were smeared with blood.

'What happened?' Hana gasped, running to put her arms around her cousin.

'She was out looking for new greens. I found her lying on the ground – I thought she was dead!' Sada's face contorted in grief. She was speaking rapidly, almost incoherently. 'And look at this – look at her neck!'

On Ryl's pale neck, in the centre of the blood, Hana could just make out two small marks. They looked like the marks of sharp teeth – but only two teeth.

'It had to be an animal,' Ket breathed from behind Hana. 'But what animal only leaves the marks of two teeth?'

Hana's heart felt tight and oddly heavy at once – like a stone falling inside her. Sada was already speaking.

'It wasn't an animal! She says it was a man, a boy! She says he threw her down and bit her – and he – drank her blood.' Sada began to sob, clutching Ryl to her. 'Why would he want to do that? Oh, please, somebody help me! My daughter's been hurt!'

Ryl just stared dazedly over her mother's arm.

Ket said faintly, 'A boy . . .'

Hana gulped and said, 'Let's take her to Old Mother . . .' But then she stopped and looked toward the river.

The men were driving the stranger up the bank. He was snarling, terrified and angry, but when he saw Ryl, his expression changed.

He stared at her, his wounded animal eyes sick and dismayed. To Hana, it seemed as if he could hardly stand to look at her, but he couldn't look away. His gaze was fixed on the little girl's throat.

And then he turned away, his eyes shut, his head falling into his hands. Every movement showed anguish. It was as if all the fight had gone out of him at once.

Hana looked back and forth in horror from the girl with blood on her throat to the stranger with blood on his mouth. The connection was obvious and nobody had to make it out loud.

But *why*? she thought, feeling nauseated and dizzy. Why would anybody want to drink a girl's blood? No animal and no human did that.

He must be a demon after all.

Arno stepped forward. He gripped Ryl's chin gently, turning her head toward the stranger.

'Was he the one who attacked you?'

Ryl's dazed eyes stared straight ahead – and then she suddenly seemed to focus. Her pupils got big and she looked at the face of the stranger.

Then she started screaming.

Screaming and screaming, hands flying up to cover her eyes. Her mother began to sob, rocking her. Some of the men began to shout at the stranger, jabbing spears at him, overcome with shock and horror. All the sounds merged together in a terrifying cacophony in Hana's head.

Hana found herself trembling. She reached automatically for little Ryl, not knowing how to comfort her. Ket was crying. Sada was wailing as she held her child. People were streaming out of the limestone cave, yelling, trying to find out what all the noise was about.

And through it all, the stranger huddled, his eyes shut, his face a mask of grief.

Arno's voice rose above the others. 'I think we hunters know what to do with him. This is no longer a matter for shamans!' He was looking at Hana as he said it.

Hana looked back. She couldn't speak. There was no reason for her to care what happened to the stranger – but she did care. He had hurt her cousin . . . but he was so wretched, so unhappy.

Maybe he couldn't help it, she thought suddenly. She didn't know where the idea came from, but it was the kind of instinct that made Old Mother say she should be a shaman. Maybe . . . he didn't want to do it, but something drove him to. And now he's sorry and ashamed. Maybe . . . oh, I don't know!

Still trembling, she found herself speaking out loud again. 'You can't just kill him. You have to take him to Old Mother.'

'It's none of her business!'

'It's her business if he's a demon! You're just co-leader, Arno. You take care of the hunting. But Old Mother is the leader in spiritual things.'

Arno's face went tight and angry. 'Fine, then,' he said. 'We take him to Old Mother.'

Jabbing with their spears, the men drove the stranger into the cave. By then, most of the people of the clan had gathered around and they were muttering angrily.

Old Mother was the oldest woman in the clan – the great grandmother of Hana and Ryl and almost everybody. She had a face covered with wrinkles and a body like a dried stick. But her dark eyes were full of wisdom. She was the clan's shaman. She was the one who interceded directly with the Earth Goddess, the Bright Mother, the Giver of Life who was above all other spirits.

She listened to the story seriously, sitting on her leather pallet while the others crowded around her. Hana edged close to her and Ryl was placed in her lap.

'They want to kill him,' Hana murmured in the old woman's ear when the story was over. 'But look at his eyes. I know he's sorry, and I think maybe he didn't mean to hurt Ryl. Can you talk to him, Old Mother?'

Old Mother knew a lot of different languages; she'd travelled very far when she had been young. But now, after trying several, she shook her head.

'Demons don't speak human languages,' Arno said scornfully. He was standing with his spear ready although the stranger squatting in front of the old woman showed no signs of trying to run away.

'He's not a demon,' Old Mother said, with a severe glance at Arno. Then she added slowly, 'But he's certainly not a man, either. I'm not sure what he is. The Goddess has never told me anything about people like him.'

'Then obviously the Goddess isn't interested,' Arno said with a shrug. 'Let the hunters take care of him.'

Hana gripped the old woman's thin shoulder.

Old Mother put a twig-like hand on Hana's. Her dark eyes were grave and sad.

'The one thing we *do* know is that he's capable of great harm,' she said softly. 'I'm sorry, child, but I think Arno is right.' Then she turned to Arno. 'It's getting dark. We'd better shut him up somewhere tonight; then in the morning we can decide what to do with him. Maybe the Goddess will tell me something about him as I sleep.'

But Hana knew better. She saw the look on Arno's face as he and the other hunters led the stranger away. And she heard the cold and angry muttering of others in the clan.

In the morning the stranger would die. Unpleasantly, if Arno had his way.

It was probably what he deserved. It was none of Hana's business. But that night, as she lay on her leather pallet underneath her warm furs, she couldn't sleep.

It was as if the Goddess were poking her, telling her that something was wrong. Something had to be done. And there was nobody else to do it.

Hana thought about the look of anguish in the stranger's eyes.

Maybe . . . if he went somewhere far away . . . he couldn't hurt other people. Out on the steppes there were no people to hurt. Maybe that was what the Goddess wanted. Maybe he was some creature that had wandered out of the spirit world and the Goddess would be angry if he were killed.

Hana didn't know; she wasn't a shaman yet. All she knew was that she felt pity for the stranger and she couldn't keep still any longer.

A short time before dawn she got up. Very quietly, she went to the back of the cave and picked up a spare waterskin and some hard patties of travelling food. Then she crept to the side cave where the stranger was shut up.

The hunters had set a sort of fence in front of the cave, like the fences they used to trap animals. It was made of branches and bones lashed together with cords. A hunter was beside the fence, one hand on his spear. He was leaning back against the cave wall, and he was asleep with his mouth open.

Hana edged past him. Her heart was pounding so loudly she was certain it would wake him up. But the hunter didn't move.

Slowly, carefully, Hana pulled one side of the fence outward.

From the darkness inside the cave, two eyes gleamed at her, throwing back the light of the fire.

Hana pressed fingers against her mouth in a sign to be quiet, then beckoned.

It was only then that she realized exactly how dangerous what she was doing was. She was letting him out – what was to stop him from rushing past her and into the main cave, grabbing people and biting them?

But the stranger did no such thing. He didn't move. He sat and his two eyes glowed at Hana.

He's not going to come, she realized. He *won't*.

She beckoned again, more urgently.

The stranger still sat. Hana's eyes were getting used to the darkness in the side cave and now she could see that he was shaking his head. He was determined to stay here and let the clan kill him.

Hana got mad.

Balancing the fence precariously, she jabbed a finger at the stranger, then jerked a thumb over her shoulder. You – out! the gesture meant. She put behind it all the authority of a descendant of Old Mother's, a woman destined to be co-leader of the clan someday.

And when the stranger didn't obey immediately, she reached for him.

That scared him. He shrank back, seeming more alarmed than he had at anything else that had happened so far. He seemed afraid for her to touch him.

Afraid he might hurt me, Hana thought. She didn't know what put the idea into her mind. And she didn't waste time wondering about it. She simply pressed her advantage, reaching for him again, using his fear to make him go where she wanted him to.

She herded him into the main cave and through it. They both moved like shadows among the shelters built along either side of the cave, Hana feeling certain that they were about to be caught any minute. But nobody caught them.

When they got outside she guided him toward the river. Then she pointed downstream. She put the food and the waterskin in his hands and made far-flung gestures that meant, Go far away. *Very* far away. Very, *very* far. She was going into a pantomime indicating what Arno would do with his spear if the stranger ever came back when she noticed the way he was looking at her.

The moon was up and so bright that she could see every detail of the strange boy's face. And now he was looking at her steadily, with the quiet concentration of a hunting animal, a carnivore. At the same time there was something bleak and terribly human in his eyes.

Hana stopped her pantomime. All at once, the space around the cave seemed very large, and she felt very small. She heard night noises, the croaking of frogs and the rushing of the river, with a peculiar intensity.

I should never have brought him out here. I'm *alone* with him out here. What was I thinking?

There was a long pause while they stood looking at each other silently. The stranger's eyes were very dark, as bottomless and ageless as Old Mother's. Hana could see that his eyelashes were long and she realized again, dimly, that he was handsome.

He lifted the packet of travelling food, looked at it, then

with a sudden gesture he threw it on the ground. He did the same with the waterskin. Then he sighed.

Hana was bristling, going from fear to annoyance and back again. What was he doing? Did he think she was trying to poison him? She picked up the food packet, broke a piece of travelling food off and put it in her mouth. Chewing, she extended the packet toward him again. She made gestures from packet to mouth, saying out loud, 'You need to eat food. Eat! Eat!'

He was watching her steadily. He took the packet from her, touched his mouth, and shook his head. He dropped it at his feet again.

He means it isn't food to him.

Hana realized it with a shock. She stood and stared at the strange boy.

The food isn't food to him and the water isn't drink. But Ryl's blood . . . he drank that.

Blood is his food and drink.

There was another long pause. Hana was very frightened. Her mouth was trembling and tears had come to her eyes. The stranger was still looking at her quietly, but she could see the fangs indenting his lower lip now and his eyes were reflecting moonlight.

He was looking at her throat.

We're out here alone . . . he could have attacked me at any time, Hana thought. He could attack me right now. He looks very strong. But he hasn't touched me. Even though he's starving, I think. And he looks so grieved, so sad . . . and so hungry.

Her thoughts were tumbling like a piece of bark tossed on the river. She felt very dizzy.

It hurt Ryl . . . but it didn't *kill* Ryl. Ryl was sitting up and eating before we all went to sleep tonight. Old Mother said she's going to get well.

If it didn't kill her, it wouldn't kill me.

Hana swallowed. She looked at the strange boy with the glowing animal eyes. She saw that he wasn't going to move toward her even though a fine trembling had taken over his body and he couldn't seem to look away from her neck.

What good does it do to send him off starving? There's no other clan near here. He'll just have to come back. And I was right before; he doesn't want to do it, but he *has* to do it. Maybe somebody put a curse on him, made it so he starves unless he drinks blood.

There's nobody else to help him.

Very slowly, her eyes on the stranger, Hana lifted the hair from one side of her neck. She exposed her throat, leaning her head back slightly.

Hunger sparked in the strange boy's eyes – and then something blazed in them so quickly and so hot that it swallowed up the hunger. Shock and anger. He was staring at her face, now, not her neck. He shook his head vehemently, glaring.

Hana touched her neck and then her mouth, then made the far-flung gestures. Eat. Then go away.

And for the Goddess's sake, hurry up, she thought, shutting her eyes. Before I panic and change my mind. She was crying now. She couldn't help it. She clenched her fists and her teeth and waited grimly, trying to hang on to her resolve.

When he touched her for the first time, it was to take her hand.

Hana opened her eyes. He was looking at her with such infinite sadness. He smoothed out her fist gently, then kissed her hand. Among any people, it was a gesture of gratitude . . . and reverence.

And it sent startling tingles through Hana. A feeling

that was almost like shivers, but warm. A lightness in her head and a weakness in her legs. A sense of awe and wonder that she'd only ever felt before when Old Mother was teaching her to communicate with the Goddess.

She could see startled reaction in the stranger's eyes, too. He was feeling the same things, and they were equally new to him. Hana *knew* that. But then he dropped her hand quickly and she knew that he was also afraid. The feelings were dangerous – because they drew the two of them together.

One long moment while they stood and she saw moonlight in his eyes.

Then he turned to go.

Hana watched him, her throat aching, knowing he was going to die.

And somehow that wrenched her insides in a way she'd never experienced before. Although she kept herself standing still, with her head high, she could feel the tears running down her cheeks. She didn't know why she felt this way – but it hurt her terribly. It was as if she were losing something . . . infinitely precious . . . before she'd had a chance to know it.

The future seemed grey, now. Empty. Lonely.

Cold and desolate, she stood by the rushing river and felt the wind blow through her. So alone . . .

'Hannah! Hannah! Wake up!'

Someone was shouting, but it wasn't a voice from her cave. It sounded – faraway – and seemed to come from all directions, or maybe from the sky itself.

And it was saying her name wrong.

'Hannah, wake up! Please! Open your eyes!' The faraway voice was frantic.

And then there was another voice, a quiet voice that seemed to strike a chord deep inside Hana. A voice that was even less like sound, and that spoke in Hana's mind.

Hannah, come back. You don't have to relive all this. Wake up. Come back, Hannah – now.

Hana of the Three Rivers closed her eyes and went limp.

CHAPTER

6

Hannah opened her eyes.

'Oh, thank God,' Paul said. He seemed to be almost crying. 'Oh, thank God. Do you see me? Do you know who you are?'

'I'm wet,' Hannah said slowly, feeling dazed. She touched her face. Her hair was dripping. Paul was holding a water glass. 'Why am I wet?'

'I had to wake you up.' Paul sagged to the floor beside the couch. 'What's your name? What year is it?'

'My name is Hannah Snow,' Hannah said, still feeling dazed and bodiless. 'And it's—' Suddenly memory rushed out of the fog at her. She sat bolt upright, tears starting to stream from her eyes. 'What *was* all that?'

'I don't know,' Paul whispered. He leaned his head against the couch, then looked up. 'You just kept talking – you were telling that story as if you were there. It was really *happening* to you. And nothing I could do would break the trance. I tried everything – I thought you were never going to come out of it. And then you started sobbing and I couldn't make you stop.'

'I *felt* as if it were happening to me,' Hannah said. Her head ached; her whole body felt bruised with tension.

And she was reeling with memories that were perfectly real and perfectly hers . . . and impossible.

'That was like no past life regression I've ever read about,' Paul said, his voice agitated. 'The detail . . . you knew everything. Have you ever studied – is there any way you could have known those kinds of things?'

'No.' Hannah was just as agitated. 'I've never studied humans in the Stone Age, and this was *real*. It wasn't something I was making up as I was going along.'

They were both talking at once. 'That guy,' Paul was saying. 'He's the one you're afraid of, isn't he? But, look, you know, regression is one thing . . . past lives is another thing . . . but *this* is crazy.'

'I don't believe in vampires,' Hannah was saying at the same time. 'Because that's what that guy was supposed to be, wasn't it? Of course it was. Caveman vampire. He was probably the first one. And I don't believe in reincarnation.'

'Just plain crazy. This is crazy.'

'I *agree*.'

They both took a breath, looking at each other. There was a long silence.

Hannah put a hand to her forehead. 'I'm . . . really tired.'

'Yeah. Yeah, I can understand that.' Paul looked around the room, nodded twice, then got up. 'Well, we'd better get you home. We can talk about all this later, figure out what it really means. Some kind of subconscious fixation . . . archetypical symbolism . . . something.' He ran out of air and shook his head. 'Now, you feel all right, don't you? And you're not going to worry about this? Because there's nothing to worry about.'

'I know. I know.'

'At least we know we don't have to worry about vampires attacking you.' He laughed. The laugh was strained.

Hannah couldn't manage even a smile.

There was a brief silence, then Paul said, 'You know, I think I'll drive you home. That would be good. That would be a good idea.'

'That would be fine,' Hannah whispered.

He held out a hand to help her off the couch. 'By the way, I'm really sorry I had to get you all wet.'

'No. It was good you did. I was feeling so awful – and there were worse things about to happen.'

Paul blinked. 'I'm sorry?'

Hannah looked at him helplessly, then away. 'There were worse things about to happen. Terrible things. Really, really awful things.'

'How do you know that?'

'I don't know. But there were.'

Paul walked her to her doorstep. And Hannah was glad of it.

Once inside the house, she went straight down the hall to her mother's study. It was a cluttered comfortable room with books piled on the floor and the tools of a paleontologist scattered around. Her mother was at her desk, bending over a microscope.

'Is that you, Hannah?' she asked without looking up. 'I've got some marvellous sections of haversian canals in duckbill bones. Want to see?'

'Oh . . . not now. Maybe later,' Hannah said. She wanted very much to tell her mother about what had happened, but something was stopping her. Her mother was so sensible, so practical and intelligent . . .

She'll think I'm crazy. And she'll be right. And then she'll be appalled, wondering how she could have given birth to an insane daughter.

That was an exaggeration, and Hannah knew it, but

somehow she still couldn't bring herself to tell. Since her father had died five years ago, she and her mother had been almost like friends, but that didn't mean she didn't want her mother's approval. She did. She desperately wanted her mother to be proud of her, and to realize that she could handle things on her own.

It had been the same with the notes – she'd never told about finding them. For all her mom knew, Hannah's only problem was bad dreams.

'So how did it go tonight?' her mother asked now, eye still to the microscope. 'That Dr Winfield is so young – I hope he's not too inexperienced.'

Last chance. Take it or lose it. 'Uh, it went fine,' Hannah said weakly.

'That's good. There's chicken in the crockpot. I'll be out in a little while; I just want to finish this.'

'OK. Great. Thanks.' Hannah turned and stumbled out, completely frustrated with herself.

You know Mom won't really be awful, she scolded herself as she fished a piece of chicken out of the crockpot. So *tell* her. Or call Chess and tell *her*. They'll make things better. They'll tell you how impossible all this stuff about vampires and past lives is . . .

Yes, and that's the problem.

Hannah sat frozen, holding a fork with a bite of chicken on it motionless in front of her.

I don't believe in vampires or reincarnation. But I know what I saw. I know things about Hana . . . things that weren't even in the story I told Paul. I know she wore a tunic and leggings of roe deer hide. I know she ate wild cattle and wild boar and salmon and hazel nuts. I know she made tools out of elk antler and deer bone and flint . . . God, I could pick up a flint cobble and knock off a set of blades and scrapers right now. I *know* I could. I can feel how to in my hands.

She put the fork down and looked at her hands. They were shaking slightly.

And I know she had a beautiful singing voice, a voice like crystal . . .

Like the crystal voice in my mind.

So what do I do when they tell me it's impossible? Argue with them? Then I'll *really* be crazy, like those people in institutions who think they're Napoleon or Cleopatra.

God, I hope I haven't been Cleopatra.

Half laughing and half crying, she put her face in her hands.

And what about *him?*

The blond stranger with the bottomless eyes. The guy Hana didn't have a name for, but Hannah knew as Thierry.

If the rest of it is real, what about him?

He's the one I'm afraid of, Hannah thought. But he didn't seem so bad. Dangerous, but not evil. So why do I think of him as evil?

And why do I want him anyway?

Because she did want him. She remembered the feelings of Hana standing next to the stranger in the moonlight. Confusion . . . fear . . . and attraction. That magnetism between them. The extraordinary things that happened when he touched her hand.

He came to the Three Rivers and turned her life upside down . . . *The Three Rivers*. Oh, God, why didn't I think of that before? The *note*. One of the notes said. 'Remember the Three Rivers.'

OK. So I've remembered it. So what now?

She had no idea. Maybe she was supposed to understand everything now, and know what to do . . . but she didn't. She was more confused than ever.

Of course, a tiny voice like a cool dark wind in her brain said, *you didn't remember* all *of it yet. Did you? Paul woke you up before you got to the end.*

Shut up, Hannah told the voice.

But she couldn't stop thinking. All night she was restless, moving from one room to another, avoiding her mother's questions. And even after her mother went to bed, Hannah found herself wandering aimlessly through the house, straightening things, picking up books and putting them down again.

I've got to sleep. That's the only thing that will help me feel better, she thought. But she couldn't make herself sit, much less lie down.

Maybe I need some air.

It was a strange thought. She'd never actually felt the need to go outside for the sole purpose of breathing fresh air – in Montana you did that all day long. But there was something pulling at her, drawing her to go outside. It was like a compulsion and she couldn't resist.

I'll just go on the back porch. Of course there's nothing to be scared of out there. And if I go outside, then I'll *prove* there isn't, and then I can go to sleep.

Without stopping to consider the logic of this, she opened the back door.

It was a beautiful night. The moon threw a silver glow over everything and the horizon seemed very far away. Hannah's backyard blended into the wild bluestem and pine grass of the prairie. The wind carried the clean pungent smell of sage.

We'll have spring flowers soon, Hannah thought. Asters and bluebells and little golden buttercups. Everything will be green for a while. Spring's a time for life, not death.

And I was right to come out. I feel more relaxed now. I can go back inside and lie down . . .

It was at that moment that she realized she was being watched.

It was the same feeling she'd been having for weeks, the feeling that there were eyes in the darkness and they were fixed on her. Chills of adrenalin ran through Hannah's body.

Don't panic, she told herself. It's just a feeling. There's probably nothing out here.

She took a slow step backward toward the door. She didn't want to move too quickly. She had the irrational certainty that if she turned and ran, whatever was watching her would spring out and get her before she got the door open.

At the same time she edged backward, her eyes and ears were straining so hard that she saw grey spots and she heard a thin ringing. She was trying, desperately, to catch some sign of movement, some sound. But everything was still and the only noises were the normal distant noises of the outdoors.

Then she saw the shadow.

Black against the lighter blackness of the night, it was moving among the bluestem grass. And it was big. Tall. Not a cat or other small animal. Big as a person.

It was coming toward her.

Hannah thought she might faint.

Don't be ridiculous, a sharp voice in her head told her. *Get* inside. *You're standing here in the light from the windows; you're a perfect target. Get inside* fast *and lock the door.*

Hannah whirled, and knew even as she did it that she wouldn't be fast enough. It was going to jump at her exposed back. It was going to . . .

'Wait,' came a voice out of the darkness. 'Please. Wait.'

A male voice. Unfamiliar. But it seemed to grab Hannah and hold her still.

'I won't hurt you. I promise.'

Runrunrunrun! Hannah's mind told her.

Very slowly, one hand on the door knob, she turned around.

She watched the dark figure coming out of the shadows to her. She didn't try to get away again. She had a dizzying feeling that fate had caught up with her.

The ground sloped, so the light from the house windows showed her his boots first, then the legs of his jeans. Normal walking boots like any Montanan might wear. Ordinary jeans, long legs. He was tall. Then the light showed his shirt, which was an ordinary T-shirt, a little cold to be walking around at night in, but nothing startling. And then his shoulders, which were nice ones.

Then, as he stepped to the base of the porch, she saw his face.

He looked better than when she had seen him last. His white-blond hair wasn't crazily messed up; it fell neatly over his forehead. He wasn't splattered with mud and his eyes weren't wild. They were dark and so endlessly sad that it was like a knife in the heart just to see him.

But it was unmistakably the boy from her hypnosis session.

'Oh, God,' Hannah said. 'Oh, God.' Her knees were giving out.

It's real. It's *real*. He's real and that means . . . it's all true.

'Oh, *God*.' She was trembling violently and she had to put pressure on her knees to keep standing. The world was changing around her, and it was the most disorienting thing she'd ever experienced. It was as if the fabric of her universe was actually moving – pulsing and shifting to accommodate the new truths.

Nothing was ever going to be the same again.

'Are you all right?' The stranger moved toward her and Hannah recoiled instinctively.

'Don't touch me!' she gasped, and at the same moment her legs gave out. She slid to the floor of the porch and stared at the boy whose face was now approximately level with hers.

'I'm sorry,' he almost whispered. 'I know what you're going through. You're just realizing now, aren't you?'

Hannah said, whispering to herself, 'It's all true.'

'Yes.' The dark eyes were so sad.

'It's . . . I've had past lives.'

'Yes.' He squatted on the ground, looking down as if he couldn't keep staring at her face anymore. He picked up a pebble, examined it. Hannah noticed that his fingers were long and sensitive-looking.

'You're an Old Soul,' he said quietly. 'You've had lots of lives.'

'I was Hana of the Three Rivers.'

His fingers stopped rolling the pebble. 'Yes.'

'And you're Thierry. And you're a . . .'

He didn't look up. 'Go on. Say it.'

Hannah couldn't. Her voice wouldn't form the word.

The stranger – Thierry – said it for her. 'Vampires are real.' A glance from those unfathomable eyes. 'I'm sorry.'

Hannah breathed and looked down at him. But the world had finished its reshaping. Her mind was beginning to work again.

At least I know I'm not crazy, she thought. That's some consolation. It's the universe that's insane, not me.

And now I have to deal with it, somehow.

She said quietly, 'Are you going to kill me now?'

'God – no!' He stood up fast, uncoiling. Shock was

naked on his face. 'You don't understand. I would never hurt you. I . . .' He broke off. 'It's hard to know where to begin.'

Hannah sat silently, while he looked around the porch for inspiration. She could feel her heart beating in her throat. She'd told Paul that this boy had killed her, kept killing her. But his look of shock had been so genuine, as if she'd hurt him terribly by even suggesting it.

'I suppose I should start by explaining exactly what I am,' he said. 'And what I've done. I made you come outside tonight. I influenced you. I didn't want to do it, but I had to talk to you.'

'Influenced me?'

It's a mental thing. I can also just communicate this way. It was his voice, but his lips weren't moving.

And it was the same voice she'd heard at the end of her hypnotic session, the voice that wasn't Paul's. The one that had spoken in her head, saying, *Hannah, come back. You don't have to relive this.*

'You were the one who woke me up,' Hannah whispered. 'I wouldn't have come back except for you.'

'I couldn't stand to see you hurting like that.'

Can somebody with his eyes be evil?

He was obviously a different sort of creature than she was, and every move he made showed the grace of a predator. It reminded her of how the wolves had moved – they had *rippled*. He did, too, his muscles moving so lightly under his skin. He was unnatural – but beautiful.

Something struck her. 'The wolves. I picked up a silver picture frame to bash them with. Silver.' She looked at him. 'Werewolves are real.' At the last moment her voice made it a statement instead of a question.

'So much is real that you don't know about. Or that you haven't remembered yet. You were starting to remember with that shrink. You said I was a Lord of the Night World.'

The Night World. Just the mention of it sent prickles through Hannah. She could almost remember, but not quite.

And she knew it was crazy to be kneeling here having this conversation. She was talking to a *vampire*. A guy who drank blood for a living. A guy whose every gesture showed he was a hunter. And not only a vampire, but the person her subconscious had been warning her about for weeks. Telling her to be afraid, be very afraid.

So why wasn't she running? For one thing, she didn't think her legs would physically support her. And for another, well, somehow she couldn't stop looking at him.

'One of the werewolves was mine,' he was saying quietly. 'She was here to find you – and protect you. But the other one . . . Hannah, you have to understand. I'm not the only one looking for you.'

To protect me. So I was right, Hannah thought. The grey female was on my side. She said, 'Who else is looking?'

'Another Night Person.' He looked away. 'Another vampire.'

'Am I a Night Person?'

'No. You're a human.' He said it the way he said everything, as if reminding her of terrible facts he wished he didn't have to bring up. 'Old Souls are just humans who keep coming back.'

'How many times have I come back?'

'I . . . I'd have to think about it. Quite a few.'

'And have *you* been with me in all of them?'

'Any of them I could manage.'

'What do the rest of the notes mean?' Hannah had been gathering speed, and now she was shooting questions at him in machine-gun fashion. She thought she was in control, and she hardly noticed the hysterical edge to her own voice. '*Why* am I telling myself I'll be dead before I'm seventeen?'

'Hannah . . .' He reached out a hand to calm her.

Hannah's own hand moved by reflex, coming up to ward his off. And then their fingers touched, bare skin to bare skin, and the world disappeared.

CHAPTER 7

It was like being struck by lightning. Hannah felt the current through her body, but it was her mind that was most affected.

I know you! It was as if she had been standing in a dark landscape, lost and blind, when suddenly a brilliant flash illuminated everything, allowing her to see farther than she'd ever seen before. She was trembling violently, pitching forward even as he fell toward her. Electricity was running through every nerve in her body and she was shaking and shaking, overcome by waves of the purest emotion she'd ever felt.

Fury.

'You were supposed to be there!' She got out in a choked gasp. 'Where *were* you?'

You were supposed to be with me – for so long! You're *part* of me, the part I've always vaguely missed. You were supposed to be around, helping out, picking me up when I fell down. Watching my back, listening to my stories. Understanding things that I wouldn't want to tell other people. Loving me when I'm stupid. Giving *me* something to take care of and be good to, the way the Goddess meant women to do.

Hannah—

It was the closest thing to a mental gasp Hannah could imagine, and with it she realized that somehow they were directly connected now. He could hear her thoughts, just as she could hear his.

Good! she thought, not wasting time to marvel over this. Her mind was raging on.

You were my flying companion! My playmate! You were my other half of the mysteries! We were supposed to be sacred to each other – *and you haven't been there!*

This last thought she sent squarely toward him. And she felt it hit him, and felt his reaction.

'I've *tried*!'

He was horrified . . . guilt-stricken. But then, Hannah could sense that this was pretty much the usual state for him, so it didn't affect him quite as much as it might have someone else. And beneath the horror was an astonishment and burgeoning joy that sent a different kind of tingle through her.

'You *do* know me, don't you?' he said quietly. He pushed her back to look at her, as if he still couldn't believe it. 'You remember . . . Hannah, how much do you remember?'

Hannah was looking at him, studying him . . . Yes, I know that bone structure. And the eyes, especially the eyes. It was like an adopted child discovering a brother or sister and seeing familiar features in an unfamiliar face, tracing each one with wonder and recognition.

'I remember . . . that we were meant for each other. That we're' – she came up with the word slowly – '*soulmates.*'

'Yes,' he whispered. Awe was softening his features, changing his eyes. The desperate sadness that seemed so much a part of them was lightening. 'Soulmates. We were destined for each other. We should have been together down the ages.'

They were supporting each other now, Hannah kneeling on the porch and Thierry holding her with one knee on a step. Their faces were inches apart. Hannah found herself watching his mouth.

'So what happened?' she whispered.

In the same tone, without moving back, he whispered, 'I screwed up.'

'Oh.'

Her initial fury had faded. She could *feel* him, feel his emotions, sense his thoughts. He was as anguished at their separation as she was. He wanted her. He loved her . . . adored her. He thought of her the way poets think of the moon and the stars – in ridiculous hyperbole. He actually saw her surrounded by a sort of silvery halo.

Which was completely silly, but if he wanted to think of her that way – well, Hannah wouldn't object. It made her want to be very gentle with him.

And right now she could feel his warm breath. If she leaned forward just an inch her top lip would touch his bottom lip.

Hannah leaned forward.

'Wait—' he said.

That was a mistake, saying it out loud. It moved his lips against hers, turning it from a touch into a kiss.

And then, for a while, neither of them could resist. They needed each other so desperately, and the kiss was warm and sweet. Hannah was flooded with love and comfort and joy.

This was meant to be.

Hannah was dizzy but still capable of thought. I knew life had something wonderful and mysterious to give me. Something I could sense but not see, something that was always just out of reach.

And here it is. I'm one of the lucky ones – I've found it.

Thierry wasn't as articulate. All she could hear him think was, *Yes.*

Hannah had never been so filled with gratitude. Love spilled from her and into Thierry and back again. The more she gave, the more she got back. It was a cycle, taking them higher and higher.

Like flying, Hannah thought. She wasn't dizzy anymore. She was strangely, clear and calm, as if she were standing on a mountain top. Infinite tenderness . . . infinite belonging. It was so good it hurt.

And it made her want to give more.

She knew what she wanted. It was what she'd tried to give him the first time, when she knew he would die without her. She'd wanted to give him what all women could give.

Life.

She was only a girl now, not ready for the responsibilities that would come with making new life from her body. But she could give Thierry life another way.

She pulled back to look at him, to see bruised dark eyes filled with aching tenderness. Then she touched his mouth with her fingertips.

He kissed them. Hannah ignored the kiss and poked a finger in.

Shock flared in Thierry's eyes.

There. That was it. The long canine tooth, just barely sharp. Not yet the tooth of a predator, of a fox or a lynx or wolf. She ran her finger against it.

The shock turned to something else. A glazed look. Need mixed with pure terror.

Thierry whispered. 'Don't, Hannah, please. You don't know—'

Hannah tested the tip of the tooth with her thumb. Yes, it was sharper now. Longer, more delicate. It would look like the tooth of an arctic fox in her palm – milky-white, translucent, elegantly curved.

Thierry's chest was heaving. 'Please stop. I – I can't—'

Hannah was enthralled. I don't know why people are afraid of vampires, she thought. A human could tease or torture a vampire this way, driving him insane – if she were cruel.

Or she could choose to be kind.

Very gently, Hannah reached with her other hand. She touched the back of Thierry's neck, bringing just the slightest pressure to bear. But he was so obedient to her touch – it was easy to guide his mouth to her throat.

Hannah . . .

She could feel him trembling.

Don't be afraid, she told him silently. And she pulled him closer.

He grabbed her shoulders to push her away – and then just hung on. Clinging desperately, helplessly. Kissing her neck over and over. She felt his control break . . . and then felt the sharpness of teeth.

It wasn't like pain. It was like the tenderness, a hurting that was good.

And then . . . devastating bliss.

Not a physical feeling. It was emotional. They were completely together, and light poured through them.

How many lives together have we missed? How many times have I had to say, 'Maybe in the next life?' How did we ever manage to come apart?

It was as if her question went searching through both their minds, soaring and diving, looking for an answer on its own. And Thierry didn't put up any resistance. She knew that he couldn't; he was as caught up as she was in what was happening between them, as overwhelmed.

There was nothing to stop her from finding the answer.

This revelation didn't come all in one blinding illumination. Instead it came in small flashes, each almost too brief to understand.

Flash. Thierry's face above her. Not the gentle face she had seen by the porch. A savage face with an animal light in the eyes. A snarling mouth . . . and teeth red with blood.

No . . .

Flash. Pain. Teeth that tore her throat. The feel of her blood spilling warm over her neck. Darkness coming.

Oh, God, no . . .

Flash. A different face. A woman with black hair and eyes full of concern. 'Don't you know? He's evil. How many times does he have to kill you before you realize that?'

No, no, no, no . . .

But saying no didn't change anything.

It was the truth. She was seeing her own memories – seeing things that had really happened. She *knew* that.

He'd killed her.

Hannah, no—

It was a cry of anguish. Hannah wrenched herself away. She could see the shock in Thierry's eyes, she could feel him shaking.

'You really did it,' she whispered.

'Hannah—'

'That's why you woke me up from the hypnosis! You didn't want me to remember! You knew I'd find out the truth!' Hannah was beside herself with grief and anger. If she hadn't trusted him, if everything hadn't been so perfect, she wouldn't have felt so betrayed. As it was, it was the greatest betrayal of her life – of all her lives.

It had all been a lie – everything she'd just been feeling. The togetherness, the love, the joy . . . all false.

'Hannah, that wasn't the reason. . . .'

'You're evil! You're a killer!' She told me, Hannah thought. The woman with black hair; she told me the truth. Why didn't I remember her? Why didn't I listen this time?

She could remember other things now, other things the woman had said. 'He's unbelievably cunning . . . he'll try to trick you. He'll try to use mind control . . .'

Mind control. Influencing her. He'd *admitted* that.

And what she'd been feeling tonight was some sort of trick. He'd managed to play on her emotions . . . God, he'd even gotten her to offer him her blood. She'd let him *bite* her, drink from her like some parasite . . .

'I hate you,' she whispered.

She saw how that hurt him; he flinched and looked away, stricken. Then he gripped her shoulders again, his voice soft. 'Hannah, I wanted to explain to you. Please. You don't understand everything . . .'

'Yes, I do! I *do*! I remember everything! And I understand what you really are.' Her voice was as quiet as his, but much more intense. She shrugged her shoulders and shifted backward to get away from him. She didn't want to feel his hands on her.

He looked jolted. Unbelieving. 'You remember . . . everything?'

'Everything.' Hannah was proud and cold now. 'So you can just go away, because whatever you've got planned won't work. Whatever – tricks – you were going to use . . .' She shook her head. 'Just go.'

For just a second, a strange expression crossed Thierry's face. An expression so tragic and lonely that Hannah's throat closed.

But she couldn't let herself soften. She couldn't give him a chance to trick her again.

'Just stay away from me,' she said. With all the

confusion and turmoil inside her, that was the only thing she could keep clear in her mind. 'I never want to see you again.'

He had gotten control of himself. He looked shell-shocked but his eyes were steady. 'I've never wanted to hurt you,' he said quietly. 'And all I want to do now is protect you. But if that's what you want, I'll go away.'

How could he claim he'd never wanted to hurt her? Didn't killing her count? 'That *is* what I want. And I don't need your protection.'

'You have it anyway,' he said.

And then he moved, faster than she could ever hope to move, almost faster than thought. In an instant, he was close to her. His fingers touched her left cheek, light as a moth's wings. And then he was taking her hand, slipping something on her finger.

'Wear this,' he said, no louder than a breath. 'It has spells to protect you. And even without the spells, there aren't many Night People who'll harm you if they see it.'

Hannah opened her mouth to say she wasn't afraid of any Night People except him, but he was still speaking. 'Try not to go out alone, especially at night.'

And then he was gone.

Like that. He was off her porch and out somewhere in the darkness, not even a shadow, just *gone*. If she hadn't had a fleeting impression of movement toward the prairie, she would have thought he had the ability to become invisible at a moment's notice.

And her heart was pounding, hurting, filling her throat so she couldn't breathe.

Why had he touched her cheek? Most people didn't touch the birthmark; they treated it like a bruise that might still hurt. But his fingers hadn't avoided it. The caress had been gentle, almost sad, but not frightened.

And why was she still standing here, staring into the darkness as if she expected him to reappear?

Go *inside*, idiot.

Hannah turned and fumbled with the back door, pulling at the knob as if she'd never opened it before. She shut the door and locked it, and again she found herself as clumsy as if she'd never worked a lock or seen this one in her life.

She was beyond screaming or crying, in a state of shock that was almost dream-like. The house was too bright. The clock on the kitchen wall was too loud. She had the distracted feeling that it wasn't either night or daytime.

It was like coming out of a theatre and being surprised to find that it's still light outside. She felt that this couldn't be the same house she'd left an hour ago. *She* wasn't the same person who had left. Everything around her seemed like some carefully staged movie set that was supposed to be real, but wasn't, and only she could tell the difference.

I feel like a stranger here, she thought, putting one hand to her neck where she could just detect two little puncture marks. Oh, God, how am I ever going to know what's real again?

But I should be happy; I should be grateful. I probably just saved my own life out there. I was alone with a vicious, evil, murderous monster, and . . .

Somehow the thought died away. She couldn't be happy and she didn't want to think about how evil Thierry was. She felt hollow and aching.

It wasn't until she stumbled into her own bedroom that she remembered to look down at her right hand.

On the fourth finger was a ring. It was made of gold and either white gold or silver. It was shaped like a rose, with the stem twining around the finger and back on itself in an intricate knot. The blossom was inset with tiny stones – black transparent stones. Black diamonds? Hannah wondered.

It was beautiful. The craftsmanship was exquisite. Every delicate leaf and tiny thorn was perfect. But a black flower?

It's a symbol of the Night World, her mind told her. *A symbol of people who've been made into vampires.*

It was the cool wind voice back again. At least she understood what it was saying this time, the last time, when it had given her advice about silver and wolves, she had been completely confused.

Thierry wanted her to wear the ring; he claimed it would protect her. But knowing him, it was probably another trick. If it had any spells on it, they were probably spells to help him control her mind.

It took nearly an hour to get the ring off. Hannah used soap and butter and Vaseline, pulling and twisting until her finger was red, aching, and swollen. She used a dental pick from her fossil-collecting kit to try to pry the coils of the stem apart. Nothing worked, until at last the pick slipped and blood welled up from a shallow cut. When the blood touched the ring it seemed to loosen, and Hannah quickly wrenched it off.

Then she stood panting. The struggle with the little band of metal had left her exhausted and unable to focus on anything else. She threw the ring in her bedroom wastebasket and stumbled toward bed.

I'm tired . . . I'm so tired. I'll think about everything tomorrow, try to sort out my life. But for now . . . please just let me sleep.

She could feel her body vibrating with adrenalin after she lay in bed, and she was afraid that sleep wouldn't come. But tense as she was, her mind was too foggy to stay awake. She turned over once and let go of consciousness.

Hannah Snow fell asleep.

* * *

Hana of the Three Rivers opened her eyes.

Cold and desolate, Hana stood by the rushing river and felt the wind blow through her. So alone.

That was when Arno burst out of the bushes on the riverbank.

There were several hunters with him and they all had spears. They charged after the stranger at full speed. Hana screamed a warning, but she knew he didn't have a chance.

She could hear a few minutes of chaos far away in the dark. And then she saw the stranger being driven back, surrounded by Arno's hunters.

'Arno – don't hurt him! Please!' Hana was speaking desperately, trying to block the men's way back. 'Don't you see? He could have hurt me and he didn't. He isn't a demon! He can't help being the way he is!'

Arno shouldered her aside. 'Don't think you're going to get away without being punished, either.'

Hana followed them up to the cave, her stomach churning with fear.

By the time everyone who'd been awakened by Arno's hunters understood what was happening, the sky outside had turned grey. It was almost dawn.

'You said we should wait and see if the Earth Goddess would tell you something about the demon while you slept,' Arno said to Old Mother. 'Has she?'

Old Mother glanced at Hana sorrowfully, then back at Arno. She shook her head. Then she started to speak, but Arno was already talking loudly.

'Then let's kill him and get it over with. Take him outside.'

'No!' Hana screamed. It didn't do any good. She was caught and held back in strong hands. The stranger gave

her one look as he was driven outside in a circle of spears.

That was when the real horror began.

Because of something that Hana had never imagined, something she was sure even the shamans had never heard of.

The stranger was a creature that wouldn't die.

Arno was the first to jab with his spear. The whitish-grey flint spearhead went into the stranger's side, drawing blood. Hana saw it; she had run out of the cave, still trying to find a way to stop this.

She also saw the blood stop flowing as the wound in the boy's side closed.

There were gasps from all around her. Arno, looking as if he couldn't believe his eyes, jabbed again. And watched, mouth falling open, as the second wound bled and then closed. He kept trying. Only the wounds where a spear was driven into the wooden shaft stayed open.

One of the women whispered, 'He *is* a demon.'

Everyone was frightened. But nobody moved away from the stranger. He was too dangerous to let go. And there were lots of them, and only one of him.

Hana saw something happening in the faces of her clan. Something new and horrible. Fear of the unknown was changing them, making them cruel. They were turning from basically good people, people who would never torture an animal by prolonging its death, into people who would torture a man.

'He may be a demon, but he still bleeds,' one of the hunters said breathlessly, after a jab. 'He feels pain.'

'Get a torch,' somebody else said. 'See if he burns!'

And then it was terrible. Hana felt as if she were in the middle of a storm, able to see things but buffeted this way and that, unable to *do* anything about it. People were running. People were getting torches, stone axes, different kinds of flint knives. The clan had turned into a huge entity feeding off its own violence. It was mindless and unstoppable.

Hana cast a desperate look toward the cave, where Old Mother lay confined to her pallet. There was no help from that direction.

People were screaming, burning the stranger, throwing stones at him. The stranger was falling, bloody, smoke rising from his burns. He was lying on the ground, unable to fight back. But still, he didn't die. He kept trying to crawl away.

Hana was screaming herself, screaming and crying, beating at the shoulders of a hunter who pulled her back. And it went on and on. Even the young boys were brave enough now to run forward and throw stones at the stranger.

And he still wouldn't die.

Hana was in a nightmare. Her throat was raw from screaming. Her vision was going grey. She couldn't stand to watch this anymore; she couldn't stand the smell of blood and burning flesh or the sound of blows. But there was nowhere to go. There was no way to get out. This was her life. She had to stay here and go insane . . .

CHAPTER 8

Hannah sat up in bed, gasping.

For several moments she didn't know where she was. Through a gap in her curtains she could see the grey light of dawn – just like Hana's grey dawn – and she thought she still might be in the nightmare. But then, slowly, objects in the room became clear. Her bookshelves, crammed with books and crowned with one near-perfect trilobite fossil on a stand. Her dresser, its top piled with things that belonged in other places. Her posters of *Velociraptor* and *T. Rex*.

I'm me. I remember me.

She had never been so happy to be herself, or to be awake.

But that dream she'd just had, that had happened to her. A long time ago, sure, but nothing like so long ago as, say, when the *T. Rex* had been alive. Not to mention the trilobite. A few thousand years was yesterday to Mother Earth.

And it was all real, she knew that now. She accepted it. She had fallen asleep and her subconscious had pulled back the veil of the past and allowed her to see more of Hana's story.

Thierry, she thought. The people of Hana's clan tortured him. God knows for how long – I'm just glad I didn't have to watch more.

But it puts sort of a different twist on things, doesn't it?

She still didn't know how the story ended. She wasn't sure she *wanted* to know. But it was hard to blame him for whatever had happened afterward.

An awful feeling was settling in Hannah's stomach. All those things I said to him, terrible things, she thought. Why did I say all that? I was so angry, I lost control completely. I hated him and all I cared about was hurting him. I really thought he must be evil, pure evil.

I told him to go away forever.

How could I have done that? He's my soulmate.

There was a strange emptiness inside her, as if she'd been hollowed out like a tree struck by lightning.

Inside the emptiness, a voice like a cool dark wind whispered, *But you told Paul that he kept killing you over and over. Is* that *justifiable? He's a vampire, a predator, and that makes him evil by nature. Maybe he can't help being what he is, but there's no reason for you to be destroyed again because of it. Are you going to let him kill you in this life, too?*

She was torn between pity for him and the deep instinct that he was dangerous. The cool wind voice seemed to be the voice of reason.

Go ahead and feel sorry for him, it said. *Just keep him far away from you.*

She felt better having come to a decision, even if it was a decision that left her heart numb. She glanced around the room, focused on the clock by her bedside, and blinked.

Oh, my God – school.

It was quarter to seven and it was a Friday. Sacajawea High seemed light-years away, like someplace she'd visited in a past life.

But it's not. It's *your* life, now, the only one that counts. You have to forget all that other stuff about reincarnation and vampires and the Night World. You have to forget about *him*.

You sent him away and he's gone. So let's get on with living in the normal world.

Just thinking this way made her feel braced and icy, as if she'd had a cold shower. She took a real shower, dressed in jeans and a denim shirt, and she had breakfast with her mother, who cast her several thoughtful glances but didn't ask any questions until they were almost finished.

Then she said, 'Did everything go all right at Dr Winfield's yesterday evening?'

Had it only been yesterday evening? It seemed like a week ago. Hannah chewed a bite of cornflakes and finally said, 'Uh, why?'

'Because he called while you were in the shower. He seemed . . .' Her mother stopped and searched for a word. '*Anxious*. Worse than worried but not as bad as hysterical.'

Hannah looked at her mother's face, which was narrow, intelligent, and tanned by the Montana sun. Her eyes were more blue than Hannah's grey, but they were direct and discerning.

She wanted to tell her mother the whole story – but when she had time to do it, and after she'd had time to think it out. There was no urgency. It was all behind her now, and it wasn't as if she needed advice.

'Paul's anxious a lot,' she said judiciously, sticking to the clean edge of truth. 'I think that's why he became a psychologist. He tried a sort of hypnosis thing on me yesterday and it didn't exactly work out.'

'Hypnosis?' Her mother's eyebrows lifted. 'Hannah, I don't know if you should be getting into that—'

'Don't worry; I'm not. It's over. We're not going to try it again.'

'I see. Well, he said for you to call him to set up another appointment. I think he wants to see you soon.' She reached over suddenly and took Hannah's hand. 'Honey, are you feeling any *better*? Are you still having bad dreams?'

Hannah looked away. 'Actually, I sort of had one last night. But I think I understand them better now. They don't scare me as much.' She squeezed her mother's hand. 'Don't worry, I'm going to be fine.'

'All right, but—' Before her mother could finish the sentence a horn honked outside.

'That's Chess. I'd better run.' Hannah gulped down the dregs of her orange juice and dashed into her bedroom to grab her backpack. She hesitated a split second by the wastebasket, then shook her head.

No. There was no reason to take the black rose ring with her. It was *his*, and she didn't want to be reminded of him.

She slung the backpack over her shoulder, yelled goodbye to her mother, and hurried outside.

Chess's car was parked in the driveway. As Hannah started toward it she had an odd impression. She seemed to see a figure standing behind the car – a tall figure, face turned toward her. But her eyes were dazzled by the sun and at that instant she involuntarily blinked. When she could see again, there was nothing in that spot except a little swirl of dust.

'You're late,' Chess said when Hannah got in the car. Chess, whose real name was Catherine Clovis, was petite and pretty, with dark hair cut in a cap to frame her face. But just now her slanted green cat-eyes and Mona Lisa smile reminded Hannah too much of Ket. It was disconcerting; she had to glance down to make sure Chess wasn't wearing a deer-skin outfit.

'You OK?' Now Chess was looking at her with concern.

'Yeah.' Hannah sank back against the upholstery, blinking. 'I think I need to get my eyes checked, though.' She glanced at the spot where the phantom figure had been – nothing. And Chess was just Chess: smart, savvy, and faintly exotic, like an orchid blooming in the badlands.

'Well, you can do it when we go shopping this weekend,' Chess said. She slanted Hannah a glance. 'We *must* go shopping. Next week's your birthday and I need something new to wear.'

Hannah grinned in spite of herself. 'Maybe a new necklace,' she muttered.

'What?'

'Nothing.' I wonder what happened to Ket, she thought. Even if Hana died young, at least Ket must have grown up. I wonder if she married Ran, the guy who wanted to 'mate' her?

'Are you *sure* you're OK?' Chess said.

'Yeah. Sorry; I'm a little brain-dead. I didn't sleep well last night.' Her plan for Chess was exactly the same as for her mother. Tell her everything – in a little while. When she was less upset about it.

Chess was putting an arm around her, steering skilfully with the other. 'Hey, we've got to get you in shape, kid. I mean, first it's your birthday, then graduation. Isn't that psychologist doing anything to help?'

Hannah muttered, 'Maybe too much.'

That night, she was restless again. The school day had passed uneventfully. Hannah and her mother had had dinner peacefully. But after her mother went out to a meeting with some local rockhounds, Hannah found herself wandering around the house, too wound up to read or watch TV, too distracted to go anywhere.

Maybe I need some air, she thought – and then she caught herself and gave a self-mocking grin.

Sure. Air. When what you're *really* thinking is that he just might be out there. Admit it.

She admitted it. Not that she thought Thierry was very likely to be hanging around her backyard, considering what she'd said to him.

And why should you *want* to talk to him? she demanded of herself. He may not be completely and totally and pointlessly evil, but he's still no boy scout.

But she couldn't shake a vague feeling of wanting to go outside. At last she went out on the porch, telling herself that she'd spend five minutes here and then go back inside.

It was another beautiful night, but Hannah couldn't enjoy it. Everything reminded her too much of him. She could feel herself softening toward him, weakening. He had looked so stricken, so devastated, when she told him to go away . . .

'Am I interrupting?'

Hannah started. She wheeled toward the voice.

Standing on the other side of the porch was a tall girl. She looked a year or so older than Hannah, and she had long hair, *very* long hair, so black that it seemed to reflect moonlight like a raven's wing. She was extraordinarily beautiful – and Hannah recognized her.

She's the one from my vision. That flash of a girl telling me that Thierry was cunning. She's the one who warned me about him.

And she's the figure I saw behind Chess's car this morning. She must have been watching me then.

'I'm sorry if I scared you,' the girl said now, smiling. 'You looked so far away, and I didn't mean to startle you. But I'd really like to talk to you if you have a few minutes.'

'I . . .' Hannah felt strangely tongue-tied. Something about the girl made her uncomfortable, in a way that went beyond the dream-like weirdness of recognizing somebody she'd never seen in her present life.

But she's your friend, she told herself. She's helped you in the past; she probably wants to help you again now. You should be grateful to her.

'Sure,' Hannah said. 'We can talk.' She added somewhat awkwardly, 'I remember you.'

'Wonderful. Do you really? That makes everything so much easier.'

Hannah nodded. And told herself again that this girl was her friend, and nobody to be hostile to or wary of.

'Well . . .' The girl glanced around the porch, where there was clearly no place to sit. 'Ah . . .'

Hannah was embarrassed, as if the girl had asked, 'Do you entertain all your visitors outside?' She turned around and opened the back door. 'Come on in. We can sit down.'

'Thank you,' the girl said and smiled.

In the bright fluorescent lights of the kitchen, she was even more beautiful. Hauntingly beautiful. Exquisite features, skin like silk. Lips that made Hannah think of adjectives like full and ripe. And eyes that were like nothing Hannah had ever seen before.

They were large, almond-shaped, heavy-lashed, and luminous. But it wasn't just that. Every time Hannah looked, they seemed to be a different colour. They changed from honey to mahogany to jungle-leaf green to larkspur purple to misty blue. It was amazing.

'If you remember me, then you must know what I'm here about,' the girl said. She rested an elbow on the kitchen table and propped her chin on her fist.

Hannah said one word. 'Thierry.'

'Yes, From the way you say that, maybe you don't need my advice after all.' The girl had an extraordinary voice as well; low and pleasant, with a faint husky throb in it.

Hannah lifted her shoulders. 'Well, there's still a lot I don't know about him – but I don't need anybody to tell me that he's dangerous. And I've already told him to go away.'

'Have you really? How remarkably brave of you.'

Hannah blinked. She hadn't thought of it as being so brave.

'I mean, you do realize how powerful he is? He's a Lord of the Night World, the head of all the made vampires. He could' – the girl snapped her fingers – 'call out a hundred little vampires and werewolves. Not to mention his connection with the witches in Las Vegas.'

'What are you trying to say? That I *shouldn't* have told him to go away? I don't care how many monsters he can call out,' Hannah said sharply.

'No. Of course you don't. Like I said, you're brave.' The girl regarded her with eyes the deep purple of bittersweet nightshade. 'I just want you to realize what he's capable of. He could have this whole county wiped out. He can be very cruel and very childish – if he doesn't get what he wants he'll simply go into a rage.'

'And does he do that a lot – go into rages?'

'All the time, unfortunately.'

I don't believe you.

The thought came to Hannah suddenly. She didn't know *where* it came from, but she couldn't ignore it. There was something about this girl that bothered her, something that felt like a greasy stone held between the fingers. That felt like a lie.

'Who are you?' she said directly. When the girl's eyes – now burnt sienna – lifted to hers this time, she held them. 'I mean, why are you so interested in me? Why are you even *here*, in Montana, where I am? Is it just a coincidence?'

'Of course not. I came because I knew that he was about to find you again. I'm interested in you because, well, I've known Thierry since his childhood, before he became a vampire, and I feel a certain obligation to stop him.' She smiled, meeting Hannah's steady gaze easily. 'And my name . . . is Maya.'

She said the last words slowly, and she seemed to be watching Hannah for a reaction. But the name didn't mean anything to Hannah. And Hannah simply couldn't figure out whether this girl called Maya was lying or not.

'I know you've warned me about Thierry before,' she said, trying to gather her thoughts. 'But I don't remember anything about it except you telling me. I don't even know *what* you are – I mean, are you somebody who's been reincarnated like me? Or are you . . . ?' She left the question open-ended. As a matter of fact, she knew Maya wasn't human; no human was so eerily beautiful or supernaturally graceful. If Maya claimed she *was*, Hannah would know for sure it was a deception.

'I'm a vampire,' Maya said calmly and without hesitation. 'I lived with Thierry's tribe in the days when you lived with the Three Rivers clan. In fact, I'm the one who actually made him into a vampire. I shouldn't have done it; I should have realized he was one of those people who couldn't handle it. But I didn't know he'd go crazy and become . . . what he is.' She looked off into the distance. 'I suppose that's why I feel responsible for him,' she finished softly. Then she looked back at Hannah. 'Any other questions?'

'Hundreds,' Hannah said. 'About the Night World, and about what's happened to me in past lives—'

'And I'm afraid I'm not going to be able to answer most of them. There are rules against talking about the Night World – and anyway, it's safer for you not to know. As for your past lives, well, you don't really *want* to know what he's done to you each time, do you? It's too gruesome.' She leaned forward, looking at Hannah earnestly. 'What you should do now is put the past behind you and forget about all this. Try to have a happy future.'

It was exactly what Hannah had decided to do earlier. So why did she feel like bristling now? She weighed different responses and finally said, 'If he wants to kill me so much, why didn't he just do it last night? Instead of talking to me.'

'Oh, my dear child.' The tone was slightly patronizing, but seemed genuinely pitying. 'He wants you to *love* him first, and then he kills you. I know, it's sick, it's twisted, but it's the way he is. He seems to think it has to be that way, since it was that way the first time. He's obsessed.'

Hannah was silent. Nothing inside her stood up to say that this was a lie. And the idea that Thierry was obsessed certainly rang true. At last she said slowly, 'Thank you for coming to warn me. I do appreciate it.'

'No, you don't,' Maya said. 'I wouldn't either if someone came to tell me things I didn't want to hear. But maybe someday you *will* thank me.' She stood. 'I hope we won't have to meet again.'

Hannah walked her to the back door and let her out.

On the porch, Maya turned. 'He really is insane, you know,' she said. 'You'll probably begin to have doubts again. But he's obsessive and unstable, just like any stalker;

and he's really capable of anything. Don't be fooled.'

'I don't think I'm ever going to see him again,' Hannah said, unreasonably annoyed. 'So it's going to be kind of hard to fool me.'

Maya smiled, nodded, then did the disappearing act. Just as Thierry had, she turned and simply melted into the night.

Hannah stared out into the darkness for a minute or so. Then she went back into the kitchen and called Paul Winfield's number.

She got his answering machine. 'Hi, this is Hannah, and I got your message about making another appointment. I was wondering if we could maybe do it tomorrow – or anyway some time over the weekend. And . . .' She hesitated, wondering if it was something she should say in person, then shrugged. Might as well give him time to prepare. 'And I'd like to do another regression. There are some things I want to figure out.'

She felt better after she hung up. One way or another, she would get at the truth.

She headed into her bedroom with a faint, grim smile.

And stopped dead on the threshold.

Thierry was sitting on her bed.

For a moment Hannah stood frozen. Then she said sharply, 'What are you doing here?' At the same time, she glanced around the room to see how he had gotten in. The windows were shut and only opened from inside.

He must have walked in while I was in the kitchen talking with Maya.

'I had to see you,' Thierry said. He looked – strange. His dark eyes seemed hot somehow, as if he were burning inside. His face was tense and grim.

'I told you to keep away from me.' Hannah kept fear out of her voice, but she was scared. There was a sort of electricity in the air, but it wasn't a good electricity. It was purely dangerous.

'I know you did, and I tried. But I can't stay away, Hannah. I just can't. It makes me . . . crazy.'

And with that, he stood up.

Hannah's heart seemed to jump into her throat and stay there, pounding hard. She fought to keep her face calm.

He's fast, a little voice in her head seemed to say, and with relief she recognized the dark wind voice, the cool voice of reason. *There's no point in running from him, because he can catch you in a second.*

'You have to understand,' Thierry was saying. 'Please try to understand. I *need* you. We were meant to be together. Without you, I'm nothing.'

He took a step toward her. His eyes were black and fathomless, and Hannah could almost feel their heat. Obsessed, yes, she thought. Maya was right. He may put on a good front, but underneath he's just plain crazy. Like any stalker.

'Say you understand,' Thierry said. He reached a pleading hand toward her.

'I understand,' Hannah said grimly. 'And I still want you to go away.'

'I can't. I have to make sure we'll be together, the way we were meant to be. And there's only one way to do that.'

There was something different about his mouth. Two delicate fangs were protruding, indenting his lower lip.

Hannah felt a cold fist close over her heart.

'You have to join the Night World, Hannah. You have to become like me. I promise you, once it's over, you'll be happy.'

'Happy?' A wave of sickening revulsion swept over

Hannah. 'As a monster like you? I was *happy* before you ever showed up. I'd be happy if you'd just keep out of my life forever. I—'

Stop talking! The cool wind voice was screaming at her, but Hannah was too overwrought to listen.

'You're disgusting. I *hate* you. And nothing can ever make me love you ag—'

She didn't get to finish. In one swift movement, he was in front of her. And then he grabbed her.

CHAPTER 9

'You'll change your mind,' Thierry said.

An instant later everything was chaos. Thierry had one hand in her hair, twisting her head to the side, exposing her neck. His other arm was keeping both her arms trapped against her body. Hannah was twisting, struggling – and it wasn't doing any good. He was unbelievably strong.

She felt the warmth of breath on her neck . . . and then the sharpness of teeth.

'Don't fight.' Thierry's muffled voice came to her. 'You'll only make it hurt worse.'

Hannah fought. And it did hurt. The pain of having blood drawn out against her will was like nothing she'd ever felt. It was as if her soul was being pulled out of her body, a pain that radiated down her neck and through her left shoulder and arm. It turned her vision grey and made her feel light-headed.

'I – *hate* – you,' she got out. She tried to reach for him with her mind, to see if she could hurt him that way . . . but it was like running up against an obsidian wall. She could feel nothing of Thierry in the contact, just smooth black hardness.

Forget about that, the cool wind voice said. *And don't faint; you've got to stay conscious. Think about your room. You need wood; you need a weapon. Where . . . ?*

The desk.

Even as she thought it, Thierry's grip on her was shifting. He was forcing her to turn so she faced away from him, still holding her in an iron grip with one arm. She had no idea what he was doing with the other arm until he spoke again.

'I have to give you back something for what I took.'

And then the other arm was in front of Hannah, wrist pressing to her mouth. She still didn't really understand – she was dazed with pain and loss of blood – until she felt warm liquid trickling into her mouth and tasted a strange exotic taste.

Oh, God – *no.* It's his *blood.* You're drinking vampire blood.

She tried not to swallow, but the liquid kept flowing in, choking her. It didn't taste at all like blood. It was rich and wild and burned slightly – and she could almost feel it changing her.

You've got to stop this, the cool wind voice told her. *Now.*

With a violent wrench that almost dislocated her shoulder, Hannah got one arm free. Then she started to fight hard, not because she wanted to get away, but because she wanted to keep Thierry occupied in holding her. While they were struggling, she surreptitiously reached out with her free hand.

I can't feel it. She threw her body back and forth, trying to get Thierry to move closer to the desk. Just a little farther . . . there. There!

Her fingers were on her desk. She stomped on Thierry's foot to keep him distracted. She heard a snarl of pain and Thierry shook her, but her fingers kept groping across the desk until they found something smooth and long, with a pointed graphite end.

A pencil.

Hannah curled her fingers, gathering the pencil into her fist. She was gasping with effort, which meant more of the strange blood was flowing into her mouth.

Now think. *Visualize his hand. Picture the pencil going right in, all the way through. And now* strike.

Hannah brought the pencil up with all her strength, driving it into the back of Thierry's hand.

She heard a yelp of pain and outrage – and at the same instant she felt a stab of pain herself. She'd driven the pencil all the way through his hand and jabbed her own cheek.

She didn't spend time worrying about it. The iron grip on her had loosened. She slammed a foot into Thierry's shin and spun away as he jerked back.

The desk! You need another weapon!

Even as the voice was telling her, Hannah was reaching for her desk, gathering a random handful of pens and pencils. Thank God for her habit of losing pencils, which was the reason she had to keep so many. As soon as she had them, she twisted to dart across the room, getting her back to a wall. She faced Thierry, panting.

'This next one goes right into your heart,' she told him, pulling one pencil out of the handful and holding it in her fist. Her voice was soft and ragged, but absolutely deadly in its conviction.

'You hurt me!' Thierry had pulled the pencil out and was staring at the wound. His face was contorted, his eyes blazing with animal pain and fury. He looked like a stranger.

'Right,' Hannah said, panting. 'And if you come close to me again, I'll kill you. That's a promise. Now get the *hell* out of my house and out of my life!'

Thierry stared back and forth from her to his hand. Then he snarled – really snarled, his upper lip lifting, his teeth bared. Hannah had never seen a human face look so bestial.

'You'll be sorry,' he said, like a child in a temper tantrum. 'And if you tell anybody about this, I'll kill them. I will. It's Night World law.'

Then he did the fade-out thing. Hannah blinked and he wasn't there. He must have backed up down the hall, but she didn't hear a door open or close.

It was several minutes before she could loosen her grip on her pencil or step away from the wall. When she could, it was to stumble toward the phone. She pressed the speed dial for Chess's number.

Busy.

Hannah dropped the phone. She was swaying on her feet, feeling sick and giddy, but she headed for the dining room. There, keeping one of the windows shut, was a wooden dowel, the remnant of some long-past safety craze of her mother's. Hannah broke it over her knee and carried one splinter-ended piece with her to the garage.

The dusty old Ford was parked there, the one her father had driven before he died. Hannah found the keys and started for Chess's house. She could think of only one thing: she didn't want to be alone.

Grey spots danced in front of her eyes as she drove. She kept imagining things rushing at her from the prairie.

Stay awake. Just stay awake, she told herself, biting her lip hard enough to draw blood.

There! There's the house up ahead. You can see the light. All you have to do is get there.

She stepped on the accelerator. And then everything went grey.

* * *

Thierry looked around the resort lobby, then glanced at his watch. He'd been doing that every five minutes for about the last twelve hours, and his nerves were starting to fray.

He didn't like leaving Hannah alone. Of course, the ring would protect her when she was away from the house, and the amulet he'd buried in her backyard would protect the house itself. It was a strong amulet, made for him by Grandma Harman, the oldest and most powerful witch in the world, the Crone of the Inner Circle. It set wards around the house, so that no Night Person could enter without a direct invitation from somebody who lived inside.

He still didn't like leaving Hannah alone.

Only a little while longer, he told himself. It had taken him most of last night and all of today to call in enough of his own people to set up a plan for watching over Hannah.

She'd told him to go away, and he had. Her word was law to him. But that didn't mean he couldn't have her guarded. She need never realize that there were Night People around her, watching and waiting in the shadows – and ready to fight to the death if any danger appeared.

Lupe had been right. He couldn't deal with this alone. And now he was going to have to rely on other people to keep Hannah safe.

Thierry looked at his watch again. It was nine o'clock at night, and he was almost tempted to give up on Circe. But only a witch of her power could set up the kind of heavy-duty wards that would protect Hannah wherever she went in Amador County.

He kept waiting. As he did, he stared at a gun rack on the wall and tried to keep his brain turned off. It didn't work.

Ever since he'd awoken Hannah from her hypnotic trance, he'd been trying very hard not to think about the old days. But now, he found himself being irresistibly drawn back, not only thinking about them, but reliving them. Travelling back in his mind to the stupid young man he had been . . .

He hadn't been the first vampire. He didn't have that distinction.

He had only been the second.

He'd grown up in the tribe of Maya and Hellewise. *The* Maya and Hellewise, the twin daughters of Hecate Witch Queen. The Maya and Hellewise who would go down as the two greatest figures in Night World history; Hellewise Hearth-Woman as the ancestress of the Harman family, the most famous of the living witches, and Maya as the ancestress of both the lamia and the made vampires.

But of course he knew nothing about that at the time.

All he knew was that they were both pretty girls. Beautiful. Hellewise had long yellow hair and deep brown eyes. Maya had long black hair and eyes that glittered in different colours like the changing lights in a glacier. He liked both sisters very much.

Maybe that was his downfall.

He'd been a very ordinary fellow, with a good throwing arm, a delicate touch in carving ivory, and a vague longing to see the world. He'd taken it for granted that his tribe was special, that they could influence the weather and summon animals from the forest. They were the witch people, they'd been granted special powers, and that was all. It wasn't anything to worry about.

And, like everyone else, he knew that Maya was doing experiments in the forest, using her powers to try and become immortal. But that didn't worry him particularly either . . .

I was very young and very, very stupid, Thierry thought.

That had been the real downfall of the tribe. Maya's desire to become immortal. Because she'd been willing to pay any price for it, even to the point of becoming a monster and leaving a curse on all her descendants. Maybe if Thierry and the other witch people had realized that, they could have stopped her before it happened.

Because Maya had finally found the right spell to achieve immortality. The problem was that to do it, she had to steal the babies of the tribe. All four of them. She took them out to the forest, did the spell, and drank their blood. Thierry and the rest of the tribe found the four little bled-out bodies later.

Hellewise had cried all night. Thierry, who couldn't understand how the pretty girl he liked could have done something so awful, cried, too. Maya herself had disappeared completely.

But a few nights later she came to Thierry. He was keeping watch outside the cave when she appeared silently beside him.

She had changed.

She wasn't the pretty girl he knew anymore. She was stunningly, dazzlingly beautiful. But she was different. She moved with the grace of a night time predator, and her eyes reflected the firelight.

She was very pale, but that only made her more lovely. Her mouth, which had always been soft and inviting, seemed red as blood. And when she smiled at him, he saw her long pointed teeth.

'Hello, Theorn,' she said, that was his name back then. 'I want to make you immortal.'

Thierry was scared out of his mind.

He had no idea what she'd become – some weird creature with unnatural teeth. But he knew he had no desire at all to be like her.

'I really think it's unfair, the way you go back and forth between me and Hellewise,' she said casually, sitting down on the bare earth. 'So I've decided to resolve the question. You're going to be mine, now and forever.'

She reached out and took his hand. Her fingers were very slender and very cold, and unbelievably strong. Thierry couldn't pull away. He stared at his hand with his mouth open like the idiot he was.

This was the time he should have started yelling, thrashing, doing anything to attract attention and get away. But Maya seemed to hold him with her eyes like a snake holding a bird. She was unnatural and evil . . . but she was so beautiful.

It was the first and the last time that Thierry would be fascinated by the beauty of pure evil, but it was enough. He was doomed from that moment. He'd doomed himself.

An instant of hesitation. He would pay for it for unimaginable years in the future.

'It's not so bad,' Maya was saying, still fixing him with her terrible and lovely eyes. 'There are a few things I had to figure out – a few things I didn't expect. I thought drinking the blood of the babies would be the end of it, but no.'

Thierry felt sick.

'I've got these teeth for a reason, apparently. It seems I have to drink the blood of a mortal creature every day, or I die. It's inconvenient, but I can live with it.'

Thierry whispered something beginning with, 'Oh, Hecate, Dark Mother—'

'Now, stop that!' Maya made a sharp gesture. 'No

praying, please, and especially not to that old harridan. I'm not a witch anymore. I'm something completely new, I suppose I should think of a name for myself. Night-hunter . . . blood-drinker . . . I don't know, the possibilities are endless. I'm going to start a new race, Theorn. We'll be better than the witches, stronger, faster – and we'll live forever. We'll never die, so we'll rule everyone. And you're going to be my first convert.'

'No,' Thierry said. He still thought he had a choice.

'Yes. I'm going to have a baby, not with you, I'm afraid; I don't think you'll be able to, and the baby will have my blood. And I'm going to give my blood to other people the way I'll give it to you now. Someday there won't be anyone in the world who won't have my blood. It's a nice thought, isn't it?' She rested her chin on a fist and her eyes glittered.

'Hellewise will stop you,' Thierry said flatly.

'My sister? No, I don't think so. Especially not since I'll have you to help me. She likes you, you know. It will be hard for her to kill somebody she likes so much.'

'She won't have to. *I'll* kill you,' Thierry snarled.

Maya laughed out loud.

'You? *You*? Don't you know yourself yet? You're not a killer, you don't have the guts for it. That will change, of course, after I give you my blood. But you won't want to kill me then. You'll join me – and be happy. You'll see.' She dusted off her hands as if a difficult negotiation had been accomplished and terms had been reached. 'Now. Let's do it.'

He was strong. He had that good throwing arm – he was dead accurate with a spear or a killing stick. But she was so much stronger that she could handle him like a baby. The first thing she did was clamp a hand across his mouth, because by this time it had occurred even to stupid

Thierry that he was in very bad trouble, and that he needed help.

There was no sound of a struggle as she dragged him off into the bushes.

'I'm afraid this is going to hurt,' she said. She was lying on top of him, her eyes glittering into his. She was excited. 'At least, all the animals I've caught seem to have found it very unpleasant. But it's for your own good.'

Then she ripped his throat out.

That was what it felt like. And that was when he realized what those long canine teeth were for. Like any lynx or cave lion or wolf, she needed teeth to tear.

Through the black waves of shock and pain, he heard her drinking.

It lasted a long time. But finally, mercifully, he realized that he was dying. He took comfort in the thought that the horror would soon be over.

He couldn't have been more wrong. The horror was just beginning.

When Maya lifted her head, her mouth was scarlet with his blood. Dripping. She wasn't beautiful any longer, she was simply fiendish.

'Now,' she said. 'I'm going to give you something that will make it all better.'

She pulled back and placed a fire-hardened splinter of wood at her own throat. She smiled at him. Maya had always been physically brave. And then, with a gesture almost of ecstasy, she plunged the splinter in, sending blood spurting and spilling.

Then she fell on top of him again.

He didn't mean to swallow the blood that filled his mouth. But everything was so grey and unreal – and he still had enough survival reflex left to not want to drown in it. The warm, strange-tasting liquid went down his throat. It burned like fermented-berry wine.

After she made him drink, he realized to his relief that he was still dying. He didn't know that he wasn't going to stay dead. He felt her carrying him farther into the forest, he was completely limp now and didn't put up any resistance – and then everything went black.

When he woke up, he'd been buried.

He clawed himself up out of the shallow grave and found himself looking into the astonished face of his brother Conlan. The tribe had buried him in the traditional way – in the soft dirt at the back of the cave.

In the minute before his brother could yell in surprise, Thierry was at his throat.

It was animal instinct. A thirst inside of him like nothing he had ever known. A pain that was like being underwater – being strangled – gasping for air. It made him desperate, made him insane. He didn't think at all.

He simply tried, mindlessly, to tear at his brother's throat.

What stopped him was someone calling his name. Calling it over and over, in great pain. When he looked around, he saw Hellewise, her brown eyes huge and spilling with tears, her mouth trembling.

The expression on her face would haunt him forever.

He ran out of the cave and kept running. Behind him, just faintly, he could hear Hellewise's voice, 'Theorn, I'll stop her. I swear to you, I'll stop her.'

He realized later that it was all Hellewise could offer him. She knew that his curse was permanent. What he was now, he would be forever.

There wasn't a name for it then, but he was the first made vampire. Maya, who would have a son just as she promised, was the first of the lamia, the family vampires who could grow up and have children. And her son, Red

Fern, would be the ancestor of the Redfern family, the most powerful lamia family in the Night World.

Thierry didn't know any of that as he ran. He only knew he had to get away from people, or he would hurt them.

Maya caught up with him while he was frantically trying to quench his thirst by drinking from a stream.

'You're going to make yourself sick,' she said, inspecting him critically. 'You can't drink that. It's blood you need.'

Thierry jumped up, shaking with fury and hatred and weakness all mixed together. 'What about *yours*?' he snarled.

Maya laughed. 'How sweet. But it won't do. You need the blood of living creatures.' She wasn't at all afraid of him, and he remembered how strong she had been. He was no match for her.

He turned and began to stumble off.

Maya called after him, 'You can't do it, you know. You can't get away from me. I've *chosen* you, Theorn. You're mine, now and forever. And in the end you'll realize that and join me.'

Thierry kept going. He could hear her laughing as he went.

He lived on the steppes for several weeks, wandering across the high windswept grasslands. He was more an animal than anything resembling a person. The thirst inside him made him desperate, until he stumbled over a rabbit. The next instant he found that he was holding it, biting into its throat. His teeth were like Maya's now – long, sensitive, and perfect for tearing or puncturing. And she was right, only the blood of a living creature could help the burning, suffocating feeling inside him.

He didn't catch food very often. Every time he drank it

reminded him of what he was.

He was starving when he finally came to the Three Rivers.

He didn't see the little girl out picking spring greens until he was on top of her. He burst out of a pile of brush, panting with thirst like a wounded deer – and there she was, looking up at him. And then everything went dark for a while.

When he came to himself, he stopped drinking. He needed the food, he would die in terrible agony without it – but he dropped the girl and ran. Hana's people found him a little while later.

And they did exactly what he'd expected any tribe to do – they saw that he was an abomination and brandished spears at him. He expected them to kill him at any minute. He didn't realize yet, and neither did they, that a creature like him took some killing.

And then he saw Hana.

CHAPTER 10

The first sight of her broke through his animal state and gave him enough mind to stand up like a man. She reminded him of Hellewise. She had that same look of tender courage, that same ageless wisdom in her eyes. Any woman could be pretty by virtue of regular features. But Hana was beautiful because her soul showed in her face.

Seeing her made him ashamed. Seeing her defend him, intercede on his behalf as she was so obviously doing, made him angry.

He resisted when she sneaked him out of the cave and tried to send him back into the world. Didn't she understand? It was best for him to die. As long as he was loose, no child, no woman, no man was safe. Even as he stood there in the moonlight with her, he was trembling with need. The bloodlust was trying to unbalance his mind, and it was all he could do not to grab *her* and bite into her soft throat.

When she offered him her throat, he almost cried. It wasn't a sacrifice to turn her down and walk away. It was the only right thing to do, the only thing he could do.

And then the hunters came.

His mind was unbalanced by the torture. It was that simple. Not that it was an excuse, there was no excuse for what followed. But during the endless time while Hana's clan burned and stabbed and beat him, he lost all contact with the person he thought of as himself. He became an animal, as mindless as the mob that was trying to kill him.

As an animal, he wanted two things: to survive and to strike out at the people who were hurting him. And there was a way to do both.

Throats. White throats, spurting dark blood. The image came to him slowly in his haze of pain. He didn't have to lie here and take this. He was wounded, but there was still a granite core of strength inside him. He could fight back, and his enemies would give him life.

The next time a spear jabbed at him, he grabbed it and pulled.

It belonged to the broad-shouldered hunter, the one who'd led the others to him. Thierry grabbed the man as he stumbled forward, wrestling him to the ground. And then, before anyone in the crowd had time to react, he darted for the hunter's throat, for the big vein that pulsed just under the skin.

It was all over in a minute. He was drinking deep, deep, and gaining strength with every swallow. The clan of the Three Rivers was staring at him in paralyzed shock.

It felt good.

He tossed the dead man aside and reached for another.

When several hunters came at him at once, he knocked them apart and killed them, one, two, three. He was a very efficient killer. The blood made him supernaturally strong and fast, and the bloodlust gave him motivation. He was like a wolf set loose in a herd of antelope – except that for a long time nobody in the clan had the sense to run. They kept coming at him, trying to stop him, and he kept killing.

It was a slaughter. He killed them all.

He was drunk with blood and he gloried in it, in the animal simplicity of it, the power it gave him. Killing *was* glory. Killing to eat, killing for revenge. Destroying the people who hurt him. He didn't ever want to stop.

He was drinking the last drops from the veins of a young girl when he looked down and saw it was Hana.

Her clear grey eyes were wide open, but the light in them was beginning to go dark.

He'd killed her.

In one blinding instant he wasn't an animal anymore. He was a person. And he was looking down at the one person who had tried to help him, who had offered him her blood to keep him alive.

He raised his eyes and saw the devastation he'd left in the cave. It wasn't just this girl. He'd murdered most of her tribe.

That was when he knew the truth. He was damned. Worse than Maya. He'd committed a crime so monstrous that he could never be forgiven, never be redeemed. He had joined evil in the end, just as Maya had promised he would.

No punishment could be too great for him – but then, no punishment would make the slightest difference anyway, not to these people or to the dying girl in his arms.

For just an instant some part of him pushed away at the feelings of guilt and horror. All right, you're evil, it said. You might as well go ahead and *be* evil. Enjoy it. Have no regrets. It's your nature, now. Give in.

Then the girl in his arms stirred.

She was still conscious, although barely. Her eyes were

still open. She was looking up at him . . .

In that moment, Thierry felt a shock that was different from anything he'd ever felt before.

In those large grey eyes, in the pupils which were hugely dilated as if to catch every last ray of light before death, he saw . . . himself.

Himself and the girl, walking together, hand in hand through the ages. Joined. Shifting scenes behind them, different places, different times. But always the two of them, tied with an invisible bond.

He *recognized* her. It was almost as if all those different ages had already happened, as if he were only remembering them. But he knew they were in the future. He was looking down the corridor of time, seeing what *should have been.*

She was his soulmate.

She was the one who was supposed to have walked with him through different lives, being born and loving and dying and being born again. They'd been born *for* each other, to help each other grow and blossom and discover and evolve. They should have had many lives together.

And none of it was going to happen. He was an immortal creature – how could he die and be born again? And she was dying *because* of him. He'd destroyed it all, everything. He'd killed his destiny.

In the enormity of it, he sat silent and stunned. He couldn't say, 'I'm sorry.' He couldn't say, 'What have I done?' There was nothing that he could say that wasn't so trivial as to be demeaning to her. He simply sat and shook, looking down into her eyes. He had an endless feeling of falling.

And then Hana spoke.

I forgive you.

It was just a whisper, but he heard it in his mind, not with his ears. And he understood it, even though her language was different from his. Thierry reeled with the discovery that he could talk to her. Oh, Goddess, the chance at least to tell her how he would try to atone for this by spilling out his own blood . . .

You can't forgive me. He could see that she understood his own hushed answer. He knew he didn't deserve forgiveness. But part of him wanted her to realize that he had never meant this to happen. *I wasn't always like this. I used to be a person –*

We don't have time for that, she told him. Her spirit seemed to be reaching toward him, drawing him into her, facing him in a still and separate place where only the two of them existed. He knew then that she had seen the same thing he had, the same corridor of time.

She was gentle, but so sad. *I don't want you to die. But I want you to promise me one thing.*

Anything.

I want you to promise me you'll never kill again.

It was easy to promise. He didn't plan to live . . . no, she didn't want him to die. But he couldn't live without her and he certainly couldn't live after what he'd done.

He'd worry about it later, about how to deal with the long grey stretch of future waiting for him. For now, he said, *I'll never kill again.*

She gave him just the faintest of smiles.

And then she died.

The grey eyes went fixed and dark. Unseeing. Her skin was ghostly white and her body was absolutely still. She seemed smaller all at once as her spirit left her.

Thierry cradled her, moaning like a wounded animal. He was crying. Shaking so hard he almost couldn't keep hold of her. Helpless, pierced by love that felt like a spear, he reached out to gently push her hair off her face. His thumb stroked her cheek – and left a trail of blood.

He stared at it in horror. The mark was like a blaze of red against her pale skin.

Even his love was deadly. His caress had branded her.

The few survivors of Hana's clan were on the move, surrounding Thierry, panting and gasping with their spears ready. They sensed that he was vulnerable now.

And he wouldn't have lifted a hand to stop them . . . except that he had made a promise to Hana. She wanted him alive to keep it.

So he left her there. He picked up her still, cooling body and carried it toward the nearest hunter. The man stared at him in fear and disbelief, but he finally dropped his spear to take the dead girl. And then Thierry walked out of the cave and into the merciless sunlight.

He headed for his home.

Maya caught up with him somewhere on the steppes, appearing out of the tall, ripping grass. 'I told you how you'd end up. Now forget that washed-out blonde and start enjoying life with me.'

Thierry didn't even look at her. The only thing he could imagine doing with Maya was killing her . . . and he couldn't do that.

'Don't walk away from me!' Maya wasn't laughing now. She was furious. Her voice followed him as he kept going. 'I *chose* you, Theorn! You're mine. You *can't* walk away from me!'

Thierry kept going, neither slower nor faster, letting her voice blend into the humming of the insects on the grassland. But her mental voice followed him.

I'll never let you get away. You'll always be mine, now and forever.

Thierry travelled fast, and in only a few days, he

reached home and the person he'd come to see.

Hellewise looked up from her drying herbs and gasped.

'I'm not going to hurt you,' he said. 'I need your help.'

What he wanted from her was a spell to sleep. He wanted to sleep until Hana was born again.

'It could be a long time,' Hellewise said when he told her the whole story. 'It sounds as if her soul has been damaged. It could be hundreds of years – even thousands.'

Thierry didn't care.

'And you might die,' Hellewise said, looking at him steadily with her deep, soft brown eyes. 'And with what you've become – I don't think creatures like you are reborn. You would just . . . die.'

Thierry simply nodded. He was only afraid of two things: that Maya would find him while he was asleep, and that he wouldn't know when to wake up.

'I can arrange the second,' Hellewise said quietly. 'You're linked anyway; your souls are one. When she's born again, voices from the Other Side will whisper to you.'

Thierry himself figured out how to solve the first problem. He dug himself a grave. It was the only place where he could count on being safe and undisturbed.

Hellewise gave him an infusion of roots and bark and Thierry went to sleep.

He slept a long time.

He slept straight through the epic battle when Hellewise drove Maya and her son Red Fern out of the tribe and away from the witches. He slept through the origins of the Night World and thousands of years of human change. When he finally woke up, the world was a different place, with civilizations and cities. And he knew that somewhere Hana had been born in one of them.

He began to look.

He was a wanderer, a lost soul with no home and no

people. But not a killer. He learned to take blood without killing, to find willing donors instead of hunting terrified prey.

He looked in every village he passed, learning about the new world surrounding him, surviving on very little, searching every face he saw. Lots of communities would have been glad to adopt him, this tall young man with dusty clothes and far-seeing eyes. But he only stayed long enough to make sure that Hana wasn't there.

When he did find her it was in Egypt, the Kingdom of the Two Lands. She was sixteen. Her name was Ha-nahkt.

And Thierry would have recognized her anywhere, because she was still tall, still fair-haired and grey-eyed and beautiful.

Except for one thing.

Across her left cheek, where his fingers had smeared her own blood the night that he had killed her, was a red mark like a bruise. Like a stain on her perfect skin.

It was a sort of psychic brand, a physical reminder of what had happened in her last life. A permanent wound. And it was his fault.

Thierry was overcome with grief and shame. He saw that the other girl, Ket, the friend who had been with Hana in the last life, was with her again now. She had friends. Maybe it was best to leave her alone in this life, not even try to speak to her.

But he had forgotten about Maya.

Vampires don't die.

Life is strange sometimes. It was just as Thierry was thinking this that a figure walked into the lobby. Still half in his daydream of the past, he was expecting it to be Circe, so for a moment he was simply confused. Then his heart rate picked up and every muscle in his body tensed violently.

It was Maya.

He hadn't seen her for over a hundred years. The last time had been in Quebec, when Hannah had been named Annette.

And Maya had just killed her.

Thierry stood up.

She was as beautiful as ever. But to Thierry it was like the rainbow on oil scum. He hated her more than he had ever imagined he could hate anyone.

'So you found me,' he said quietly. 'I knew you'd show up eventually.'

Maya smiled brilliantly. 'I found *her* first.'

Thierry went still.

'That amulet was a very good one. I had to wait around to catch her alone so she could invite me inside.'

Thierry's heart lurched. He felt a physical wrench, as if something in him were actually trying to get out, trying desperately to get to Hannah – now.

How could he have been so stupid? She was too innocent; of course she would invite someone into her house. And she thought of Maya as a friend.

The ring should have offered at least a measure of protection from mind control, but only if Hannah had kept it on. Thierry realized now that she probably hadn't.

His voice a bare whisper, he said, 'What did you do to her?'

'Oh, not much. Mostly it was just conversation. I mentioned that you were likely to get rough with her if things didn't go your way.' Maya tilted her head, eyes on his face, looking for a reaction.

Thierry didn't give it to her. He just stood, watching her silently.

She hadn't changed in thousands of years. She *never* changed, never grew, never got tired. And she never gave up. He didn't think she was capable of it.

Sometimes he thought he should just tie himself to her at the waist and find a bottomless pit to jump into. Rid the world of its two oldest vampires and all the problems Maya caused.

But there was his promise to Hannah.

'It doesn't matter what you say to her,' he said stonily. 'You don't understand, Maya. This time is different. She remembers and—'

'And she hates you. I know. Poor baby.' Maya made a mock-sympathetic face. Her eyes sparkled peacock blue.

Thierry gritted his teeth. 'And I've come to a decision,' he went on evenly. 'The cycle has to be broken. And there *is* a way to do it.'

'I know,' Maya said before he could finish. 'You can give her up. Give in to me—'

'Yes.' This time he cut her off. And the look of astonishment that flared in her eyes was worth it. 'At least, yes to the first part,' he finished. 'I'm giving her up.'

'You're not. You can't.'

'She's happy in this life. And she – doesn't want me.' There. It had been hard to say, but he'd gotten it out. 'She remembers everything – I don't know why, but she does. Maybe because she's so close to her original form. Maybe somehow the memories are closer to the surface. Or maybe it's the hypnosis. But in any case, she doesn't want me anymore.'

Maya was watching him, fascinated, her eyes the violet of deep twilight, her lips parted. Suddenly, she looked beyond him and smiled secretly. 'She remembers everything? You really think so?'

Thierry nodded. 'All I've ever brought her is misery and pain. I guess she realizes that.' He took a breath, then caught Maya's eyes again. 'So I'm ending the cycle . . . now.'

'You're going to walk away.'

'And so are you. She's no threat to you anymore. If you want something from me, the only person to deal with is me. You can try any time you like in Vegas.' He gazed at her levelly.

Maya threw back her head and let out ripples of musical laughter.

'Oh, why didn't you tell me before? You could have saved me some trouble . . . but on the other hand, her blood was very sweet. I wouldn't have missed—'

She broke off, then, because Thierry slammed her against the oak-panelled wall of the lobby.

In one instant, his control had disappeared. He was so angry that he couldn't speak out loud.

What did you do to her? What did you do? He shouted the words telepathically as his hands closed around Maya's throat.

Maya just smiled at him. She was the oldest vampire, and the most powerful. In every vampire who came after her, her blood had been diluted, half as strong, a quarter as strong, an eighth. But she was the original and the purest. She wasn't afraid of anyone.

Me? I *didn't do anything,* she said, answering him the same way. *I'm afraid* you *were the one who attacked her. She seemed very unhappy about it; she even stabbed you with a pencil.* Maya lifted a hand and Thierry saw a neat dark hole puncturing it, faintly ringed with blood.

The power of illusion, he thought. Maya could appear as anyone and anything she wanted. She had talents that usually only belonged to werewolves and shapeshifters. And of course she was a witch.

She really has extraordinary spirit, Maya went on. *But she's all right – you didn't exchange as much blood as you'd planned. The pencil, you see.*

People were gathering behind Thierry, murmuring anxiously. They were about to interfere and ask him to please let go of the girl he was strangling.

He ignored them.

Listen to me, he told Maya, staring into her mocking golden eyes. *Listen, because I'm never going to say this again. If you touch Hannah again – ever – in any life – I will kill you.*

'I'll kill you,' he whispered out loud, to emphasize it. 'Believe me, Maya, I'll do it.'

Then he let her go. He had to get to Hannah. Even a small exchange of blood with a vampire could be dangerous, and Maya's blood was the most potent on earth. Worse, he'd already taken some of Hannah's blood last night. She could be critically weak now . . . or starting to change.

He wouldn't think about that.

You won't, you know. Maya's telepathic voice followed him as he made for the door. *You won't kill me. Not Thierry the compassionate, Thierry the good vampire, Thierry the saint of Circle Daybreak. You're not capable of it. You* can't *kill.*

Thierry stopped on the threshold and turned around. He stared directly into Maya's eyes.

'Try me.'

Then he was outside, moving quickly through the night. Even so, Maya got the last word.

And, of course, there's your promise . . .

CHAPTER 11

Hannah stirred.

She vaguely felt that something was wrong, something needed doing. Then she remembered. The car! She had to stay awake, had to keep the car on the road . . .

Her eyes flew open.

She was already off the road. The Ford had gone roving over the open prairie, where there was almost nothing to hit except sagebrush and tumbleweeds. It had ended up with its front bumper against a prickly pear, bending the cactus at an impossible angle.

The night was very quiet. She looked around and found that she could see the light of Chess's house, behind her and to the left.

The engine was off. Hannah turned the key in the ignition, but only got a grinding sound.

Now what? Should I get out and walk?

She tried to concentrate on her body, to figure out how she felt. She ought to feel terrible, after all, she'd lost blood and swallowed who knew what kind of poison from Thierry's veins.

But instead she only felt strangely dizzy, slightly dreamy.

I can walk. I'm fine.

Holding on to her length of dowel, she got out of the car and started toward the light. She could hardly feel the rough ground and the bluestem grass under her feet.

She had gone about a hundred yards toward the light when she heard a wolf howl.

It was such a distinctive sound – and so incongruous. Hannah stopped in her tracks. For a wild moment she wondered if coyotes howled.

But that was ridiculous. It was a wolf, just like the wolves that had attacked her at Paul's. And she didn't have anything made of silver.

Just keep walking, she thought. She didn't need the cool wind voice to tell her that.

Even in her light-headed state, she was frightened. She'd seen the savagery of teeth and claws close up. And the part of her that was Hana of the Three Rivers had a gut-deep fear of wild animals that the civilized Hannah Snow could never begin to approach.

She gripped her stick in a clammy palm and kept walking grimly.

The howl sounded again, so close that Hannah jumped inside her skin. Her eyes darted, trying to pick objects out in the darkness. She felt as if she could see better than usual at night – could the vampire blood have done that? But even with her new vision, she couldn't spot anything moving. The world around her was deserted and eerily quiet.

And the stars were very far away. They blazed in the sky with a cold blue light as if to show how distant they were from human affairs.

I could die here and they'd go right on shining, Hannah thought. She felt very small and very unimportant – and very alone.

And then she heard a breath drawn behind her.

Funny. The wolf howls had been so loud, and this was so soft . . . and yet it was much more terrifying. It was close – intimate. A *personal* sound that told her she definitely wasn't alone.

Hannah whirled with her stick held ready. Her skin was crawling and she could feel a wash of acid from her stomach, but she meant to fight for her life. She was at one with the cool wind voice; her heart was dark and cold and steely.

A tall figure was standing there. Starlight reflected off pale blond hair.

Thierry.

Hannah levelled her stick.

'What's the matter? Come back for more?' she said, and she was pleased to find her voice steady. Husky, but steady. She waved her stick at him to show what kind of 'more' she meant.

'Are you all right?' Thierry said.

He looked – different from the last time she'd seen him. His expression was different. His dark eyes seemed pensive again, the sort of expression a star might have if it cared about anything that was going on underneath it. Infinitely remote, but infinitely sad, too.

'Why should you care?' A wave of dizziness went through her. She fought it off – and saw that he was stepping toward her, hand reaching out. She whipped the stick up to the exact level of his hand, an inch from his palm. She was impressed with herself for how fast she did it. Her body was moving the way it had with the werewolves, instinctively and smoothly.

I suppose I had a life as a warrior, she mused. I think that's where the cool wind voice comes from, just the way the crystal voice comes from Hana of the Three Rivers.

'I do care,' Thierry said. His voice said he didn't expect her to believe it.

Hannah laughed. The combination of her dizziness and her body instinct was having an odd effect. She felt brashly, stupidly overconfident. Maybe this is what drunk feels like, she thought, her mind wandering again.

'Hannah—'

Hannah made the stick whistle in the air, stopping him from coming any closer to her. 'Are you *crazy*?' she said. There were tears in her eyes. 'Do you think that you can just attack me and then come back and say 'I'm sorry' and it's all going to be OK? Well, it isn't. If there was ever anything between us, it's all over now. There is no second chance.'

She could see his face tense. A muscle twitched in his tight jaw. But the strangest thing was that she could have sworn he had tears in his eyes, too.

It infuriated her. How dare he pretend to be hurt by her, after what he'd done?

'*I hate you.*' She spat the words with a force that startled even her. 'I don't need you. I don't want you. And I'm telling you for the third time, *keep the hell away from me.*'

He had opened his mouth as if he were about to say something, but when she got to 'I don't need you,' he suddenly shut it. When she finished, he looked away, across the shortgrass prairie.

'And maybe that's best,' he said almost inaudibly.

'For you to keep away?'

'For you to hate me.' He looked at her again. Hannah had never seen eyes like that before. They were impossibly distant and shattered and still . . . like the peace after a war that killed everyone.

'Hannah, I came to tell you that I *am* going away,' he went on. His voice was like his eyes, bloodless and quenched. 'I'm going home. I won't bother you again. And you're right; you don't need me. You can live a long and happy life without me.'

If he expected her to be impressed, she wasn't. She wouldn't believe words from him anymore.

'There's just one thing.' He hesitated. 'Before I go, would you let me look at you? At your neck. I want to make sure that' – another fleeting hesitation – 'that I didn't hurt you when I attacked you.'

Hannah laughed again, a short, sharp bark of a laugh. 'How stupid do you think I am? I mean, *really*.' She laughed again and heard an edge of hysteria in it. 'If you want to do something for me, you can turn around and *go*. Go away forever.'

'I will.' There was so much strain on his face. 'I promise. I'm just worried about you getting indoors before you faint.'

'I can take care of myself. I don't need any help from you.' Hannah was feeling dizzier by the minute, but she tried not to let it show. 'If you would just leave, I'll be fine.'

In fact, she knew she wasn't going to be fine. The grey spots were swarming in front of her eyes again. She was going to pass out soon.

Then I'd better start for Chess's, she thought. It was insanity to turn her back on him, but it was worse insanity to stand here until she collapsed at his feet.

'I'm leaving now,' she said, trying to sound clear and precise and unlike someone who was about to fall over unconscious. 'And I don't want you to follow me.'

She turned and started walking.

I will not faint, I will not faint, she told herself grimly. She swung her stick and tried to take deep breaths of the cool night air. But tufts of grass seemed to be trying to trip her up with every step and the entire landscape seemed to rock every time she looked up.

I . . . will . . . not . . . faint. She knew her life depended on it. The ground seemed rubbery now, as if her feet were sinking into it and then rebounding. And where was the light that marked Chess's house? It had somehow gotten over to the right of her. She corrected her course and stumbled on.

I will not faint . . .

And then her legs simply melted. She didn't *have* legs. The rest of her fell slowly toward the ground. Hannah managed to break her fall with her arms. Then everything was still and dark.

She didn't go out completely. She was floating in darkness, feeling woozy even though she was lying down, when she sensed someone beside her.

No, she thought. Get the stick. He'll bite you; he'll kill you.

But she couldn't move. Her hand wouldn't obey her.

She felt a gentle hand brush her hair off her face.

No . . .

Then a touch on her neck. But it was only gentle fingers, running lightly over the skin where she'd been bitten tonight. They felt like a doctor's fingers, exploring to diagnose. She heard a sigh that sounded like relief, and then the fingers trailed away.

'You'll be all right.' Thierry's voice came to her softly. She realized he didn't think she could hear him. He thought she was unconscious. 'As long as you stay away from vampires for the next week.'

Was that a threat? Hannah didn't understand. She braced herself for the piercing pain of teeth.

Then she felt him touch her again, just his fingertips brushing her face. The touch was so immeasurably gentle. So tender.

No, Hannah thought. She wanted to move, to kick him

away. But she couldn't.

And those delicate fingers were moving on, tracing her features one by one. With the lightest of touches that sent helpless chills through her.

I hate you, Hannah thought.

The touch followed the curve of her eyebrow, trailed down her cheek to her birthmark. Hannah shivered inwardly. It sketched the line of her jaw, then moved to her lips.

The skin was so sensitive here. Thierry's fingers traced the outline of her lips, the join between upper and lower. The chills became a fluttering inside Hannah. Her heart swelled with love and longing.

I won't feel this way. I *hate* you . . .

But a voice was whispering in her mind, a voice she hadn't heard in what seemed like a long time. A crystal voice, soft but ringing.

Feel him. Does this feel like that other one? Sense him. Does he smell the same, sound the same . . . ?

Hannah didn't know what to make of the words and didn't want to. She just wanted Thierry to stop.

The fingers brushed over her eyelashes, thumb stroking over the fragile skin of her eyelids as if to keep them shut. Then she felt him bend closer.

No, no, no . . .

Warm lips touched her forehead. Again, just the barest touch. Then they were gone.

'Goodbye, Hannah,' Thierry whispered.

Hannah felt herself lifted. She was being carried in strong gentle arms, moving swiftly and smoothly.

It was harder for her to stay conscious than it had been before. She had a strange feeling of tranquillity, of security. But she fought to open her eyes just a crack.

She wanted to see his hands. She didn't think there

had been enough time for the pencil wound to heal completely.

If the pencil wound was there.

But her eyes wouldn't open – not until she felt herself being lowered and placed on solid ground. Then she managed to lift heavy eyelids and dart a glance at his hands.

There were no marks.

The knowledge burned through her, but she didn't have any strength left. She felt her eyes lapsing shut again. Dimly, very far away, she could hear the faint echo of a doorbell.

Then a soft voice in her head. *You don't have to be afraid anymore. I'm going away – and so is* she.

Don't go. Wait. I have to talk to you. I have to ask you . . .

But she could feel cold air all around her and she knew he was gone.

A moment later she heard the door open, and the sound of Chess's mother gasping. She was on the Clovis's doorstep. People were shaking her, talking to her.

Hannah wasn't interested in any of it. She let the darkness take her.

It was when she let go completely that she began to dream. She was Hana of the Three Rivers and she was seeing the end of her own life.

She saw the bruised and bloody figure of Thierry rising up to kill his torturers. She felt it as her turn came. She looked up and saw his savage face, saw the animal light in his eyes. She felt her life flow away.

Then she saw the end of the story. The glimpse of the corridor through time, the recognition of her soulmate. The forgiveness and the promise.

And then just shadows. But Hannah slept peacefully in the shadows until morning, unafraid.

The first thing Hannah saw when she woke up was a pair of glowing green cat-eyes looking down at her.

'How do you feel?' Chess asked.

She was lying in Chess's bed. Sunlight was streaming in the window.

'I . . . can't tell yet,' Hannah said. Disjointed images were floating in her head, not quite forming a whole picture.

'We found you last night,' Chess said. 'You ran your dad's car off the road, but you managed to make it here before you collapsed.'

'Oh . . . yeah. I remember.' She *did* remember; the pieces of the puzzle suddenly clicked together. Maya. Thierry. The attack. The car. Thierry again. And finally her dream. Her own voice saying, 'I forgive you.'

And now he was gone. He'd gone home, wherever home was.

She had never felt so confused.

'Hannah, what *happened*? Are you sick? We didn't know whether to take you to a hospital last night or what. But you didn't have a fever and you seemed to be breathing fine, so my mom said you could just sleep a while.'

'I'm not sick.' This was the time to tell Chess everything. After all, that was the reason she'd been running to Chess in the first place last night.

But now . . . now in the bright morning light, she didn't want to tell Chess. It wasn't just that it might put Chess in danger, either from Thierry or the Night World in general. It was that Hannah didn't *need* to talk about it; she could cope on her own. It wasn't Chess's problem.

And I don't even know the truth yet, Hannah thought.

But *that* is going to change.

'Hannah, are you even listening to me?'

'Yeah. I'm sorry. And I'm OK; I felt kind of dizzy last night, but now I'm better. Can I use your phone?'

'Can you *what*?'

'I have to call Paul – you know, the psychologist. I need to see him, fast.'

She jumped up, steadied herself against a brief wave of giddiness, and walked past Chess, who was watching her in bewilderment.

'No,' Paul said. 'No, it's absolutely out of the question.' He waved his hands, then patted his pockets nervously, coming up empty.

'Paul, please. I *have* to do this. And if you won't help me, I'll try it on my own. I think self-hypnosis should work. I've been doing a pretty good job of dreaming the past lately, anyway.'

'It's . . . too . . . dangerous.' Paul said each word separately, then sank into his chair, hands at his temples. 'Don't you *remember* what happened the last time?'

Hannah felt sorry for him. But she said ruthlessly, 'If I do it on my own, it may be even more dangerous. Right? At least if you hypnotize me you can be there to wake me up. You can throw a glass of water in my face again.'

He looked up sharply. 'Oh, yeah? And what if it doesn't work this time?'

Hannah dropped her eyes. Then she raised them and looked at Paul directly. 'I don't know,' she admitted quietly. 'But I've still got to try. I have to know the truth. If I don't, I really think I may go insane.' She didn't say it melodramatically. It was a simple statement of fact.

Paul groaned. Then he grabbed a pen and started chewing on it, glancing around the room. 'What is it that you would want to know? Just presuming that I agreed to help you.' His voice sounded squashed.

Hannah felt a surge of relief. 'I want to know about this woman who keeps warning me,' she said. 'Her name is Maya. And I want to know how I die in my other lives.'

'Oh, terrific. That sounds like fun.'

'I *have* to do it.' She took a deep breath. She wouldn't let herself look away from him, even though she could feel the warmth as her eyes filled. 'Look, I know you don't understand. And I can't explain to you how important it is to me. But it is . . . important.'

There was a silence, then Paul said, 'All right. All right. But only because I think it's safer for you to be with somebody.'

Hannah whispered, 'Thank you.'

Then she blinked and unfolded a piece of paper. 'I wrote down some questions for you to ask me.'

'Great. Wonderful. I'm sure you'll be getting your degree in psychology soon.' But he took the paper.

Hannah walked over to the couch and got herself settled. She shut her eyes, telling her muscles to relax.

'OK,' Paul said. His voice was very slightly unsteady, but Hannah could tell he was trying to make it soothing. 'I want you to imagine a beautiful violet light . . .'

CHAPTER 12

She was sixteen and her name was Ha-nahkt. She was a virgin priestess dedicated to the goddess Isis.

She was wearing a fine linen shift that fell from her waist to her ankles. Above the waist, she wore nothing except a deep silver collar strung with beads of amethyst, carnelian, turquoise, and lapis lazuli. There were two silver bracelets on her upper arms and two on her wrists.

Morning was her favourite time.

This morning she carefully placed her offering in front of the statue of Isis. Lotus blossoms, small cakes, and beer. Then, facing south, she began the chant to wake the goddess up.

> 'Awaken, Isis, Mother of the Stars,
> Great of Magic,
> Mistress of all the World,
> Sovereign of her father,
> Mightier than the gods,
> Lady of the Waters of Life,
> Powerful of Heart,
> Isis of the Ten Thousand Names . . .'

A step sounded behind her and she broke off short, feeling startled and annoyed.

'I'm sorry. Did I disturb you?'

It was a woman, a beautiful woman with long black hair.

'You're not allowed in here,' Ha-nahkt said sharply. 'Only priests and priestesses . . .' Her voice trailed off as she looked at the woman more closely. Maybe she *is* a priestess, she thought. There's something in her face . . .

'I just want to talk to you,' the woman said. Her voice was husky and persuasive, almost mesmerizing. 'It's very important.' She smiled and Ha-nahkt felt hairs stir at the back of her neck.

If she's a priestess, I bet she's a priestess of Set. Set was the most evil of all the gods – and one of the most powerful. Ha-nahkt could sense power in this woman, no question about that. But evil? She wasn't sure.

'My name is Maya. And what I have to tell you may save your life.'

Ha-nahkt stood still. Part of her wanted to run from Maya, to go and get her best friend Khet-hetepes. Or, better yet, one of the senior priestesses. But another part of her was curious.

'I really shouldn't stop in the middle of the chant,' she began.

'It's about the stranger.'

Ha-nahkt lost her breath.

There was a long moment of silence, and then she said, 'I don't know what you're talking about.' She could hear the shake in her own voice.

'Oh, yes, you do. The stranger. Tall, blond, handsome . . . and with such sad dark eyes. The one you've been meeting on the sly.'

Ha-nahkt could feel the shaking take over her whole body. She was a priestess, sworn to the goddess. If anyone found she'd been meeting a man . . .

'Oh, don't worry, little one,' Maya said and laughed. 'I'm not here to turn you in. Just the opposite, in fact. I want to help you.'

'We haven't done anything,' Ha-nahkt faltered. 'Just kissed. He says he doesn't want me to leave the temple. He isn't going to stay long. He says he saw me, and he just had to speak to me.'

'And no wonder,' Maya said in a cooing tone. She touched Ha-nahkt's hair lightly and Ha-nahkt moved instinctively away. 'You're such a pretty girl. Such unusual colouring for this part of the world. I suppose you think you love him.'

'I *do* love him,' Ha-nahkt blurted before she could stop herself. Then she lowered her voice. 'But I know my duty. He says that in the next world we'll be together.' She didn't want to tell the rest of it, the remarkable things she'd seen with the stranger, the way she'd *recognized* him. The way they were destined for each other.

'And you believed him? Oh, my dear child. You're so innocent. I suppose that comes from living your life in a temple.' She gazed around thoughtfully, then looked back at Hannah. Her face became grave and regretful.

'I hate to have to tell you this,' she said. 'But the stranger does *not* love you. The truth is that he's a very evil man. The truth is that he's not a man at all. He's an Ur-Demon and he wants to steal your *sa*.'

Oh, Isis, Ha-nahkt thought. *Sa* was the breath of life, the magical force that allowed you to live. She'd heard of demons who wanted to steal it. But she couldn't believe it of the stranger. He seemed so gentle, so kind . . .

'It's true,' Maya said positively. She glanced at Ha-nahkt sideways. 'And you know it is, if you think about it. Why else would he want to taste your blood?'

Ha-nahkt started and flushed. 'How do you know—?' She stopped and bit her lip.

'You've been meeting him at night by the lotus pool, when everyone else is asleep,' Maya said. 'And I suppose you thought it wouldn't hurt to let him drink a little of your blood. Not much. Just a bit. It was exciting. But I'm telling you the truth, now – it *will* hurt you. He's a demon and he wants you dead.'

The husky, mesmerizing voice went on and on. It was telling all about Ur-Demons who drank blood, and men and women who could change into animals, and a place called the World of the Night, where they all lived. Ha-nahkt's head began to spin.

And her heart shattered.

Literally. She could feel the jagged pieces of it every time she tried to breathe. A priestess didn't cry, but tears were forcing themselves out of her closed lids.

Because she couldn't deny that the stranger did act a little like an Ur-Demon. Why else *would* he drink blood?

And the things she'd seen with him, the feeling of destiny . . . that must have all been magic. He had tricked her with spells.

Maya seemed to have finished her story. 'Do you think you can remember all that?' she asked.

Ha-nahkt made a miserable gesture. What did it matter if she remembered it? She only wanted to be left alone.

'Look at me!'

Ha-nahkt glanced up, startled. It was a mistake. Maya's eyes were strange; they seemed to turn different colours from moment to moment, and once Hanahkt met them, she couldn't look away. She was caught in a spell, and she felt her will slipping.

'Now,' Maya said, and her eyes were deep gold and ancient as a crocodile's. 'Remember all that. And remember this. Remember . . . how he kills you.'

And then the strangest thing of all happened.

It suddenly seemed to Ha-nahkt that she was two people. One of them was her ordinary self. And the other was a different self, a distant self, who seemed to be looking on from the future. At this moment, Ha-nahkt and the future self were seeing different things.

Ha-nahkt saw that Maya was gone and the temple was empty. And then she saw that someone else was walking in. A tall figure, with light hair and dark fathomless eyes – the stranger. He smiled at her, walked toward her with his arms held out. He grasped her with hands that were as strong as a demon's. Then he showed his teeth.

The future self saw something else. She saw that Maya never left the temple. She saw Maya's face and body ripple as if they were made of water – and then change. It was as if there were two images, one on top of the other. The outward image was of the stranger, but it was Maya underneath.

That's it. That's how she did it.

The voice came from outside Ha-nahkt, and she didn't understand it. She didn't have time to think about it, either, because the next instant she felt the tearing pain of teeth.

Oh, Isis, Goddess of Life, guide me to the other world . . .

'That's how she did it,' Hannah breathed.

She was sitting up on the couch. She knew who she was, and more, she knew who she'd been.

It was another of those blinding flashes of illumination. She felt as if she were standing at the end of the corridor of time and looking back at a hundred different versions of herself. They each looked slightly different, and they wore different clothes, but they were all her. Her name had been Hanje, Anora, Xiana, Nan Haiane, Honni, Ian,

Annette. She had been a warrior, a priestess, a princess, a slave. And right now she felt she had the strength of all her selves.

At the far end of the corridor, back where it was misty and blurry and faintly tinted pink and blue, she seemed to see Hana smiling at her. And then Hana turned and walked away, her task accomplished.

Hannah took a deep breath and let it out.

'She did it with illusions,' she said, hardly aware that she was talking out loud. 'Maya. And she's done it before, of course. Maybe every time. What do you do with somebody who keeps killing you over and over? Never letting you live to your seventeenth birthday? Trying to destroy you, not just your life, but your heart . . . ?'

She realized that Paul was staring at her. 'You want me to answer that?'

Hannah shook her head even as she went on talking. 'Goddess – I mean, God – she must hate me. I still don't understand why. It must be because she wants Thierry herself, or maybe just because she wants him miserable. She wants him to know that I'm terrified of him, that I hate him. And she *did* it. She convinced me. She convinced my subconscious enough that I started warning myself against him.'

'If any of this is true, which I'm not going to admit for a second, because they would definitely take my licence away – then I can tell you one thing,' Paul said. 'She sounds very, very dangerous.'

'She is.'

'Then why are you so happy?' he asked pathetically.

Hannah glanced at him and laughed. She couldn't hope to explain it.

But she was more than happy, she was exalted. She was buoyant, ecstatic, over the moon.

Thierry wasn't evil. She had the confirmation of a hundred selves whispering it to her. Maya was the enemy, the snake in the garden. Thierry was exactly what he'd told her he was. Someone who had made a terrible mistake and had spent millennia paying for it – and searching for her.

He *is* gentle and kind. He does love me. And we *are* destined for each other.

I've got to find him.

The last thought came as an additional bright revelation, but one that made her sit up and go still.

She had no idea how.

Where had he gone? Home. Where was home? She didn't know.

It could be anywhere in the world.

'Hannah . . .'

'Wait,' Hannah whispered.

'Look, Hannah, I think we should maybe do some work on this. Talk about it, examine your feelings . . .'

'No, hush!' Hannah waved a hand at him. 'She gave me a clue! She didn't mean to, but she gave me a clue! She said he had connections with witches in Vegas.'

'Oh, my God,' Paul muttered. Then he jumped up. 'Hannah, where are you going?'

'I'm sorry.' She darted back into the office, threw her arms around him, and gave him a kiss. Then, smiling into his startled face, she said, 'Thank you. Thank you for helping. You'll never know how much you've done for me.'

'I need money.'

Chess blinked, but went on looking at her intently.

'I know it isn't fair to ask you without explaining why. But I *can't* tell you. It would be dangerous for you. I just have to ask you to trust me.'

Chess kept looking at her. The slanted green eyes searched Hannah's face. Then, without a word, she got up.

Hannah sat on Chess's crisp white-on-white coverlet and waited. After a few minutes Chess came back into the room and settled her own petite self on the bed.

'Here,' she said, and plunked down a credit card. 'Mom said I could use it to get some things for graduation. I figure she'll understand – maybe.'

Hannah threw her arms around her. 'Thank you,' she whispered. 'I'll pay it back as soon as I can.' Then she burst out, 'How can you be so nice? I'd be yelling to know what was going on.'

'I *am* going to yell,' Chess said, squeezing her back. 'But more than that. I'm going with you.'

Hannah drew back. How could she explain? She knew that by going to Las Vegas she would be putting her own life in danger. From Maya, certainly. From the Night World, probably. Even from the witches Thierry had connections with, possibly.

And she couldn't drag Chess into that.

'I've got something I want you to hang on to,' she said. She reached into her canvas bag and pulled out an envelope. 'This is for you and for my mom – just in case. If you don't hear from me by my birthday, then I want you to open it.'

'Didn't you hear me? I'm going *with* you. I don't know what's been going on with you, but I'm not going to let you run off on your own.'

'And I can't take you.' She caught the glowing cat-eyes and held them. 'Please understand, Chess. It's something I have to do alone. Besides, I need you here to cover for me, to tell my mom I'm at your house so she doesn't worry. OK?' She reached out and gave Chess a tiny shake. 'OK?'

Chess shut her eyes, then nodded. Then she sniffled, her chin trembling.

Hannah hugged her again. 'Thank you,' she whispered. 'Let's be best friends forever.'

Monday morning, instead of going to school, Hannah started for Billings airport. She was driving the Ford – her mom had fixed it over the weekend. Her mom thought she was spending the next couple of days with Chess to study for finals.

It was frightening but exhilarating to fly on a plane by herself, going to a city she'd never been to before. All the time she was in the air, she was thinking, Closer, closer, closer – and looking at the black rose ring on her finger.

She'd fished it out of her bedroom wastebasket. Now she turned her hand this way and that to see the black gems catch the light. Her chest tightened.

What if I can't find him? she thought.

The other fear she didn't want to admit, even to herself. What if she did find him, and he didn't want her anymore? After all, she'd only told him that she hated him a few dozen times and ordered him to stay away from her forever.

I won't think about that. There's no point. First I have to track him down, and after that what happens, happens.

The airport in Las Vegas was surprisingly small. There were slot machines all over. Hannah collected her one duffel bag at the luggage carousel and then walked outside. She stood in the warm desert air, trying to figure out what to do next.

How do you find witches?

She didn't know. She didn't think they were likely to be listed in the phone book. So she just trusted to luck and headed where everybody else was heading – the Strip.

It was a mistake from the beginning, and that afternoon and night were among the worst times in her life.

It didn't start off so bad. The Strip was gaudy and glittery, especially as darkness fell. The hotels were so bizarre and so dazzling that it took Hannah's breath away. One of them, the Luxor, was shaped like a giant black pyramid with a Sphinx in front of it. Hannah stood and watched coloured lasers dart from the Sphinx's eyes and laughed.

What would Ha-nahkt have thought of *that*?

But there was something almost sickening about all the lights and the hustling after a while. Something . . . unwholesome. The crowds were so thick, both inside the hotels and out on the street, that Hannah could hardly move. Everyone seemed to be in a rush – except the people nailed in front of slot machines.

It feels . . . greedy, Hannah decided finally, searching in her mind for the right word. All these people want to win free money. All these hotels want to take their money. And of course, the hotels are the winners in the end. They've built a sort of Venus' flytrap to lure people here. And some of these people don't look as if they can afford to lose.

Her heart felt physically heavy and her lungs felt constricted. She wanted Montana and a horizon so far away that it pried your mind open. She wanted clean air. She wanted *space*.

But even worse than the atmosphere of greed and commercialism was the fact that she wasn't finding any witches.

She struck up conversations a few times with desk clerks and waitresses. But when she casually asked if there were any odd people in town who practised witchcraft, they looked at her as if she were crazy.

By nine o'clock that night she was dizzy, exhausted, and sick with defeat.

I'm never going to find them. Which means I'm never going to find him.

She collapsed on a bench outside the Stardust Hotel, wondering what to do next. Her legs hurt and her head was pounding. She didn't want to spend Chess's mom's money on a hotel – but she'd noticed police officers making people move on if they tried to sleep on the street.

Why did I come here? I should have put an ad in the paper: 'Desperately Seeking Thierry'. I should have known this wouldn't work.

Even as she was thinking it, something about a boy in the crowd caught her eye.

He wasn't Thierry. He wasn't anything like Thierry. Except for the way he moved.

It was that same rippling grace she'd seen in both Thierry and Maya, an easy control of motion that reminded her of a jungle cat. And his face . . . he was almost eerily good-looking in a ragamuffin way.

When he glanced up toward the Stardust's tall neon sign, she thought she could see light reflect from his eyes.

He's one of them. I know it. He's one of the Night People.

Without stopping to think, she jumped up, slung her bag over her shoulder, and followed him.

It wasn't easy. He walked fast and she had to keep dodging tourists. He was headed off the Strip, to one of the quiet dimly-lit streets that ran parallel to it.

It was a whole different world here, just one block away from the glitter and bustle. The hotels were small and in poor repair. The businesses seemed to be mostly pawnshops. Everything had a dingy depressed feeling.

Hannah felt a prickling down her spine.

She was now following the only figure on a deserted

street, Any minute now, he'd realize she was tailing him – but what could she do? She didn't dare lose sight of him.

The boy seemed to be leading her into worse and worse areas – *sleazy* was the word for them, Hannah thought. The streetlights were far apart here with areas of darkness in between.

All at once he took a sharp left turn, seeming to disappear behind a building with a sign that read, DAN'S BAIL BONDS. Hannah jogged to catch up to him and found herself staring down a narrow alley. It was extremely dark. She hesitated a moment, then grimly took a few steps forward.

On the third step, the boy appeared from behind a Dumpster.

He was facing her, and once again Hannah caught the flash of eyeshine. She stood very still as he walked slowly toward her.

'You following me or something?' he asked. He seemed amused. He had a sharp face with an almost pointed chin and dark hair that looked uncombed. He was no taller than Hannah, but his body seemed tough and wiry.

It's the Artful Dodger, Hannah thought.

As he reached her, he looked her up and down. His expression was a combination of lechery and hunger. Gooseflesh blossomed on Hannah's skin.

'I'm sorry,' she said, trying to make her voice quiet and direct. 'I *was* following you. I wanted to ask you something – I'm looking for someone.'

'You found him, baby,' the boy said. He darted a quick glance around as if to make sure that there was nobody in the alley with them.

And then, before Hannah could say another word, he knocked her into the wall and pinned her there.

CHAPTER 13

'Don't fight,' he panted into her face. 'It'll be easier if you just relax.'

Hannah was frightened – and furious. 'In your dreams,' she gasped and slammed a knee into his groin. She hadn't survived Maya and come thousands of miles to be killed by some weasel of a vampire.

She could feel him trying to do something to her mind – it reminded her of the way Maya had captured Ha-nahkt's eyes. Some kind of hypnosis, she supposed. But she'd had enough of hypnosis in the last week. She fought it.

And she fought with her body, unskilfully maybe, but with utter conviction. She head-butted him on the nose when he tried to get close to her neck.

'Ow!' The Artful Dodger jerked back. Then he got a better grip on her arm. He pulled the wrist toward him and Hannah suddenly realized what he was doing. There were nice accessible veins there. He was going to draw blood from her wrist.

'No, you don't,' she gasped. She had no idea what would happen if she lost any more blood to a vampire. Thierry had said she wasn't in danger as long as she kept away from them for the next week, so she presumed that if she didn't stay away, she *was* in danger. And she was already noticing little changes in herself: her ability to see better in the dark, for instance.

She tried to wrench her arm out of the boy's grip – and then she heard a gasp. Suddenly she realized that he wasn't holding her as tightly, and he wasn't trying to pull her wrist to him. Instead he was just staring at her hand.

At her ring.

The expression on his face might have been funny if Hannah hadn't been shaking with adrenaline. He looked shocked, dismayed, scared, disbelieving, and embarrassed all at once.

'Who – who – who *are* you?' he spluttered.

Hannah looked at the ring, and then at him. Of course. How could she have been so stupid? She should have mentioned Thierry right away. If he was a Lord of the Night World, maybe everybody knew him. Maybe she could skip the witches altogether.

'I told you I was looking for somebody. His name is Thierry Descouedres. He gave me this ring.'

The Artful Dodger gave a kind of moan. Then he looked up at her from under his spiky bangs. 'I didn't hurt you, did I?' he said. It wasn't a question, it was a demand for agreement. 'I didn't do anything to you.'

'You didn't get the chance,' Hannah said. But she was afraid the boy might just take off running, so she added, 'I don't want to get you in trouble. I just want to find Thierry. Can you help me?'

'I . . . help you. Yeah, yeah. I can be a big help.' He hesitated, then said, 'It's kind of a long walk.'

A walk? Thierry was *here*? Hannah's heart leaped so high that her whole body felt light.

'I'm not tired,' she said, and it was true. 'I can walk anywhere.'

* * *

The house was enormous.

Magnificent. Palatial, even. Awe-inspiring.

The Artful Dodger abandoned Hannah at the beginning of the long palm-tree-lined drive, blurting. 'That's it,' and then scampering off into the darkness. Hannah looked after him for a moment, then grimly started up the drive, sincerely hoping that it *was* it. She was so tired that she was weaving and her feet felt as if they'd been pounded with stones.

As she walked up to the front door, though, her doubts disappeared. There were black roses everywhere.

There was an arch-shaped stained-glass window above the double doors, showing a black rose that had the same intricately knotted stem as the one on Hannah's ring. The same design had been worked into the crowns over the windows. It was used like a family crest or seal.

Just seeing all those roses made Hannah's heart beat faster.

OK, then. Ring the doorbell, she told herself. And stop feeling like some Cinderella who's come to see what's keeping the prince.

She pushed the doorbell button, then held her breath as chimes echoed distantly.

Please. Please answer . . .

She heard footsteps approaching and her heart *really* started to pound.

I can't believe it's all been this easy . . .

But when the door opened, it wasn't Thierry. It was a college-age guy with a suit, brown hair pulled back into a short ponytail, and dark glasses. He looked vaguely like a young CIA agent, Hannah thought wildly.

He and Hannah stared at each other.

'Uh, I'm here to . . . I'm looking for Thierry Descouedres,'

Hannah said finally, trying to sound confident.

The CIA guy didn't change expression. When he spoke, it wasn't unkindly, but Hannah's heart plummeted.

'He's not here. Try again in a few days. And it's better to call one of his secretaries before showing up.'

He started to shut the door.

A wave of desperation broke over Hannah.

'Wait!' she said, and she actually stuck her foot in the doorway. She was amazed at herself.

The CIA guy looked down at her foot, then up at her face. 'Yes?'

Oh, God, he thinks I'm a nuisance visitor. Hannah suddenly had a vision of swarms of petitioners lined up at Thierry's house, all wanting him to do something for them. Like supplicants waiting for an audience with the king.

And I must look like riffraff, she thought. She was wearing Levis and a shirt that was sweaty and wrinkled after tramping around the Strip all day. Her boots were dusty. Her hair was limp and dishevelled, straggling over her face.

'Yes?' the CIA guy said again, politely urgent.

'I . . . nothing.' Hannah felt tears spring to her eyes and was furious with herself. She hid them by bending down to pick up her duffel bag, which by now felt as if it were loaded with rocks.

She had never been so tired. Her mouth was dry and cottony and her muscles were starting to cramp. She had no idea where to find a safe place to sleep.

But it wasn't the CIA guy's problem.

'Thank you,' Hannah said. She took a deep breath and started to turn away.

It was the deep breath that did it. Someone was crossing the grand entrance hall behind the CIA guy and the breath delayed Hannah long enough that they saw each other.

'Nilsson, *wait*!' the someone yelled and came bounding over to the door.

It was a girl, thin and tanned, with odd silvery-brown hair and dark amber eyes. She had several yellowing bruises on her face.

But it was her expression that startled Hannah. Her amber eyes were wide and sparkling in what looked like recognition, her mouth was open in astonishment and excitement. She was waving her arms.

'That's her!' she yelled at the CIA guy, pointing to Hannah. 'It's her! It's *her*.' When he stared at her, she hit him in the shoulder. '*Her!*'

They both turned to stare at Hannah. The CIA guy had an expression now. He looked stunned.

Hannah stared back at them, bewildered.

Then, seeming dazed, the CIA guy very slowly opened the door. 'My name is Nilsson, miss,' he said. 'Please come inside.'

Stupid me, Hannah thought. Almost as an afterthought, she pushed straggling hair off her left cheek, away from her birthmark. I should have told them who I was. But how could I know they would understand?

Nilsson was talking again as he gently took her bag. 'I'm very sorry, miss, I didn't realize . . . I hope you won't hold this—'

'Nobody knew you were *coming*,' the girl broke in with refreshing bluntness. 'And the worst thing is that Thierry's gone off somewhere. I don't think anybody knows where or when he'll be back. But meanwhile you'd better stay put. I don't want to think about what he'd do to us if we lost you.' She smiled at Hannah and added, 'I'm Lupe Acevedo.'

'Hannah Snow.'

'I know.' The girl winked. 'We met before, but I

couldn't exactly introduce myself. Don't you remember?'

Hannah started to shake her head – and then she blinked. Blinked again. That silvery-brown colouring . . . those amber eyes . . .

'Yeah,' Lupe said, looking hugely delighted. 'That was me. That's how I got these bruises. The other wolf got it worse, though. I ripped him a new—'

'Would you like something to drink?' Nilsson interrupted hastily. 'Or to eat? Why don't you come in and sit down?'

Hannah's mind was reeling. That girl is a werewolf, she thought. A *werewolf*. The last time I saw her she had big ears and a bushy tail. Werewolves are real.

And this one protected me.

She said dizzily, 'I . . . thank you. I mean, you saved my life, didn't you?'

Lupe shrugged. 'Part of the job. Want a Coke?'

Hannah blinked, then laughed. 'I'd kill for one.'

'I'll take care of it,' Nilsson said. 'I'll take care of everything. Lupe, why don't you show her upstairs?' He hurried off and opened a cellular phone. A moment later several other guys dressed like him came running. The strange thing was that they were all very young, all in their late teens. Hannah caught snatches of frantic-sounding conversation.

'Well, try *that* number—'

'What about leaving a message with—'

'Come on,' Lupe said, interrupting Hannah's eavesdropping. With that same cheerful bluntness she added, 'You look like you could use a bath.'

She led Hannah past a giant white sculpture toward a wide curving staircase. Hannah glimpsed other rooms opening off the hallway. A living room that looked as big as a football field, decorated with white couches, geometric furniture, and abstract paintings. A dining room with a mile-long table. An alcove with a grand piano.

Hannah felt more like Cinderella than ever. Nobody in Medicine Rock had a grand piano.

I didn't know he was so rich. I don't know if I can deal with this.

But when she was installed in a sort of Moorish fantasy bathroom, surrounded by jungly green plants and exotic tiles and brass globe lights with cut-out star shapes, she decided that she could probably adjust to living this way. If forced.

It was heaven just to relax in the Jacuzzi tub, drinking a Coke and breathing in the delicious scent of bath salts. And it was even better to sit up in bed afterward, eating finger sandwiches sent up by 'Chef' and telling Lupe how she came to be in Las Vegas.

When she was done, Lupe said, 'Nilsson and everybody are trying to find Thierry. It may take a little while, though. See, he just stopped off for a few minutes on Saturday, and then he disappeared again. But meanwhile, this house is pretty well protected. And all of us will fight for you, I mean, fight to the death, if we have to. So it's safer than most other places.'

Hannah felt a roiling in her stomach. She didn't understand. Lupe made it sound as if they were in some castle getting ready for a siege. 'Safe from . . . ?'

Lupe looked surprised. 'From *her* – Maya,' she said, as if it should be obvious.

Hannah had a sinking feeling. I should have known, she thought. But all she said was, 'So you think I'm still in danger from her.'

Lupe's eyebrows shot up. She said mildly, 'Well, sure. She's going to try to kill you. And she's awfully good at killing.'

Especially me, Hannah thought. But she was too tired to be much afraid. Trusting to Lupe and Nilsson and the rest of Thierry's household, she fell asleep that night as soon as her head touched the pillow.

She woke up to see sunshine. It was reflecting off the bedroom walls, which were painted a softly burnished gold. Weird but beautiful, Hannah thought, looking dreamily around at ebony furniture and decorative tribal masks. Then she remembered where she was and jumped out of bed.

She found clean clothes – her size – lying on an elaborately carved chest. She had just finished pulling them on when Lupe knocked on the door.

'Lupe, have they—'

Lupe shook her silvery-brown head. 'They haven't found him yet.'

Hannah sighed, then smiled, trying not to look too disappointed.

Lupe made a sympathetic face. 'I know. While you wait, though, you might like to meet some people.' She grinned. 'They're sort of special people, and it's a secret that they're even here. But I talked to them last night, and they all decided that it would be OK. They all want to meet you.'

Hannah was curious. 'Special people? Are they humans or . . . uh . . . ?'

Lupe grinned even more widely. 'They're both. That's why they're special.' As she talked, she was leading Hannah downstairs and through miles of hallway. 'They did something for me,' she said, not smiling now, but serious. 'They saved my life and my mom's life. See, I'm not a pure-bred werewolf. My dad was human.'

Hannah looked at her, startled.

'Yeah. And that's against the laws of the Night World. You can't fall in love with a human, much less marry them. The other werewolves came one night and killed my dad. They would have killed my mom and me, too, but Thierry got us out of the city and hid us. That's why I'd do anything for him. I wouldn't be alive if it wasn't for him . . . and Circle Daybreak.'

She had paused by the door of a room located toward the back of the house. Now, she opened the door, gave Hannah a funny little nod and a wink, and said, 'You go meet them. I think you'll like each other. You're their type.'

Hannah wasn't sure what this meant. She felt shy as she stepped over the threshold and looked around the room.

It was a den, smaller than the front living room, and more cozy, with furniture in warm ochers and burnt siennas. A breakfast buffet was set out on a long sideboard made of golden pine. It smelled good, but Hannah didn't have time to look at it. As soon as she came in the room, every head turned and she found a dozen people staring at her.

Young people. All around her age. Normal-type teenagers, except that a surprising number of them were extremely good-looking.

Behind her, the door closed firmly. Hannah felt more and more as if she'd just walked out on stage and forgotten her lines.

Then one of the girls sitting on an ottoman jumped up and ran to her. 'You're Hana, aren't you?' she said warmly.

'Hannah. Yes.'

'I can't believe I'm really meeting you! This is so exciting. Thierry's told us all about you.' She put a gentle hand on Hannah's arm. 'Hannah, this is Circle Daybreak.

And my name is Thea Harman.'

She was almost as tall as Hannah was, and the yellow hair spilling over her shoulders was a few shades darker than Hannah's. Her eyes were brown and soft and somehow wise.

'Hi, Thea.' Somehow Hannah felt instinctively at ease with this girl. 'Lupe was telling me about Circle Daybreak, but I didn't exactly understand.'

'It started as a sort of witch organization,' Thea said. 'A witch circle. But it's not just for witches. It's for humans and vampires and werewolves and shapeshifters . . . and, well, anybody who wants to help Night People and humans get along. Come and meet the others and we'll try to explain.'

A few minutes later, Hannah was sitting on a couch with a plate of eggs Benedict, being introduced.

'This is James and Poppy,' Thea said. 'James is a Redfern on his mother's side, which makes him a descendant of Maya's.' She glanced at James with gentle mischief.

'I didn't pick my parents. Believe me, I didn't,' James said to Hannah. He had light brown hair and thoughtful grey eyes. When he smiled it was impossible not to smile back.

'Nobody would have picked your parents, Jamie,' Poppy said, elbowing him. She was very small, but there was a kind of impish wisdom in her face. Her head was a tangle of copper curls and her eyes were as green as emeralds. Hannah found her elfin beauty just a little scary . . . just a little inhuman.

'They're both vampires,' Thea said, answering Hannah's unspoken question.

'I didn't used to be,' Poppy said. 'James changed me because I was dying.'

'What's a soulmate for?' James said, and Poppy poked

him again and then grinned at him. They were obviously in love.

'You're – soulmates?' Hannah spoke softly, wistfully.

It was Thea who answered. 'That's the thing, you see – something is causing Night People to find human soulmates. We witches think that it's some Power that's waking up again, making it happen. Some Power that's been asleep for a long time – maybe since the time when Thierry was born.'

Now Hannah understood why Lupe had said she was Circle Daybreak's type of people. She was part of this.

'But, that's wonderful,' she said, speaking slowly and trying to gather her thoughts. 'I mean . . .' She couldn't exactly explain *why* it was so wonderful, but she had a sense of some immense turning point being reached in the world, of some cycle that was about to end.

Thea was smiling at her. 'I know what you mean. We think so, too.' She turned and held out a hand to a very tall boy with a sweet face, sandy hair, and hazel eyes. 'And this is *my* soulmate, Eric. He's human.'

'Just barely,' a boy from the other side of the room said. Eric ignored him and smiled at Hannah.

'And this is Gillian and David,' Thea said, moving around the circle. 'Gillian's a distant cousin of mine, a witch, and David's human. Soulmates, again.'

Gillian was tiny, with white-blonde hair that fit her head like a silky cap and deep violet eyes. David had dark hair, brown eyes, and a lean tanned face. They both smiled at Hannah.

Thea was moving on. 'And next comes Rashel and Quinn. Rashel is human, she used to be a vampire hunter.'

'I still am. But now I just hunt *bad* vampires,' Rashel said coolly. Hannah had an instinctive feeling of respect for her. She was tall and seemed to have perfect control of her body. Her hair was black and her eyes were a fierce and blazing green.

'And Quinn's a vampire,' Thea said.

Quinn was the boy who'd made the barely-human remark. He was very good-looking, with clean features that were strongly chiselled but almost delicate. His hair was as black as Rashel's, and his eyes were black, too. He flashed Hannah a smile that, while beautiful, was slightly unnerving.

'Quinn's the only one here who can compete with you as far as the past goes,' Thea added. 'He was made into a vampire back in the sixteen hundreds, by Hunter Redfern.'

Quinn flashed another smile. 'Did you have a life in colonial America? Maybe we've met.'

Hannah smiled in return, but she was also studying him with interest. He didn't look older than eighteen.

'Is that why everybody here looks so young?' she asked. 'All the staff, I mean, Nilsson and the other guys in suits. Are they all vampires?'

Thea nodded. 'All made vampires. Lamia, like James, can grow up if they want. But once you make a human into a vampire they stop ageing – and you can't make somebody over nineteen into a vampire. Their bodies can't make the change. They just burn out.'

Hannah felt an odd chill, almost of premonition. But before she could say anything, a new voice interrupted.

'Speaking of the lamia, isn't anybody going to introduce *me*?'

Thea turned toward the window. 'Sorry, Ash, but if you're going to sleep over there, you can't blame us for forgetting you.' She looked at Hannah. 'This is another Redfern, a cousin of James's. His name is Ash.'

Ash was gorgeous, lanky and elegant, with ash-blond hair. But what startled Hannah as he got up and unhurriedly walked to meet her was his eyes.

They were like Maya's eyes, shifting colour from moment to moment. The resemblance was so striking that it was a moment before Hannah could take his hand.

He's got Maya's genes, Hannah thought. He smiled at her, then sprawled on the loveseat.

'We're not all of Circle Daybreak, of course,' Thea said. 'In fact, we're some of the newest members. And we're from all over the country – North Carolina, Pennsylvania, Massachusetts, everywhere. But Thierry called us together specially, to talk about the soulmate principle and the old Powers awakening.'

'That was last week, before he found out about you,' copper-haired Poppy said. 'And before he ran off. But we've been talking without him, trying to figure out what to do next.'

Hannah said, 'Whatever it is, I'd like to help you.'

They all looked pleased. But Thea said, 'You should think about it first. We're dangerous people to know.'

'We're on everybody's hit list,' Rashel, the black-haired vampire hunter, said dryly.

'We've got the whole Night World against us,' Ash said, rolling his ever-changing eyes.

'Against *us*. You just said "us".' James turned on his cousin triumphantly, as if he'd just won a point in an argument. 'You admit you're a part of us.'

Ash looked at the ceiling. 'I don't have any choice.'

'But *you* do, Hannah,' Thea interrupted. She smiled at Hannah, but her soft brown eyes were serious. 'You don't have to be in any more danger than you are now.'

'I think—' Hannah began. But before she could finish, there was an explosion of noise from somewhere outside.

CHAPTER 14

'Stay here,' Rashel said sharply, but Hannah ran with the rest of them toward the front of the house. She could hear a ferocious snarling and barking outside, a very familiar sort of sound.

Nilsson and the other CIA guys were running around. They looked grim and efficient, moving fast but not frantically. Hannah realized that they knew how to do this sort of thing.

She didn't see Lupe.

The snarling outside got louder, building to a volley of short barks. There was a yelp – and then a scrambling noise. After a moment of silence there came a sound that lifted the hair on Hannah's forearms – a wild and eerie and beautiful sound. A wolf howling. Two other wolf voices joined the first, chording, rising and falling, interweaving with each other. Hannah found herself gasping, her entire skin shivering. Then there was one long sustained note and it was over.

'Wow,' the tiny blonde called Gillian whispered.

Hannah rubbed her bare arms hard.

The front door opened. Hannah felt herself looking toward the ground, but nothing four-legged came in.

Instead it was Lupe and two guys, all dishevelled, flushed, and grinning.

'It was just some scouts,' Lupe said. 'We ran them off.'

'Scouts from Maya?' Hannah said, feeling a tightness in her stomach. It really was true, then. Maya was trying to storm the house to get to her.

Lupe nodded. 'It'll be OK,' she said almost gently. 'But I think all of you better stay inside today. You can watch movies or play games in the game room.'

Hannah spent the day talking with the Circle Daybreak members. The more she found out about them, the more she liked them. Only one thing made her uncomfortable. They all seemed to defer to her – as if, somehow, they expected her to be wiser or better because of her former lifetimes. It was embarrassing, because she knew she wasn't.

She tried to keep her mind off Thierry . . . and Maya.

But it wasn't easy. That night she found herself walking restlessly through the house. She wound up in a little ante-room on the second floor that looked down on the enormous living room.

'Can't relax?'

The lazy murmur came from behind her. Hannah turned to see Ash, his lanky elegant body propped against a wall. His eyes looked silver in the dimly lit room.

'Not really,' Hannah admitted. 'I just wish they'd find Thierry. I've got a bad feeling about it.'

They stood for a moment in silence. Then Ash said, 'Yeah, it's hard to be without your soulmate. Once you've found them, I mean.'

Hannah looked at him, intrigued. The way he said that . . .

She spoke hesitantly. 'This morning Thea said you were all here because you had human soulmates.'

He looked across the room at French doors that led to a balcony. 'Yes?'

'And – well . . .' Maybe she's *dead*, Hannah thought suddenly. Maybe I shouldn't ask.

'And you want to know where mine is,' Ash said.

'I didn't mean to pry.'

'No. It's OK.' Ash looked out at the darkness beyond the French doors again. 'She's waiting, I hope. I've got some things to put right before I see her.'

He didn't seem scary anymore, no matter how his eyes changed. He seemed – vulnerable.

'I'm sure she *is* waiting,' Hannah said. 'And I'll bet she'll be glad to see you when you've put things right.' She added quietly, 'I know I'll be glad to see Thierry.'

He glanced at her, startled, then smiled. He had a very nice smile. 'That's true, you've been in her shoes, haven't you? And Thierry's certainly tried to make up for his past. I mean, he's been doing good works for centuries. So maybe there's hope for me after all.'

He said it almost mockingly, but Hannah caught an odd glistening in his eyes.

'You're like her, you know,' he added abruptly. 'Like my – like Mary-Lynnette. You're both . . . wise.'

Before Hannah could think of something to say to that, he nodded to her, straightened up, and went back into the hallway, whistling softly through his teeth.

Hannah stood alone in the dim room. For some reason, she felt better suddenly. More optimistic about the future.

I think I'll be able to sleep tonight. And tomorrow, maybe Thierry will be here.

She clamped down hard on the rush of hope that filled her at the thought. Hope . . . and concern. After all she'd said to him, she couldn't be absolutely sure how Thierry would receive her.

What if he doesn't want me after all?

Don't be silly. Don't *think* about it. Go outside and get a breath of air, and then go to bed.

Later, of course, she realized just how stupid she had been. She should have known that getting a breath of fresh air only led to one thing in her life.

But at the moment it seemed like a good idea. Lupe had warned her not to open any outside doors – but the French doors only led to a second-floor balcony overlooking the backyard. Hannah opened them and stepped out.

Nice, she thought. The air was just cool enough to be pleasant.

From here she could look across dark stretches of grass to flood-lit palm trees and softly splashing fountains. Although she couldn't see Thierry's people, she knew they were out there, stationed around the grounds, watching and waiting. Guarding her. It made her feel safe.

Nothing can get to the house with them around it, she thought. I can sleep just fine.

She was about to turn and go back inside when she heard the scratching.

It came from above her. From the roof. She glanced up and got the shock of this particular lifetime.

There was a bat hanging from the roof.

A bat. A *bat*.

A huge bat. Upside down. Its leathery black wings were wrapped around it and its small red eyes shone at her with reflected light.

Wild thoughts tumbled through Hannah's mind, all in a fraction of an instant. Maybe it's a decoration . . . no, idiot, it's *alive*. Maybe it's somebody to guard me. God, maybe it's *Thierry* . . .

But all the while, she knew. And when the instant of

paralysis passed and she could command her body again, she sucked in a deep breath to scream an alarm.

She never got the chance to make a sound. With a noise like an umbrella opening, the bat unfolded its wings suddenly, displaying an amazingly large span of black membrane.

At the same moment something like sheet lightning seemed to hit Hannah, a blinding surge of pure mental energy. She saw stars, and then everything faded to darkness.

Something hurt.

My head, Hannah thought slowly. And my back.

In fact, she hurt all over. And she was blind, or she had her eyes shut. She tried to open them and nothing changed. She could feel herself blinking, but she could only see one thing.

Blackness. Utter, complete blackness.

She realized then that she'd never seen real darkness before. In her bedroom at night there was always some diffused light showing at the top of her curtains. Even outdoors there was always moonlight or starlight, or if it were cloudy, the reflection of human lights, however faint.

This was different. This was *solid* darkness. Hannah imagined she could feel it pressing against her face, weighing down on her body. And no matter how wide she opened her eyes or how fixedly she stared, she couldn't see even the slightest glimmer breaking it.

I will not panic, she told herself.

But it was hard. She was fighting an instinctive fear, hardwired into the brain since before the Stone Age. All humans panicked in complete blackness.

Just breathe, she told herself firmly. *Breathe*. OK. Now. You've got to get out of here. First things first. Are you hurt?

She couldn't tell. She had to shut her eyes in order to sense her own body. As she did, she realized that she was sitting up, instinctively huddling into herself to keep safe from the darkness.

OK. I don't think you're hurt. Let's try standing up. Very slowly.

That was when the real shock came.

She couldn't stand up.

She *couldn't*.

She could move her arms and even her legs. But when she tried to lift her body, even to shift position slightly, something bit into her waist, keeping her immobile.

With a crawling feeling of horror, Hannah put her hands to her waist and felt the rough texture of rope.

I'm tied. I'm *tied* . . .

There was something hard against her back. A tree? Her hands flew to feel it. No, not a tree – too regular. Tall, but squarish. A post of some kind.

The rope seemed to be wound many times around her waist, tightly enough that it constricted her breathing a little. It bound her securely to the post. And then it fastened above or far behind her somewhere, she couldn't find any knots with her fingers.

It felt like very strong, very sturdy rope. Hannah knew without question that she wasn't going to be able to wiggle out of it or untie it.

The post seemed very sturdy, too. The ground under Hannah was dirt and rock.

I'm alone, she thought slowly. She could hear her own gasping breath. I'm all alone . . . and I'm tied here in the dark. I can't move. *I can't get away*.

Maya put me here. She left me to die all alone in the dark.

For a while, then, Hannah simply lost control. She

screamed for help and heard her voice echo oddly. She pulled and twisted at the rope with her fingers until her fingertips were raw. She threw her whole body from one side to the other, trying to loosen the rope or the post, until the pain in her waist made her stop. And finally she gave in to the galloping fear inside her and sobbed out loud.

She had never, ever, felt so desolate and alone.

In the end, though, she cried herself out. And when she'd gasped to a stop, she found that she could think a little.

Listen, girl. You've got to get a grip. You've got to help yourself, because there's nobody else to do it.

It wasn't the cool wind voice or even the crystal voice – because they were both just part of her now. It was Hannah's own mental voice. She had accepted all her past selves and their experiences, and in return she felt she could call on at least some of their wisdom.

OK, she thought grimly. No more crying. Think. What can you tell about your situation?

I'm not out in the open. I know because there's no light at all and because of the way my voice echoed. I'm in a big . . . room or something. It's got a high ceiling. And the floor is rock.

Good. OK, do you hear anything else?

Hannah listened. It was hard to concentrate on the silence around her – it made her own breathing and heartbeat seem terrifyingly loud. She could feel her nerves stretch and fray . . . but she held on, ignoring her own noises and trying to reach out into the darkness with her ears.

Then she heard it. Very far away, a sound like a faucet dripping slowly.

What the hell? I'm in a big black room with a

rock floor and a leaky faucet.

Shut up. Keep concentrating. What do you smell?

Hannah sniffed. That didn't work, so she took long breaths through her nose, ignoring the pain as her midsection pressed against the rope.

It's musty in here. Dank. It smells damp and cold.

In fact, it was very cold. Her panic had kept her warm before, but now she realized that her fingers were icy and her arms and legs were stiff.

OK, so what have we got? I'm in a big black *refrigerated* room with a high ceiling and a stone floor. And it's musty and damp.

A cellar? A cellar without windows?

But she was just fooling herself. She knew. The skin of her face seemed to sense the pressure of tons of rock above her. Her ears told her that that musical dripping was water on rock, very far away. Her nose told her that she wasn't in any building. And her fingers could feel the natural irregularity of the ground underneath her.

She didn't want to believe it. But the knowledge crowded in on her, inescapable.

I'm in a cave.

A cave or a cavern. Anyway, I'm *inside* the earth. God knows how deep inside. Deep enough and far enough that I can't see any light from an entrance or vent hole.

Very deep inside, her heart told her.

She was in the loneliest place in the world. And she was going to die here.

Hannah had never had claustrophobia before. But now she couldn't help feeling that the mass of rock around and above her was trying to crush her. It could fall in at any minute, she thought. She felt a physical pressure, as if she were at the bottom of the ocean. She began to have trouble breathing.

She had to get her mind off it. She *refused* to turn into that screaming, gibbering thing in the darkness again. Worse than the thought of dying was the thought of going insane down here.

Think about Thierry. When he finds out you're missing he'll start looking for you. You *know* that. And he won't give up until he finds you.

But I'll be dead by then, she thought involuntarily.

This time, instead of fear, the idea of her death brought a strange poignant lineliness.

Another life where I missed him, she thought. She blinked against tears suddenly. Oh, God. Great.

It's so *hard*. So hard to keep hoping that someday it's going to work out. But I'll meet him again in my next life. And maybe I won't be so stupid then; I won't fall for Maya's tricks.

It'll be harder for him, I guess. He'll have to wait and get through the years day by day. I'll just go to sleep and eventually wake up somewhere else. And then someday he'll come for me and I'll remember . . . and then we'll start all over.

I really did try this time, Thierry. I did my best. I didn't mean to mess things up.

Promise me you'll look for me again.

Promise you'll find me. I promise I'll wait for you.

No matter how long it takes.

Hannah shut her eyes, leaning back against the post and almost unconsciously touching the ring he'd given her. Maybe next time she'd remember it.

Suddenly she didn't feel sad or afraid anymore. Just very tired.

Eyes still shut, she grinned weakly. I feel old. Like Mom's always complaining she feels. Ready to turn this old body in and get a new . . .

The thought broke off and disappeared.

Was that a *noise*?

Hannah found herself sitting up, leaning forward as far as the rope would allow, straining her ears. She thought she'd heard . . . *yes*. There it was again. A solid echoing sound out in the darkness.

It sounded like footsteps. And it was coming closer.

Yes, yes. I'm rescued, I'm saved. Hannah's heart was pounding so hard that she could hardly breathe to yell. But at last, just as she saw a bobbing point of light in the blackness, she managed to get out a hoarse squawk.

'Thierry? Hello? I'm over here!'

The light kept coming toward her. She could hear the footsteps coming closer.

And there was no answer.

'Thierry . . . ?' Her voice trailed off.

Footsteps. The light was big now. It was a beam, a flashlight. Hannah blinked at it.

Her heart was slowly sinking until it seemed to reach stone.

And then the flashlight was right in front of her. It shone in her face, dazzling her eyes. Another light snapped on, a small camping lantern. Vision rushed back to Hannah, sending information surging to her brain.

But there was no happiness in it. Hannah's entire body was ice cold now, shivering.

Because of course it wasn't Thierry. It was Maya.

CHAPTER 15

'I hope I didn't disturb you,' Maya said.

She put down the lantern and what looked like a black backpack. Then she stood with her hands on her hips and looked at Hannah.

I will not cry. I won't give her the satisfaction, Hannah thought.

'I didn't know vampires could really change into bats,' she said.

Maya laughed. She looked beautiful in the pool of lantern light. Her long black hair fell in waves around her, hanging down her back to her hips. Her skin was milky-pale and her eyes looked dark and mysterious. Her laughing mouth was red.

She was wearing designer jeans and high-heeled snakeskin boots. Funny, Hannah had never noticed any of Maya's clothes before. Usually the woman herself was so striking that it was impossible to focus on how she was dressed.

'Not all vampires can shapeshift,' Maya said. 'But, then, I'm not like other vampires. I'm the first, my darling. I'm the original. And I have to say I'm getting really sick of *you*.'

The feeling is mutual, Hannah thought. She said, 'Then why don't you leave me alone? Why don't you leave me and Thierry alone?'

'Because, then, my sweetpea, I wouldn't *win*. And I have to win.' She looked at Hannah directly, her face oddly serious. 'Don't you understand that yet?' she said softly. 'I have to win, because I've given up too much to lose. It can't all be for nothing. So winning is all there is.'

Hannah's breath was taken away.

She hadn't expected a coherent answer from Maya . . . but she'd gotten one. And she did understand. Maya had devoted her life to keeping Hannah and Thierry apart. Her *long* life. Her thousands of years. If she lost at this point, that life became meaningless.

'You don't know how to do anything else,' Hannah whispered slowly, figuring it out.

'Oh, enough of the press conference. I know how to do lots of things, you'll find that out. I'm through fooling around with you, cupcake.'

Hannah ignored the threat – and the insulting endearment. 'But it won't do you any good,' she said, genuinely bewildered, as if she and Maya were discussing whether or not to go shopping together. 'You're going to kill me, sure, I understand that. But it won't help you get Thierry. He'll just hate you more . . . and he'll just wait for me to come back.'

Maya had knelt by the backpack, rummaging in it. Now she looked up at Hannah and smiled – a strange slow smile.

'Will he?'

Hannah stared at those red lips, feeling as if someone were pouring ice water down her backbone. 'You know he will. Unless you kill him, too.'

The lips curved again. 'An interesting idea. But not

quite what I had in mind. I need him alive; he's my prize, you see. When you win, you need a prize.'

Hannah was feeling colder and colder inside. 'Then he'll wait.'

'Not if you're not coming back.'

And how do you arrange *that*? Hannah thought. God, maybe she's going to keep me *alive* here . . . tied up and alive until I'm ninety. The idea brought a wave of suffocating fear. Hannah glanced around, trying to imagine what it would be like to spend her life in this place. In this cold, dark, horrible . . .

Maya burst into laughter.

'You can't figure it out, can you? Well, let me help.' She walked to where Hannah was sitting and knelt. 'Look at this. Look, Hannah.'

She was holding up an oval hand mirror. At the same moment she shone the flashlight on Hannah's face.

Hannah looked into the mirror – and gasped.

It was her face . . . but not her face. For one instant she couldn't put her finger on the difference – all she could think was that it was *Hana's* face, Hana of the Three Rivers. And then she realized.

Her birthmark was gone.

Or . . . *almost* gone. She could still see a shadow of it if she turned her head to one side. But it had faded almost to invisibility.

God, I'm good-looking, Hannah thought numbly. She was too dazed to feel either vain or humble. Then she realized it wasn't just the absence of the birthmark that made her look beautiful.

Even in the unnatural beam of the flashlight she could tell that she was pale. Her skin was creamy, almost translucent. Her eyes seemed larger and brighter. Her mouth seemed softer and more sensuous. And there was an indefinable *something* about her face . . .

I look like Poppy, she thought. Like Poppy, the girl with the copper hair. The vampire.

Wordlessly, she looked at Maya.

Maya's red lips stretched in a smile.

'Yes. I exchanged blood with you when I picked you up last night. That's why you slept so long . . . you probably don't realize it, but it's afternoon out there. And you're changing already. I figure one more exchange of blood . . . maybe two. I don't want to rush things. I can't have you dying *before* you become a vampire.'

Hannah's mind was reeling. Her head fell back weakly to rest against the post. She stared at Maya.

'But *why*?' she whispered, almost pleadingly. 'Why make me a vampire?'

Maya stood. She walked over to the backpack and carefully tucked the mirror inside. Then she pulled out something else, something so long that it was sticking out of the top of the pack. She held it up.

A stake. A black wooden stake, like a spear, about as long as Maya's arm. It had a nice pointed end on it.

'Vampires don't come back,' Maya said.

Suddenly there was a roaring in Hannah's ears. She swallowed and swallowed. She was afraid she was going to faint or be sick.

'Vampires . . . don't . . . ?'

'It's an interesting bit of trivia, isn't it? Maybe it'll be on *Jeopardy!* someday. I have to admit, I don't exactly understand the logistics, but vampires don't reincarnate, not even if they're Old Souls. They just die. I've heard it suggested that it's because making them vampires takes their souls away, but I don't know . . . Does Thierry have a soul, do you think?'

Everything was whirling around Hannah now. There

was nothing solid, nothing to hang on to.

To die . . . she could face that. But to die forever, to go *out* . . . what if vampires didn't even go to some other place, some afterlife? What if they just suddenly *weren't*?

It was the most frightening thing she had ever imagined.

'I won't let you,' she whispered, hearing her own voice come out hoarse and ragged. 'I won't—'

'But you can't stop me,' Maya said, amused. 'Those ropes are hemp – they'll hold you when you're a vampire as well as when you're human. You're helpless, poor baby. You can't do anything against me.' With a look of pleasure in her own cleverness, she said, 'I finally found a way to break the cycle.'

She left the backpack and knelt in front of Hannah again. This time when the red lips parted, Hannah saw long sharp teeth.

Hannah fought. Even knowing that it was hopeless, she did everything she could think of, lashing out at Maya with the strength of sheer desperation. But it wasn't any good. Maya was simply that much stronger than she was. In a matter of minutes, Hannah found herself with both hands pinned and her head twisted to one side, her throat exposed.

Now she knew why Maya had forced her to drink vampire blood before. It hadn't just been random cruelty. It was part of a plan.

You can't do this to me. You *can't*. You can't kill my soul . . .

'Ready or not,' Maya said, almost humming it.

Then Hannah felt teeth.

She struggled again, like a gazelle in the jaws of a lioness. It had no effect. She could feel the unique pain of her blood being drawn out against her will. She could feel Maya drinking deeply.

I don't want this to be happening . . .

At last the pain faded to a drowsy sort of ache. Hannah's mind felt dopey, her body numb.

Maya was wrestling her into a different position, tilting Hannah's head back and pressing her wrist to Hannah's mouth.

I won't drink. I'll let myself drown first. At least I'll die before I'm a vampire . . .

But she found that it wasn't that easy to will yourself into dying from lack of air. Eventually, she choked and swallowed Maya's blood. She wound up coughing and sputtering, trying to clear her throat and get air.

Maya sat back.

'There,' she said, slightly breathless. She shone the flashlight into Hannah's face again.

'Yes.' She looked judicial, like a woman considering a turkey in the oven. 'Yes, it's going very well. Once more should do it. You'd be a vampire now, if we hadn't wasted so much time since the first exchange.'

'Thierry will kill you when he finds out,' Hannah whispered.

'And break his sacred promise? I don't *think* so.' Maya smiled and got up again, pottering with her backpack. 'Of course, this wouldn't be happening if he hadn't broken his promise to *me*,' she added, almost matter-of-factly. 'He told me that you wouldn't come between us anymore. But the next time I turn around – there you are! Shacked up in his house, no less. He should have known better.'

Hannah stared at her. 'He didn't even know I was there. Maya, don't you realize that? He didn't know—'

Maya cut her off with a gesture. 'Don't expect me to believe anything you say. Not at this point.' She straightened up, looked at Hannah, then sighed. She switched off the lantern and picked up the flashlight. 'I'm afraid I'm going to have to leave you for a while, now. I'll be back tonight to finish this little job. Don't worry, I won't be late . . . after all, I have a deadline to meet. Tomorrow's your birthday.'

'Maya . . .' I have to keep her here talking, Hannah thought. I have to make her understand that Thierry didn't break his promise.

She was trying to ignore the chilling question that ran just under her thoughts. What if Thierry had been serious about what he'd told Maya? If he really wanted to be with Maya as long as Hannah was no longer between them?

'Can't stay; must fly,' Maya said, trilling laughter again. 'I hope you won't be too lonely. By the way, I wouldn't rock that pole too much. This is an abandoned silver mine, and that whole structure is unstable.'

'Maya—'

'See you later.' She picked up the backpack and walked away.

She ignored Hannah's yells. And eventually, when Hannah couldn't see the beam of the flashlight anymore, she stopped yelling.

She was in the dark again.

And weaker. Drained emotionally and drained of vitality by what Maya had done. She felt sick, feverish, and itchy as if there were bugs crawling under her skin.

And she was alone.

Almost, *almost*, she gave in to the panic again. But she was afraid that if she lost control this time, she'd never get it back. She'd be insane by the time Maya returned.

Time. That's it, girl, you've got some time. She's not coming back until tonight, so get your head clear and start using the time you have.

But it's so dark . . .

Wait. Did she take the lantern with her? She turned it

off, but did she *take* it?

With the utmost caution, Hannah felt around her with her hands. Nothing, but then she couldn't lean very far because of the rope.

OK. Try your feet. *Carefully*. If you kick it away, it's all over.

Hannah lifted one leg and began to gently pat the foot down toward the ground. Little pats, slow pats. About the third time she did it, her foot hit something that fell over.

That's it! Now nudge it toward you. Careful. Careful. Closer . . . almost . . . now around to your side . . .

Got it! Hannah reached out and grabbed the lantern, holding it desperately with both hands like somebody holding a radio while sitting in the bathtub. Don't drop it . . . find the switch.

Light blossomed.

Hannah kissed the lantern. She actually kissed it. It was an ordinary battery-operated fluorescent camping lantern, but she felt as if she were holding a miracle.

Light made such a difference.

OK. Now look around you. What can you do to help yourself here?

But looking around made her heart sink.

The cavern she was in was irregular, with uneven walls and overhanging slabs of rock. A silver mine, Maya had said. That meant the place was probably blasted out by humans.

On either side of her, Hannah could see more posts like the one she was tied to. They seemed to form a kind of scaffolding against the wall. So miners can get to it, I guess, she thought vaguely. Or maybe to help hold the roof up, or both.

And it's unstable.

As a last resort, she could simply do her best to bring

the whole thing down. And then pray she died quickly.

For now, she kept looking.

The wall on her right, the only one she could see in the pool of lantern light, was surprisingly variegated. Even beautiful. It wasn't just rough grey rock; it was rough grey rock veined with milky-white and pale pink quartz.

Silver comes in quartz sometimes, Hannah thought. She knew that much from her mom's friends, the rockhounds.

But that doesn't do me any good. It's pretty, but useless.

She was starting to panic again. She had a light, but what good was it? She could see, but she had nothing to work with.

There's got to be *something* here. Rocks. I've got rocks and that's it. Hannah shifted to get away from one that was bruising her thigh. Maybe I can throw rocks at her . . .

Not rocks. Quartz.

Suddenly Hannah's whole body was tingling. Her breath was stopped in her lungs and her skin felt electrified.

I've got quartz.

With shaking hands, she put the lantern down. She reached for an angular chunk of rock on the ground beside her.

Tears sprang to her eyes.

This is a quartz nodule. It's crystal. Fine-grained. Workable.

I know how to make a tool out of this.

She'd never done it in this life, of course. But Hana of the Three Rivers had done it all the time. She'd made knives, scrapers, drills . . . and hand-axes.

She would have preferred flint to work with; it fractured much more regularly. But quartz was fine.

I can feel in my hands how to do it . . .

OK. Stay calm. First, find a hammer stone.

It was too easy. There were rocks all around her. Hannah picked up one with a slightly rounded surface, weighed it in her hand. It felt good.

She pulled her legs in, set the angular chunk in front of her, and started working.

She didn't actually make a hand-axe. She didn't need to. Once she had bashed off a few flakes with long sharp edges, she started sawing at the rope. The flakes were wavy and irregular, but they were as sharp as broken glass and quite sufficient to cut the hemp.

It took a long time, and twice she had to make new flakes when the ones she was using blunted. But she was patient. She kept working until she could pull first one length of rope, then another and another free.

When the last strand parted, she almost screamed in sheer joy.

I'm free! I did it! I did it!

She jumped up, her weakness and fever forgotten. She danced around the room. Then she ran back and picked up her precious lantern.

And now – I'm out of here!

But she wasn't.

It took a while for the realization to dawn. First, she walked back in the direction that Maya had come. She found what felt like miles of twisting passageways, sometimes so narrow that the walls almost brushed her shoulders, and so low that she had to duck her head. The rock was cold – and wet.

There were several branching passages, but each one led to a dead end. And it was only when Hannah got to the end of the main passage that she realized how Maya had gotten into the mine.

She was standing below a vertical shaft. It soared maybe a hundred feet straight up. At the very top, she could see reddish sunlight.

It was like a giant chimney, except that the walls were nowhere near that close to each other. And nowhere near irregular enough to climb.

No human could get out this way.

I suppose they had some sort of elevator or something when the mine was working, Hannah thought dazedly. She was sick and numb. She couldn't believe that her triumph had turned into this.

For a while she shouted, staring up at that square of infuriating, unattainable sunlight. When she got so hoarse she could scarcely hear herself anymore, she admitted that it was no use.

Nobody is going to come and rescue you. OK. So you have to rescue yourself.

But all I've got is rocks . . . No.

No, I'm free now. I can move around. I can get to the scaffolding.

I've got rocks – and wood.

Hannah stood paralyzed for a second, then she clutched the lantern to her chest and went running back down the passageway.

When she got to her cavern, she examined the scaffolding excitedly.

Yes. Some of this wood is still good. It's old, but it's hard. I can work with this.

This time, she made a real hand-axe, taking special care to fashion the tip, making it thin and straightedged and sharp. The final tool was roughly triangular and heavy. It fit comfortably in her hand. Hana would have been proud of it.

Then she used the axe to chop off a length of wood from the creaking, groaning scaffolding. All the while she did it she whistled softly, hoping she wasn't going to bring the whole structure down on her head.

She used the axe to shape the length of wood, too, making it round, about as thick as her thumb and as long as her forearm. She knocked off a quartz scraper to do the finer shaping.

Finally she used a flake to hone one end of the stick to a point. She ground it back and forth against an outcrop of gritty stone to bring it to maximum smoothness and sharpness.

Then she held out the finished tool and admired it.

She had a stake. A very good stake.

And Maya was going to get a surprise.

Hannah sat down, turned the lantern off to conserve the battery, and began to wait.

CHAPTER 16

It was a very long time before Hannah heard footsteps again.

She distracted herself during the long wait by whistling songs under her breath and thinking about the people she loved.

Her mother. Her mother didn't even miss her yet, didn't know she was gone. But by tomorrow she would. Tomorrow was May first, Hannah's birthday, and Chess would give her mother the letter.

Chess, of course. Hannah wished now that she'd spent more time saying goodbye to Chess, that she'd explained things better. Chess would have been fascinated. And she had a right to know she was an Old Soul, too.

Paul Winfield. That was strange – she'd only known him a week. But he'd tried to help her. And at this moment, he knew more about Hannah Snow than anyone else in Montana.

I hope he doesn't start smoking again if he finds out I'm dead.

Because that was probably how she would end up. Hannah had no illusions about that. She had a weapon – but so did Maya, and Maya was much faster and stronger.

She was no match for Maya under the best of circumstances, much less when she was weak and feverish. The best she could hope for was to get Maya to kill her while she was still human.

She thought about the Circle Daybreak members. They were good people. She was sorry she wouldn't have the chance to know them better, to help them. They were doing something important, something she instinctively sensed was necessary right now.

And she thought about Thierry.

He'll have to go wandering again, I guess. It's too bad. He hasn't had a very happy life. I was starting to think I could take that sadness out of his eyes . . .

When she heard a noise at last, she thought it might be her imagination. She held her breath.

No. It's footsteps. Getting closer.

She's coming.

Hannah shifted position. She had stationed herself near the mouth of the cavern; now she took a deep breath and eased herself into a crouch. She wiped her sweaty right palm on her jeans and got a better grip on her stake.

She figured that Maya would shine the flashlight toward the pole where Hannah had been tied, then maybe take a few steps farther inside the cavern, trying to see what was going on.

And then I'll do it. I'll come out of the darkness behind her. Jump and skewer her through the back. But I've got to time it right.

She held her breath as she saw light outside the mouth of the cavern. Her greatest fear was that Maya would *hear* her.

Quiet . . . quiet . . .

The light came closer. Hannah watched it, not moving. But her brain was clicking along in surprise. It wasn't the slanted, focused beam of a flashlight. It was the more diffuse pool of light from a lantern.

She's brought another one. But that means . . .

Maya was walking in.

Walking quickly, and not pausing. She couldn't shine the light onto the pole yet. And she didn't seem anxious to – apparently it didn't occur to her that she needed to check on Hannah. She was that confident.

Hannah cursed mentally. She's going too far – she's out of range. Get up!

Her plan in ruins, she flexed her knees and stood. She heard a crack in her knee joint that sounded as loud as a gunshot.

But Maya didn't stop. She kept going. She was almost at the pole.

As silently as she could, Hannah headed across the cavern. All Maya had to do was turn around to see her.

Maya was at the pole. She was stopping. She was looking from side to side.

Hannah was behind her.

Now.

Now was the time. Hannah's muscles could feel how she had to stab, to throw her weight behind the thrust so that the stake went in under Maya's left shoulder blade. She knew how to do it . . .

But she couldn't.

She couldn't stab somebody in the back. Somebody who wasn't menacing her at the moment, who didn't even know they were in danger.

Oh, my God! Don't be stupid! *Do* it!

Oh, my Goddess! a voice echoed back in her head. *You're not a killer. This isn't even self-defence!*

Frustrated almost to the point of hysteria, Hannah heard herself let out a breath. It was wet. She was crying.

Her arm drooped. Her muscles collapsed. She wasn't doing it. She couldn't do it.

Maya slowly turned around.

She looked both beautiful and eerie in the lantern light. She surveyed Hannah up and down, looking in particular at the drooping stake.

Then she looked at Hannah's face.

'You're the strangest girl,' she said, in what seemed to be genuine bewilderment. 'Why didn't you do it? You were smart enough to get yourself out and make yourself a weapon. Why didn't you have the guts to finish it?'

Hannah was asking herself the same thing. Only with more expletives.

I am going to die now, she thought. And maybe die for good – because I don't have guts. Because I couldn't kill somebody I know is completely evil and completely determined to kill me.

That's not ethics. That's *stupid*.

'I suppose it's that Egyptian temple training,' Maya was saying. 'Or maybe the life when you were a Buddhist – do you remember that? Or maybe you're just weak.'

And a victim. I've spent a couple thousand years being a victim – yours. I guess I've got my part down perfect by now.

'Oh, well. It doesn't really matter why,' Maya said. 'It all comes down to the same thing in the end. Now. Let's get this over with.'

Hannah stared at her, breathing hard, feeling like a rabbit looking at a headlight.

Nobody should live as a victim. Every creature has a right to fight for its life.

But she couldn't seem to get her muscles to move anymore. She was just too tired. Every part of her hurt, from her throbbing head to her raw fingertips to her bruised and aching feet.

Maya was smiling, fixing her with eyes that shifted from lapis-lazuli blue to glacier green.

'Be a good girl, now,' she crooned.

I don't want to be a good girl . . .

Maya reached for her with long arms.

'Don't touch her!' Thierry said from the cavern mouth.

Hannah's head jerked sideways. She stared at the new pool of light on the other side of the cave. For the first few seconds she thought she was hallucinating.

But, no. He was there. Thierry was standing there with a lantern of his own, tall and almost shimmering with coiled tension, like a predator ready to spring.

The problem was that he was too far away. And Maya was too fast. In the same instant that it took Hannah to make her brain believe her eyes, Maya was moving. In one swift step, she was behind Hannah, with her hands around Hannah's throat.

'Stay where you are,' she said. 'Or I'll break her little neck.'

Hannah knew she could do it. She could feel the iron strength in Maya's hands. Maya didn't need a weapon.

Thierry put the lantern down and raised his empty hands. 'I'm staying,' he said quietly.

'And tell whoever else you've got in that tunnel to go back. All the way back. If I see another person, I'll kill her.'

Without turning, Thierry shouted. 'Go back to the entrance. All of you.' Then he looked at Hannah. 'Are you all right?'

Hannah couldn't nod. Maya's grip was so tight that she could barely say, 'Yes.' But she could look at him, and she could see his eyes.

She knew, in that moment, that all her fears about him not wanting her anymore were groundless. He loved her.

She had never seen such open love and concern in anyone's face before.

More, they *understood* each other. They didn't need any words. It was the end of misunderstandings and mistrust. For perhaps the first time since she had been Hana of the Three Rivers, Hannah trusted him without reservation.

They were in accord.

And neither of them wanted this to end with a death.

When Thierry took his eyes from Hannah's, it was to look at Maya and say, 'It's over, now. You have to realize that. I've got twenty people down here, and another twenty on the surface waiting.' His voice became softer and more deliberate. 'But I give you my word, you can walk out of here right now, Maya. Nobody will touch you. All you have to do is let Hannah go first.'

'Together,' Hannah said, coughing as Maya's hands tightened, cutting off her breath. She gasped and finished, 'We go out together, Thierry.'

Thierry nodded and looked at Maya. He was holding his hand out now, like someone trying to coax a frightened child. 'Just let her go,' he said softly.

Maya laughed.

It was an unnatural sound, and it made Hannah's skin crawl. Nothing sane made a noise like that.

'But that way, I won't *win*,' Maya said, almost pleasantly.

'You can't win anyway,' Thierry said quietly. 'Even if you kill her, she'll still be alive –'

'Not if I make her a vampire first,' Maya interrupted.

But Thierry was shaking his head. 'It doesn't matter.' His voice was still quiet, but it was filled with the authority of absolute conviction, a kind of bedrock certainty that held even Hannah mesmerized.

'Even if you kill her, she'll still be alive – here.' He

tapped his chest. 'In me. I keep her here. She's *part* of me. So until you kill me, you can't really kill her. And you can't win. It's that simple.'

There was a silence. Hannah's own heart was twisted with the force of her love for him. Her eyes were full.

She could hear Maya breathing, and the sound was ragged. She thought that the pressure of Maya's hands was infinitesimally less.

'I could kill you both,' Maya said at last in a grating voice.

Thierry lifted his shoulders and dropped them in a gesture too sad to be a shrug. 'But how can you win when the people you hate aren't there to see it?'

It sounded insane – but it was true. Hannah could feel it hit Maya like a well-thrown javelin. If Maya couldn't have Thierry as her prize, if she couldn't even make him suffer, what was the point? Where was the victory?

'Let's stop the cycle right here,' Thierry said softly. 'Let her go.'

He was so gentle, and so reasonable, and so tired-sounding. Hannah didn't see how anyone could resist him. But she was still surprised at what happened next.

Slowly, very slowly, the hands around her neck loosened their grip. Maya stepped away.

Hannah sucked in a deep breath. She wanted to run to Thierry, but she was afraid to do anything to unbalance the delicate stalemate in the cavern. Besides, her knees were wobbly.

Maya was moving around her, taking a step or two in front of her, facing Thierry directly.

'I loved you,' she said. There was a sound in her voice Hannah had never heard before, a quaver. 'Why didn't you ever understand that?'

Thierry shook his head. 'Because it's not true. You

never loved me. You wanted me. Mostly because you couldn't have me.'

There was a silence then as they stood looking at each other. Not because they understood each other too well for words, Hannah thought. Because they would never understand each other. They had nothing to say.

The silence stretched on and on – and then Maya collapsed.

She didn't fall down. But she might as well have. Hannah saw the life go out of her – the *hope*. The energy that had kept Maya vibrant and sparkling after thousands of years. It had all come from her need to win . . . and now she knew she'd lost.

She was defeated.

'Come on, Hannah,' Thierry said quietly. 'Let's go.' Then he turned to shout back into the tunnel behind him. 'Clear the way. We're all coming out.'

That was when it happened.

Maya had been standing slumped, her head down, her eyes on the ground.

Or on her backpack.

And now, as Thierry turned away, she flashed one glance at him and then moved as fast as a striking snake. She grabbed the black stake and held it horizontally, her arm drawn back.

Hannah recognized the posture instantly. As Hana of the Three Rivers she'd seen hunters throw spears all the time.

'Game over,' Maya whispered.

Hannah had a fraction of a second to act – and no time to consider. All she thought was, *No.*

With her whole weight behind the thrust, she lunged at Maya. Stake first.

The sharp wooden point went in just under Maya's

shoulder blade. She staggered, off balance, her throw ruined. The black stake went skittering across the rough stone floor.

Hannah was off balance, too. She was falling. Maya was falling. But it all seemed to be happening in slow motion.

I've killed her.

There was no triumph in the thought. Only a sort of hushed certainty.

When the slow-motion feeling ended, she found herself the way anybody finds themself after a fall. On the ground and surprised. Except that Maya was underneath her, with a stake protruding from her back.

Hannah's first frantic thought was to get a doctor. She'd never seen someone this badly hurt before – not in this life. There was blood seeping out of Maya's back around the makeshift stake. It had gone in very deep, the wood piercing vampire flesh like razor-sharp steel through a human.

Thierry was beside her. Kneeling, pulling Hannah slightly away from Maya's prone form, as if she might still be dangerous.

Hannah reached for him at the same time, and their hands met, intertwined. She held on tight, feeling a rush of warmth and comfort from his presence.

Then Thierry gently turned Maya onto her side.

Hair was falling across Maya's face like a black waterfall. Her skin was chalky white and her eyes were wide open. But she was laughing.

Laughing.

She looked at Hannah and laughed. In a thick choking voice, she gasped. 'You had guts – after all.'

Hannah whispered, 'Can we do anything for her?'

Thierry shook his head.

Then it was terrible. Maya's laugh turned into a gurgle. A trickle of blood ran out of the side of her mouth. Her body jerked. Her eyes stared. And then, finally, she was still.

Hannah felt her own breath sigh out.

She's dead. I killed her. I killed someone.

Every creature has the right to fight for its life – or its loved ones.

Thierry said softly, 'The cycle is broken.'

Then he let Maya's shoulder go and her body slumped down again. She seemed smaller now, shrunken. After a moment Hannah realized it wasn't an illusion. Maya was doing what all vampires do in the movies. She was falling in on herself, her tissues collapsing, muscle and flesh shrivelling. The one hand Hannah could see seemed to be wasting away and hardening at the same time. The skin became yellow and leathery, showing the form of the tendons underneath.

In the end, Maya was just a leather sack full of bones.

Hannah swallowed and shut her eyes.

'Are you all right? Let me look at you.' Thierry was holding her, examining her. Then when Hannah met his eyes, he looked at her long and searchingly and said with a different meaning, 'Are you all right?'

Hannah understood. She looked at Maya and then back at him.

'I'm not proud of it,' she said slowly. 'But I'm not sorry, either. It just – had to be done.' She thought another moment, then said, getting out each word separately, 'I refuse to be . . . a victim . . . anymore.'

Thierry tightened his arm around her. '*I'm* proud of you,' he said. Then he added, 'Let's go. We need to get you to a healer.'

They walked back through the narrow passageway,

which was no longer dark because Thierry's people had placed lanterns every few feet. At the end of the passage, in the room with the vertical shaft, they had set up some sort of rope and pulley.

Lupe was there, and Nilsson, and the rest of the CIA group. So were Rashel and Quinn. The fighters, Hannah thought. Everyone called and laughed and patted her when she came in with Thierry.

'It's over,' Thierry said briefly. 'She's dead.'

Everyone looked at him and then at Hannah. And somehow they knew. They all cheered and patted her again. Hannah didn't feel like Cinderella anymore; she felt like Dorothy after killing the Wicked Witch.

And she didn't like it.

Lupe took her by the shoulders and said excitedly, 'Do you know what you've done?'

Hannah said, 'Yes. But I don't want to think about it anymore right now.'

It wasn't until they'd hauled her up the vertical shaft that it occurred to her to ask Thierry how he'd found her. She was standing on an inconspicuous hillside with no buildings or landmarks around. Maya had picked a very good hiding place.

'One of her own people sold her out,' Thierry said. 'He got to the house about the same time I did this evening, and he said he had information to sell. He was a werewolf who wasn't happy with how she'd treated him.'

A werewolf with black hair? Hannah wondered. But she was too sleepy suddenly to ask more questions.

'Home, sir?' Nilsson said, a little breathlessly because he'd just come up the shaft.

Thierry looked at him, laughed, and started to help Hannah down the hill. 'That's right. Home, Nilsson.'

CHAPTER 17

'I need to call my mom,' Hannah said.

Thierry nodded. 'But maybe wait until she's up. It's not dawn yet.'

They were at Thierry's house, in the elegant bedroom with the softly burnished gold walls. The window had just begun to turn grey.

It was so good to rest, to let go of tension, to feel her battered body relax. It was so good to be *alive*. She felt as if she'd been reborn and was looking at the world with wide new eyes. Even the smallest comforts – a hot drink, a fire in the fireplace – were immeasurably precious.

And it was good to be with Thierry.

He was sitting on the bed, holding her hand, watching her as if he couldn't believe she was real.

The healer had come and gone, and now it was just the two of them. They sat together quietly, not needing words. They looked into each other's eyes, and then they were reaching for each other, holding each other. Resting like weary travellers in each other's arms.

Hannah leaned her forehead against Thierry's lips.

It's over, she thought. I was right when I told Paul the apocalypse was coming – but it's over now.

Thierry stirred, kissing the hair on her forehead. Then he spoke, not out loud but with his mental voice. As soon as Hannah heard it, she knew he was trying to say something serious and important.

You know, you came very close to becoming a vampire. You're going to be sick for a few days while your body shifts back to human.

Hannah nodded without pulling away to look at him. The healer had told her all that. She sensed that there was something more Thierry wanted to say.

And . . . well, you still have a choice, you know.

There was a silence. Then Hannah did pull away to look at him. 'What do you mean?'

He took a deep breath, then said out loud, 'I mean, you can still choose to be a vampire. You're right on the edge. If you want, we can make you change over.'

Hannah took a long breath of her own.

She hadn't thought about this – but she was thinking now. As a vampire, she'd be immortal; she could stay with Thierry continuously for who knew how many thousands of years? She would be stronger than a human, faster, telepathic.

And perfect physically. Involuntarily, her hand went to her left cheek, to her birthmark.

The doctors couldn't take it away. But becoming a vampire would.

She looked directly at Thierry. 'Is that what you want? For me to become a vampire?'

He was looking at her cheek, too. Then he met her eyes.

'I want what *you* want. I want you to be happy. Nothing else matters to me.'

Hannah took her hand away.

'Then,' she said very softly, 'if you don't mind, I'll stay human. I don't mind the birthmark. It's just – part of me, now. It doesn't bring up any bad memories.' After a moment, she added, 'All humans are imperfect, I guess.'

She could see tears in Thierry's eyes. He gently lifted her hand and kissed it. He didn't say anything, but something about his expression made Hannah's throat and chest fill with love.

Then he took her in his arms.

And Hannah was happy. So happy that she was crying a little, too.

She was with her flying companion – her playmate. The one who was sacred to her, who was the other half of the mysteries of life for her. The one who would always be there for her, helping her, watching her back, picking her up when she fell down, listening to her stories – no matter how many times she told them. Loving her even when she was stupid. Understanding her without words. Being inside the innermost circle in her mind.

Her soulmate.

Things are going to be all right now, she thought.

Suddenly it was as if she could see the corridor of time again, but this time looking forward, not back.

She would go to college and become a paleontologist. And she and Thierry would work with Circle Daybreak and the Old Powers that were rising. They would be happy together, and they would help the world through the enormous changes that were coming.

The sadness would go out of Thierry's eyes.

They would love and discover and learn and explore. And Hannah would grow up and get older, and Thierry would love her just the same. And then one day, being human, she would go back to Mother Earth, like a wave going out to the ocean. Thierry would grieve for her – and wait for her.

And then they would start all over again.

One lifetime with him was enough, but Hannah sensed that there would be many. There would always be something new to learn.

Thierry moved, his breath warming her hair. 'I almost forgot,' he whispered. 'You're seventeen today. Congratulations.'

That's right, Hannah thought. She looked toward the window, startled and overwhelmed. The sky was turning pink now. She was seeing the dawn of her seventeenth birthday – something that had never happened before.

I've changed my destiny.

'I love you,' she whispered to Thierry.

And then they just sat together, holding each other as the room filled with light.

Collect the Night World series

NIGHT WORLD
L.J. Smith

The Night World is a secret society of vampires, werewolves, witches and creatures of darkness – a place where it is too dangerous to fall in love . . .

Read the third compelling volume of Night World:
HUNTRESS, BLACK DAWN and WITCH LIGHT

In *Huntress*, Jez Redfern is wild and dangerous, and the leader of a gang of Night World vampires. But Jez discovers a shocking secret, and faces a terrifying choice: she must either remain a deadly crusader of evil, or fight to protect innocent mortals from her former friends . . . But can she resist her instinct for blood?

In *Black Dawn*, Maggie Neely's biggest worry is leading her soccer team to victory – until her brother Miles goes missing. Maggie must find him. Her search leads her to the vampire Delos, to whom she is strangely attracted. But while Delos lives, Miles could be lost forever. Can Maggie bring herself to destroy him? Or will Delos get to Maggie first?

In *Witch Light*, Keller is part shape-shifter, part panther. She is searching for a new Wild Power. But can the dizzy human girl, Iliana, really be it? And then there's the dashing, romantic Galen. Keller has strong feelings for him, but he's destined to be Iliana's soulmate. Can Keller keep away? Or will she break her promise and fall in love?